JN294318

WASEDA University Academic Series

早稲田大学学術叢書

23

Negotiating History

From Romanticism to Victorianism

Rieko Suzuki

Waseda University Press

Negotiating History
From Romanticism to Victorianism

Rieko SUZUKI is Assistant Professor of English and English Literature at the Faculty of Law, Waseda University, Tokyo.

First published in 2012 by
Waseda University Press Co., Ltd.
1-1-7 Nishiwaseda
Shinjuku-ku, Tokyo 169-0051
www.waseda-up.co.jp

© 2012 by Rieko Suzuki

All rights reserved. Except for short extracts used for academic purposes or book reviews, no part of this publication may be reproduced, stored in a retrieval system or transmitted in any form whatsoever—electronic, mechanical, photocopying or otherwise—without the prior and written permission of the publisher.

ISBN 978-4-657-12703-7

Printed in Japan

In Memory of my grandfather
Sagenta Harasawa

Table of Contents

Note on the Texts

I have used the texts of Shelley's poems in the following priority (either for scholarly reasons or for their level of circulation): *The Poems of Shelley* (Matthews and Everest 1989, 2000); *Shelley's Poetry and Prose* (Reiman and Fraistat 2002); *The Poetical Works* (Hutchinson and Matthews 1971). For Shelley's prose, I have applied the same rule to the above with the addition of *The Complete Works of Percy Bysshe Shelley* (Julian edition).

In Chapter 1 on 'The Triumph of Life', I have used Reiman's text in *Shelley's Poetry and Prose.* Although G.M. Matthews' text offers a competing version of 'The Triumph' to Reiman's with insightful and suggestive variant readings, I chose Reiman's over Matthews' text due to the wide circulation of the former, and more importantly as their different readings do not have direct bearing on my argument. I have also consulted the facsimile copy of the manuscript of 'The Triumph of Life' (*The Bodleian Shelley Manuscript,* Vol. 1), which was useful in shedding light on Shelley's original intentions that became neatly edited by Mary Shelley and her succeeding editors.

In Chapter 3 where Shelley's texts are used as sources of influence on Browning, I have used the version that Browning is likely to have read: for example, 'Hymn of Apollo' and 'Sonnet: Political Greatness' in *The Miscellaneous Poems* (1826); *Alastor, or The Spirit of Solitude* (except for the 'Preface', which was not included in this volume), 'The Triumph of Life', and 'Julian and Maddalo' in *The Posthumous Poems* (1824); 'Letter to Maria Gisborne' in *The Poetical Works of Percy Bysshe Shelley* (1839); and 'Peter Bell the Third' in its manuscript state or in the one volume edition of *The Poetical Works* (1840). Browning also possessed the following volumes: *Adonais* (1821), *The Cenci* (1821?), *Epipsychidion* (1821), *Prometheus Unbound* (1820), *The Revolt of Islam; A Poem in Twelve Cantos* (1818), and *Rosalind and Helen* (1819).[1]

I have used the text included in *The Novels and Selected Works of Mary Shelley* (Crook 1996) for *Valperga, or, The Life and Adventures of Castruccio, Prince of Lucca* mainly because it is widely accepted as the authorial version. I have also consulted three other editions (Curran 1997; Rajan 1998; Rossington 2000) for further reference.

The general rule I have applied to the choice of texts for the poems of Robert Browning was to use the first edition because Browning himself valued it over revised versions. Thus, for *Sordello* and other relevant poems, I have used *The Poems of Browning* (Woolford and Karlin 1991), which adopts the same policy (i.e. of using the texts in their first edition). Otherwise, I have used *The Poems* (Pettigrew and Collins 1996) and in the case of *The Ring and the Book*, *The Poetical Works of Robert Browning* (Hawlin and Burnett 1998). Browning's prose work, 'Essay on Shelley', which I refer to in Chapter 3 is the text included in the appendix to *The Poems* (Pettigrew and Collins 1996).

The section entitled 'Feminism' in Chapter 3 was published in *Studies in Browning* (2001) in a slightly altered form as 'Recovering the Female Voice: the "sad disheveled ghost" in Browning's Sordello'.

Note

1. See *Collections*, pp. 177–79 (A2092, A2097, A2100, A2109, A2115, A2117, A2120, A2121). For Shelley 1839, T.J. Wise claims 'that Browning possessed Mrs. Shelley's 4-vol. edition of 1839'; see Pottle 68.

Abbreviations

Collections	=	The Browning Collections: A Reconstruction With Other Memorabilia
Correspondence	=	The Brownings' Correspondence
Trumpeter	=	Browning's Trumpeter: the Correspondence of Robert Browning and Frederick J. Furnivall 1872–1889
Hood	=	Letters of Robert Browning Collected by Thomas J. Wise
New Letters	=	New Letters of Robert Browning
MSJ	=	The Journals of Mary Shelley: 1814–1844
Julian edition	=	The Complete Works of Percy Bysshe Shelley
BSM	=	The Bodleian Shelley Manuscripts
PBSL	=	The Letters of Percy Bysshe Shelley
PWS	=	The Poetical Works: Shelley
SPP	=	Shelley's Poetry and Prose

Acknowledgements

This book is based on the PhD thesis I submitted to the University of Manchester. I would like to thank my supervisor, John Woolford, both, for seeing me through the three texts and for sharing his expertise in and appreciation of Browning's art with me. I am indebted to his comments and his advice, without which I would not be where I am today. Mike Rossington of the University of Newcastle was also instrumental in identifying problems in the Shelleys' texts and helping me deal with them. I owe my present interest in Mary Shelley to his compassionate critical reading of her works; it goes without saying that my passion for Shelley's poetry has been enhanced by his knowledge and appreciation of his art. I am grateful to Toshi Takamiya of Keio University for his support over the years in my academic pursuit. My thanks go to Paul Dawson and Joe Phelan who were the examiners of my PhD thesis. Joe Phelan was especially helpful in offering advice on how to proceed with the book.

Many people with whom I have come into contact over the years have contributed to the formation of my thoughts through feedback at conferences and more extensive discussions from which I have gained greater depth of knowledge in my chosen field. My thanks go also to Isobel Armstrong, Bernard Beatty, Jim Chandler, Nora Crook, Bill Goldman, Jerome de Groot, Harry Harootunian, Danny Karlin, Britta Martens, Nick Roe, Sharon Ruston, Alastair Thomson, and Tim Webb.

Staff at various libraries have kindly assisted me in consulting materials for my thesis. I would like to thank in particular: The Bodleian Library, The British Library (London) Cambridge University Library,

John Rylands (University) Library of Manchester (Deansgate), Keio University Library, The Literary and Philosophical Society of Newcastle upon Tyne, Reading University Library, The Robinson Library of the University of Newcastle upon Tyne, Senate House, and Waseda University Library. I am grateful to Dr. Barker-Benfield of the Department of Special Collections & Western Manuscripts of The Bodleian Library for allowing me to consult the manuscript of 'The Triumph of Life'. I have also received assistance through BARS that covered trips from London to The Bodleian Library.

Finally, I would like to thank Waseda University Press, and in particular, Susumu Itō, Atsushi Kanamaru, and Steve Walsh.

INTRODUCTION

TEXTS: 'THE TRIUMPH OF LIFE', *VALPERGA*, AND *SORDELLO*

This book initially began as a way of bridging the two literary periods—Romantic and Victorian—that seemed to call out for continuity despite their differences in politics and sensibility. As soon as any text or author becomes discussed under the labels of 'Romanticism' or 'Victorianism', it immediately gains the association of a set of political and cultural values that is not always accurate in reflecting what that text manifests. This owes much to the practice we have become accustomed to in literary history of pigeonholing authors and texts according to the literary period in which they wrote. While some periods, for example, the eighteenth century to the Romantic period, have gained greater understanding in their subtle transition or fusion of the one into the other, others are still suffering from oversimplification due to periodisation. The Romantic to the Victorian period still sadly seems to belong to the latter category. Although there have been attempts to bring the two disciplines together through conferences, they are not altogether the friendliest of neighbours: Victorianism prides on discarding Romantic sensibility and political immaturity or irresponsibility as the basis of its solidification. Reflecting the sceptical reticence with which critics have come to treat the term 'Romanticism,' I would like to look to the texts themselves for the articulation of a set of concerns and values that make them Romantic. In locating the shift from one -ism to the other, I believe that it is possible to locate the initial questioning of, distancing from, and gesture toward a revision of Romanticism in the texts themselves. As examples, I focus on P.B. Shelley's 'The Triumph of Life,' Mary Shelley's *Valperga* and Robert Browning's *Sordello*. While 'The Triumph' and *Sordello* can partly be explained by what Bloom calls the anxiety of influence in Browning's break away from high Romanticism to Victorianism, I would also argue that the growing popularity of the novel as a literary genre had a considerable influence on the young Browning and that Mary Shelley's historical novel served as an important mediation in Browning's remodelling of Romanticism.

Of course, these are by no means the only texts worth examining as examples that demonstrate strained aspects of Romanticism that problematise the status of poets and art in an increasingly industrialised and commercialised society; but the way in which *Valperga* and *Sordello* respond to, and attempt at advancing one's understanding and judgement of, the viability of the poetic agency, which concerned Shelley in 'The Triumph,' allows us to see one kind of development beyond the failure of Romanticism. The literary influence of Shelley on the young Browning needs no explanation here as it has been recounted numerous times in Browning studies; equally established is the close literary bonding between the Shelleys in their daily reading to their composition. Because the two influences were prominent and direct, they enable a tighter association of texts than otherwise possible and the change in aesthetic taste more tangible.

The Shelleys shared a common interest and aspiration from the very onset of their literary career. Having educated himself in the tradition of the Enlightenment thinkers, Shelley responded immediately to Godwin's *Political Justice* and became a self-willing disciple: Shelley's early pamphleteering activism gave way to political gradualism, which Godwin expounded in his treatise. As Shelley stated in his 'Preface' to *Prometheus*

Unbound, his 'passion for reforming the world' lay at the heart of his Romantic programme. What I mean by Romantic programme (for lack of a better word) is Percy Shelley's enactment of apocalyptic history through his own mythmaking: the works in question concern the unlocking of the mind from the fetters of a social and political value system that had become corrupt or unworkable, which would further instigate a collapse of the social fabric that sustained it and thereby inaugurate a new society.[1] This can be traced in his epic-scale works from *Queen Mab* to his 'first serious appeal to the Public', *The Revolt of Islam,* and to *Prometheus Unbound*, which he claimed as 'the best thing I ever wrote'.[2] Shelley also engaged in voicing his prophetic visions in the 'popular songs wholly political, & destined to awaken & direct the imagination of the reformers' written in the wake of the Peterloo Massacre (*PBSL* 2: 191).[3] Shelley often presents societal transition through the time sequence of past, present, and future, for example, in *Queen Mab* and *Prometheus Unbound*; however, the futurity that promises such a utopian society is one that belongs to an apocalyptic vision that is divorced from any specificity of time.[4] Both *The Revolt of Islam* and *The Mask of Anarchy* draw on the book of Revelation in their prophetic representation of what remains unrealised in the poem but awaits the maturation of time. At the crux of these poems exists the Poet (that is Shelley himself) who is regarded as the very agent of enacting such change (moral and social), the views of which he was to voice most clearly in *A Defence of Poetry*:

> Poets are the hierophants of an unapprehended inspiration, the mirrors of the gigantic shadows which futurity casts upon the present, the words which express what they understand not, the trumpets which sing to battle and feel not what they inspire: the influence which is moved not, but moves. Poets are the unacknowledged legislators of the World. (*SPP* 535)

The politicised role of the Poet as a liberator of society as well as humanity, which Shelley subscribed to, found a prototype in Prometheus as the champion of human aspiration and social regeneration in the face of political and moral adversity.[5] Mary Shelley was quick to respond to this by openly admitting the association of the Romantic prototype with Prometheus in her highly popular novel *Frankenstein*.[6] What is more, the fact that Mary Shelley dedicated her first novel to her father, William Godwin, is suggestive: while Mary Shelley identified Frankenstein's aspiration for human improvement even in the face of adversity and hardship, she also questioned the egoistic desires that sustain such a project as being essentially antisocial and inhumane. In *Frankenstein*, Mary Shelley's critique targeted at the legacy of elitist Enlightenment thinkers finds a clear voice from which Godwin does not evade. Unlike Percy Shelley's wholehearted embrace of Godwinian principles, Mary Shelley, no doubt, was in a position to see in practice how they were exercised (or not exercised) both in real life and in times that saw his creed becoming increasingly eclipsed by the philosophical radicalism of the utilitarian school.

Even if Percy and Mary Shelley did not always agree on the moral implications of Prometheanism when framed in gendered contexts, its political and charismatic appeal was central to their writings.[7] If Mary Shelley explored the negative and destructive potential of Prometheanism in *Frankenstein*, then Percy Shelley exploited its full emancipatory energy in *Prometheus Unbound*. Reading the works of the Shelleys in this light has all too often led to the assumption that Mary Shelley's early novels demonstrate a feminist critique of masculine egotism that becomes tied in with Prometheanism while Percy Shelley's poetry celebrates its idealism at all cost.[8]

I would like to read the works of the Shelleys against the grain by firstly demonstrating how much Mary Shelley had in fact invested in Percy Shelley's Promethean project to liberate the minds and political state of a people.[9] The reason for my choice of one of Mary Shelley's early novels, *Valperga, or, The Life and Adventures of Castruccio, Prince of Lucca*, as the text for examination is that it most directly engages with the issues that Shelley's Romantic programme raises: the role of a poet and poetry in effecting social change, the relationship between poetry and political, psychological freedom, the poetic agency and the making of history, and 'imagination' and 'love' as the alternative means to government over 'power'. It is no surprise that much of what Shelley articulated in the *Prometheus Unbound* volume that dealt with 'liberty and liberation' and in *A Defence of Poetry* should find its utterance in *Valperga*, which was written at around the same time. The belief that *Valperga* marks a break of dialogue between the Shelleys is another misunderstanding caused largely by overemphasising Mary Shelley's feminist critique targeted at her surrounding male Romantics. *Valperga* is a highly complex novel that demands reading on different levels if one is to achieve anything close to a satisfactory understanding of the text; what feminist reading takes to be Mary Shelley's articulation of the problematic of her own repressed authorship or female subjectivity can readily be translated into that of the writer-reader relationship (which Shelley faced) or of the viability of a poetic agent in a commercial society. Therefore, to read this novel as a simple feminist critique of masculine egotism (however useful and illuminating this is) limits the social and political scope, which Mary Shelley incorporates in this historical romance as a way of engaging in contemporary politics.[10] Mary Shelley's *Valperga* directly addresses the political issues concerning the state of post-Napoleonic Europe under the guise of the factional feud between republicanism and imperialism of the Italian Middle Ages: the heroine, Euthanasia, who represents the liberal effort, comes to a head-on clash with the imperialist aggression of Castruccio's force. The tragic failure of republicanism not only reflects that of the uprisings in Europe in 1820 during the period in which Mary Shelley spent writing the novel, but also the literary career of Percy Shelley, whose best intention to emancipate through his writings the human mind from misguided passions that license social and political oppression had gone largely unnoticed.[11]

Secondly, I would like to question the status of Percy Shelley's idealism, which is often seen to exist autonomously, as in the case of *Prometheus Unbound*. In tracing the literary trajectory of Percy Shelley, one is prone to overlook the complex interrelations among texts (especially within single volumes of collected works designed by Shelley himself) that sustain certain aesthetics and ideas as a whole.[12] When, for example, *Prometheus Unbound* is read within the framework of the 1820 volume that contains other poems that complement it, a slightly different picture emerges;[13] furthermore, if one takes into account other poems that Shelley was working on while writing *Prometheus Unbound*, the confident optimism that it first promised gives way to a realisation of the kind of pressure under which Shelley laboured.[14] This is not to say that Shelley's idealism is undermined in any way; rather it is to emphasise how precariously such utopian politics was allowed to exist in the first place. Shelley's next major work, *The Cenci*, demonstrates the ease with which Shelley was able to delineate 'the sad reality' of 'Equal, unclassed, tribeless and nationless' man, as opposed to the previous cosmological drama.[15]

To appreciate that Shelley at no point in his literary career held a position that was free from scepticism that encroached upon his idealism, gives his last poetical work, 'The Triumph of Life', a different kind of meaning.[16] In the past, the interpretative dispute has been over its aesthetic status: whether it signified an imaginative growth or decline, which, in its indecisiveness, had further invited a deconstructive reading that divorced the text from any kind of meaning altogether.[17] It is possible to see 'The Triumph' as a solidification of his previous poetic exercise—in both style and aesthetics. Indeed, the reason why critics hailed 'The Triumph' as Shelley's best effort was to do with the intensifying and consolidating aspect of his art that works on his previous poetic experiments.[18] But above all, 'The Triumph' invites a reading against the backdrop of Prometheanism; the fall, which Rousseau is depicted as having undergone in the poem, gains momentum when juxtaposed to the height from which he fell.[19] Its power lies in the way Shelley's idealistic vision is made to co-habit in a world in which such idealism is continuously being eroded by a force that exists beyond one's control.[20] This is not, however, to authorise a reading of 'The Triumph of Life' as his last statement as has often been the case simply because it was his last major poetic effort. It might be telling of the kind of both personal and public pressure under which he was increasingly becoming strained, but as Rousseau's own solipsistic account of history demonstrates, '"The Triumph of Life" is a criticism, not of life, but of a certain way of looking at life' (Roberts 762). The significance of perspective is central to Shelley's oeuvre, especially in the *Prometheus Unbound* volume;[21] 'The Triumph,' in which the persona is carefully deployed to stand at a distance from Rousseau so that they are not one and the same, is no exception. However compelling and seductive Rousseau's self-defeating testimony might be, there is no reason to believe that the narrator must follow his steps.[22]

If Mary Shelley's novel is best read with, and against, Shelleyan Romanticism, Robert Browning's early career demonstrates a similar involvement and investment in it. Mary Shelley and Browning are arguably the two most sympathetic and critical readers of Shelley even if Mary Shelley's gender and Browning's Victorian sensibility bring out differences from his high-Romantic stance. Little has been said on the relationship between these two writers; however, there is no evidence that they had any direct contact on Mary Shelley's return to England after Shelley's death in Italy; Browning's rather condescending comments in a letter regarding Mary Shelley suggest that he was not in the same mind about Mary Shelley as he was about Shelley.[23] This is a curious fact, as Browning's inclination toward realism has something in common with Mary Shelley's preference for the real rather than the 'theoretical and the ideal.'[24] My choice of text for Browning, *Sordello,* is not only set in medieval Italy, but also utilises the Guelph-Ghibelline strife to map out the contemporary politics. Dante is directly invoked, as he is in *Valperga,* as the inaugurator of the Italian Renaissance and one who was, like the protagonist-troubadour Sordello, interested in politics.[25] Although there are traces in *Sordello* that suggest Browning's familiarity with *Valperga,* no full-drawn conclusion can be made at this point that he had read it.[26] In *Sordello,* Browning interestingly reverses the conventional gender roles (as deployed in Mary Shelley's novel), so that the hero is made into a vulnerable feeling youth, whereas the heroine acts out the power-crazed politician. Whether this is a direct response to Mary Shelley's *Valperga,* or part of the general feminisation of poetic subjectivity, is pure speculation.[27]

Browning's early works have been discussed primarily in relation to Romanticism and Shelley's influence in particular.[28] Browning's own testimony of having immersed himself in Shelley's poetry itself speaks for the latter's presence in his early works.[29] Although Browning's emulation of Shelley's poetic style and thematic preoccupation has been commented on in great length, there are still voids that need to be addressed. For example, while *Pauline* and *Paracelsus* (to a lesser extent) have enjoyed critical attention, attempted to elucidate the Shelleyan tone and persona detectible in the poems, *Sordello* has been dismissed as a break from that influence.[30] For this, Browning's own gesture to release himself from his idol at the very beginning of the poem has much to answer.[31] My argument, however, is that while *Sordello* shies away from the overt lyricism of Romantic self-revelation characteristic in the works of Shelley and Byron, its thematic preoccupation remains intact; if anything, Shelleyan Prometheanism comes under full scrutiny in *Sordello*.[32]

It becomes clear as the poem progresses, and Browning's own relation to his chosen genre—epic narrative romance—turns problematic, that the poem's underlying theme is not love romance or the chivalric accomplishment of the troubadour, Sordello, but his Promethean impulse that fails to materialise in the political arena of the Italian Middle Ages.[33] That Browning chose an unknown troubadour over a successful poet such as Dante as the protagonist of his poem aligns with Browning's preference for failed heroes.[34] In explaining Browning's strong interest in them, one might add to the list of reasons provided by previous critics the legacy of political and poetic failure that consumed idealists such as Shelley.[35] However much *Sordello* deviates from Browning's previous practices, the protagonist remains a Romantic who strives to achieve self-fulfilment as a means to social betterment (although this is not the case from the beginning of the poem). What is understood to be Browning's revisionary attempt at Shelleyan poetics in the poem arises not solely from his disagreement with Shelley or the development of his distinct poetic identity, but also as a way of salvaging Prometheanism in an age that had overshadowed its potential.[36]

Browning's determination not to follow Shelley in his lyrical self-expression at the beginning of *Sordello* triggers Browning to work on a new poetic style that would accommodate his altered view on the role of his audience.[37] The conscientious move away from his previous works that emulated Shelley's poetry can partly be described in terms of Browning's later polarisation of 'subjective' and 'objective' poets.

However, as Browning himself comments in his essay on Shelley, the poetic characteristics of a poet are not always as clear-cut as the two terms suggest, and are often a matter of emphasis rather than strict identification.[38] In Browning's gesture toward 'objective' from 'subjective' poetry in *Sordello*, he seeks his model in Shelley's middle style as opposed to the high style that he initially attempted to emulate. It is a curious fact that while Browning vigorously scrutinised the moral and political implications of Shelleyan Prometheanism in the 1830s through his surrogate Sordello, he also looked to Shelley for the alternative poetics that would supplant his apocalyptic and transcendent view of poetry. This aspect of Browning's engagement with Shelley's poetry has attracted little attention in the past. This book aims to address this neglect, which has gone unnoticed precisely because Shelley's influence on Browning, although unquestionable, has tended to fix upon the more prominent aspect of that relationship.

While *Sordello* still engages in Romanticism, it also departs from it as Browning consolidates his own poetics during the course of the poem. Sordello's self-absorbed life in the beginning in which he mingles with nature is a scathing criticism of Wordsworth, whose retreat from the real world into the Lakes denoted the elder poet's apostasy and shying away from taking political responsibility.[39] Sordello's appropriation of Apollo has direct resonance that recalls Shelley's 'Hymn of Apollo'; it provides Browning with a means of critiquing the poet's own stance at deification. That Browning detected a certain arrogance and transgression in the Romantic poets, such as Byron and Shelley, in assuming godhead is clear. Browning exploits his surrogate Sordello to expose what he saw as problematic in the Romantic bard; in recasting his protagonist-poet, he assimilates the moral judgement and work ethic of the Protestant tradition. Browning's rejection of eighteenth-century philosophy (i.e. French materialism) in a gesture toward his Christian faith is a clear break from Shelley who among other things was, no doubt, a disciple of that tradition. Browning's attempt to recover spirituality in the form of an institutionalised religion (even in its instability) reflects a general cultural shift that became Victorianism. The success of the novel as a literary genre in the Victorian period also accounts for the stylistic idiosyncrasies of

Sordello and its emulation of realism. The Romantic and Victorian sensibilities co-exist in *Sordello*, which partly explains the difficulty and confusion that is often associated with the poem.

CONTEXTS: HISTORICAL BACKGROUND

The Shelleys pursued their early careers in the aftermath of the Napoleonic wars, which was marked by reactionary politics at home, and imperial aggression on the continent, fuelled by opportunism. Although the French rule under Napoleon had faced Italian resistance, as an act of foreign aggression, it nevertheless had contributed to 'the development of Italian national sentiment.'[40] Napoleon's policies aimed at centralisation had an effect of evoking the idea of a unified Italy among the Italians; by the same token, however, writers were quick to respond to what looked like a cultural colonisation 'by resurrecting that "cultural nationalism" which had first appeared in Italy during the Renaissance' (Duggan 96).

When the coalition army finally defeated Napoleon, Italy found itself once again in the hands of the Austrians, who ensured their power over the region at the peace settlement of Vienna in 1815 by restoring the deposed rulers—Victor Emmanuel I to Turin, Ferdinand II to Florence, the Pope to Rome, and afterwards, Ferdinand IV to Naples—and placing Lombardy and Venice under their own direct control. The Austrian presence in Italy reversed the progressive values that the French Revolution had promoted, by insisting on the 'superior merits of tradition, authority, and hierarchy, sanctioned by religion' (Duggan 100; Holt 38). Thus, the former supporters of liberty were forced either into exile or underground: Foscolo, Rossetti, Panizzi, and Berchet are some of the famous poets and scholars who arrived in England and through whom the British intelligentsia was kept up to date on the Italian political scene (Brand 3). In Italy, secret societies became 'the main vehicles for liberal dissent after 1815' (Duggan 43). Although attempts to subvert this backward regime did take place, most notably in Naples in the summer of 1820, the insurgents lacked a coherent goal and thereby could not sustain their political power (Duggan 48).[41]

When the Shelleys moved in 1818 to Italy as the place of their permanent residence, they came to a country that did not yet know itself as a unified nation, with stifled energy that would occasionally unleash itself only to be crushed by the Austrian military. As a fervent advocate of liberty, Shelley took the destiny of Italy upon himself; his exiled status further enhanced his sense of alienation and political frustration and he aligned himself ever closer to Italy's own poets of the past—Dante and Petrarch. 'Lines Written Among the Euganean Hills' laments the degradation of the Italian city-states, especially Venice, which had once been a 'Sun-girt City' but 'Now is come a darker day'; 'Ode to the West Wind' envisages political hope through the seasonal cycle; and while 'Ode to Liberty' celebrates the uprising in Spain, 'Ode To Naples' rejoices in a revolution that followed in Naples. That Shelley staged his composition of his cosmological drama *Prometheus Unbound* in terms of tyrannical oppression and liberation from it in Rome is suggestive; it is also telling that he insisted on the inspiration of his other masterpiece on patriarchal tyranny, *The Cenci*, as being his Roman experience.[42] Much of Shelley's poetry is inextricable from the Italian political scene of the early nineteenth century and the rich Italian historical arena in which past examples could be found.

While Shelley responded to the political developments on the Continent with some urgency, he never lost sight of the events that were taking place at home. In the years following the Congress of Vienna, England was becoming increasingly reactionary in fear of a mob rule: the attempt by the government to root out any cause of public agitation culminated in what came to be known as the 'Peterloo Massacre'. The summer following the Shelleys' departure from England, a crowd of 60,000 working men in Manchester gathered in St. Peter's Field to hear Henry Hunt address them on parliamentary reform; it was disrupted by a group of soldiers who charged into the crowd killing approximately 15 and injuring 500 people. Shelley was informed of this event through the *Examiner* a few days later and had finished writing his poem on the event, *The Mask of Anarchy*, by September. His critique is targeted at the Foreign Secretary, Castlereagh, who led England through the Napoleonic Wars and took oppressive measures both in Ireland and at home, and at the Home secretary, Sidmouth, who used government spies and informants to repress and eradicate radical activities. Shelley composed a number of poems on the state of England in 1819: 'Lines Written during the Castlereagh Administration' (or 'To Sidmouth and Castlereagh'), 'Men of England: A Song', 'A New National Anthem', 'England in 1819', 'Ballad of the Starving Mother' as well as *The Mask of Anarchy*.[43] The group of poems indicates a pivotal significance for 1819—as a historical moment that defines itself against the past and the future, what James Chandler calls a 'case' of Romantic historicism.[44]

Mary Shelley was no less political than Shelley in her writings: *Frankenstein* is no doubt a statement on the French Revolution even if it resists being read solely on those terms; her second novel, *Valperga*, directly raises political issues, however displaced in time. Mary Shelley's novels demonstrate not only an awareness of but also a willingness to directly engage in the socio-political debate of the early nineteenth century; it is no wonder then that such words as 'liberty' and 'tyranny' run as leitmotifs through *Valperga*. It is, however, Mary Shelley who directly dealt with the theme of Italian struggle for freedom, not simply on an abstract, but also on a more pragmatic, level. *Valperga,* no doubt, draws its inspiration from Sismondi's *Histoire des Républiques Italiennes du Moyen Âge,* in which the development of Italian history from a feudalistic age to the birth of republicanism—in Florence, for instance—is delineated and in which Dante is made to play a central role:

> The other nations of Europe were yet immersed in barbarism, when Italy, where the light of civilization had never been wholly eclipsed, began to emerge from the darkness of the ruin of the Western Empire, and to catch from the East the returning rays of literature and science. At the beginning of the fourteenth century Dante had already given a permanent form to the language which was the offspring of this revolution; he was personally engaged in those political struggles, in which the elements of the good and evil that have since assumed a more permanent form were contending; his disappointment and exile gave him leisure to meditate, and produced his *Divina Comedia*. (*Valperga* 7)

Although Mary Shelley depicts her heroine, Euthanasia, with much sympathy, as the Countess of Valperga who seeks to retain her political autonomy against a fierce factional contest that has little to do with the welfare of the people but all to do with partisan interest, her idealistic independence looks hopelessly unrealistic. In the years that were spent in writing *Valperga*, Mary Shelley saw the uprisings in Spain and in Naples that were in the end short-lived. As the failure drove Shelley to despondency and scepticism over the fate of Italy, Mary Shelley seemed to have encoded the inevitability of failure of such autonomous government in the face of imperial aggression. Given the time in which *Valperga* was written, it is difficult to dismiss the growing awareness of national sentiment and solidarity that would become the movement toward national unification, *Risorgimento*. That the idea of an Italian unity came from Sardinia-Piedmont, the sole independent Italian state, which sought to annex Lombardy in an attempt to rival the Austrian power, reverberates in *Valperga*: Galeazzo Visconti of Milan, the chief power of Lombardy, suggests the usurpation of Florence to Castruccio (who had recently settled on a peace agreement with Florence) as a means of unifying Tuscany and eventually Italy. Although the impulse for unification is not identical—Visconti's attempt being in alliance with the Holy Roman Emperor whereas *Risorgimento* was a break away from the Austrian domination—the necessity of collective power nonetheless resonates as the only realistic means of rivalling an imperialist power.

In Browning's *Sordello*, the question of Italian nationalism becomes a central issue as opposed to what was merely implied in *Valperga*. The protagonist-troubadour, Sordello, figures as the failure to achieve Italian unification—both politically and aesthetically. That Dante is regarded as the one who inaugurated the Italian Renaissance in a similar way in which Mary Shelley saw his role is clear: Browning implies this in the text by stating that Sordello's efforts (spent in vain) will be superseded by those of his successor. What Browning dramatises, as in the case of Euthanasia in *Valperga*, is an individual who is at odds with historical necessity, who cannot assimilate him/herself to the collective force at work. Whereas Euthanasia attempts to transform society through the imagination and love—the very creeds of Godwin and Percy Shelley—Sordello seeks to inaugurate a New Jerusalem by means of his apocalyptic vision—a legacy of Shelleyan Prometheansim. For this reason, neither of the works is ultimately about Italian nationalism; it concerns the Romantic programme (of which both protagonists are agents) and its viability as a means of changing society.

Browning's reading of Dante's *Divina Comedia* (in which Sordello briefly appears) with his Italian teacher, Angelo Cerutti, is thought to have influenced his choice of material for his narrative poem *Sordello*.[45] It is not a coincidence perhaps that Browning's longest poem on Italy (with the exception of *The Ring and the Book*) and contemporary politics should owe its inspiration to Cerutti, an Italian living in London with an in-depth knowledge of Italian history and culture. Although Cerutti came to England for financial rather than political reasons, the growing number of Italian exiles that came to England in the 1820s fleeing the oppression of a foreign rule in Italy, could not have escaped Browning's attention. Browning, through his Italian tutor, or simply through his growing interest in Italy, must have become aware of their presence in London with a mission 'to awaken the English public generally to a sense of Italy's wrongs by publishing books, pamphlets and articles of a political nature' (Brand 33). Among such exiles, Foscolo and Panizzi were particularly active in making their views known to the public.[46]

Their mission to inform the English public of the state of political oppression (the word used by Panizzi in his article in the *Edinburgh Review* in 1832) in Italy duly reflects the political developments in Italy in the 1820s. In Lombardy, Piedmont, and the Papal States, the Austrians had strengthened their control over the activities of secret societies and had sentenced prominent liberals to long-term imprisonment; in the case of Santarosa's conspirators, ninety-seven were condemned to death.[47] The most famous secret society, the *Carbonari*, which mainly operated in southern Italy, was successful in bringing about the 1831 revolutions but proved again short-lived owing to 'the inability of the different cities to lay aside their rivalries and make a common cause' (Duggan 107). The failure of the 1831 insurrections marked a turning point in the Italian liberal movement, which afterwards was to be led by Giuseppe Mazzini, a young member of the *Carbonari*. Mazzini, who became an exile in the same year for his hand in an uprising in Liguria, formed a secret society called Young Italy that was to have a considerable impact on the nationalist movement.[48] Mazzini inaugurated a new historical epoch by emphasising the importance of the 'collective struggle' of the people over the 'struggle for individual rights' and of 'duties' rather than 'rights' (Duggan 108, 109); this shift in emphasis signified his break away from the French model on which much of the past revolutionary ethos had been based. His further exile to England in 1837 made his ideas particularly current through his friendship with the Carlyles and with Browning.[49]

Browning wrote a number of poems on the Italian question, beginning with *Sordello*; his trip to Italy in 1838 was the first of many he was to make to that country, which he would eventually choose as the destination of his elopement with Elizabeth Barrett and the place of their residence. *Pippa Passes*, which Browning is thought to have conceived in the year following his first visit to Italy, deals not only with the Italian locale—Asolo in the Veneto—but also with Italian nationalism; 'Italy in England' written a few years later dramatises the struggle for Italian unification known as the *Risorgimento*. Whether the latter poem was actually based on Mazzini's pamphlet, *Ricordi dei Fratelli Bandiera*, remains to be proven; however, its compassionate depiction of the political struggle, by an Englishman, was enough to impress Mazzini. Browning continued to write on the *Risorgimento* in the 1850s in Italy—for example, *Old Pictures* and *De Gustibus*—and further into 1860, in *Prince Hohenstiel*.[50]

If the Italian setting provided Browning with the framework for his radical politics in *Sordello*, he drew his material from the English political debates of the 1830s. The most direct medium through which he acquainted himself with various political issues was W.J. Fox's *The Monthly Repository*. Fox shared Browning's dissenting background and his radical politics appealed to Browning: through Fox, the poet was to become acquainted with political and social thinkers of the day, such as J.S. Mill, Thomas Carlyle, Leigh Hunt, and Harriet and James Martineau.[51] *Monthly Repository* prided itself on the fusion of literature and politics with the most notable contributor of this kind being the author of *Corn Law Rhymes,* Ebenezer Elliot. When the editorship passed from Fox to R.H. Horne and then to Leigh Hunt in 1837, the latter attempted to resuscitate the principles on which he had founded *The Examiner* 29 years before—that is, the 'combination of a love of literature with politics' (Mason 266, 268). Browning therefore would have felt at home with such issues as Parliamentary reform, the repeal of the Corn Laws and Chartist movements, which, however indirectly, became assimilated into his poetry.[52]

NAPOLEON

If the French Revolution was the grand theme of the nineteenth century, then Napoleon is undoubtedly the exponent of it who dominated the public imagination. As the first- and second-generation Romantics demonstrate, the persona of Napoleon was bound up with the ethos of the French Revolution and its failure, so much so that one's assessment of his character became a tool by which the conservatives and radicals came to position themselves in the political arena of post-revolutionary England. Whereas the Lake poets saw Napoleon as Satanic in the years that followed Napoleon's peninsular campaigns and did not spare any words of eulogy for Wellington's defeat of Napoleon in 1814, Byron refused to do just that, which outraged Scott in his review of Byron's *Childe Harold,* Canto III in the Tory *Quarterly Review* of 16 October 1816 (Bainbridge 159). That Byron omitted homage to Wellington was scandalous in the patriotic climate that followed the Battle of Waterloo; among the flood of poems written on the topic, it stood out as being perniciously subversive. Not only did Byron have a personal investment in the figure of Napoleon, whose theatricality on the world stage appealed to his own self-projected image, but Napoleon's potential role as the liberator of the people and nations had also struck a chord in his liberal impulses. Hazlitt went even further by identifying Napoleon with Milton's Satan whose heroic defiance in the face of opposition aligned him as one fighting for the cause of the people (Bainbridge 188). The radicals saw more danger in the reactionary climate of post-Waterloo England than in Napoleon's military aggression, which disgraced his initial reputation as the liberator.

While Napoleon was used to justify and endorse the reactionary climate in England by the Lake poets, Byron and Hazlitt endeavoured to place his shortcomings in a larger framework, thereby emphasising a more significant issue at stake—the cause of liberty—which in their eyes was being conveniently brushed aside by their opponents. Against such party politics, the Shelleys and Browning took an interest in Napoleon as the man whose personal fault was seen to reflect a problem endemic to the nature of power.

In understanding Napoleon—both as a potential liberator and as a tyrant—his historical presence posed a dilemma for P.B. Shelley that would become generalised into 'how power and will/In opposition rule our mortal day' (ll. 228–9). That the *beau idéal* of the French Revolution became disgraced by Napoleon's military aggression rather than promoted by it (as was first thought) is being referred to here. As Shelley places Napoleon in a group of the 'The great, the unforgotten' whose tragedy lay in their inability to 'know themselves' (l. 209) and whose 'might/Could not repress the mutiny within' (ll. 212–13), Shelley probes further into the mind of the figure. In 'Sonnet: To the Republic of Benevento' (or 'Sonnet: Political Greatness'), which was written around the same time as 'Lines Written on Hearing the News of the Death of Napoleon', Shelley takes this further by stating what Napoleon failed to achieve in terms of his personality. It is possible to detect in Shelley's use of rhetoric here an echo of Walter Savage Landor's eulogy of Napoleon in *Gebirus*, written in 1798 (a year after Napoleon's deliverance of the Italians from the Austrians). Despite Landor's slighting of the epic genre, he depicts Napoleon as the hero of the poem by deliberately distinguishing him as 'man', as opposed to Gebirus, who is designated as 'Prince' or 'King' (Bainbridge 43). Landor's refusal to attach any hereditary title to Napoleon makes him a republican hero who corresponds to another such figure, George Washington, whom he likewise addresses as 'O Man!' (l. 59) in his 'Ode to General Washington'.[53]

In the sonnet, it is instructive that Shelley uses 'man' in a similar way to Landor, undermining the 'force or custom' that produces social titles of any kind in defining 'political greatness':

> Man who *man* would be,
> Must rule the empire of himself; in it
> Must be supreme, establishing his throne
> On vanquished will,—quelling the *anarchy*
> Of hopes and fears,—being himself alone.—
> (*SPP* 327; ll. 10–14) [emphases added][54]

Shelley's possible allusion here to Napoleon as the failed case is acute if one recalls 'Ode to Liberty' in which Napoleon is addressed as 'The Anarch' (l. 175). What Shelley dramatises here is the dichotomy of the private and the public: even Napoleon, who was successful in conquering the external sphere by using his military skills, is not guaranteed to rule over 'the empire of himself'.

In Mary Shelley's *Valperga*, Castruccio Castracani figures as the Napoleonic figure whose sole ambition is to leave his mark in history. Castruccio contemplates self-aggrandizement at age seven:

> [...] imagination, ever at work, pictured his future life, brilliant with glowing love, transcendant with glory and success. Thus, in solitude, while no censuring eye could check the exuberant vanity, he would throw his arms to the north, the south, the east, and the west, crying,—'There—there—there, and there, shall my fame reach!'—and then, in gay defiance, casting his eager glance towards heaven:—'and even there, if man may climb the slippery sides of the arched palace of eternal fame, there also will I be recorded'.[55] (23)

One of the objectives of the novel is, no doubt, to delineate a character whose political ambition gradually overtakes his individuality: Mary Shelley gives a meticulous account of this process, to which various personal influences and political circumstances contribute. As John Gibson Lockhart refers to Mary Shelley's 'perpetual drumming at poor Bonaparte' in his review of *Valperga* in *Blackwood's Edinburgh*

Magazine, it does not take much for the reader to make the connection between the power-crazed Castruccio Castracani and Napoleon Bonaparte.[56] Despite Mary Shelley's denial of this association, the fact that she made this historical figure (who had little in common with Napoleon except for his outstanding military skills) a tragic hero raises the question of where that inspiration came from. Byron is a possible model; but as mentioned earlier, Byron's self-projected image itself owed much to Napoleon, whose theatrical presence Byron attempted to emulate in his writing. Mary Shelley's harsh treatment of Castruccio, which was noted by the same reviewer in the *Blackwood's*, reads like a condemnation of the 'will to power' that overcame Napoleon and Castruccio alike as a futile passion that defeats itself in the end, as the inscription of his tombstone succinctly tells:

> Lo, by the fame of my deeds, I live and shall live, the glory of Italian soldiery, the paragon of the Lucchese, the pride of Tuscany Castruccio, son of Gerio, of the family of the Antelminelli. I lived, I sinned, I suffered; I yielded to Nature. Men of good will, help a devout soul in need, mindful that in short while ye are to die. (326)

Castruccio and Napoleon similarly become victims of time by succumbing to the worldly power that is only defined by temporality. Dante, on the other hand, figures in the novel as the poet whose poetry will continue to inspire across Time; P.B. Shelley likewise gave him a privileged status in *A Defence of Poetry*:

> The poetry of Dante may be considered as the bridge thrown over the stream of time, which unites the modern and antient world. The distorted notions of invisible things which Dante and his rival Milton have idealized, are merely the mask and the mantle in which these great poets walk through eternity enveloped and disguised.
>
> (*SPP* 526)

The dichotomy into 'men of action' (such as Castruccio and Napoleon), and 'poets' and 'philosophers' is central to 'The Triumph of Life', *Valperga*, and *Sordello*: whereas the Shelleys see the division as a sad reality in which 'Good and the means of good' are 'made irreconcilable' (ll. 230–1), Browning takes this further into pragmatic politics that aim to reduce the gap rather than eliminate it.

If Napoleonic men of action and Dantean poet stand in contrast to one another in the works of the Shelleys, their mutual exclusion becomes questioned in Browning's *Sordello*. Browning sets out by creating two characters that enact these two roles: Salinguerra, whose sole ambition is to serve Ecelin and his Ghibelline party and Sordello, who, as the forerunner of Dante, is given a chance to inaugurate the Italian Renaissance but fails. What deserves attention is the fact that politics, which governs 'men of action', becomes an immediate problem for the poets, too. In other words, poets are not excused from the real world to retreat into their ideal haven as Sordello does near the beginning of the poem. Browning refuses to see the world divided into the 'real' and the 'ideal': such demarcation has no meaning in his politics. What the poem addresses through Salinguerra and Sordello is the way in which such a schism may be avoided. This, to a certain degree, reflects the change of climate in the radical cause that took place between the Shelleys' compositions in the beginning of the 1820s and Browning's during the late 1830s.

Individual power is undermined considerably if one compares Castruccio to Salinguerra: whereas the former still retains a glamour and power that is reminiscent of Napoleon, the heroic impact of the latter lessened considerably, as his self-imposed subservience to Ecelin demonstrates. One is able to detect a change in ethos that initially owed itself to the French Revolution. As the Italian revolutionist Mazzini came to emphasise the 'collective struggle' over the 'struggle for individual rights', and 'duties' over 'rights', Browning similarly voiced this epistemological shift by punishing Sordello for his refusal to accept his limited role in history. That collectivism was seen to be equally important as individualism is apparent in Browning's own authorial voice, which breaks through in the poem: 'that collective man/Outstrips the individual!' (v 95–6). As J.S. Mill stated in his essay 'Civilization', social progress was seen to go hand in hand with the transference of power from individuals to the masses, which is duly reflected here. What is also worth noting is the epistemological shift that had taken placed since high Romanticism when the Godwinian idea of individual freedom was still predominant as the basic criteria of social progress, as in the case of the Shelleys. Browning's emphasis on collective will, however, is not necessarily only historically specific; it also denotes Browning's challenge against a prevalent historiography that only deals with individuals and their contribution to the making of history while neglecting the role played by their fellow men.

If the Shelleys believed that Napoleon was a victim of his own 'will to power', which turned his initial heroism into self-aggrandizement, then Browning was more cautious about interpreting his downfall as the result of a change in his character. Forster's *Life of Strafford*, which Browning assisted in writing, provides us with an insight into his views on historical figures such as Wentworth, whose character remains an enigma at best.[57] What Browning attempts to uncover through this prose work is the consistency of an individual mind that is not understood as such but instead becomes misinterpreted owing to the incomprehensible nature of his actions—in this case, Wentworth's relentless support for the weak and worthless King:

> [...] he [Wentworth] was consistent to himself throughout. I have always considered that much good worth is thrown away upon what is usually called 'apostacy'. In the majority of cases, if the circumstances are thoroughly examined, it will be found that there has been 'no such thing'. (Furnivall 60–61)

Not only does Browning argue for the consistency of individual character, but he also criticises the historian whose critical insight does not reach beyond 'their dispensation of good and evil fame' and who capitalises on recounting a 'complete change' in character that 'has commonly no mean influence on the nature of their award' (Furnivall 61).

Browning's scepticism about historical representation as historical truth is not far off from recent critiques of the status of historical discourse and knowledge: that is, historical representation is seen to be not so much about historical truth but historical myth or fabrication 'shaped according to teleological and often ideological designs' (Bainbridge 5). Napoleon is a compelling example because he provided the historical arena in which people from opposite political camps could participate to position themselves through their representations of him, which in effect had little to do with the 'real' Napoleon but all to do with their exercise of imagination and fabrication to endorse their ideological views.

ROMANTIC HISTORIOGRAPHY

As they tell the history of Western civilisation or of the Italian Middle Ages, all three texts do so by interweaving the private and public histories between which the protagonists negotiate. P.B. Shelley's 'The Triumph of Life' characteristically opens with a symbolic description of the sunrise that can be interpreted as either the dawn of civilisation or the emergence of the life principle in the form of sun worship. Just as the narrator cannot join in to celebrate life as all other natural forms do, his psychological *impasse* becomes translated into that of historical progress. The narrator's guide in the poem, who takes the figure of the historical Rousseau, likewise recounts his own past in an allegorical narrative; when he is left behind by the 'shape all light', which possibly represents his narcissistic desire in the guise of the imagination, he finds himself left in 'a public way', where he is reduced to 'a root'. That private histories correspond to public histories in the way Shelley depicts in 'The Triumph of Life' is not a novel practice for him; indeed, its genealogy can be traced back to 'Lines written among the Euganean Hills', where his personal loss converges with that of the Italian past. Shelley's reading of history as at once consisting of the private and public resonates in Mary Shelley's *Valperga*. Castruccio's ruthless usurpation of the castle and the surrounding province that belongs to the heroine, Euthanasia, gains sentimental significance as it symbolises his violation and betrayal of their love compact. It is of interest that Mary Shelley chose to delineate Castruccio's imperialist aggression through his exploitation of the female. Yet, it also tells the history of the ideological contest—between republicanism and imperialism—that characterised the Italian Middle Ages.

Browning seems to invert Mary Shelley's depiction of gender roles in *Sordello*: the troubadour-protagonist, Sordello, shows signs of femininity by being deeply affected by the pillage scene of Ferrara whereas his 'out-soul' Palma stands as a masculine will-to-power who is not only indifferent to human misery but whose sole intent is to make Sordello 'king'. Although Sordello's conversion to a Guelph does not materialise into taking action simply because he cannot convince Palma and Salinguerra to fight on the side of the people, his failure as a political leader has much to do with his lack of means of achieving it. That Sordello could not find his Beatrice figure resonates in the poem as another cause of his underachievement compared to Dante's in his *Divine Comedy*. The 'man of action', Salinguerra, unlike Mary Shelley's Castruccio, devotes himself to the house of Romano simply because his political ambition has been crippled by his loss of his wife and son (which he was led to believe by Ecelin's deceiving wife). Browning's emphasis on the femininity in men and masculinity in women makes the point that the traditional grouping of masculinity with the public sphere and femininity with the private does not hold and that they are not necessarily gender specific.

All three texts—'The Triumph of Life', *Valperga*, and *Sordello*—are examples of Romantic historiography that endorse a set of aesthetic values set against those of Enlightenment historiography. Rather than dealing with 'society in a mass' and eliciting 'generalities of historical abstraction', Godwin, for example, called for the importance of representing 'the materials of which it [society] is composed': 'the operation of human passions [...] the empire of motives [...] the influence that one human being exercises over another'.[58] Furthermore, Carlyle was to push this notion forward by claiming that the historical process was 'the essence of innumerable biographies'.[59] Indeed, as all three texts engage in delineating the history of the West or of the Italian Middle Ages, they do so through the personal lives of the individuals.

In 'The Triumph of Life', Shelley deliberately invokes Enlightenment historiography by opening his poem with what may be understood to be the dawn of civilisation; instead of continuing his narrative of universal history, Shelley turns his critical attention to Rousseau, who serves as a useful link between the *philosophes* and the Romantics such as himself.

Despite Rousseau's encounter with the 'shape all light', which again seems to invoke the Enlightenment by Shelley's use of 'light', Rousseau is found by the narrator on the side of the public way, spiritually emptied without hope or will to follow the 'chariot of life'. As Rousseau's dominating pessimism in the poem invited critics to read the poem as Shelley's own statement on personal and public failure, it is easy to translate Rousseau's scepticism toward life into that of the narrator and further into Shelley's own view. However, the carefully constructed framework—a vision of a dream within a dream—will not allow such a simplistic equation to pass without some doubts: the narrator is distanced from Rousseau in his state of suspension; although he shares Rousseau's pessimism, he has not yet awoken from his dream-vision to experience it in reality. Shelley is at once empathising with Rousseau and distancing himself from him in the knowledge that the irony and scepticism with which the *philosophes* came to view society must be scrutinised, but not identified with, if one is to overcome their failure.[60]

Mary Shelley's *Valperga* is in line with Godwin's idea of history in that she deliberately set out to anatomise the characters and their influence on one another, so that the inner dramas of the two heroines set against the making of a tyrant in the hero make up her history of the Italian Middle Ages. Equally deserving attention are Scott's techniques in his portrayal of the historical past: 'the depiction of the variety, color, and vividness of the historical field';[61] but more importantly 'his capacity to give living human embodiment to historical-social types'.[62] *The Literary Gazette* praised the section on Euthanasia's court 'for its vivid picture of the manners of the age' while *The Literary Register of the Fine Arts, Sciences, and Belles Lettres* went so far as to say that 'The principal merit of this novel consists [...] in its faithful delineation of the character and manners of the people of the age of which it treats'.[63] For all her success in typecasting characters—the shrewd and greedy Benedetto Peppi, the treacherous and cruel Galeazzo Visconti, the heretical Beatrice, and the Dantean Euthanasia, to name a few—Mary Shelley's motive behind her historical novel has more in common with Godwin's than Scott's: the novel is used as a means to engage in the political discourse of a liberal dissent.[64]

Browning similarly exploited his historical material to depict the present. Although there is no doubt, especially in his adoption of a six-book structure, that Browning owed his idea of historical romance to Scott, his divergence from Scott's historical novels is as clear as Mary Shelley's in *Valperga*. If P.B. Shelley's 'The Triumph of Life' suffers from the subjective solipsism 'of high romantic tradition' then Mary Shelley's *Valperga* introduces judgement through the heroine, Euthanasia, which privileged the female control over cultural morality.[65] Browning's *Sordello* presents the Romantic bard of subjective solipsism only as a means to convert him into a new type of poet who reflects not only Browning's revisionary outcome of his poetics—his abandonment of the 'subjective' in favour of the 'objective'—but also the change in aesthetic taste—for example, preference for realism over idealism, factual over subjective history—that became prominent as the century progressed.

In considering these three texts as cases of Romantic historiography, what is noticeable is that they are unable to deliver what they set out to produce: 'The Triumph of Life' fails to become Petrarch's *Trionfi*, as a historical vision that embodies ontological and teleological values as defined in the latter work; both *Valperga* and *Sordello* are tragedies that disappoint one's expectation of a romance. At the heart of these three texts, it is possible to argue for the presence of a trauma that subverts the generic expectations; they only reach textual completion owing to their formal restraint (either of accidental truncation or of their romance format).

If one were to adopt Gary Handwerk's argument that '[t]rauma is [...] one of the two characteristic patterns of historicity for Romanticism' then 'The Triumph of Life', *Valperga*, and *Sordello* are no exception.[66] Handwerk utilises trauma theory to analyse Godwin's historical novel *Mandeville* as a case that demonstrates 'the limits of Godwin's liberal imagination in its inability to conceive recursiveness except as traumatic repetition' (Handwerk 93). These three texts suffer from a similar kind of traumatic repetition in that they are unable to imagine a successful social revolution that will emancipate them from stasis. As Cathy Caruth defines trauma in *Unclaimed Experience: Trauma,*

Narrative, and History, 'recursiveness' is one of its characteristic manifestations:

> trauma describes an overwhelming experience of sudden or catastrophic events in which the response to the event occurs in the often delayed, uncontrolled repetitive appearance of hallucinations and other intrusive phenomena.[67]

At the heart of trauma lies the inaccessibility of an event as historical process thereby creating a lacuna in the historical narrative that one tells. What the three texts have in common is the absence of an event, which becomes repeatedly referred to but never directly engaged with. We read instead the recurrence of stasis, which narrator and protagonist alike have fallen into: in 'The Triumph', the narrator is in a paralysed state in which he is unable to act; the ones who do act in *Valperga* do so toward social destruction while the heroine, Euthanasia, remains in resolute inaction (except when she is called to defend her castle on one occasion and Castruccio's life on another); Sordello is weighed down by his paramount task of self-revelation, which disables him from acting. Because all three protagonists are unable to act, the stories centre on that stasis creating a narrative pattern that might be understood as being recursive: 'The Triumph' repeats the narrator's frustrated liberal imagination in a deadlock through Rousseau; Euthanasia's emotional outpouring of her faith in, and betrayal by, Castruccio becomes repeated in Beatrice's narrative; Sordello's inability to act translates into the author's inability to write his 'poem about a poet writing poems'.[68] They all deal with trauma of one form or another: at a more general level, the failure of the French Revolution no doubt lurks in the background of their inability to tell a successful story of social transformation; yet, they are also deeply crippled by personal anxieties that surface in the text.

A series of lyrics P.B. Shelley composed while he was working on 'The Triumph of Life' offers clues to the narrator's paralysed state that disables historical progress in the poem: lyrics written for Jane Williams, which are conventionally understood to be love poems, create a problematic blockage for Shelley's own historical narrative that was until that point defined by his marital partnership with Mary Shelley. In understanding the emotional outpourings by two women that dominate *Valperga*, *Mathilda* offers a useful insight: Mary Shelley temporarily left *Valperga* to write her novella in the summer of 1819 when she was on the brink of deep depression after losing her son William. She blamed P.B. Shelley for the death of her two children, which happened within a space of a year; the lack of sympathy from her father, William Godwin, was also causing her great mental pain. That she felt betrayed by her father and emotionally unassisted by her male companion surfaces in the novella. Although the heroine's emotions that govern *Mathilda* at the expense of its plot become assimilated into the story of Castruccio Castracani and his romantic intrigues with Euthanasia and Beatrice in *Valperga*, its historical narrative remains far from stable: the two private histories of the heroines stand in contest with the public history of Castruccio's deeds. The main plot, despite what the title suggests—*The Life and Adventures of Castruccio*—is the betrayal of the two heroines by the hero to which their narratives repeatedly return.

In the case of Browning's *Sordello*, its poetic crisis may best be understood in relation to Browning's engagement with Romantic poetry and Romanticism at large. That Browning felt the necessity to dismiss Shelley at the beginning of the poem is suggestive:

> —thou, spirit, come not near
> Now—nor this time desert thy cloudy place
> To scare me, thus employed, with that pure face! (i 60–62)

That Shelley is clearly a threat to Browning, which Bloom explains as 'the anxiety of influence' exercised by one strong poet over another who comes after him, is maintained throughout the poem in Browning's extensive influence by, and revision of, Shelleyan poetics. It is not, however, simply a Oedipal contest between the two poets that defines Browning's poetic struggle; the failure of the Romantic poets to assimilate poetry into politics through their appeal to the audience had a scarring effect on the succeeding poets, including Browning, who began their careers by grappling with the idea of the role of a poet in an industrial society. Therefore, it is not surprising when the authorial voice breaks through the romance narrative in order to redefine his poetics. However idiosyncratic this practice may be, Browning exploits his poem to work out his revisionary process. Thus, the romance narrative becomes Browning's own initiation into his poetic identity.

Romantic Historicism

Taking my cue from James Chandler's *England in 1819*, in which Chandler makes a convincing case for Romantic historicism by focusing on the literature published in 1819, I would like to argue that a similar self-consciousness over one's historical moment prevails in 'The Triumph', *Valperga*, and *Sordello*. Although the radical momentum dwindled to some extent in the years following 1819, as Chandler noted on the reversal of Shelley's ideals in 'The Triumph' written in 1822 (Chandler 29), both 'The Triumph' and *Valperga* nevertheless demonstrate their sustaining engagement with 'the spirit of the age', however gloomy it might have become. They are not concerned solely with the state of Britain, but of Europe at large: the Shelleys came to see an epochal transition taking place on a pan-European scale from feudalistic imperialism to democratic liberalism, which was interlinked with the rise of nationalism. In expectation of such a change, which was first introduced by the French Revolution, the Shelleys naturally found themselves at a pivot in history that would either inaugurate a new age or lapse back into the feudal past. What Shelley stated in the 'Preface' to *The Revolt of Islam*, which was written a few years before in 1817 as a response to the aftermath of the failure of the French Revolution, gains particular relevance here:

> But on the first reverses of hope in the progress of French liberty, the sanguine eagerness for good overleapt the solution of these questions, and for a time extinguished itself in the unexpectedness of their result. Thus many of the most ardent and tender-hearted of the worshippers of public good, have been morally ruined by what a partial glimpse of the events they deplored, appeared to show as the melancholy desolation of all their cherished hopes. Hence gloom and mis-

> anthropy have become the characteristics of the age in which we live, the solace of a disappointment that unconsciously finds relief only in the wilful exaggeration of its own despair. (Everest 2000, p. 37)

That the followers of the *philosophes* fell into scepticism and irony with which they came to see history as a result of the events that followed the French Revolution imposes a threat on liberals such as Shelley, who came to acknowledge that progress must be accompanied by the dissemination of ideas as well as practical means to achieving it. In the years that followed the political uprisings in Italy and Spain that ended in failure, the urgency for Shelley to reassess the Revolutionary ethos must have been especially acute. In *Valperga*, Mary Shelley likewise questions the validity of individualistic liberalism that seeks to maintain itself where collective interests operate as the primary motive in society. As opposed to the Romantic idea of societal progress that was defined by Godwin's *Political Justice* in the 1790s, the utilitarian school of thought, which sought to advance collective over individual interest, gained momentum that would materialise itself in the reform acts of the nineteenth century.

Browning's *Sordello* is a good example in which such a shift in radicalism from individualism to collectivism occurs: the source of this influence is no doubt J.S. Mill and Thomas Carlyle, who were leading figures in engaging the public in the 'spirit of the age' through their writings.[69] They seized the notion of historical self-consciousness that emerged with the Peterloo Massacre and transformed it into the 'Condition-of-England' question that would define the age in which they lived. Browning takes this on board when he refuses to write a romance of nobility and turn a blind eye to the reality that besets those members of society whose interests are underrepresented; he also punishes his troubadour-protagonist for not accepting his assigned role in the gradual societal change. Browning inherits the historical self-consciousness that marked the writings of the Shelleys in its urgency for societal transformation; he replaces their reliance on individual courage and aspiration with collective understanding and action. Browning's *Sordello*, therefore, should be understood as a cultural product that materialised as an effect of the rise of Romantic historicism and as a solution to the impasse into which Romantics such as the Shelleys had fallen.

NOTES

1. Both Shelley's apocalyptic vision and his mythmaking as they relate to history are topics of book-length study in themselves. What concerned critics such as Harold Bloom and Ross Greig Woodman, for example, had been Shelley's ontological probing into what art does or undoes: for example, Bloom reads Shelley's mythopoeic work, *Prometheus Unbound,* as engaging in the replacement of what Martin Buber calls 'I-It' with 'I-Thou'—that is, the attempt to recover 'relationship' from 'experience' (what would be the secularised version of redemption from the Fall); Woodman sees Shelley's apocalyptic vision as essentially pagan in that the recovery of man's divinity is to be achieved by Eros, who 'remove[s] all the veils which separate him from Dionysus, the archetype of his own divine nature' (70). See Bloom 1959; Woodman 70.

   On the other side of the spectrum, there has been a vigorous attempt to place Shelley's mythmaking and apocalyptic history in the social and political contexts of the early nineteenth century. Marilyn Butler argues that Shelley's use of Zoroastrian dualism provided him with a compelling myth that validated his hopes for political reversal in favour of liberalism. Stephen C. Behrendt inaugurates a collection of essays in 'Introduction: History, Mythmaking and Romantic Artist' that highlight the reciprocal nature of myth and history in that '[i]f myth may be pressed into service to enhance history and historical consciousness, so also may history function to enhance myth' (20); that is to say, myth must continually be updated in order to retain its universal appeal while history must be *imagined,* for which myth becomes a useful tool, if artists were to serve as active agents in the making of its future. James Chandler argues that through Shelley's use of traditional tropes (of both pagan and Biblical origin) in 'Ode to the West Wind,' Shelley conceives himself as being 'led by the events of post-Revolution history to construct an account whereby he and post-Revolution history make each other.' See Butler 1982, p. 58; Behrendt 13–32 (20); Chandler 554.
2. Everest et al. 2000, p. 44; *PBSL* 2: 164.
3. Steven Goldsmith discriminates the apocalyptic rhetoric Shelley used for *Prometheus Unbound* from that of 'Popular Songs' arguing that while the former works toward political transcendence the latter inscribe the politically underrepresented into history (234–42).
4. Bryan Shelley emphasises Shelley's political disillusionment as a significant factor in embracing apocalyptic vision (150).
5. See Stuart Curran's 'The Political Prometheus.'
6. The full title of Mary Shelley's novel is *Frankenstein; or, The Modern Prometheus.*

7. While *Frankenstein* is the most obvious example of Prometheanism that went wrong, in her other two early novels, *Valperga* (which will be discussed further in chapter 2) and *The Last Man,* the protagonists likewise are characterised by their Promethean effort, which similarly becomes crushed either by masculine aggression or by an epidemic that is beyond human control.
8. For a feminist reading of Mary Shelley's early works, see Gilbert and Gubar; Mellor, *Mary Shelley*; Poovey.

   While Shelley critics are generally more sceptical of the status of Shelley's idealism, more often than not Mary Shelley critics identify unequivocally Shelley's poetry with the Romantic ideal. See, for example, Blumberg 77; Mellor, *Mary Shelley* 79.
9. Mary Poovey is in accordance with Gilbert and Gubar in reading Mary Shelley's early novels as manifesting her 'anxiety of authorship' under the shadow of 'the conventional ideal of the self-effacing woman' on the one hand, and 'the masculine image of the poet' on the other (for which 'Percy Shelley's image of the artist as priest-lawgiver-prophet' would be an immediate example); see Poovey 261. Although Poovey's argument is persuasive in the case of *Frankenstein* and *The Last Man*, in *Valperga* the gender issue seems to be more complex. For example, Betty T. Bennett, in reading Euthanasia as a Promethean figure whose active political role offsets her romantic role as the heroine, insists that the 'novel owes far more to Shelley's Promethean ideal, in which love becomes the means of developing a viable alternative to the existing social structure, and to Godwin and Wollstonecraft, who advocated the need for alternative social structures'; see Reiman 1978, p. 356.
10. Bennett argues that

    > [...] Mary Shelley's operative theme is political, that her criticism of fourteenth-century Italy differs little from her criticism of fourteenth-century England (and by implication, of nineteenth-century Europe), and that these works [*Valperga* and *Perkin Warbeck*], whatever their stylistic shortcomings, are written in the tradition of social reform, particularly influenced—as were the efforts of so many other reformers of the time—by Godwin and Wollstonecraft. (Reiman 1978, p. 356)

11. Percy Shelley's letters of his last years have in general a pessimistic tone that denote his disappointment with the reading public:

    > I am speaking literally, infirm of purpose. I have great designs, and feeble hopes of ever accomplishing them. [...] To be sure, the reception the public have given me might [go] far enough to damp any man's enthusiasm. (8 November 1820; *PBSL* 2: 244–45)

> My 'Cenci' had, I believe, a complete failure—at least the silence of the bookseller would say so. [...] With no strong personal reasons to interest me, my disappointment on public grounds has been excessive. (?14 May 1821; 2: 290–91)

> As to the Poem I send you, I fear it is worth little. Heaven knows what makes me persevere (after the severe reproof of public neglect) in writing verses; and Heaven alone, whose will I execute so awkwardly, is responsible for my presumption. (16 July 1821; 2: 309)

> I write nothing, and probably shall write no more. It offends me to see my name classed among those who have no name. If I cannot be something better, I had rather be nothing, and the accursed cause to the downfall of which I dedicated what powers I may have had—flourishes like a cedar and covers England with its boughs. (11 August 1821; 2: 331)

12. For example, Shelley's collections of 1816, 1819, and 1820.
13. The 1820 collection contains *Prometheus Unbound*, 'The Sensitive Plant', 'A Vision of the Sea', 'Ode to Heaven', 'An Exhortation', 'Ode to the West Wind', 'An Ode [Written, October 1819, before the Spaniards had recovered their liberty]', 'The Cloud', 'To a Skylark' and 'Ode to Liberty'.

    Neil Fraistat examines the *Prometheus Unbound* volume 'as one of the greatest poetic collections of the age' that 'ranks with *Lyrical Ballads* and Keats's *Lamia*' (187) in *The Poem and the Book: Interpreting Collections of Romantic Poetry*. Fraistat begins by reminding the readers of the importance that Shelley himself stressed of the choice and ordering of the poems included in the volume; his contention is to discuss not only the interrelation of the poems but 'the collection as a whole [...] as an integral unit' (143). Against often-held views that Shelley was an easy optimist, Fraistat concludes that 'the nine accompanying poems work largely to destabilize the victorious ending of 'Prometheus Unbound' (149); that 'there can be nothing static in the 1820 volume about Shelley's symbols or the world they represent'; (175) and finally, what the volume as a whole suggests is that 'the Promethean paradise must be perpetually remade, or again it will be lost' (186).
14. 'Julian and Maddalo', which was composed around the same time as *Prometheus Unbound* Acts II and III, would be an obvious example; it demonstrates Shelley's self-awareness regarding his idealistic outlook (represented in Julian), which verges on insanity on one hand (as in the Maniac) and Byronic pessimism (as in Maddalo) on the other. Shelley was also planning to add all of his 'saddest verses raked up into one heap' (*PBSL* 2: 593) to the publication of *Julian and Maddalo* and *Athanase* (which never materialised); one such verse, 'Misery.—A Fragment', the intermediate fair copy of which appears 'in Nbk 8 on leaves left blank after

the fair copy of PU II ii' (p. 701) is particularly suggestive in that part of it (ll. 28–9) echoes certain phrasing from *Prometheus Unbound* (II i 8–10 or possibly vice versa). Everest argues that 'Misery' was 'most probably written in June 1819 in Livorno, following the death of William Shelley aged 3½ in Rome on 7 June and prompted at least in part by the severe effect of that catastrophe on Mary's spirits and on her attitude to S' (701). As Everest also asserts, 'by August 1819 at least S. 'was working simultaneously on the fairly substantial additional passages for Act II [...] and various lyrical passages of Act IV', thereby making the echo between 'Misery' and *PU* either way plausible. See editors' introduction to *Prometheus Unbound, Julian and Maddalo*, and *Misery.—A Fragment* (Everest et al. 2000).

15. *The Cenci* was written in Monte Nero 'from the end of June until the middle of August' and 'a version of it, seems to have been written by the middle of July'; see Everest et al. 2000, p. 714; *PBSL* 2:115. Whereas Shelley spent intermittently over a year from the summer of 1818 to the end of 1819 in working on *Prometheus Unbound*, Shelley boasted to Peacock that 'my work on the Cenci [...] was done in two months'; see the introductions to *Prometheus Unbound* and *The Cenci* in Everest et al. 2000; *PBSL* 2:115.
16. Tilotamma Rajan makes a similar point in *Dark Interpreter: the Discourse of Romanticism* when she asserts that Shelley's move away from idealism in 'The Triumph of Life' is symptomatic of Shelley's own divide between scepticism and idealism that manifested itself as early as *Alastor*, and that 'The Triumph of Life' does not necessarily replace the idealism expounded, for example, in *A Defence of Poetry*, but reaffirms it by realising that 'the deconstructive Dionysiac element' is inherent in it. (60, 71)
17. Those who argue for a positive development in the continuation of the poem include Reiman and Duffy, while those upholding a negative decline include Bloom, Allott, and Pyle: see Reiman 1965; Duffy; Pyle 94–128; Bloom 1959; Alott 239–78. For the deconstructive reading of the poem, see de Man, 1979, pp. 39–73; J. Hillis Miller 1993, pp. 218–40.
18. T.S. Eliot in 'Talk of Dante' hailed it as 'Shelley's greatest tribute to Dante', and 'also the greatest' of his poems (110); Harold Bloom in *Shelley's Mythmaking* similarly praised its artistic achievement when he claimed that '[t] he full implications latent in all of Shelley's mythmaking are finally visualised in this account of the triumph of life over almost all human integrity and aspiration' (221).
19. The figure of Rousseau in the poem despairs over his own fall:

    And if the spark with which Heaven lit my spirit
    Earth had with purer nutriment supplied

    'Corruption would not now thus much inherit
    Of what was once Rousseau—(ll. 201–204)

The association of Rousseau with Prometheus was made explicitly, for example, by Mary Wollstonecraft; see *Mary and The Wrongs of Woman* 89–90.

20. In *Adonais*, Shelley refers to 'the contagion of the world's slow stain' from which Keats 'is secure' (*SPP* 422; ll. 356–7).
21. Fraistat writes '[i]n the *Prometheus Unbound* volume, as demonstrated graphically in the 'Ode to Heaven', Perspective is everything' (Fraistat 1985, p. 175).
22. Rousseau urges the speaker to

    follow thou, and from spectator turn
    Actor or victim in this wretchedness

    'And what thou wouldst be taught I then may learn
    From thee. (ll. 305–308)

23. The editors of *New Letters* maintain that '[i]t is probable that Browning did not know Mrs. Shelley personally, and judging from the suggested motto one may doubt that he was well acquainted with her characteristic literary work' (33). The 'motto' refers to 'Mrs. Shelley and the very few Imaginative Romancists [sic]', who where among eleven other authors and subjects Browning suggested in his letter of Autumn 1843 to Richard Hengist Horne for his *A New Spirit of the Age* (London, 1844).

    Browning hardly mentions Mary Shelley in his letters, which makes a stark contrast to his constant reference to Percy Shelley, and even to William Godwin and Mary Wollstonecraft. Of the few that reveal Browning's attitude toward Mary Shelley is firstly his scathing remark on Mary Shelley's altered lifestyle that complied with Victorian propriety and respectability:

    > Oh that book [Mary Shelley's *Rambles in Germany and Italy in 1840, 1842 and 1843*]—does one wake or sleep? The 'Mary dear' with the brown eyes, and Godwin's daughter and Shelley's wife, and who surely was something better once upon a time—and to go thro' Rome & Florence & the rest, after what I suppose to be Lady Londonderry's fashion: the intrepidity of the commonplace quite astounds me—(letter of 11 September 1845 to Elizabeth Barrett Barrett).

    Secondly, Browning's unfavourable remark on Mary Shelley's literary ability:

    > I believe I have seen somewhere that the translation ['Relation' of the Cenci affair] was made by Mrs. Shelley—the note appended to an omitted passage seems a womanly performance. (letter of 25 October 1876 to H. Buxton Forman)

    Correspondence 11: 69–70; Hood 33.
24. Mary Shelley's high praise of *The Cenci* can be ascribed to its realism—that it depicts real emotions rather than 'metaphysical' or 'abstract' concepts; see 'Note on *The Cenci*, By Mrs. Shelley' in *PWS* 334–37 (335).

25. Sordello's career is measured against Dante's, whom he predates only to be overtaken: 'Sordello, thy forerunner, Florentine!' (i 348); 'I [Sordello] die then! Will the rest agree to die?/Next Age or no? Shall its Sordello try/ Clue after clue and catch at last the clue/I miss' (iii 182–4). See Woolford and Karlin 1991, 1: 365, 534–5.
26. Apart from the common plot of *Valperga* and *Sordello*—the protagonist's romantic involvement with his/her enemy (i.e. supporting the opposite political belief) that leads to a tragic ending—there are resemblances in some of the characters: Palma and Euthanasia have similar physical features; Sordello and Castruccio in their youth both demonstrate keen sensibility and passion for self-aggrandizement; Castruccio's later career has much in common with Salinguerra who is depicted as a Machiavellian warlord.

    David E. Latané notes the similarities between the two texts: 'Mary Shelley's *Valperga* offers interesting parallels to *Sordello*, since it is the story of a Prince of Lucca who begins life as a sensitive youth and terminates it as a Machiavellian strongman'; see Latané 1987, p. 141.
27. Alfred Tennyson, for example, wrote a series of poems in the thirties in which he used a female voice to express his own poetic or sexual anxiety: for example, see 'Mariana', 'The Lady of Shalott', and 'Mariana in the South'.

    In examining a series of poems, Arthur Hallam wrote in the thirties and later on women—'Claribel', 'Lilian', 'Isabel', 'Mariana' and 'Adeline'—Isobel Armstrong draws attention to Hallam's praise of women, whom he saw as being 'nearer to life of the affections and the senses, because, less amenable to the power of reflection than men' (1993, p. 49). Armstrong offers a more problematic case for Tennyson's use of the female in 'Mariana' in his exploration 'of damaged female sexuality' that is characterised by 'repetition of single feeling' (50).
28. While it is impossible to mention all the works that refer to Shelley's influence on the young Browning and his early works, those that deal with it in some length include Pottle; Norman 83–106; Collins 1965, pp. 151–60; Bloom 1971; Keenan 119–145; Yetman; Ryals 1976, pp. 231–45; Maynard 1977, pp. 193–219; Cundiff; Tucker 119–45; Woolford 1988, ch. 1.
29. Browning first encountered Shelley's poetry in late 1826 or in 1827 through his cousin, James Silverthorne, who gave him a copy of Shelley's *Miscellaneous Poems* (1826); on reading this pirated edition of Shelley's poems, mostly taken from *Posthumous Poems* (1824), he became captivated by the newly discovered poet and wrote to the *Literary Gazette* with the intention of finding out where he could find more of Shelley's works; on finding a publisher in Covent Garden who stocked them, his mother

was sent for to fetch what volumes she could get hold of, which included *Queen Mab*. This famous story has been recounted by numerous biographers including Orr 1908, pp. 37–40; Griffin and Minchin 51–53; DeVane 1955, pp. 9–10; Maynard 1977, pp. 193–200; Ryals 1993, p. 6.

Even after Browning's conscientious distancing from Shelley, his former idol continued to play on Browning's mind well into his later years, if somewhat problematically. Traces of Shelley's presence in, and influence on, Browning's later works include: *Memorabilia* (included in the *Men and Women* volume), in which Browning recounts an emotional incident of coming across a stranger in a bookshop who happened to be talking about his conversation in the past with Shelley; *The Ring and the Book* (1: 744, 760–71), in which the mage talks about raising a ghost and the resuscitation of life—a clear reference to Mary Shelley's *Frankenstein* and also to Percy Shelley's own scientific interest and immersion in the occult on which Frankenstein's early career is based; *Cenciaja* (published in 1876), a work partly based on Shelley's *Cenci*, which Browning refers to as 'your superb/Achievement' (ll. 17–8). On discovering Shelley's treatment of his first wife, Harriet, through the private letters that came into his hands, Browning significantly altered his views on 'Shelley the *man*' and 'even the *poet*'; he blamed Shelley's action, which he condemned as 'wholly inexcusable', to Shelley being 'half crazy' at the time; however, Browning never publicly denounced him. See Pettigrew and Collins 1: 643, 2: 473; Hawlin and Burnett 43–44; *The Poems* 2: 473; Hood 222–3, 242–3.

30. Browning names Shelley in *Pauline* as the 'Sun-treader' (l. 151); what follows is Browning's lament for the loss of Shelley's life—'Thou art gone from us' (l. 152)—complemented by the inspiration that Shelley's poetry continues to exercise on Browning—'But thou art still for me' (ll. 162, 168); Browning's affirmation of Shelley's immortality in 'that one so pure as thou/ Could never die' (ll. 208–9). See Woolford and Karlin 1991, 1: 36–39.
31. Browning addresses Shelley at the beginning of Book I: 'thou, spirit, come not near/Now—nor this time desert thy cloudy place/To scare me, thus employed, with that pure face!' (i 60–62); in the 1863 edition of *Poetical Works*, Browning writes, 'Shelley departing', in the running-titles; see Woolford and Karkin 1991, 1: 398.
32. As I will discuss in chapter 3, Sordello's attempt to 'build Rome' (i.e. an ideal polity based on the model of republican Rome) in the face of imperial expansion fed on self-aggrandizement easily translates itself into Promethean effort as Romantics such as Shelley understood it.
33. The authorial voice breaks through the narrative halfway through Book 3 when Browning himself dispels the illusion that he conjures up as the 'archimage' (i.e. the epic romance of *Sordello*) with a strong allusion to Archimago

in Spenser's *Faerie Queene*. This gesture becomes the turning point in the poem's aesthetics and politics as I will discuss further in chapter 3.

34. In addition to Pauline and Paracelsus as a failure of one kind or another, there are a host of apostates who figure in his early works: Strafford in *Strafford* (1837), Charles in *King Victor and King Charles* (1842), Djabal in *The Return of the Druses* (1843), Colombe and Valence in *Colombe's Birthday* (1844), Wordsworth in *The Lost Leader* (1845), Chiappino in *A Soul's Tragedy* (1845), and the speaker of *The Italian in England* (1845). John Woolford discusses Browning's 'near-obsession with apostates from its principles' in relation to what he calls 'embarrassment at power'; see Woolford 1998, pp. 18–22.

35. The most pervasive case put forward with regard to Browning's preoccupation with failure would be Harold Bloom's reading of 'Childe Roland to the Dark Tower Came', which sees the poem as concerning the repressed anxiety that seeks to cover up its purposelessness in the wake of his abandonment of Shelleyan ideals:

    > There is perhaps a darker source in the guilt or shame of identifying the precursor with the ego ideal, and then living on in the sense of having betrayed that identification by one's own failure to have become oneself, by a realization that the ephebe has betrayed his own integrity and betrayed also the covenant that first bound him to the precursor.

    See 'Browning: Good Moments and Ruined Quests' included in Bloom 1979, pp. 123–147 (125). Bloom worked out his ideas on 'Childe Roland' in a series of writings: See Bloom 1971, 1976.

36. The most convincing instance of this would be 'The Triumph of Life', which Browning most likely read in the *Posthumous Poems* that he owned:

    > As for the early editions of Shelley. They were obtained for me some time before 1830 (or even earlier) in the *regular way*, from Hunt and Clarke, in consequence of a direction I obtained from the *Literary Gazette*. I still possess *Posthumous Poems*, but have long since parted with *Prometheus Poems*, *Rosalind* and [sic] *Helen*, *Six Weeks' Tour*, *Cenci*, and the *Adonais*. (Robert Browning to Thomas J. Wise dated 3 March 1886; Hood 246)

37. In delineating the development of poetic style from epic to drama (exemplified in the works of Dante and Shakespeare respectively), Browning further alludes to the 'psychological perception' of which *Sordello* will stand as a model (Woolford and Karlin 1991, 1: 693):

    > How we attained to talk as brothers talk,
    > In half-words, call things by half-names [...]
    >
    > 'tis but brother's speech

> We need, speech where an accent's change gives each
> The other's soul—no speech to understand
> By former audience—need was then expand,
> Expatiate—hardly were they brothers! true—
> Nor I lament my less remove from you,
> Nor reconstruct what stands already (v 605–6, 615–21)

While Browning subscribes to a Wordsworthian poetics that emphasises the equality between poet and reader, he advocates the language of suggestion over Wordsworth's common speech; see Woolford and Karlin 1991, 1: 698.

David E. Latané, Jr. writes 'Browning's Sordello [...] represents a culmination of sorts of the troping of style to represent the necessity of fitting the audience to the poem—the reciprocity between intended reader and poetic form is one of its themes' (Latané 1987, p. 24).

38. Browning writes in his 'Essay on Shelley'—an introduction to Shelley's letters (which later turned out to be forgeries):

> Nor is there any reason why these two modes of poetic faculty [i.e. subjective and objective] may not issue hereafter from the same poet in successive perfect works, examples of which, according to what are now considered the exigencies of art, we have hitherto possessed in distinct individuals only. (1003)

Although Browning depicts Shelley as primarily a 'subjective poet' who concerns himself with 'the absolute Divine mind' (1003), he attributes 'objectivity' to some of his works as well: '[i]t would be easy to take my stand on successful instances of objectivity in Shelley: there is the unrivalled 'Cenci'; there is the 'Julian and Maddalo' too' (1012). See 'Browning's Introductory Essay' (Pettigrew and Collins 1: 1001–1013).

39. Browning's portrayal of a nature poet who is characterised by 'his roves/ Among the hills and valleys, plains and groves' (ii 270–1) not only suggests an anti-social behaviour but it also implies a self-serving egotism that contains a potential danger of succumbing to the seduction of political power when given the chance. The association of the two strongly implies Wordsworth as Shelley understood him. See chapter 3.

40. See Duggan 96. Following the lead of past historians, Edgar Holt equally stresses the significance of the French influence in Italy, which 'was one of the determining factors of the Risorgimento' (Holt 20).

41. Holt likewise argues that the lack of an 'idea of promoting Italian unity or of driving the Austrians out of the peninsula' had relevance to the failure of the Neapolitan rising (53).

42. Shelley writes in his 'Preface' to *Prometheus Unbound*:

> This Poem was chiefly written upon the mountainous ruins of the Baths of Caracalla, among the flowery glades, and thickets of

> odoriferous blossoming trees, which are extended in ever winding labyrinths upon its immense paltforms and dizzy arches suspended in the air. The bright blue sky of Rome, and the effect of the vigorous awakening of spring in that divinest climate, and the new life with which it drenches the spirits even to intoxication, were the inspiration of this drama. (Everest et al. 2000, 2: 473)

Similarly, Shelley alludes to his Roman experience as the source of inspiration for *The Cenci*:

> This national and universal interest which the story produces and has produced for two centuries, and among all ranks of people in a great City, where the imagination is kept for ever active and awake, first suggested to me the conception of its fitness for a dramatic purpose. (Everest et al. 2000, p. 729)

43. Some of these poems appear under slightly different titles according to different editions: see *PWS*, *SPP*, Webb 1995.
44. Chandler argues that 'Shelley was drawn into the powerful historical contemporaneity of a hyperactive public sphere that made Peterloo thinkable in the first place' and that 'Shelley's 1819 comments [...] can be seen as part of a cycle of intensifying self-consciousness about the historical state of the representation' that becomes tied in with 'anachronism' or 'a measureable form of dislocation.' See Chandler 80, 107.
45. Jacob Korg states that 'Browning probably first encountered the figure of Sordello while reading Dante with Cerutti' (Korg 16).
46. As an early reader of Byron, Browning would have come across Ugo Foscolo's essay on the six greatest contemporary poets in *Historical Illustrations of the Fourth Canto of Childe Harold's Pigrimage* published in 1818. Foscolo's *Epochs of the Italian Language* (1818) and *Essays on Petrarch* (1821) would have appealed to Browning, who was reading classical Italian texts with Cerutti. See Wicks 21; Cambon 25.
47. Santarosa, a cavalry officer, staged a coup in 1821 in Piedmont, but could not gain the support of the moderates and the rising failed soon after the King's abdication (Duggan 104).
48. G.F.-H Berkeley argues for the importance of Mazzini's conception of the role of Italy to inaugurate a new age of 'free nations' over that of the 'free individual,' which was seen to be the achievement of the French Revolution (Berkeley 1968, p. 13).
49. For Mazzini's acquaintance with the Carlyles, see Smith 29–31.
50. 'Old Pictures in Florence' is a poem included in *Men and Women* (1855)—one of the few poems spoken in the poet's own voice. In elaborating his views on Florentine art, Browning begins by referring to Giotto's unfinished bell-tower, which provides an example that illustrates his point that the art of imperfection is superior to that of Greek perfection. Browning's

association of Florentine art with its republican past further leads him to meditate on the existing political state of Italy and its future liberation from the Austrian rule. 'De Gustibus', which also appears in *Men and Women*, again concerns Italy, not from a public or propagandistic perspective, but from Browning's own personal attachment. *Prince Hohenstiel-Schwangau, Saviour of Society*, on the other hand, recounts the political career and enigmatic character of Napoleon III, whose support for the Italian cause proved to be disappointing for those fighting for Italy's liberation; Browning further suggests the casualness with which Napoleon compromised his ideals.

51. Ryals 1993, p. 33.
52. See the editors' notes to *Paraclesus* in Woolford and Karlin 1991, 1: 107.
53. See Landor 3: 438.
54. There is a strong echo of Milton's Satan here (i.e. 'being himself alone'); see 3.441–2, 3.667, 4.917, 4.935 of *Paradise Lost*.
55. Browning similarly depicts Sordello as being fascinated by the idea of dominating the world:

    So lives he [Sordello]: if not careless as before,
    Comforted: for one may anticipate,
    Rehearse the future; be prepared when fate
    Startle, real places of enormous fames,
    Estes abroad and Eccelins at home
    To worship him, Mantuas, Veronas, Rome
    To witness it. (i 844–51)

56. *Blackwood's Edinburgh Magazine* 13 (March 1823): 283–93
57. *Life of Strafford* was originally intended as part of the *Lives of Eminent British Statesmen* for Lardner's *Cabinet Cyclopædia*, which had been undertaken by John Forster; when Forster fell ill soon after beginning the Life of Strafford 'for which he had made full collections and extracts', Browning stepped in to complete it. The extent of Browning's contribution is still unresolved; his own comments on, and various speculations based on the content and stylistic characteristics of, the work remain the only source of information. See Furnivall v–xii (v).

    John Woolford maintains that the quoted passage can reasonably be ascribed to Browning on the basis of subject and wording—for example, 'apostacy' and 'no such thing' (private communication).
58. William Godwin, 'Of History and Romance' (362).
59. On Carlyle's Romantic concept of history, see White 1975, p. 68.
60. White writes: 'And what it [nineteenth-century historical thought] objected to most in Enlightenment historiography was its *essential irony*,

just as it objected to most in its cultural reflection was its *skepticism*' (1975, p. 47).

In glossing one of the 'apocryphal passages' (the term which Reiman uses 'to designate those passages of three or more complete lines in "The Triumph" MS that were at one time part of the text but were later cancelled or superceded') that draw on recent history, Donald H. Reiman reads Rousseau's 'contemptuous attitude toward history' ('And if I [Rousseau] sought those joys which now are pain,/If he [Voltaire] is captive to the car of life,/'Twas that we feared our labour wd be vain'; *TLA*-'B', ll. 25–27) as a warning for 'the Poet' who adopts a similar view, which holds a wider implication in that 'Shelley's generation [...] can learn from the mistakes of that age's earlier generations (those of Rousseau, Voltaire and of Wordsworth)'. See 'Appendix C: Apocryphal Passages' included in *BSM* 1:332, 334–5.

61. White 1975, p. 14.
62. Lukács 1976, p. 35.
63. *The Literary Gazette,* n.s. (28 August 1823): 82–84; *The Literary Register of the Fine Arts, Sciences, and Belles Lettres* 36 (8 March 1823): 151–52.
64. Betty T. Bennett stresses the political significance of *Valperga* and *Perkin Warbeck* over their emulation at Scott's 'romance' of 'idealised love stories'.
65. See Gibson 1987, p. 27; Mellor, 'A Criticism of Their Own' (Beer 30).
66. See his chapter on 'History, trauma, and the limits of the liberal imagination: William Godwin's historical fiction' in Rajan 1998, pp. 64–85.
67. Caruth 11.
68. Lionel Stevenson's words in 'The Key Poem of the Victorian Age' (278).
69. Miscellaneous essays written by Thomas Carlyle appeared in the *Edinburgh Review* and *Fraser's Magazine* while those by J.S. Mill were published in the *London and Westminster Review* and the *Monthly Repository* in the late 1820s to the 1830s.

Chapter 1

P.B. Shelley's 'The Triumph of Life'

Introduction

P.B. Shelley's last attempt, which was hailed by both T.S. Eliot and Harold Bloom as his greatest effort, has also proven to be one of his most disputed poems, with interpretations varying from Shelleyan optimism to self-destructive pessimism. That the poem was left unfinished when the poet drowned in the bay of Spezia and that the present text as we know it today was reconstructed out of the debris in which it remained, firstly by Mary Shelley and subsequently by modern scholars, accounts for the difficulties in explicating the text.[1] This status of the poem, however, has given much more scope for reader-participation than is usually allowed, so that the text has, without deliberate intention on Shelley's part, become palimpsest-like with layers of inscriptions attempting to complete the poem. The irony is that such an endeavour has often resulted in self-reflection: the ideologies that critics have endorsed in their readings highlighting their own beliefs. For instance, the biographical reading of the poem famously undertaken by G.M. Matthews and Donald H. Reiman accentuates their respective understanding of the man and poet in 1822; the deconstructive reading of the poem equally proved self-gratifying in identifying the limitation set by itself.[2]

The difficulty of reading 'The Triumph of Life', apart from the ambiguity regarding its ideology, can partly be explained by the way in which it engages with the literary as well as the socio-political history of the West as it tells its own story.[3] It does so in a cryptic manner: the poem opens with a sunrise, which is being contrasted with the troubled psyche of the speaker-narrator that remains aloof amidst the sun's celebratory act of unmasking the natural world. The speaker-narrator is not only antithetical to his natural surrounding but finds himself equally averse to his own vision, which consists of a historical pageant. The crux of the poem in which Rousseau gives his own account of history reinforces the very psychological displacement the speaker-narrator was subjected to in the beginning. The poem attempts to be a social satire, mocking the socio-political value system that feeds the individual will-to-power on the one hand, and fosters blind subjection on the other; but its inability to become one projects the speaker-narrator's own anxiety over his divided self.

In spite of its overtly political concerns, 'The Triumph of Life' is also a private poem that requires to be read as one. The very fact that Shelley's composition of it was accompanied by repeated draftings of his lyrics to Jane Williams testifies to his preoccupation with her at the time. The significance of this implies an ideological dilemma: the private and the public are tied in together as always in Shelley's works so that one problem easily becomes that of the other. For this, one only needs to look at the 'Lines Written Among the Euganean Hills' in which he vacillates between his lament for the degraded political state of the Italian cities and for the loss of his own happiness. The contrast between the natural and the human world, which Shelley repeatedly uses in his poems, is particularly compelling because the former promises regeneration whereas the latter is deprived of such assurance. In the poem, whatever owes itself to human construction—ideology, love, and language—fails; and it is only nature that remains uncorrupted. For this reason, 'The Triumph' is arguably the most pessimistic of Shelley's poems but also the most engaging in its honesty and effort to come to terms with both private and political failure.

The Triumph of Life

Shelley's use of the Italian literary tradition in the poem is immediately recognisable, from the title evoking Petrarch's *Trionfi* to its adopted rhyme scheme of the *terza rima* employed by both Dante and Petrarch. It is not limited to the stylistic aspect but also reflects the political as well as philosophical orientation of the works of the two Italian poets.[4] Both Dante and Petrarch were exiled from their native city, and Shelley's deliberate choice to model 'The Triumph' on their works, which were shaped by their circumstances, signifies the leitmotif of his poem—the alienated self in exile. That, for both Dante and Petrarch, their political displacement triggered them to write an epic-vision provides a subtext for Shelley's attempt at the genre; however, his failure to deliver that becomes the epistemology of Romantic historiography—the exposure of the fragmented self in discordance with tradition, society, and history.

The ambiguity regarding both the poem's aesthetics and ideology has largely to do with the title and what Shelley means by 'Life'. His scepticism regarding language as a valid means to an ontological inquiry makes his argument tantalizing and elusive. Shelley clearly sees 'Life' in dual opposing terms, whether as an extension of his Platonic ideas, or, as the most effective way of questioning the linguistic system that defines our social existence. As Paul de Man insists, 'The Triumph' is largely to do with language, in the sense that it is a protest against linearity in time for which language stands as the prime example: because civilisation is only possible through language, there is no escape from it; yet Shelley attempts that impossibility of delineating the a-temporal space through language. Its effect, according to de Man, is that Shelley ends up deconstructing himself and signposting 'death' instead of 'life'. What is worth noting is the tantalising effect of words that prove revelatory of the intermediate state between 'life' and 'death'. Metaphor serves to open up that possibility through the difference created in the mind by the overlapping of two signified objects. The association of the two, however, is an arbitrary one that is prone to collapse if it does not become metonymical. The effect of metaphor is to create a hovering state in which the mind does not know which to attach itself to.[5]

'Life', as it appears in Shelley's works, can mean almost anything from generative impulse to spiritual decay; and 'The Triumph of Life' should be read with this sense of uncertainty or ambiguity. Shelley deviates significantly from, for instance, Petrarch's clear-cut rendition of the triumphs, whereby Love, Death, Fame, Time, and Eternity are given logical hierarchical positioning according to their fixed values. This not only reflects a medieval world-view, but it also demonstrates his belief in the unity of the signifier and the signified without which such faith cannot be successfully communicated. Shelley's 'Life', therefore, is not a concrete concept that overcomes or becomes overcome by others; it denotes the collapse of such a fixed value system and embraces scepticism as the best faith one can adopt in order to reach the truth.

Shelley's relativist world-view does not, however, conceal his revolutionary mind that seeks to re-write the linguistic code according to a new social and political order:

> Philosophy, impatient as it may be to build, has much work yet remaining as pioneer for the overgrowth of ages. It makes one step towards this object however; it destroys error, and the roots of error. It leaves, what is too often the duty of the reformer in political and ethical questions to leave, a vacancy. It reduces the mind to that freedom in which it would have acted, but for the misuse of words and signs, the instruments of its own creation.—By signs, I would be understood in a wide sense, including what is properly meant by that term, and what I peculiarly mean. In this latter sense almost all familiar objects are signs, standing not for themselves but for others, in their capacity of suggesting one thought which shall lead to a train of thoughts.—Our whole life is thus an education of error.[6]

'The Triumph' seeks to expose the socio-political values that developed with language as a corrupted system that requires renovation; for this end, Rousseau bears a particular significance as the precursor-guide to the speaker-narrator.

It is no accident that Shelley chose Rousseau as the central figure of the poem: Rousseau as the Enlightenment philosopher who was believed by Shelley's contemporaries to have triggered the French Revolution was also an exponent of sensibility as the popularity of his novel *La Nouvelle Héloïse* testifies. As his treatise *The Essay on the Origin of Languages* gave Derrida the perfect opportunity to apply a deconstructive reading to his text, Rousseau's theory of language serves as an uncanny precursor to the successive critique on language, which 'The Triumph' first incorporates, then successively invites in contemporary criticism.

In his *Essay on the Origin of Languages*, Rousseau attempts to outline the development of language, which he believes corresponds with that of society, from its primitive state to a more mature state of civilisation. Just as he saw the social malaise in the over-refined society to which he belonged, he detected a corruption in the modern languages (especially French), which have become, as it were, a mere form detached from content; just as the excess of wealth and abuse of power have resulted in a political subversion as in the French Revolution, by the same token the overreaching refinement of language brought moral degradation due to its servitude to decorum rather than meaning. Such a critique on the divorce of the nominal from the semantic aspect of language is at the heart of Shelley's political works, such as 'The Mask of Anarchy' and 'The Triumph.' In the latter, Shelley delineates that fall from prelapsarian bliss in which desire and pleasure were one, as depicted in the allegorical picture of the sun bestowing life on the natural world: with the introduction of the speaker-narrator, however, harmony gives way to division—of night and day, the outer and inner self. Such a fall is depicted twice: first by the narrator and second by Rousseau in his autobiographical account of his story. What the insistence on such experience points to is the inadequacy of the mind (which works through language alone) to recapitulate the original state. The poem casts a downward trajectory from the unifying beginning to the decaying end, be it that of society, or the life of an individual, through the course of which the very notion of 'Life' transforms itself to mean 'Death'.

DREAM-VISION

What follows the cosmic staging of the opening in which the speaker-narrator undergoes a vertiginous sensation ('before me fled/The night; behind me rose the day; the Deep//Was at my feet, and Heaven above my head', ll. 26-28) is 'a strange trance' that 'over my fancy grew', but 'Which was not slumber' due to its very nature.[7] The speaker-narrator, at this point, is seeing two visions at the same time: one of his surrounding landscape and the other of his imaginary construct, but these, nevertheless, appear equally real. The 'waking trance' is further given a Platonic overtone by the way it is 'recovered' rather than 'discovered':

> and I knew
> That I had felt the freshness of *that* dawn,
> Bathed in the *same* cold dew my brow and hair
> And sate as thus upon that slope of lawn
>
> Under the *self same* bough (ll. 33-37)
> [emphases added]

Not only does the past perfect tense of this sentence make it clear that the experience is not of an immediate but of a reiterative nature, but the italicised words also reinforce it as being *déjà vu*.

There is a clear break in the poem, which occurs after the introduction of the 'Vision' and before the actual description of it, being the pageant as witnessed by the speaker-narrator. It signifies a changing mode from describing a familiar landscape to narrating a visionary vista. As much as Shelley reinforces this transition by inserting the break so that there is no going back, he also reaffirms to the readers that there is little concern for going astray; for we have been told that the very nature of the trance restores rather than destabilises the former senses of the speaker-narrator. The readers are thus invited to take part in a vision over which we hold a privileged vantage-point: we know that it is genuine to the extent that it is revealing of a certain kind of truth, but not to the extent that it becomes threatening. This framework—a vision triggered by the half-slumberous state of the speaker-narrator—gives a sense of security to the otherwise uncontrollable sequence of events.

Shelley's interest in the Spanish dramatist Calderón de la Barca is known to have been sparked off sometime in 1819 through his reading of his plays in Spanish with Maria Gisborne, a momentum that even led to his own translation of *El Mágico Prodigioso* in 1822.[8] Calderón offered Shelley a different perspective from that of high-minded seriousness to work out his thoughts and ideas, and the significance of Shelley's immersion in Calderón during these years preceding his death cannot be over-emphasised: 'it is almost certainly his reading of Calderón which gave unity and force to this conception of the world as transient, a bubble, an empty vision.'[9] If Calderón's general influence over Shelley's poetry is one of tone and attitude, it extends itself to the thematic level in 'The Triumph of Life'. There are two leitmotifs in 'The Triumph' that are possible echoes of Calderón's plays: first, *El Mágico Prodigioso*, which Shelley called the Spanish *Faust*, and second, *La Vida es Sueño*, in which Calderón uses a 'dream' as a metaphor for 'Life'.

Despite its happy ending in the manner of a Shakespearian comedy, *La Vida es Sueño* (*Life is a Dream*) questions the referential and value system by which we live and through which alone we perceive reality. Segismund comes to doubt what he sees (once he is allowed outside the prison) only because he has been secluded from society since his birth by his father owing to an evil omen portending Segismund's revolt against him. Because he eluded social education owing to his seclusion, Segismund is able to reverse reality and fantasy by naming the very social code which makes up the former as the latter. To him, the referential and value system by which people live their lives is no less ludicrous and delusive than his own fantasy world of isolated madness. He gains this insight, interestingly, at the expense of a dream: his father experiments how Segismund would act when brought back into society, but safeguards himself by making his son believe that it is only a dream in case his behaviour proves to be unfavourable. So as Segismund's father literally stages life as a dream, that stability of a dream within reality is subverted by Segismund, only to emphasise the fragility of such a construct when faced with an ontological probing into the nature of human existence:

> It is a singular world we live in—and
> Experience has taught me one thing alone that life
> Is made up of strange unconnected dreams.
> Man thinks he is—and dreams of that he is
> And never wakes to know he does but dream.
> Some dream they're kings, and in a vain delusion
> But tyrannize to serve—and the applauses
> Of men are written in the clouds, and death
> Scatters the breath to less than air. The miser
> Consumes his life in dreaming he is rich
> His golden dreams but add unto his cares.
> The poor man dreams he suffers from the scorn
> Of the world, and calls it misery to live.
> And all, to sum up all, dream that they are
> None understanding what or why he is.
> What is this life—that we should covet it?
> What is this life that we should cling to it?
> A phantom haunted frenzy—a false nature
> A vain and empty shadow, all the good
> We prize or aim at only turns to evil—
> All life and being are but dreams and dreams
> Themselves are but the memory of other dreams.[10]

This quasi-Platonic notion that the life in this world lacks the authenticity of existence and meaning has strong bearing on 'The Triumph of Life'; that this sense is further intensified by the disappointment and frustration an idealist of Shelley's type is bound to experience in the real world has something in common with Calderón's essentially religious outlook on life that downplays its worldly values.[11] Even if Shelley found it impossible to share his Catholicism, Calderón's spiritual appeal in the face of his own disillusionment with the real world must have struck a chord.[12]

Furthermore, Calderón's experimentation with the metaphysical aspect of life (rather than a dogmatic preaching of it) no doubt found its correlative in Shelley himself if one considers for a moment the passion with which he pursued these philosophical questions throughout his career.

In an essay entitled 'On Life', Shelley similarly explores the meaning of 'Life'. He begins by drawing our attention to its inexplicable nature that can best be described as 'the great miracle'; and continues to argue that the reason why it does not 'absorb and overawe' us is because '[t]he mist of familiarity obscures from us the wonder of our being' (*SPP* 505). Shelley is no doubt using Platonic diction when he claims that 'We live on, and in living we lose the apprehension of life' (506). Yet, this observation is not grounded in any ontological or teleological conviction regarding human existence: 'For what are we? Whence do we come, and whither do we go? Is birth the commencement, is death the conclusion of our being? What is birth and death?' (506) After his speculation on scepticism, materialism, and immaterialism, Shelley is left with the conviction that none of the dogmatic theories explain the nature of life satisfactorily, and Sir W. Drummond's *Academical Questions* is cited as the only exception to an otherwise deficient philosophical system. The reason he gives for this lies at the core of his idealism:

> man is a being of high aspirations 'looking both before and after,' whose 'thoughts that wander through eternity,' disclaim alliance with transience and decay, incapable of imagining to himself annihilation, existing but in the future and past, being, not what he is, but what he has been, and shall be. Whatever may be his true and final destination, there is a spirit within him at enmity with change and extinction [nothingness and dissolution]. (506)

Shelley stresses the need for the human mind to attribute meaning to life and believe in the immortality of human efforts ('the character of all life and being')—whether those of an individual or collective power—as opposed to being satisfied with one's concerns alone. The mind that is capable of discerning the past, present and future, in terms of one's moral life or that of mankind at large is what Shelley attributes to poets as he develops this notion in *A Defence of Poetry*. In other words, he refutes all philosophical systems that deny the spiritual continuum of human life; yet explication of a system that does incorporate it is also beyond the scope of language: 'We are on that verge where words abandon us, and what wonder if we grow dizzy to look down the dark abyss of—how little we know' (508).

If metaphysics fall short in explaining 'Life', through its fixed systems that delimit the scope of what that nomenclature might entail, poetry serves as an alternative means to express the 'wonder' and 'mystery' that lie at the heart of such an inquiry. Through the use of metaphor, poetry temporarily creates a new possibility of cognitive association, by destabilising the relationship between signifier and signified without total collapse. This hovering state in which the semiotic and the semantic aspects of language negotiate permeates 'The Triumph' in more senses than one. If the poem's thematic preoccupation is with language as an act of socialisation, then de-socialisation, or the breaking down of language followed by reorganisation, signifies a possible re-structuring of society. The repeated reminder that the poem vacillates between reality and unreality only to lose the boundary that distinguishes the two reinforces this ultimately subversive stance in uncertainty: the speaker-narrator is awake yet dreams; Rousseau does not know whether he wakes or dreams. In other words, the void between meaning and non-meaning is the realm that 'The Triumph' exploits in order to examine the implications of language and furthermore those of the referential and value system in society.

The poem can arguably be classified as a social satire because what the speaker-narrator envisions is not a fanciful construct of the mind but a depiction of reality, which is more *real* than mimesis. The poem, which requires to be read at a latent level, shares the subliminal quality of a dream, yet, at the same time, exhibits an intense contemplation of reality. Shelley gives his own explanation of this state in 'On Life':

> Those who are subject to the state called reverie feel as if their nature were dissolved into the surrounding universe, or as if the surrounding universe were absorbed into their being. They are conscious of

> no distinction. And these are states which precede or accompany or follow an unusually intense and vivid apprehension of life. (507)

As with the introduction of the speaker-narrator's waking-dream, we are led to his 'unusually intense and vivid apprehension of life.' A familiar enough yet significant point that Shelley makes in relation to this power is the detrimental effect that language exerts over man's relationship with his surroundings. As we grow up, 'this power commonly decays' because, as children, we 'less habitually distinguished all that we saw and felt from ourselves' (507). Language educates us into the social code by which we live, and consequently we 'become mechanical and habitual agents' (507-8). Rousseau interestingly acts out this trajectory in the poem; he is unable to undo experience and retrieve his former blissful state.

'The Triumph' functions as a social satire to the extent that it exposes falsehood in various disguises: the ignorant crowd commits follies without knowing what they do; the historical figures whose will to power distinguishes them from the crowd eventually succumb to the 'Conqueror' owing to their lack of self-knowledge:

> they who wore
> Mitres and helms and crowns, or wreathes of light,
> Signs of thought's empire over thought; their lore
>
> Taught them not this—to know themselves; their might
> Could not repress the mutiny within,
> And for the morn of truth they feigned, deep night
>
> Caught them ere evening. (ll. 209-15)

The poem, however, cannot sustain its satirical stance in the end because what it ultimately purports is a tragedy of how 'all the good/We prize or aim at turns to evil.' Men are helpless because they have no control over good and evil:

> And much I grieved to think how power and will
> In opposition rule our mortal day—

> And why God made irreconcilable
> Good and the means of good (ll. 228-31)

Shelley's emphasis on the inextricability of 'good' and 'evil' suggests his inclination towards Manichaeanism; but the point is that men cannot have access to a complete control over these conflicting forces at work. What men can do is only to hope that 'good' will prevail over 'evil' in the end. Such frail conviction disables the poem from completing a task in the manner of *Trionfi*, in which Petrarch presents a world-view based on hierarchical values. Faced with an existential crisis, the poem does not have a ready answer to overcome it.

On a more personal level, the poem engages with a tragedy that is a direct legacy of Romanticism, which Rousseau embodies and, to a certain degree, the speaker-narrator adopts. Their own symbolic accounts resonate with each other: they are both initially in harmony with nature, but their spiritual communion with nature turns into alienation, and in the case of Rousseau, into both spiritual and physical corruption. The mistake that both personae commit is to compare their creativity with that of the sun; such acts of self-deification prove to be fatal, in a literal sense, as they become subjected to seasonal decay irrespective of their will. 'The Triumph' dramatises the tragic mortality of men compared to the immortality of nature. While nature is ever capable of regeneration, it becomes an act of perversion if attempted by men:

> the marble brow of youth was cleft
> With care, and in the eyes where once hope shone
> Desire like a lioness bereft
>
> Of its last cub, glared ere it died (ll. 523-26)

The symbolic act of the 'Sun' unmasking darkness from 'Earth' with which the poem opens becomes a tragic event for men because the very act exposes men's follies or reveals their mortality. In either case, unmasking connotes an entirely different significance in 'The Triumph' from that given in *Prometheus Unbound*, which will be dealt with in further detail in the following section.

If the epic-visions of Dante and Petrarch provided the framework of 'The Triumph', then Calderón offered the materials with which to work out its own problems. The common consequence of these borrowings was that 'The Triumph' fell short of the optimistic conviction that enabled previous poets to complete their epic-visions successfully. It significantly denotes the fragment epistemology of Romanticism that Shelley came to inherit; it also points to a modernity in which only relativist values can suffice. Shelley, writing within the tradition of epic-vision, ironically denounces its anachronism as an invalid form. What Shelley contributed to it, in effect, is the honesty of having failed to achieve that task.

Masquerade/Pageant/Mask

Shelley suggests in *Prometheus Unbound* and in a 'Sonnet: Lift not the painted veil' that life is all to do with putting on a veil, covering reality by painting it with a make-believe of what we would like it to be. This he calls, paradoxically, 'Death' in *Prometheus Unbound* (3.3.113). In making sense of what Shelley means by this, it is necessary to keep in mind his intention behind this work, which is not to render real life with real people but to present a cosmic staging of the principles that, in Shelley's views, govern the world in which we live. Therefore, what he implies is, on one level, the notion that to put on a veil of deception is endemic to life, yet, on another level, that there is a greater force at work, which, operating by its own rules, will cast off the deception. So what we call life, living from day to day in disguise, is, in fact, not life in the true sense of possessing a generative power, but death. What Shelley dramatises in *Prometheus Unbound* is the generative power of 'Love', which alone can unmask the world of deception:

> The loathsome mask has fallen, the man remains,
> Sceptreless, free, uncircumscribed: but man:

> Equal, unclassed, tribeless and nationless,
> Exempt from awe, worship, degree,—the King
> Over himself; just, gentle, wise: but man (3.4.193-97)

Shelley suggests here, as Rousseau does, that man is innately good, and that the shackles of social convention alienate man from a primal stage of happiness where he is free and undivided. One can either interpret Prometheus as a victim of tyranny, or as a victim of self-afflicted alienation whereby he creates his own enemy in his mind. The significance of these views—one political and the other psychological—is that they are intricately connected. Man is a social being who makes sense of his existence in relation to the referential and value system of the society to which he belongs; for this reason, the political infrastructure not only concerns society at large but also becomes duplicated in the individual mind. When Rousseau, for instance, critiques the state of contemporary society for its excessive imbalances in wealth and power, he also brings to light the individual consciousness that sustains it:

> It is difficult to reduce to obedience a man who has no wish to command, and the most adroit politician could not enslave men whose only wish was to be free; on the other hand, inequality extends easily among ambitious and cowardly souls, who are always ready to run the risks of fortune and almost indifferent as to whether they command or obey, according to fortune's favour.[13]

A similar version of the Hegelian master-slave dialectic can be applied to *Prometheus Unbound*: the division in society between the oppressor and the oppressed becomes transformed into a division within one's own psyche. To achieve the collapse of such opposition in the mind, therefore, is to simultaneously effect a change in the social reality. Thus, *Prometheus Unbound* does not necessarily demonstrate Shelley's disengagement from taking political actions but a change in his opinion, which favours a psychological approach towards achieving social progress.

The relationship between the socio-political and the psychological aspects of human existence is further explored in Shelley's use of the masquerade. He sees a separation of the form—how one is represented in society—and the content—the self; and in his view, we are merely made into actors who play our roles according to social rules. In depicting such a divorce between form and content, Shelley employs the masquerade. Bakhtin argues that, in the Romantic period, the carnival spirit became appropriated to 'an individual carnival, marked by a vivid sense of isolation'.[14] The separation of form and content in man's existence came to be seen as being increasingly problematic: the conventions that society demands we adopt or live by begin to take on a life of their own for which the mask provides a particularly useful metaphor. The liberation that people enjoyed in the masquerade, of occupying another subject-position from the one society demands that we adopt in everyday life, is transformed into something more serious and tragic in the case of Shelley's works: the act of masking either causes suffering, or provides the means to gratifying self-interest. It causes some to suffer because they can no longer be themselves but are forced to play a role by the mask they wear. This can be attributed to either personal or domestic slavery, an instance of the latter being Beatrice in *The Cenci*:

> The crimes and miseries in which she was an actor and a sufferer are as the mask and the mantle in which circumstances clothed her for her impersonation on the scene of the world.[15]

Ultimately, the masks become the only way of distinguishing people, and take over the identities of the individuals.

Browning also explored this aspect of human existence in his later poem *Fifine at the Fair* (1872), which has direct relevance to 'The Triumph' in its depiction of the masses who are visually identified by the fixity of their expression that exposes their overriding passion:

> On each hand,
> I soon became aware, flocked the infinitude
> Of passions, loves and hates, man pampers till his mood
> Becomes himself, the whole sole face we name him by,
> Nor want denotement else, if age or youth supply

The rest of him: old, young,—classed creature: in the main
A love, a hate, a hope, a fear, each soul a-strain
Some one way through the flesh—the face, an evidence
O' the soul at work inside; and, all the more intense,
So much the more grotesque. (Collins 1996; 1712-20)

Browning, however, reverses his contemptuous attitude (adopted in the manner of Byron and Shelley) toward life as an alienation of the 'self' in its appropriation of 'form' by altering his perspective:

There went
Conviction to my soul, that what I took of late
For Venice was the world; its Carnival—the state
Of mankind, masquerade in life-long permanence
For all time, and no one particular feast-day. Whence
'Twas easy to infer what meant my late disgust
At the brute-pageant, each grotesque of greed and lust
And idle hate, and love as impotent for good—
When from my pride of place I passed the interlude
In critical review; and what, the wonder that ensued
When, from such pinnacled pre-eminence, I found
Somehow the proper goal for wisdom was the ground
And not the sky,—so, slid sagaciously betimes
Down heaven's baluster-rope, to reach the mob of mimes
And mummers; whereby came discovery there was just
Enough and not too much of hate, love, greed and lust,
Could one discerningly but hold the balance, shift
The weight from scale to scale, do justice to the drift
Of nature, and explain the glories by the shames
Mixed up in man, one stuff miscalled by different names
According to what stage i' the process turned his rough,
Even as I gazed, to smooth—only get close enough!
—What was all this except the lesson of life? (1857-78)

Browning's attitude here can be explained by his deliberate swerving away from the poetic stance of the Romantic bard who alone stood in eminence, gazing down below upon the real world, more often than not, with contempt. It also denotes a social, cultural, and political change from the Romantic to the Victorian period that is duly reflected in the aesthetics of the poem.[16]

The divergence of Browning from Shelley's appropriation of the mask, however, is not merely that of aesthetic difference: if Browning's interest in the mask was largely that of a humanist, then Shelley's preoccupation with the mask had strong political implications. In *The Mask of Anarchy*, society is portrayed as a masquerade in which 'All disguised, even to the eyes,/Like Bishops, lawyers, peers, or spies' (ll. 28-29). What is implied here is that rather than taking on a profession or a social position, people are subsumed by them. The viewer no longer sees people as individuals but as types that can be readily labelled. This denotes one's surrender to form and consequently signifies spiritual enslavement. Man can never be good or happy in the true sense, according to Shelley, unless he is totally free. What prevents man from achieving this state is the greatest enemy, which Shelley represents in *The Mask of Anarchy*. 'Anarchy' figures in the poem as the religious, judicial, as well as the feudal tyrant who seeks 'glory, and blood, and gold' (l. 65) at whatever cost. What these various occupations and social positions have in common is their subservience to 'Anarchy' in their pursuit of self-interest, which Shelley critiques as the evil motivating force of society. The masks are nothing but a mimicry, which gets reproduced so as to maintain the status quo.

Shelley uses the masque for subversive ends in 'Charles the First'. He dramatises the grotesque discrepancy between appearance and reality by juxtaposing the masque and the anti-masque, which is detected by the Second Citizen:

> Ay, there they are—
> Nobles, and sons of nobles, patentees,
> Monopolists, and stewards of this poor farm,
> On whose lean sheep sit the prophetic crows,
> Here is the pomp that strips the houseless orphan,
> Here is the pride that breaks the desolate heart.
> These are the lilies glorious as Solomon,
> Who toil not, neither do they spin,—unless
> It be the webs they catch poor rogues withal.

Here is the surfeit which to them who earn
The niggard wages of the earth, scarce leaves
The tithe that will support them till they crawl
Back to her cold hard bosom. Here is health
Followed by grim disease, glory by shame,
Waste by lame famine, wealth by squalid want,
And England's sin by England's punishment.
And, as the effect pursues the cause foregone,
Lo, giving substance to my words, behold
At once the sign and the thing signified—
A troop of cripples, beggars, and lean outcasts,
Horsed upon stumbling jades, carted with dung,
Dragged for a day from cellars and low cabins
And rotten hiding-holes, to point the moral
Of this presentment, and bring up the rear
Of painted pomp with misery!

(*PWS* 492; 1.150-174)

The masque not only serves to gratify the egos of those in power but can also be used as a device to mock false appearances, the forms which have become meaningless and obsolete. The essential nature of the mask is mimicry, and the fixed, stagnant expression of the mask enables one to identify with the social values it mimics. It thus provides a sense of security, as well as a mockery of what is being mimicked, depending on the spectator. The masque and the anti-masque together offer a critique of the ill-functioning value system and thus disturb the king and queen despite the pleasure they gain out of it:

King Thanks, gentlemen. I heartily accept
This token of your service: your gay masque
Was performed gallantly. And it shows well
When subjects twine such flowers of [observance?]
With the sharp thorns that deck the English crown.
A gentle heart enjoys what it confers,
Even as it suffers that which it inflicts,
Though Justice guides the stroke.
Accept my hearty thanks. (2.1-9)

While the masque provides a sense of security for those who wish to maintain the status quo by being reminded of the social values they represent, it also gives away its identity—a mimicry devoid of content—which the citizens easily recognise. Be it the specific time in history, the reign of Charles the First or the Peterloo Massacre, the abuse of power in its excess engenders an ultimate fixity of form, which eventually becomes defeated owing to its divorce from content. Shelley's use of the masquerade is to mock the socio-political value systems that have become divorced from reality so that they only serve to gratify those in power, and further to enlighten those who are the spectators as well as the participants of the masquerade with knowledge of what they are masking, or being masked from, so as to induce reformation or revolution of the very social and political power structure it is mimicking. In this sense, one can say that Shelley employs the masquerade to an educational end:

> The paradox of the masquerade—whether in its cultural or literary manifestation—was that it presented truth in the shape of deception, the aspirations of an era in a theater of disguise.
>
> (Castle 346)

Shelley appropriates the masquerade for similar ends in 'The Triumph of Life': its grotesque mockery and parody serve as a satirical critique of the falsehood in society. Shelley also utilises the traditional sense in which the pageant figured to give the poem an ironic overtone:

> such seemed the jubilee
> As when to greet some conqueror's advance
>
> Imperial Rome poured forth her living sea
> From senatehouse and prison and theatre
> When Freedom left those who upon the free
>
> Had bound a yoke which soon they stooped to bear.
>
> (ll. 111-16)

The pageant had always been associated with the political conquerors as a manifestation of their power over the people whom they ruled. As Shelley had already experimented with this motif in 'The Mask of Anarchy' in the form of a pageant that reinstates its subservience to 'Anarchy', 'The Triumph of Life' similarly acts out 'the victory-pageant of death-in-life.'[17] G.M. Matthews elaborates on a possible influence which the fresco in the Campo Santo at Pisa (known as 'The Triumph of Death') may have had on the composition of 'The Triumph':

> The social satire in this painting is very powerful, and Shelley might well have taken it as a homily on the vanity of wealth and rank rather than on the vanity of earthly life. Like his own 'Triumph' it seems to say: *This* kind of life is really death.[18]

According to Leigh Hunt, the revelatory and moral messages that the 'Triumphs' manifest owe their origin in the conflation of the masquerade and pageant, which was popularly performed in Italy. The first notable event took place in Florence in the time of Lorenzo de' Medici: 'a party of persons, during a season of public festivity, made their appearance in the streets, riding along in procession, and dressed up like reanimated dead bodies', and 'sung a tremendous chorus, reminding the appalled spectators of their mortality.'[19]

In 'The Triumph', the emphasis is on the act of unmasking rather than masking. While the sun in the opening unmasks the darkness to give life to the varieties of terrestrial existence, the waking trance of the speaker-narrator exposes men to their follies:

> Old age and youth, manhood and infancy,
>
> Mixed in one mighty torrent did appear,
> Some flying from the thing they feared and some
> Seeking the object of another's fear,
>
> And others as with steps towards the tomb
> Pored on the trodden worms that crawled beneath,
> And others mournfully within the gloom

Of their own shadow walked, and called it death ...
    And some fled from it as it were a ghost,
Half fainting in the affliction of vain breath. (ll. 52-61)

Men are depicted in Gothic perversity, which prevails over the entire pageant. Shelley depicts history as a world-stage on which the same follies are repeatedly committed. While the men of power lose sight of their own weaknesses in order to distinguish themselves, the ignorant mass blindly subject themselves to their transient passions and readily succumb to oppression. The fact that the car drives over the crowd while it captivates the men of power is telling of their respective involvement with life: while the unquestioning masses are eager to serve their conqueror, the great are enslaved by opportunism, which leads them to power as well as to their dethronement. Instead of revealing man's primal state of happiness in freedom when unmasked, what becomes unveiled is man's psychologically enslaved state in different disguises: 'Men [...] had become insensible and selfish: their own will had become feeble, and yet they were its slaves, and thence the slaves of the will of others: lust, fear, avarice, cruelty and fraud, characterised a race'.[20] In 'The Triumph', the masks of such evil take on a life of their own to perpetuate their influence on others when fallen 'from the countenance/And form of all' (ll. 536-7) leaving 'The action and the shape without the grace//Of life' (ll. 522-23). This is a deliberate inversion of the unmasking that takes place in *Prometheus Unbound*:

Those ugly human shapes and visages
Of which I spoke as having wrought me pain,
Past floating through the air, and fading still
Into the winds that scattered them; and those
From whom they past seemed mild and lovely forms
After some foul disguise had fallen (3.4.65-70)

The masks serve as a false perception that must be rectified in *Prometheus Unbound*; however, in 'The Triumph', they take over what they are masking, and become life itself. The extremity of Shelley's views in the latter makes the poem a severe social satire; but it does not signify his abandonment of the idealism that sustains the ideology of the former poem. Rather, he utilises the satirical mode for an educational purpose. What the participants in the pageant want is enlightenment, so that they may change the way in which they engage in history by transforming their erroneous consciousness. The emphasis Shelley laid on the enlightenment of the individual mind in order to effect a change in the social reality is reminiscent of the Godwinian idea of social progress:

> The only method according to which social improvements can be carried on, with sufficient prospect of an auspicious event, is when the improvement of our institutions advances in a just proportion to the illumination of the public understanding.[21]

One can even argue that Shelley's depiction of history as a revelation of false consciousness, serves an educational end. The 'Triumph', in this sense, does not differ from his other works, which have a clear purpose of enlightenment.

There is yet another kind of unmasking that the poem addresses. In the Sonnet 'Lift not the painted veil', Shelley depicts masking as endemic to life:

> Lift not the painted veil which those who live
> Call Life; though unreal shapes be pictured there,
> And it but mimic all we would believe
> With colours idly spread,—behind, lurk Fear
> And Hope, twin Destinies; who ever weave
> Their shadows, o'er the chasm, sightless and drear.
> (Everest 2000, p. 414; ll. 1-6)

In his metaphoric use of the veil, Shelley denotes the roles one is compelled to play in life, and at the same time, the difficulty of evading them. In the opening of 'The Triumph', the narrator's divided consciousness is set against the sun, which is ever capable of performing its task of unmasking the darkness to celebrate its own glory in giving life to the earth. The human limitation as opposed to the cosmic life of infinity is brought to the fore. The narrator is unable to switch from night to day, and these two states merge in his consciousness: he remains awake at night so that when the day arrives he is ready to rest like the stars, which 'were laid asleep'. He is unable to dispose of the melancholy that is associated with night[22] and unlike the sun, he cannot rejoice in his own creativity as the source of life. The mask cannot be cast off as it is in *Prometheus Unbound*; this is the very problem with which the narrator is confronted. The narrator's failure to psychologically liberate himself also has political implications, which become tied in with the counter-revolutionary mood of the post-Napoleonic era. As I have argued at the beginning of this section, Shelley connects both the psychological and the political strife to suggest the interconnectedness of the two aspects that govern our existence. Therefore, when Prometheus is able to rectify his erroneous consciousness, he is at the same time able to depose the tyrant. If the requirement for achieving social liberty is the consciousness of the individual, there is doubt as to the capacity of effecting such change in social reality when one is in a psychological impasse. The narrator, therefore, is unable to participate in the revolutionary energy imagined as the effect of love:

> And the love which heals all strife
> Circling, like the breath of life,
> All things in that sweet abode
> With its own mild brotherhood:
> They, not it, would change; and soon
> Every sprite beneath the moon
> Would repent its envy vain,
> And the earth grow young again. (ll. 366-373)[23]

Nietzsche, in his *Untimely Meditations*, likewise argues for his 'conception of culture as a new and improved *physics*, without inner and outer, without dissimulation and convention, culture as a unanimity of life, thought, appearance and will,' which is only conceivable in 'hopeful young people' (Nietzsche 122-123). 'The Triumph' attempts to take on board a similar faith in the regenerative force based on the youthful aspiration for transforming social reality but represents it in its negativity as an instance of failed case. To this end, Shelley's use of the mask in 'The Triumph' proves effective: the act of unmasking denotes the full generative potential of the sun, which corresponds to that in *Prometheus Unbound,* against which is depicted the human limitation that prevents the mask from being cast off. What comes into play is the notion that man is a historical phenomenon whose present state is constantly being acted upon by the past: we are shaped by our own past as well as reacting against it. The narrator's impasse dramatised in the opening is due to such contending forces of the present acting against, as well as acted upon by, the past.

Politics

In delineating Western history, the poem addresses the ignorant crowd, on the one hand, which does not directly participate in shaping history but is rather conditioned by it, and the great—be they political, ecclesiastical, or philosophical leaders—on the other, who make history, but who also have succumbed to various pitfalls. The poem can be read as a satirical account of the weaknesses exhibited by seemingly great men, and history reads like a universal world-stage on which follies are endlessly performed. The poem, however, cannot be dismissed as a mere satire, for the very cynical outlook on history demonstrated by both the speaker-narrator and Rousseau, which compels history to be read in this way, is the very problem with which the poem is engaged.[24] Despite the span of time the poem covers, from the Hellenic and Hebraic civilisation to post-Napoleonic Europe, its central focus is on the latter period. Shelley demonstrates his interest as not being that of a historiographer attempting to depict an objective portrayal of history, but in using history to his own ends—to create a future which can overcome the pessimistic mood of the post-Napoleonic era. As explicitly stated in *A Defence of Poetry*, Shelley believed the role of the poet to be that of the 'unacknowledged legislator of the world'. To this end, he invested his poetic energy, and 'The Triumph of Life' is no exception.

The poem makes a clear distinction between the men of power and poets—the former only destroy whereas the latter create. Shelley suggests the limitation of the former class in their role in history. As their sole interest is to seize power with the aid of opportunism, they are destined to be overthrown by others after gaining power: 'Their power was given/But to destroy' (ll. 292-93). What characterises them is that they have been successful in conquering the external sphere, that is, of a nation, the church or the intellect, but have failed to surmount their inner struggle, that is, to know themselves. Their neglect of conquering 'the mutiny within' eventually leads to their own dethronement:

> Man who man would be,
> Must rule the empire of himself; in it
> Must be supreme, establishing his throne
> On vanquished will,—quelling the anarchy
> Of hopes and fears,—being himself alone.—(ll. 10-14)[25]

A good example of conquerors who neglected to conquer themselves is Napoleon. Shelley seemed to have struggled over the description of Napoleon as the cancelled lines in the manuscript demonstrates:

> The latest victim/captive
> A slave who sought ...
> A willing slave who sought ...
> The latest victim
> That is Napoleon
> He The last is he: a crown sought to win[26]

Shelley's depiction of Napoleon differs from those of Byron or Hazlitt in that he does not attempt to interpret his career out of partisan interest. Although both Byron and Hazlitt acknowledged the despotism of Napoleon's rule, they nevertheless associated him with the liberal cause, the aim of which was to defeat the *ancien régime.* Napoleon served as the pivot around which both conservative and radical camps oriented themselves, so that the Lake poets, out of their conservatism, equated him with evil, and read the Battle of Waterloo as the victory of God, thereby glorifying their country and, above all, Wellington.[27] Shelley, however, refuses to assimilate Napoleon to radical politics as Hazlitt did, but instead depicts him as an example of failed personality. In so doing, he reintroduces the significance of the individual consciousness over any external social condition. That the *beau idéal* of the French Revolution ended in the hands of despotic Napoleon is a reality that radicals such as Shelley had to face up to in order to keep liberalism from going astray. The fact that Napoleon could have acted as a democratic hero instead of a power-crazed tyrant played on their minds. Shelley was understandably drawn to rationalising the act of Napoleon's fall from grace by locating the weakness within the individual mind.

Poets, Shelley states in *A Defence of Poetry*, 'are the hierophants of an unapprehended inspiration, the mirrors of the gigantic shadows which futurity casts upon the present' (535). The poets alone are in the position to guide society in its best interest with which men of power must comply. Shelley's conviction in the *Defence of Poetry*, however, is overshadowed in 'The Triumph': there is no suggestion of poets having contributed to shaping history, and Rousseau, who is confident enough to say 'there rise/A thousand beacons from the spark I bore' (ll. 206-207) also gave rise to Napoleon as a consequence of the French Revolution.[28] The role of the poet, as Shelley defined it in the *Defence of Poetry*, is being questioned here in relation to the men of power who do in fact shape history, and the doubt regarding the poet's effective role in society—in the past examples of Rousseau and Wordsworth—is the object of Shelley's critique here.[29] In one of the apocryphal passages in the manuscript, Shelley groups Rousseau and Voltaire together, and in the voice of the Rousseau suggests the common reason of their failure: 'And if I sought those joys which now are pain,/If he is captive to the car of life,/'*Twas that we feared our labour wd be vain*' (*TLA*-'B'; ll. 25-27).[30] Reiman glosses this as Rousseau's warning for the narrator who is adopting the same contemptuous attitude toward history.[31] In the final version, Voltaire is grouped with 'Frederic, Kant, Catherine, and Leopold', who are either political figures or philosophers, and the reason given for his captivity is his role as a demagogue. This shift in the reason for Voltaire's captivity is revealing of Shelley's final understanding of the *philosophes:* his failure is not due to his cynical attitude toward his achievement, but to the problematic ways in which his reasoning encouraged men of power to act on the world-stage. It is possible to argue that there are two accountable reasons behind this misuse of knowledge. The first is that Voltaire, whom Shelley considered to be one of the 'mere reasoners', neglected to abide by the superior faculty of imagination, and thus misdirected the men of power. The second is that there is an endemic problem in converting knowledge into action in the process of which the former must always be distorted or misused. There is no doubt that Shelley meant to express Voltaire's limitation as a philosopher, in which case, however, it still begs the question of how faithfully writings can be converted into actions. Shelley is keen to explore this connection between the men of power and philosophers/poets. If the men of power distort what the philosophers/poets teach, there is little hope for improving society. Shelley's treatment of Rousseau, who is given a unique status in the final version, also attests to this dilemma: 'I/Have suffered what I wrote, or viler pain!—//And so my words were seeds of misery—/Even as the deeds of others' (ll. 278-281). This can either be attributed to his personal writings, to his more overtly social writings, or to both. Rousseau was regarded as having triggered the French Revolution by some, notably by Hazlitt, and no doubt, this opinion is expressed in these words of Rousseau. The central issue that Shelley is addressing through these examples is condensed in the words of the narrator: 'And much I grieved to think how power and will/In opposition rule our mortal day—//And why God made irreconcilable/Good and the means of good' (ll. 228-231).

In *Prometheus Unbound*, at the innermost depth of Prometheus' despair in Act I, we find a similar sentiment voiced through one of the Furies: 'The good want power, but to weep barren tears./The powerful goodness want: worse need for them./The wise want love, and those who love want wisdom;/And all best things are thus confused to ill' (ll. 625-628). Prometheus has, nevertheless, voluntarily sought this pain and through its endurance aims to become a Christ-like figure: 'I would fain/Be what it is my destiny to be,/The saviour and the strength of suffering man,/Or sink into the original gulph of things' (ll. 815-18). In *Prometheus Unbound*, the world is successfully transformed into a unifying whole so that the principle of Love overrules the tyrannical force of Jupiter—the dividing agent—and it is this process which Shelley is dramatising. The focus in 'The Triumph', however, is not to demonstrate the triumphant realisation of this idealism, but to engage in the struggle to achieve it despite the discouraging environment. The poem, therefore, does not swerve away from his former beliefs, but introduces the failing energy as the focus of his attention and examination.

In accomplishing this, Shelley uses a strategy he often adopted in his other works—notably in *Alastor* and in 'Julian and Maddalo'—where he explored the full potential of the Shelleyan poet through a dialectical portrayal of two characters. The persona or the character readily identifiable with the Shelleyan poet is the frustrated poet beset by the limits of his position in society. The failed poet, by contrast, represents his poetic potential, which he demonstrates by transcending the social barrier, but at the price of death or exile.[32] Kelvin Everest convincingly argues that 'Julian and Maddalo' can be read as a social satire that demonstrates 'the damaging limitations of Julian's situation [...] as the condition of his failure' when juxtaposed with the maniac (Everest 87). My contention is to argue that Shelley's device—to create two perspectives in a subdivision of the authorial persona—highlighted by Everest is relevant to the poet's effective use of the speaker-narrator and Rousseau in 'The Triumph'. The speaker-narrator has often been interpreted as the Shelleyan poet whom no doubt he reflects to a large degree; but to treat them as one and the same is to commit a gross mistake. The narrator's state of deadlock is being dramatised in the poem only as an object of scrutiny. Rousseau, as in the case of the failed poet in *Alastor*, represents the negative potential of a poet who, because of his isolation from the world, is compelled to death or exile. The narrator is held back in his actions precisely owing to such past examples of struggle that have ended in failure, and by converting this erroneous use of the past into the very object of scrutiny, the poem provides a powerful critique of the post-Napoleonic era of despondency: Napoleon's 'grasp had left the giant world so weak//That every pigmy kicked it as it lay' (ll. 226-27). The poem, in its critique of the permeating social pessimism of its time, echoes the 'Preface' to *The Revolt of Islam* in which Shelley assigns the cause of the failure of the

French Revolution to 'a defect of correspondence between the knowledge existing in society and the improvement, or gradual abolition of political institutions' (Everest et al. 2000, p. 35). He then argues that the *beau idéal* of the Revolution cannot be accomplished overnight, since the 'misrule and superstition', which long supported the *ancien régime,* can only be corrected with time. Shelley, while acceding to gradualism, alerts the people to the danger of overreacting to the failure and abandoning the cause altogether:

> But on the first reverses of hope in the progress of French liberty, the sanguine eagerness for good overleapt the solution of these questions, and for a time extinguished itself in the unexpectedness of their result. Thus many of the most ardent and tender-hearted of the worshippers of public good, have been morally ruined by what a partial glimpse of the events they deplored, appeared to show as the melancholy desolation of all their cherished hopes. Hence gloom and misanthropy have become the characteristics of the age in which we live, the solace of a disappointment that unconsciously finds relief only in the wilful exaggeration of its own despair. (37)

It is this attitude that Shelley is critiquing in 'The Triumph'.

In 'The Triumph', both the political and the personal concerns are inextricably woven. Just as Rousseau's fall after his encounter with the 'shape all light' can be read in either aesthetic or political terms, the narrator's despair is within both the private and public domains. As previous critics have pointed out, Rousseau, like the poet in *Alastor*, represents a poet-figure who, by aspiring for idealism and experiencing disappointment, is compelled to succumb to the destructive force of Life.[33] This transition can be interpreted as a delineation of Rousseau's writings—from *Julie* to *Confessions* and finally to the *Solitary Walker*—which, to a large degree, concerns his personal life in relation to society; yet the height to which Rousseau is elevated before his fall is also suggestive of the aspiring height of the *beau idéal* of the French Revolution, and Rousseau's despair echoes the social despondency of the post-Napoleonic era. The narrator, on the other hand, who is psychologically troubled, as stated in the opening, is also disheartened by the political scenes of the past: 'and for despair/I half disdained mine eye's desire to fill//With the spent vision of the times that were/And scarce have ceased to be' (ll. 231-234). The speaker wilfully avoids engaging in the very problems which beset him, and his despair finds its correlative in Rousseau who represents both the personal and political disappointment associated with the struggle for his ideals.

Shelley uses Rousseau to represent the full potential of both the private and public aspirations of the narrator, and through a dialectical play of the two characters, he illustrates the danger, in the case of the latter, of limiting his potential by the negative implications of the former. The narrator resembles the Shelleyan poet in his psychological state of impasse but beyond which the speaker is being distanced and objectified: his despair through being confronted by the past, which demonstrates an unfavourable view of history, is being critiqued, and his struggle to win over such negative energy is sublimated into the driving force of the poem. Despite the questions of 'where', 'why', and 'how' that haunt the poem, it is not the answers that the poem addresses but the *process* in quest of them. In 'The Triumph', Shelley does not offer a clear-cut model of history, and the poem can even be interpreted as demonstrating his pessimistic attitude toward history. To read it in this light, however, is to miss the point: the double perspective he employs in the poem through the speaker-narrator and Rousseau is a device Shelley uses in order to scrutinise the erroneous consciousness that took hold of Rousseau. It also serves as a caution against a straightforward identification of the persona and the Shelleyan poet, which can be dangerously misleading. We are in the dark as to whether Shelley meant to complete the poem or not, but the fragmentary state in which it now exists effectively illustrates the significance of this process, rather than the end, at which his critical attention is being directed.

Light

What makes 'The Triumph' difficult to read as an instance of embracing a progressive mode of history, which attracted Shelley through his readings of the Enlightenment writers and Godwin, is that it resists being assimilated into a clearly defined system. Its depiction of history can be best described as resembling a Manichean outlook on the world whereby both the moral and material worlds are seen to be governed by opposing principles of evil and good. In conveying this view of history, light and dark play a central role in the poem. The most expected conclusion to be drawn from his use of the two is that light is associated with good, and dark, with evil; however, such clear-cut metaphors will not suffice in 'The Triumph.' We find that Shelley deals with different types of light as contending forces, imposing upon each other in a repetitive manner. Also, his references regarding dark are never to a complete state of darkness but to an intermediary state between light and dark. Although dark has negative implications, its impotence to exercise power means that it cannot be one of the forces of light. Shelley's complex use of light, therefore, entails a scrupulous examination of the poem's optical mode. By focussing on his methodology, I hope to reveal what is particularly unique about 'The Triumph' in relation to his previous works that are concerned with the demonstration of an apocalyptic collapse of the power-struggle between good and evil.[34]

Although the poem is permeated with light and dark imagery, they are not depicted as contending forces, but rather, different kinds of light are in contest against each other while pure darkness remains a neutral agent. For example, the 'Sun' in the opening 'sprang forth' so that 'the mask//Of darkness fell' (ll. 3-4); however, 'a cold glare, intenser than the noon/But icy cold, obscured with [ ] light/The Sun as he the stars' (ll. 77-79); furthermore, the 'shape all light' who emerged from the sun 'waned in the coming light' (l. 412). The two significant types of light, in terms of power, are those of the sun and the chariot. In their depiction, it is interesting to note that the light of the sun is always responsive to nature, whereas the light of the car is described as an alien type of light—'cold glare' (l. 77), 'severe excess' (l. 424), 'cold light' (l. 468), and 'white blaze' (l. 490).[35] The description of the latter suggests that Shelley is drawing his account from his scientific knowledge of the moon, which he mainly acquired through his reading of the works of Darwin, Newton, Herschel, and Davy. The light of the moon is characteristically intense and white, according to their discoveries, due to the lack of atmosphere, which would make the light refract and produce colour.[36] Although in *Prometheus Unbound*, the 'earth' and 'moon' are given gender roles to denote the attraction between them, Shelley suggests no such gravitational power in his use of lunar light for the chariot in 'The Triumph.' The light of the car is consistently destructive whereas the sunlight is productive. The sunlight, when brought into contact with the earthly atmosphere, creates various rays, as most notably in the instance of a rainbow, and it serves as the source of life for earthly existence.[37]

Light, furthermore, implies a dominating power, which dark lacks, and the poem may be read as a succession of violence committed by various lights.[38] De Man concentrates on the linguistic aspect of the poem and reads this violence as the positing act of language. He furthermore stresses the arbitrariness of this act:

> The positing power of language is both entirely arbitrary, in having a strength that cannot be reduced to necessity, and entirely inexorable in that there is no alternative to it. It stands beyond the polarities of chance and determination and can therefore not be part of a temporal sequence of events.
>
> (De Man 116)

De Man highlights the spontaneity and the arbitrariness of, for instance, the sun springing forth in the opening, or approach of the chariot of Life approaching, which successfully takes over what came before. He argues that these acts have no antecedents, and that they occur of their own right; it is only with hindsight that these unrelated events are stitched together in the form of a narrative, a story whose composite parts do not form a coherent story. These two powers, however, do occur in a repetition through both the narrator's and Rousseau's account whereby the sun is eclipsed by the light of the car. What should be stressed about this circular mode of history is that the powers resist being incorporated into a continuous narrative, and can only be understood as acts of violence that stand independent from cause and effect. This is suggestive of Hume's scepticism, which, for the first time, questioned the Cartesian philosophy based on the necessary connection between cause and effect.[39] There is likewise in Shelley's argument no reason to connect the lights of the sun and the chariot as related events. They simply occur to erase the other; and since we only experience what comes to pass after our birth, the sequence in which these two lights take place is always in the same order—from the sunlight to that of the car—and the state before the sunlight is only implied as darkness as in the opening before the sunrise, or possibly 'a Hell//Like this harsh world in which I wake to weep' (ll. 333-34), denoting a state under the influence of the 'cold light.'

The problem with this circular mode of production and destruction is that it does not afford credibility to the progressive model of history. In his depiction of history, Shelley associates the ignorant mass with dark—either in the form of shade or shadow. The 'multitude' prove to be powerless victims of history, while those who are chained to the car possess power but of a destructive kind. It is intriguing to note that Shelley only associates light with philosophers and poets ('wreathes of light,/ Signs of thought's empire over thought'; ll. 210-11) amongst the individuals who are given credit for their active participation in history; he further associates intellect with power but of a different kind from that of men of action. Rousseau tells the narrator of 'the spark with which Heaven lit my spirit' (l. 201) from which 'A thousand beacons' will 'rise' even after his death. This is the only account in which the power of one man affects the spread of power into the multitude. Apart from Rousseau, the light of the philosophers including Bacon (whose 'spirit [...] leapt/ Like lightening out of darkness' (ll. 269-270)) remains self-contained and its effective influence remains questionable in 'The Triumph.'

Even more problematic is the ambiguous part which the poets take in history. The hierarchy Shelley implies by his use of various lights accounts for the higher status given to those whom he considered as poets over philosophers. His definition of poets, as he states in *A Defence of Poetry*, does not confine itself to versifiers in the strictest sense; but it includes those who are able 'to apprehend the true and beautiful, in a word the good which exists in the relation, subsisting, first between existence and perception, and secondly between perception and expression' (512). As such examples, the list extends to 'the authors of language and of music, of the dance and architecture and statuary and painting', 'the institutors of laws, and the founders of civil society and the inventors of the arts of life and the teachers' of religion (512). Those who hold the highest position according to such hierarchical discrimination in 'The Triumph' are

the sacred few who could not tame
Their spirits to the Conqueror, but as soon
As they had touched the world with *living flame*

Fled back like eagles to *their native noon* (ll. 128-31)[40]
[emphases added]

The 'living flame' is a form of combustible light, which is analogous to the solar light and thus becomes 'their native noon'. It is suggested here that 'the sacred few' share a similar source of light to the sun, and if one recalls the way in which the sun is depicted as the source of creativity, both in the opening and in Rousseau's account, it becomes clear that Shelley intended to distinguish them not only by liberating them from the car but by associating them with the solar light. The same can be argued in the case of Rousseau, with the crucial difference being that the light becomes extinguished by the 'shape all light':

'And still her feet, no less than the sweet tune
To which they moved, seemed as they moved, to blot
The thoughts of him who gazed on them, and soon

'All that was seemed as if it had been not—
As if the gazer's mind was strewn beneath
Her feet *like embers*, and she, thought by thought,

'Trampled *its fires* into the dust of death (ll. 382-88)
[emphases added]

Shelley once again uses combustible light in order to depict Rousseau's thoughts; and once it becomes expunged, his mind becomes that of an entirely different nature: a *tabula rasa* on which sense-data becomes recorded. The moment his mind comes under the influence of empiricism, the 'shape all light' (an optical illusion created by the sun light reflected on the water seen through the eyes of Rousseau) wanes in the coming light of the 'cold bright car'. That he was not able to re-claim the sun as his origin as 'the sacred few' had done seems to be the reason for his eventual subordination to the car of 'Life'. Shelley's account of 'the sacred few' and the corrupted Rousseau begs the question of how one is able to sustain the level of excellence in the real world without having to quit it.

De Man explicitly expresses his distaste for 'the historicization and the aesthetification of the text', which has dominated the way in which the poem has been read in the past.[41] In other words, the central issue has been whether the poem exhibits 'a movement of growth or of degradation'; instead, De Man looks beyond to scrutinise the way in which Shelley thematises language—of figuration and disfiguration. I think it is possible to relate his argument, which is linguistic-based, to the politics of the poem. In other words, the haphazardness and the violence de Man associates with the positing power of language can also be applied to the political power in 'The Triumph'. Michel Foucault in 'Nietzsche, Genealogy, History' unfolds a similar kind of view in his argument on *Entstehung* (emergence), by cautioning us to 'avoid thinking of emergence as the final term of a historical development', and by stressing the difference of genealogy from the traditional sense of history to be its interest in 'the hazardous play of dominations' (83).[42] Foucault's idea of genealogy, especially in his examination of emergence, can be seen as the direct opposite of Godwin's gradualism and the vital role he assigned to human intellect in human progress:

> Humanity does not gradually progress from combat to combat until it arrives at universal reciprocity, where the rule of law finally replaces warfare; humanity installs each of its violences in a system of rules and thus proceeds from domination to domination. (85)

This suggests that in order to achieve political power, one must abide by the 'system of rules', and thus, the political reality can be described as an endless masquerade. It is a vicious circle that feeds itself by the self-interested individuals who seek fame and power. Just as self-interest is the enemy of progress; this in-built power structure is what Shelley sees as the obstacle to effecting change in political reality. These successive acts of domination are what the narrator deplores in his comment on the incongruity between the 'Good and the means of good' (l. 231). Despite the fact that Shelley assigned the very role of effecting this change to poets, its success remains doubtful as previous figures in the pageant show. Rousseau, in this respect, who came close to effecting a change in the political scene, is understandably given a central role in this poem.

The only part within the poem which contains a structural development is the autobiographical account given by Rousseau. The sequence from the sun light to its reflection in the well, and furthermore to the emergence of the 'shape all light' can be seen as the culmination of the poem in terms of light. This process, which leads to the 'shape all light', unlike the rising of the sun or the coming of the chariot, does not take place suddenly to replace the other, but as a result of the cooperative work of the sun, nature, and Rousseau's eyes. It is a powerful instance in which the sun, which is the source of life as well as the symbol of creativity, is reflected through the eyes of the beholder on to nature:

'And as I looked the bright omnipresence
Of morning through the orient cavern flowed,
And the Sun's image radiantly intense

'Burned on the waters of the well that glowed
Like gold, and threaded all the forest maze
With winding paths of emerald fire (ll. 343-48)

As de Man rightly argues, this section is based on reflection and mirroring—as the sunlight is reflected 'on the waters of the well', and its reflection, seen through the eyes, mirrors the shape. It is the combination of self-reflexivity in both the sun and Rousseau mediated by water which creates the ultimate form of light as designated in 'shape all light'.

The problem with the shape, however, is that it commits violence on the beholder Rousseau:

> and soon
> All that was seemed as if it had been not—
> As if the gazer's mind was strewn beneath
> Her feet like embers, and she, thought by thought,
>
> Trampled its fires into the dust of death (ll. 384-88)

The 'shape all light,' like the sun and the chariot, proves to be empowered with the ability to posit; but its imposition, in effect, invites its own destruction, as the shape, by extinguishing the thoughts of Rousseau, causes the breakdown of self-reflexivity, which sustained its existence in the first place. The shape can be interpreted, as Reiman sees it, as Julie and, therefore, Rousseau's 'vision in which he embodies his own imaginations unites all of wonderful, or wise, or beautiful, which the poet, the philosopher, or the lover could depicture' (Matthews 1989, p. 73).[43] As Shelley argues in *Alastor*, this thirst 'for intercourse with an intelligence similar to itself'—the narcissistic desire—is, in Rousseau, 'avenged by the furies of an irresistible passion pursuing him to speedy ruin' (73).[44] Shelley dramatises here the ironic way in which the intellectual light is obliterated, not by the ignorant crowd, but through its own self-reflexive power. We only need to recall how Rousseau was compelled to retreat to his imaginary world because he could not find his ideal correspondence in the real world:

> I believed that I was approaching the end of my days almost without having tasted to the full any of the pleasures for which my heart thirsted, [...] without having even tasted that intoxicating passion, the power of which I felt in my soul—a passion which, through lack of an object, was always suppressed [...] The impossibility of attaining the real persons precipitated me into the land of chimeras; and seeing nothing that existed worthy of my exalted feelings, I fostered them in an ideal world which my creative imagination soon peopled with beings after my own heart.[45]

His narcissistic desire, which he projected on to the ideal female figure, acts out the inevitable through its own self-destruction.

In political terms, the *beau idéal* of the French Revolution, inspired by Rousseau according to Hazlitt, was by the same token disgraced by Napoleon. Shelley is unable to devise a way in which the efforts of the luminaries of the world—the poets—can effect change in the political reality without them being exploited by self-interested individuals. Although the poem does not complacently embrace pessimism, the impasse of the poem best reflects his view according to which good and evil coexist without the promise of victory on either side:

> Shall we suppose that the Devil occupies the centre and God the circumference of existence, and that one urges inwards with the centripetal, whilst the other is perpetually struggling outwards from the narrow focus with the centrifugal force, and that from their perpetual conflict results that mixture of good and evil, harmony and discord, beauty and deformity, production and decay [...]?[46]

If 'The Triumph' was to be interpreted as a treatise on the Enlightenment, it implicitly critiques light as the emblem of enlightenment; instead, Shelley represents it by two types of light in the poem—the sun and the chariot—which endlessly become reproduced by successive acts of domination. It is through such contest of various lights which Shelley interprets the world; just as there is no way out from the circular mode of production and destruction, the poem is unable to define a political sphere which remains free from violence and, in effect, corruption.

Masculinity

For all his vision of an egalitarian society in which the two sexes co-operate equally,[47] 'The Triumph', one of Shelley's most politically committed poems, demonstrates the very opposite: that female performance or aspirations play little or no role in the history that he depicts. The female voice is erased from the world-stage on which, literally, great men play their parts and consequently shape history. Although Shelley is not in favour of this grand narrative consisting of men of power, even in his attempt to create an alternative version of history in which poets are made to play a central role, the female sex remains invisible. The psychological struggle that is being dramatised in 'The Triumph' is depicted as characteristically masculine: the personal state is defined against the sun—a phallic symbol used by the Enlightenment mythographers whom Shelley draws on[48]—and the political struggle is set against the male precursors of the literary tradition. This focus on the masculine mind is reminiscent of the portrayal of Prometheus in *Prometheus Unbound*: both texts suggest that only the masculine mind possesses the potential of effecting a revolutionary change, and that the female role—be it that of Asia or Jane Williams—is to assist or to participate in it emotionally.[49] The masculine mind is the centre of dramatisation to which the feminine attributes, constructed by men, contribute. This is a familiar feminist argument in current Romantic studies, which sees the male Romantic poets as being interested in the male subject-position while they objectify women as the other to subsume them as their property.[50] Thus, the significance of Asia in *Prometheus Unbound* can only be defined in relation to the part she plays in the psychological liberation of Prometheus.[51] 'The Triumph', as a version of Western history, is a one-sided story that is interested in telling the achievements and failures of masculine ambition without taking into account the female contribution to history. I will demonstrate that 'The Triumph' is an explicit instance of female exclusion and that Shelley's treatment of the female in the poem demonstrates an incongruity with his beliefs: he appropriates the female as the other onto whom the masculine ego projects itself.

I will begin my argument with the opening of the poem in which female subordination to masculine creativity or the exclusion of female gender from creativity is explicitly manifested. The sun, which is glorified as the source of life, is portrayed as a masculine force, which, through its active and imposing role, imbues earth with energy when brought into contact. Although the characterisation of the sun varies according to the discarded openings,[52] what remains unchanged is that the sun, be it an implication of God, a paternal figure, or a sexual masculine power, is designated as 'he' and never by the feminine 'she'. This is suggestive of, as Shelley, no doubt, in his symbolic use of the sun implies, the creativity of the poet,[53] and by masculinising the sun, or rather, indiscriminately taking on board the argument of the Enlightenment mythographers who see solar-worship as a form of phallicism, he is acquiescing in the denial of creativity for the female sex. Shelley's use of the sun and solar-worship proves a powerful metaphor for the artist and his creativity, but at the same time, provokes a gender issue of female exclusion. The passivity assigned to the female sex in the two versions of the discarded openings also indicates that their role in history is automatically to surrender as a victim without having the option to choose from 'actor or victim'.[54] In *A Defence of Poetry*, Shelley attributes 'the emancipation of women from a great part of the degrading restraints of antiquity' to the 'effects of the poetry of the Christian and Chivalric systems'; but what he emphasises as the effect of it is the newly born 'poetry of sexual love' written by male poets. What he seems to be suggesting is that this change, which took place within the female sex, was for the benefit of the male poets rather than for themselves: women are not given a voice of their own but merely became better objects for men who still occupied the subject-position.[55] This passivity of women is retained in 'The Triumph': Shelley does not offer an alternative role for women other than being objects of men, nor does he imply any possibility of their social participation in the future.

Amongst the great historical figures depicted in the poem, 'Catherine' alone is a female example; and even in her case, she, together with 'Frederic' and 'Leopold' are described as the 'Chained hoary anarchs' (l. 237), which sees her as a masculinised woman.[56] The captivated crew, therefore, is predominantly male, and apart from the ignorant mass, he does not refer to any female individuals. Moreover, in his depiction of the alternative class, that is, the poets who possess the potential to 'create' rather than to 'destroy', the female sex is excluded. Shelley's list includes 'the great bards of old' (l. 274), Wordsworth in the 'apocryphal passages', and Rousseau.[57] The focus is on the poets of the Revolutionary and post-Revolutionary era, who are scrutinised for their failure so that the contemporary poets, namely Shelley himself, can overcome their mistakes. This is clearly a male literary line that Shelley is establishing, and the future that lies in the speaker-narrator is further characterised by this male ambition, which he has inherited from his precursors.

The disruptive voice within the manuscript of 'The Triumph,' however, suggests the possibility of female participation, even as the object of a male ego. The lyrics are characterised by an emotionalism appropriate to the genre; and they are particularly of interest when read in the light of 'The Triumph.' In short, the lyrics represent the traditional attributes of the female gender—of feelings and emotions—which are absent in 'The Triumph.' What deserves attention is the fact that the lyrics, despite their self-contained nature, play a vital part in 'The Triumph': the emotional power of the lyrics serves as the cause of the deadlock in 'The Triumph.' The lyrics represent the invested present, which obstructs the forward movement of 'The Triumph,' and the dialectical relationship between the lyrics and 'The Triumph' is the negotiation of what might be characterised as the diachronic and the synchronic. What Nietzsche in his *Untimely Meditations* terms the *unhistorical* moment in which one loses a sense of time is applicable to the lyrics in their preoccupation with love.[58] Moreover, this *unhistorical* moment also finds its voice in 'The Triumph' when the narrator experiences vertigo: 'before me fled/The night; behind me rose the day; the Deep//Was at my feet, and Heaven above my head' (ll. 26-28). The psychological struggle to subsume the unhistorical moment into history also has political implications: that is, to unblock the impasse into which liberal efforts have fallen in the post-Napoleonic era. Indirectly, the lyrics demonstrate the vital role that emotion plays in history, and the invisible women who do in fact participate in the force of history. To reverse the argument of female exclusion, the history delineated in 'The Triumph' is a one-sided engagement in history, and only when complemented by the lyrics can it achieve its wholeness. 'The Triumph,' which is preoccupied with the historical drive, is deliberately exclusive of the historical potential of the present: 'But I, whom thoughts which must remain untold' (l. 21). His repressed 'thoughts' re-surface in the lyrics, and it is through such an indirect avenue that the poem is inclusive of the female; however, even under this light, the male subject-position remains unaltered, and the female 'other' gets subsumed as the property of the male poet.

Another instance of Shelley's use of the female gender is the 'shape all light'. Although this figure invites various interpretations as to what it actually represents,[59] her attributes and role suggest that she is a lure of some kind. The effect she has on Rousseau is worth noting: she evokes 'desire and shame', which is arguably suggestive of his sensuality. Moreover, her presence invites him to seek ontological and teleological knowledge: 'Shew whence I came, and where I am, and why—' (l. 398). Thus, Rousseau's inherent desires surface without there necessarily being a causality. Her ability to elicit and fulfil Rousseau's desires, however, at the cost of eventually denying them, reads like the seductive force of history in the guise of a female figure: just as seduction is followed by a disaster, Rousseau, after drinking the nepenthe undergoes a considerable change. The great men of power who figure in 'The Triumph', likewise, have acted according to their desires, and their ultimate determination to fulfil their ambition distinguishes them from the ignorant crowd who do not even know what they seek in 'Life'. The consequence of occupying a seemingly advantageous position in history, however, was to become chained to the car.

In addition to the character of the 'shape' as a seductress, there is another feature to her that is worth noting. The shape's luscious existence cannot be distinguished from the surrounding nature, and just as her appearance is described as an emergence from the sun, her disappearance is like the fading Lucifer.[60] Her fusion with nature adds a different dimension to her character, as being suggestive of Mother Nature; and her maternal quality (of serving as a protection) is manifested when she fades before Rousseau's eyes:

> 'So knew I in that light's severe excess
> The presence of that shape which on the stream
> Moved, as I moved along the wilderness,
>
> 'More dimly than a day appearing dream,
> The ghost of a forgotten form of sleep,
> A light from Heaven whose half extinguished beam

'Through the sick day in which we wake to weep
Glimmers, forever sought, forever lost.—
So did that shape its obscure tenour keep

'Beside my path, as silent as a ghost; (ll. 424-433)

It is instructive that the 'shape' can be interpreted as both a lure and a maternal figure: this combination can also be found in the bas-relief of History by Crodion, which depicts Clio, the Muse of History, as embodying eroticism and offering maternal sustenance.[61] Young Napoleon figures in the back, attentive to what she is about to convey. Given that Napoleon was to become one of the prominent historical figures of the nineteenth century, this representation of Napoleon and Clio is telling of how an ambitious individual becomes wrapped up in history. She seduces him so that he is driven to fulfil his desire of fame and power; she offers maternal protection as long as fortune is on his side; but just as seduction may lead to disastrous effects, she also warns him with her stern expression.

What can be said in relation to the bas-relief of History is that Shelley attributes certain female characteristics to history, and suggests that a male engagement with history is analogous to a relationship with a woman who is at once a seductress and a mother.[62] This is an appropriate example that defines the female gender as the 'other' who embodies the very qualities poets find useful in their poetic exercise. The poem clearly denies the female her subject-position and either appropriates the female to a mere object to be subsumed or excludes it completely.

CONCLUSION

'The Triumph of Life' arguably marks the end of a period of Shelley's poetical and political career, which began with *Queen Mab*, culminating in the composition of his major works of the *annus mirabilis—The Cenci*, 'The Mask of Anarchy', *Julian and Maddalo*, and *Prometheus Unbound*. These years saw Shelley, firstly, as an activist in political and religious debates—through his pamphleteering, and most notably in his direct participation in the Irish cause; his activism was then followed by his more gradualist approach, akin to Godwin's views on social reform, by probing into the psychological nature of man and its relation to society. Shelley in the meantime wrote for a diverse audience, from the masses for which *The Mask of Anarchy* was intended, to *Prometheus Unbound*, which was composed with 'the more select classes of poetical readers' in mind. As Mary Shelley notes in her introduction to the 1839 edition of Shelley's collected works, the content of his poems ranges from 'the purely imaginative' to 'those which sprang from the emotions of his heart' (*PWS* xxii); he was characteristically able to depict both the imaginary and the real. Such diversity and richness of his poetical material is indeed manifested in 'The Triumph'; it also demonstrates Shelley's experimentation with literary genre and style, which he exercised throughout his poetic career. The total sum of it is that none of the past critics have been able to categorise the poem satisfactorily, and that it is almost seen as an odd exception in his *œuvre*. 'The Triumph' is not a final testimony of the poet, as it is often considered, but a working-process, which entails his re-orientation in the midst of his existential crisis. As De Man rightly points out, there is no apparent valorisation in the poem, either in the positive or in the negative; his further analysis of the linguistic characteristics of the poem accentuates not only the random positing and erasure that language commits, but also the impossibility of eliciting the politics of the poem.

Lastly, 'The Triumph', which Donald H. Reiman argues is a private poem not intended for publication as it stands, poses the various choices in life that beset him and their consequences.[63] There is a strain of Shelley's emotional struggle that can be traced back to 'Lines Written Among the Euganean Hills', to 'all my saddest verses raked up into one heap', which Shelley intended to include in the *Julian and Maddalo* volume, and to 'Misery—A Fragment', which appears in the same notebook in which he composed *Prometheus Unbound*.[64] Even as a visionary, it was becoming increasingly hard to ignore the realities of life, which were marked by a number of domestic tragedies (i.e. the suicide of his first wife, Harriet, and the death of his and Mary's three children). Such private inner struggle no doubt played on his mind, as did the political pessimism of his age. 'The Triumph' comes at that deadlock when he could no longer continue in the same way as he had done before; this realisation that his innocence must be replaced by something other than ignorance must have made Rousseau an attractive figure to use. If Rousseau was a strategy for Shelley to re-examine himself, the speaker-narrator was the body on which to work out that process. 'The Triumph' holds a unique position in his *œuvre* not only because it was truncated by his sudden death and remains inconclusive but also because it has an urgency and sincerity that can hardly be feigned.

NOTES

1. 'The Triumph of Life', which first appeared in Mary Shelley's *Posthumous Poems* (1824), served as the basic text for 'all editions before 1960'; G. M. Matthews published '"The Triumph of Life": A New Text' (1960) as a result of his direct access to the MS since Mary Shelley in her preparation for the *Posthumous Poems*. While Donald H. Reiman's variorum edition (1965) made use of Matthews's text, it contained numerous variant readings from Matthews's. For the history of the text, see Reiman 1965, pp. 119–28.
2. Whereas the biographical reading of the poem has been put to rest after Reiman's response to Matthews, De Man's deconstructive reading of the poem has dominated the criticism of 'The Triumph': as an example of adopting De Manian approach, see Tilottama Rajan, 'The Broken Mirror: The Identity of the Text in Shelley's *Triumph of Life*' (Rajan 1990, pp. 323–49); for illustrating the limits of such reading, see Timothy Clark, 'Shelley after Deconstruction: the Poet of Anachronism' (1996, pp. 97–98).
3. The literary history is not as clearly and forcefully presented as that of socio-political history: for example, Shelley refrains from making a direct reference to Wordsworth, and he omits Milton, Shakespeare, Chaucer, etc. The reason for his underplaying of literary figures (unlike in *A Defence*) can be explained by his thematisation and problematisation of 'power' in the poem over which poets are seen to have little influence. Rousseau is clearly an exception, which may be the reason why Shelley chose him as the guide to the speaker-narrator.
4. For the influence of Dante on 'The Triumph', see Ralph Pite, 'Shelley, Dante and *The Triumph of Life*' (Clark and Hogle 197–211).
5. Paul de Man writes on 'The Triumph': 'its meaning glimmers, hovers, and wavers, but refuses to yield the clarity it keeps announcing'; see 'Shelley Disfigured' (De Man 93–123).
6. 'On Life' (*SPP* 507).
7. Ralph Pite brings to our attention the significance of Dante's *Purgatorio* in relation to Shelley's composition of 'The Triumph' and argues that 'the similarities between the opening of Shelley's poem and Dante's *Purgatorio* are striking' (Clark and Hogle 198).
8. Shelley first mentions Calderón in a letter to Thomas Jefferson Hogg dated 25 July 1819; see *PBSL* 2: 105. For Shelley's other references to, and his reading list of, the works of the Spanish dramatist, see chapters six and seven of *The Violet in the Crucible: Shelley and Translation* by Timothy Webb.

9. Webb 1976, p. 220.
10. Quoted from Webb 1976, p. 221, it appears among the drafts of *Faust* and *El MágicoProdigioso*, written in the hand of Edward Williams. Webb speculates that Shelley may have translated the passage himself, which he then entrusted Williams to record. The manuscript source is Bodleian Shelley Manuscripts adds. e.18.
11. Webb argues that '*Hellas, Adonais*, and *The Triumph of Life* are all strongly influenced by the idea that life is a dream'; although this idea is not unique to Calderón, his 'powerful and poetic exploration of this theme had its due effect on Shelley' (1976, p. 222). As an example of other possible sources that utilise the notion of 'life as a dream', Shakespeare may be given: 'We are such stuff/As dreams are made on; and our little life/Is rounded with a sleep' (*The Tempest* 4.1.156–58). This idea, however, remains localised without further development in Shakespeare.
12. Webb also notes the two-edged aspect of Calderón's influence on Shelley: 'If Calderón was partly responsible for sharpening Shelley's sense of dissatisfaction with the world, [...] it was he too who helped to direct Shelley's gaze to a region beyond the sphere of our sorrow where all the mysteries might finally be solved' (225).
13. Rousseau 1984, p. 132.
14. Bakhtin 37.
15. 'Preface' to *The Cenci* (Everest et al. 2000, p. 735).
16. The change in aesthetic taste from Romanticism to Victorianism, which Browning appropriates, will be discussed further in Chapter 3.
17. Matthews 1962, p. 124.
18. His argument is based on a suggestion made by Blunden (291). One half of this painting 'shows a party of gentlefolk flirting and making music in an orchard, while Death, a batlike woman, swoops down on them'; in the centre foreground, there is 'a pile of dead' known to be of former rulers who 'are having their souls extracted by angels or demons'; and 'another highborn party, issuing hawk-on-wrist from a mountain cleft, distantly inspect three corpses; while on the hill above, several old men follow the pastoral life in placid harmony with wild animals'. See Matthews 1962, p. 124.
19. 'Preface' to *The Descent of Liberty, A Mask* (xxii–xxiii).
20. *A Defence of Poetry* (*SPP* 524).
21. Godwin 1976, p. 273.
22. Shelley associates night with melancholy. See discarded opening 'B' and 'C' in 'Appendix B', *BSM*, vol. 1.
23. 'Lines Written among the Euganean Hills' (Everest et al. 2000, p. 443).

24. In comparison to Byron's view of history (which 'Hath but *one* page'), Paul Dawson argues that according to Shelley' it is rather our mistaken acceptance of this "law" that condemns us to repeat the past'; see '"The Mask of Darkness": Metaphor, Myth, and History in Shelley's "The Triumph of Life"' (Behrendt 238).
25. 'Sonnet: To the Republic of Benevento' (*SPP* 327).
26. *BSM* 1: 177.
27. For the manner in which Napoleon was represented by the Lakers and the radicals in their polemics over his career, see Bainbridge; see also my introduction, pp. 31–32.
28. For the idea that Rousseau was behind the French Revolution, see William Hazlitt, 'The Times Newspaper: on the Connexion between Toad-eaters and Tyrants' (*Complete Works* 4: 145–52): 'He [Burke] quarrelled with the French Revolution out of spite to Rousseau, the spark of whose genius had kindled the flame of liberty in a nation' (146).
29. Mary Shelley (less directly) and Browning problematise the effective role of a poet in society and its relation to the 'Men of Action'. See chapter 3. Although Shelley initially grouped Rousseau with Voltaire in one of the apocryphal passages (*TLA*-'B'), he held a view that distinguished him from 'mere reasoners': 'Rousseau was essentially a poet' (*Defence of Poetry* 530). Shelley originally included a reference to Wordsworth in *TLA*-'B': 'Whilst others tell our sons in prose or rhyme/ The manhood of the child' (ll. 10–11). For the term 'apocryphal passage', see Chapter 1.
30. The italicised words are those cancelled separately.
31. *BSM* 1: 334–35.
32. I owe this argument to Kelvin Everest's 'Shelley's Doubles: an Approach to *Julian and Maddalo*' (Everest 67–68).
33. I am thinking mainly of two works: Duffy and Maddox.
34. The primary example of this is *Prometheus Unbound.*
35. Clear examples of the sunlight are, firstly, the opening of the poem in which the sun performs a celebratory act of illuminating the natural world and, secondly, the vision of Rousseau's account, which describes the solar light working in unison with its natural environment.
36. See Grabo 152–53. Shelley's references to the light of the moon can also be found in *Prometheus Unbound* and in *Queen Mab.*
37. There is another simile to be drawn from Shelley's use of the 'white light' and various rays of colour: the former light is used to denote eternity, whereas the latter is employed to signify earthly life. See *Adonais*: 'Life, like a dome of many-coloured glass,/Stains the white radiance of Eternity,/ Until death tramples it to fragments'. (ll. 462–64). Interestingly, a rainbow

is formed above the chariot when Rousseau first witnesses the car: 'A Moving arch of victory, the vermilion/And green and azure plumes of Iris had/Built high over her wind-winged pavilion' (ll. 439–41). This seems to be, yet again, another instance aimed at an ironic effect: the chariot is described 'as if from some dread war/Triumphantly returning' (which is taking the lives of people).

38. I owe this argument to Paul de Man's essay, 'Shelley Disfigured'.
39. David Hume, *An Enquiry Concerning Human Understanding* bk. 1, pt. 3.
40. Reiman glosses 'the sacred few' as 'the leading representatives of the Hellenic and Hebraic civilization, among them Socrates and Jesus' (*SPP* 487).
41. De Man lists Meyer H. Abrahams and Harold Bloom as exemplary critics who have identified either 'positive or negative valorization of the movement' in the poem (299–300). To this may be added Donald H. Reiman and G.M. Matthews, whose opinions were divided on their biographical readings of the poem: while Matthews maintained that a speculative liaison between Shelley and Jane Williams existed, which signified the poet's abandonment of his former idealism, Reiman denied that any evidence exists to support the likelihood of such a relationship, arguing that Shelley remained committed to his former principles. See Matthews 1962, pp. 104–34; Reiman 1963, pp. 536–50.
42. *The Foucault Reader* 76–100.
43. See Reiman 1963, pp. 546–47.
44. Shelley similarly writes in 'On Love':

> We are born into the world and there is something within us which from the instant that we live and move thirsts after its likeness. [...] We dimly see within our intellectual nature a miniature as it were of our entire self, yet deprived of all that we condemn or despise, the ideal prototype of every thing excellent or lovely that we are capable of conceiving as belonging to the nature of man. (*SPP* 504)

45. *The Confessions of Jean-Jacques Rousseau* 396, 398.
46. 'On the Devil, and Devils' (Julian edition 7: 100).
47. In *A Defence of Poetry*, Shelley attributes '[t]he abolition of personal and domestic slavery, and the emancipation of women from a great part of the degrading restraints of antiquity' to 'the effects of the poetry of the Christian and Chivalric systems' and claims that the 'abolition of personal slavery is the basis of the highest political hope that it can enter into the mind of man to conceive' (*SPP* 524–5). *The Revolt of Islam* deals with slavery on both a personal and a societal level, the abolition of which the male and female protagonists of the poem attempt to achieve. Cythna takes the lead

in order to emancipate women: 'Can man be free if woman be a slave?' (2.43).

48. See Feldman and Richardson; especially on Richard Payne Knight and Charles Dupuis, pp. 249–56, 276–87.
49. I would argue that the disruptions within the manuscript of 'The Triumph'—'To Jane: The keen stars were twinkling', 'Lines written in the Bay of Lerici', 'Fragment: To the Moon' (I have used the titles given by Matthews in *PWS*)—stand as complementary to 'The Triumph'.
50. See 'Romanticism and the Colonization of the Feminine' by Alan Richardson in Mellor, *Romanticism and Feminism*; Mellor 1993.
51. Nigel Leask in his *British Romantic Writers and the East: Anxieties of Empire* argues that Asia is made out to play an active role *in Prometheus Unbound*; however, he is measuring her against 'the veiled maid' of *Alastor* and Cythna in *The Revolt of Islam*, and his argument still begs the question whether the education of Asia that he emphasises in 'The Role of Asia', is given the same weight as the liberation of Prometheus.
52. There are *four* extant discarded openings that are contained in *BSM*, vol. 1. I have followed Reiman's practice of designating them in the order in which they were composed as *DO*-'A' to 'D'. The italicised words are those cancelled separately in the manuscript. In *DO*-'B', the sun is given a paternal role in relation to the earth: 'the Ear<th> below/Lay *like* the fairest of the wandering Seven/*Beneath* her father's wings' (ll. 10–12); in *DO*–'C', the sun is depicted as the masculine 'he' whereas the earth is described in the feminine 'she': 'the sun came forth/Rejoicing in his splendour and the mask//Of darkness fell from the awakened earth.—/Whilst she, the fairest of the wandering Seven' (ll. 2–5); in the final version, the sun is given a god-like status: 'And in succession due, did Continent,//Isle, Ocean, and all things that in them wear/The form and character of mortal mould/Rise as the Sun their father rose' (ll. 15–18).
53. Although Rousseau's autobiographical account, in which the sun is employed as the source of human imagination, is an obvious instance of this, the opening equally suggests a strong affiliation of the sun and the mind of the poet through the contrast between the infinite creativity of the former and the limitation of the latter.
54. Rousseau tells the narrator to 'follow thou, and from spectator turn/Actor or victim in this wretchedness' (ll. 305–6).
55. Shelley mentions Dante and Petrarch as the primary examples.
56. Byron depicts her in a similar manner: 'And Catherine [...]/Though bold and bloody' (*Don Juan* 9. 70).
57. The cancelled lines in the manuscript read: 'Homer & his brethren'; see *BSM* 1: 193 (f. 33r).

58. Nietzsche lists 'love' as one of the instances of an *unhistorical* moment.
59. Whereas most critics agree on the ambivalent nature of the 'shape', Reiman argues for its benevolent character by identifying it with Julie in Rousseau's *La Nouvelle Héloïse*, while Bryan Shelley finds it unequivocally evil. See Reiman 1965; B. Shelley 162–74.
60. Her description appeals to the auditory and visual senses as well as to that of touch:

    'A shape all light, which with one hand did fling
    Dew on the earth, as if she were the Dawn
    Whose invisible rain forever seemed to sing

    'A silver music on the mossy lawn,
    And still before her on the dusky grass
    Iris her many coloured scarf had drawn.—
    * * *
    —the fierce splendour
    Fell from her as she moved under the mass

    'Of the deep cavern, and with palms so tender
    Their tread broke not the mirror of its billow,
    Glided along the river, and did bend her

    'Head under the dark boughs, till like a willow
    Her fair hair swept the bosom of the stream
    That whispered with delight to be their pillow.—(ll. 352–57, 359–66)

61. Stephen Bann in his 'Introduction' to *The Clothing of Clio* mentions the bas-relief of History by Crodion.
62. To support my view that Shelley, at some level, saw the force of history as a female figure, see the cancelled lines in the manuscript, which depict the 'the shape [...] within the car' (l. 178) as 'the mistress of the mystery'; see *BSM* 1: 171 (f.27v).
63. See 'Shelley's Manuscripts and the Web of Circumstance' (Brinkley 238).
64. There are some verbal parallels that can be noted between *Prometheus Unbound* and the 'Discarded Openings' of 'The Triumph': 'Like genius, or like joy which riseth up/As from the earth, clothing with golden clouds/ The desart of our life..../This is the season, this the day, the hour' (*PU* 1.10–13); '*It* was the year, the season & the hour/When *the* high tide of life has ceased to flow,/Its stormy reflux pauses, and *the* shore//*Looks gay* with anchored hopes, whose pennons glow/In the false wind & oer the

flattering *wave*' (*DO*-'C'). What can be deduced from such a parallel is that Shelley attempted a similar depiction of regeneration in 'The Triumph' but failed as his choice of the words 'false wind' gives away; instead, he deliberately divorced the speaker-narrator from the sun and made them contesting forces in the final version of the opening. Shelley seems to have channelled his pessimism when composing *Prometheus Unbound* into 'Misery—A Fragment'; see 'Appendix A', *BSM*, vol. 9.

Chapter 2

Mary Shelley's *Valperga*

Valperga and 'The Triumph of Life'

The last novel that Mary Shelley wrote during Percy's lifetime was *Valperga: or, The Life and Adventures of Castruccio, Prince of Lucca*, a historical romance loosely based on the life of the medieval Italian chieftain, Castruccio Castracani. Mary conceived the general idea of what was to become the novel as early as 1817, when the Shelleys were still living in England.[1] It was not, however, until two years later when they moved to Italy that she began her research on the historical background of the novel.[2] It took another year (with an interim of a year during which she worked on her novella *Mathilda*) until she began writing it. By the time *Valperga* was completed, four years had passed, and Percy had already written most of his major works, including *The Revolt of Islam*, *Julian and Maddalo*, *Prometheus Unbound*, and *The Cenci*. During the course of their partnership, the Shelleys read together, and often engaged in dialogical composition: for example, *Prometheus Unbound* makes clear reference to Shelley's *Frankenstein*, subtitled 'the modern Prometheus'; *The Cenci* and *Mathilda*, which both share the incest theme, were written in the summer of 1819. If they communicated to one another through their works, *Valperga* is no exception and especially deserves attention as it is often seen as one that marks her break away from that dialogue.[3] Interestingly, Percy's 'The Triumph,' which suffers from a similar fate, can best be understood as a response to *Valperga*.[4]

Both 'The Triumph of Life' and *Valperga* delineate history, the former being that of Western civilisation, the latter, of medieval Italy; yet, in so doing, they also question historiography that relies on great names and events as the essence of history. This is given a distinct voice in *Valperga* when the heroine, Euthanasia, defies her fate of becoming subdued to the tyrannical force of Castruccio, the usurper-to-be of her castle and dominion:

> We look back to times past, and we mass them together, and say in such a year such and such events took place, such wars occupied that year, and during the next there was peace. Yet each year was then divided into weeks, days, minutes, and slow-moving seconds, during which there were human minds to note and distinguish them, as now. We think of a small motion of the dial as of an eternity; yet ages have past, and they are but hours; the present moment will soon be only a memory, an unseen atom in the night of by-gone time. A hundred years hence, and young and old we shall all be gathered to the dust, and I shall no longer feel the coil that is at work in my heart, or any longer struggle within the inextricable bonds of fate. I know this; but yet this moment, this point of time, during which the sun makes but one round amidst the many millions it has made, and the many millions it will make, this moment is all to me. (212–13)

Mary Shelley seems to be saying here that history is not about the mass of data but is the storehouse of precedents from which one can draw an example to aid the present. In order to do so, we need to *imagine* the past so that it becomes alive to us: in *Valperga*, Shelley creates a possible scenario in the mind of the heroine—that of liberty being oppressed by tyranny. When, through her soliloquy, she is temporarily aggrandized, it also denotes liberty's defiant moment against tyranny.

The seemingly everlasting battle between liberty and tyranny is precisely the gist of history as the Shelleys saw it.[5]

In 'The Triumph', individuals whose names are unforgotten, from Hellenic and Hebraic civilisation to the present, figure as captives to the Car of Life, while the ignorant mass is portrayed as the victims of it. Percy depicts the rulers, whether they be of intellectual, religious, or political spheres, as the other side of the coin to those who are enslaved by them: the two parties are not essentially different in that they are both blind to self-knowledge and are willing victims of power. The few exceptions who are equipped with knowledge and self-will break away from the fetters and are the only ones exempted from the pageant. In this sense, the historical model, which 'The Triumph' purports, is more cyclic and linear: it demonstrates a Manichaean struggle of tyranny and liberty but with the former being more dominant than the latter. *Valperga* should be read in this light—as a critique of linear historical development and progress, most recently expounded by the Enlightenment historiographers.

'The Triumph' and *Valperga* are, on the other hand, both failed testimonies of apocalyptic history, the model of which was Percy's *Prometheus Unbound*. Not only do they use 'cars' and 'chariots' for the same end of depicting time and history but they work on Dantean allegories of hell, purgatory and paradise in an attempt to salvage their faith in love as the agent to release the world from change and corruption.[6] In *The Divine Comedy*, Dante makes Beatrice supersede Virgil as his guide to Paradise, thereby making her, or rather, his pure love for her, the key to his salvation. Prometheus, in *Prometheus Unbound*, similarly undergoes transformation—from his personal 'hell' caused by self-inflicted torture to the release of his psyche from it—with the help of Asia. In 'The Triumph' and *Valperga*, however, this model is only communicated through its negativity: just as the 'shape all light' is unable to preserve Rousseau from corruption in 'The Triumph' (or, is arguably its cause), neither Euthanasia nor Beatrice is able to save Castruccio from his own power-crazed ambition. In *Valperga*, the two heroines are powerless and vulnerable, whereas the hero remains unchecked in his weaknesses; Rousseau whose *Nouvelle Héloïse* provided an example of 'divine beauty' for the Romantics becomes the victim of a Pygmalion complex so that he is abandoned by his own creation to be reduced to an 'old root'. The disruption, which prevents these two texts functioning as a comedy in the Dantean sense, or romance in the traditional sense, becomes the point of scrutiny.

Both 'The Triumph' and *Valperga* are, on one level, coded accounts of the Shelleys' own personal histories that require to be read as such. It is no accident that *Prometheus Unbound* lurks in the background as the prototype of how things should be, as opposed to how things are,[7] depicted in the two works; for the cosmological drama of Greek gods and spirits, it is also a hopeful vision of Percy's own history. Kelvin Everest glosses the words spoken by Prometheus to Ione in the speech following his liberation—'Give her [fair Spirit] that curvèd shell, which Proteus old/Made Asia's nuptial boon, breathing within it/A voice to be accomplished' (3.3. 65–67)—as 'a fleeting identification between Prometheus and Asia, and himself [Percy] and Mary [...] with Godwin (humorously) as Proteus.[8] That Asia is vital to the release of Prometheus from his captivity points to the significance of a female agent in achieving that prophetic role that Percy took on for himself: the negative energy that pervades the time of Prometheus' confinement is only transformed and restored to his potential creativity by Asia's love for Prometheus. If one bears in mind how much the male-female relationship (although not human) shapes the course of history in *Prometheus Unbound*, the visionary failures of 'The Triumph' and *Valperga* can readily be explained on the basis of a collapsed relationship between the two sexes.

Although the 'shape all light' could be that female agent in 'The Triumph', she is also depicted as being a problematic figure who 'Trampled its [thought's] fires into the dust of death' (l. 388), transfixing Rousseau 'between desire and shame' (l. 394). That Rousseau's mind is transformed into a *tabula rasa* after following her command to 'quench thy thirst' (l. 400) demonstrates that the 'shape' is instrumental to his materialist revelation that he is no different from his fellow beings in that he is equally susceptible to the 'Car of Life'.[9] Similar disillusionment occurs in *Valperga*, for Euthanasia, when she discovers Beatrice's relationship with Castruccio and, reversely, for Castruccio, when he becomes informed of Euthanasia's part in the conspiracy against him.

> The story of Beatrice dissolved the charm; she [Euthanasia] looked on him now in the common light of day; the illusion and exaltation of love was dispelled for ever. (190–91)

> By the saints! I believed, that, if she [Euthanasia] died, like Dante's Beatrice, she would plead for me [Castruccio] before the throne of the Eternal, and that I should be saved through her. Now she is lost, and may perdition seize the whole worthless race of man, since it has fallen upon her! (312–13)

This knowledge, that the deified object of one's imagination is human after all, comes at the expense of a visionary failure, for which neither of them are prepared so that their realised world becomes a 'hell' rather than 'paradise'. That the frequent reference to Dante's *Divine Comedy*, which characterises both works, proves their preoccupation with the model, of a female guiding a male to heaven, need not be emphasised; but the extent to which it offered the Shelleys the means to write their own histories is often overlooked.[10]

What Percy described in *Valperga* as the 'romantic truth of history' might just signify this understanding—that it was an encoded history of their personal lives; to read it as such, however, also delimits the scope of the issues that the novel raises. For example, the question of female autonomy in a male-dominated society is one that not only concerns medieval Italy but also contemporary England; the heterodoxy of Beatrice and the Paterins denotes an existing problem to which Mary Shelley cannot be altogether unsympathetic coming from a dissenting background; and the problem of the political system that best fosters liberalism is one that was still hotly debated in Shelley's age. Above all, the novel speculates on the active role that poetry (most notably Dante's *Divine Comedy*) might have played were it not for the power-crazed individuals on whom it has no effect; and it problematises how the good and wise, such as Antonio dei Adimari (Euthanasia's father), Guinigi, and Euthanasia, are marginalised as political agents. In this sense, *Valperga* serves as a social critique of her own time as well as that of medieval Italy; Shelley exploits the uncanny repetition of history to valorise her own socio-political milieu.

FRANKENSTEIN, *VALPERGA*, AND *THE LAST MAN*

One of the dominant ways of reading Mary Shelley's early novels is to understand them as a series delineating her engagement with Romanticism, which, according to her view, was doomed to fail. It is remarkable that her views remained consistent so that her early premonition became a reality and then a past to be reconsidered. In *Frankenstein, or The Modern Prometheus*, which marks the beginning of Mary's literary involvement with the Byron-Shelley circle, Mary astutely identifies masculine egotism at the heart of a Romantic enterprise undertaken by men, and critiques it as a threat to domestic peace.[11] She delineates throughout her early novels a hero who pursues chimeras, whether of scientific knowledge, or of political power at the expense of domestic happiness. In her repeated attempt at unlocking, however in vain, the *impasse* of the hero (none of the heroes actually realise their potential to the full due to their moral shortcoming), her perspective undergoes transformation.

Although the novel is set in the 1790s, the issues that Frankenstein raises are hypothetical ones that belong to the future.[12] Mary notes in the introduction to her 1831 edition, that the novel 'was the offspring of happy days, when death and grief were but words, which found no true echo in my heart'.[13] The numerous losses that Mary experienced in later years then are purely post-facto. Also in the novel, the atrocious acts that Victor Frankenstein unwillingly commits through his own creation remain as a forewarning for the narrator Walton. *Valperga*, however, offers a different case, which hinges on the moment when the hero's will actuates his own tragic fall. The narrative voice does not offer a privileged retreat from the world that it depicts, as it does in *Frankenstein*; because the novel does not allow a ready remedy for the grim world it presents; it is arguably the most pessimistic of Mary's novels.[14] In *The Last Man*,

Mary once again adopts a narrative structure, which she uses in *Frankenstein*; the story is introduced through a character who witnesses the past of another with whom he comes into contact. The 'Sibyl leaves' which the narrator discovers and decodes, contain events recorded by a man belonging to the future. Mary projects in this novel the past, which she outlived as one of the few, onto the future, and thereby attempts to reconsider the past.[15] In her revisionary endeavour, she stresses the force of fatalism as the most powerful determinant of the lives of the characters and thereby underplays their will.[16]

What distinguishes *Valperga* from the other two novels is that, unlike *Frankenstein* or *The Last Man*, the time reference remains within the present: whereas *Frankenstein* is driven toward the future and *The Last Man* is drawn toward the past,[17] *Valperga* insists on being read in the present tense that precludes the future. What the novel most concerns is the culminating point that divides the world of innocence and the disillusioned world in which the three main characters find themselves equally 'lost'.[18] It deals with a historical moment when the *beau ideal* is defaced by power; in this case; by the masculine imperialism of Castruccio. It deserves attention that Mary uses medieval Italy to re-cast her own emotional and philosophical investment in what we know as Romanticism; in so doing, she not only writes the present through the past but also rewrites the past in the light of the present.

This chapter aims to elucidate the complexity of the novel, which, as suggested by various critics, cannot be fully appreciated through a simple biographical reading of the text, or by simply locating the influences of other literary techniques or ideas that are clearly present in the text.[19] In the end, Mary Shelley appropriates them according to her own political and philosophical agenda and for her artistic ends. Firstly, her re-working of genre deserves attention: under the guise of documentary history, she employs romance for the framework of her novel (which she deliberately disrupts), and fiction (including her psychological probing of the characters' minds) for the subversive ends of history. The politics of the novel affords another dimension in which Mary Shelley utilises existent models, that is, medievalism and republicanism, in order to critique and render what Romanticism in the end meant to her. The novel successfully combines the inevitable failure of Romanticism and the vulnerability of female autonomy in the public sphere: Euthanasia, as the Promethean idealist who attempts to alter society through 'love' and 'imagination', becomes crushed by masculine 'will to power'. By gendering the Romantic programme, it most effectively conveys the sense that such vision is hopeful, but must look to the future for its maturation. Mary Shelley, nevertheless, does not leave the novel on a defeatist note, but demands it that be read, through Euthanasia, as an instance of justice, which supersedes any external actions.

The novel engages in a Romantic ideal, aiming at a collapse of binary opposites (e.g. Guelphs/Ghibellines politics and public/private histories), the outcome of which is its ironic displacement and disruption; but the text never becomes subjected to cynicism because it attempts to salvage meaning from such visionary failure by privileging the author's judgment. To describe this attitude as Mary Shelley's 'anti-Romanticism' is limiting, for the process by which she reaches what appears to be her refutation of a Romantic ideal is far more complex given that the ideology she propounds is implicated in it. Rather, it would be more helpful to understand the novel as a step forward that reserves one's judgment as the salvation (but not a compromise) of Romantic failure.

History and Romance

In considering *Valperga* as a historical novel, the works of William Godwin and Sir Walter Scott bear particular significance.[20] Because Scott attracted a wide audience as a successful writer, his historical romance was a ready model for novelists writing in this genre, including Shelley. In writing *Valperga*, Shelley appropriates the framework Scott uses in *Ivanhoe*[21]: the hero returns to his native country where he becomes embroiled in a political struggle between two camps, during which he becomes romantically involved with two women of contrasting features and geological backgrounds. The outcome of *Valperga*, however, could not be more different: it questions the generic implications of 'romance' while it appropriates it, and critiques it as a gendered representation of history. Scott's aim to re-create the feudal past, or a replica of medieval romance, is achieved by stereotyping the characters: the hero proves his social status and virtue through his chivalric accomplishments, as a consequence of which a beautiful Anglo-Saxon princess is granted to him in order to secure him posterity. In fact, the character of Rowena, the heroine of the novel, is never developed and she remains merely Ivanhoe's prize.

Shelley re-figures this formula significantly, firstly by creating a female ruler who is politically autonomous: Euthanasia inherits Valperga as an heir to the castle and its dominion, and performs the task of a benevolent ruler by exercising *noblesse oblige*. Euthanasia is one of the few female characters in Shelley's work who plays an active role in the public sphere. Secondly, Shelley similarly devises a heroine of different social background; but unlike the Jewess Rebecca in *Ivanhoe*, Beatrice's genealogical background is explained in full detail, which together with the heretic sect known as the Paterins of which she becomes a member raises one of the social issues of the day that does not concern the heroine alone.[22] Whereas Scott dismisses the Jewish problem by simply removing Rebecca and her father back to Granada, Shelley reserves the potential of Beatrice as a proleptic Protestant who never succumbs to the Papal power or to Euthanasia's rationality.

On a more general level, more emphasis is placed on character development and psychological insight, which are given by the heroines themselves, than on the actions of characters (particularly that of the hero). Moreover, she makes her text a historical site where multiple narratives co-exist: for example, the Florentine Euthanasia voices the republican ideal of medieval Italy mediated by Dante's poetry, while Beatrice who is the daughter of a religious impostor, Whilhelmina of Bohemia, offers an alternative critique of that society. Scott, on the other hand, only allows one narrative, and it is one which complies with his medievalist views based on his faith in the English feudal order.

This is not to say that there is no political valorisation in *Valperga*: Shelley draws hers from the Italian republican tradition, which came into vogue through the writings of the Swiss historian Sismondi, and was mediated through the poetry of Dante. Shelley employs the Guelph-Ghibelline strife to demarcate the two political poles of republicanism and imperialism, which, in her view, have been struggling for power during the course of Western history.[23] Shelley, no doubt, takes sides with the party of liberty through her heroine, Euthanasia; but, at the same time, she is careful not to overlook the historical reality of medieval Italy. *Valperga* can be understood as one of the Romantic attempts to reflect on the recent Revolution that had shaken Europe, and to imagine a break from the impasse into which the liberal cause seemed to have fallen. It also denotes a keen awareness of the isolated attempts in Europe to gain short-lived independence from an imperial rule (i.e. Spanish and Neapolitan uprisings).

Shelley's re-writing of history is further complicated by the fact that the novel is, unlike most romances that end in a traditional happy ending, a tragedy. Not only are the heroines silenced in the kind of history they seek to promote, but they become prey to masculine imperialism. Shelley re-writes the military history of Castruccio in order to recuperate what might have been an alternative history, of those who were deprived of a voice. Her revisionary attempt cuts both ways: it questions the way history has been represented in the past through the generic packaging of romance, yet she is unable to imagine a successful republican history in which both sexes play an equal part.[24] If *Valperga* demands to be read as a romance, it does so only to critique masculine egotism, which is equated with imperialism, as an obstruction to realising ideal polity. In other words, *Ivanhoe*'s traditional quest story is transformed into the hero's political aggression; and the two heroines of *Ivanhoe* as objects of the hero's desire, one of whom is to be won as a trophy of his chivalric accomplishment, become in *Valperga*, the victims of his exploitation.

Shelley's feminist and republican recasting of Scott's patriarchal feudalism can be read at face value; however, the very fact that *Valperga* ends in a tragedy also denotes the defeat of such a revisionary attempt. Shelley effectively combines the fate of the republican ideal with that of female autonomy in that both become subjected to masculine imperialism.

Shelley's revisionary attempt in *Valperga* echoes William Godwin's re-working of genre, which he utilised for progressive ends in history.

He insists that 'mere chronicle of facts, places and dates [...] is in reality no history', and that we 'must then not rest contented with considering society in a mass, but must analyse the materials of which it is composed.'[25] In short, Godwin promotes the fictional status of *real* history, and individual over general history, partly as a reaction to the historiography of the Scottish writers such as Hume, Robertson, and Gibbon and importantly as his strategic means to create a new kind of history. Godwin's insistence on individual history rests on the belief that personal motives and intentions provide us with a clue as to how it might have been, rather than how it became through the abstraction of facts; and what is discarded in the process of it, according to Godwin, may just be the key to an alternative history.[26]

In creating a democratic history, Godwin starts out by upsetting the existent social structure: in *Caleb Williams*, for example, Godwin reverses the power between Falkland, who represents the traditional gentry class, and Caleb, the hero with a humble background. In so doing, he uses Caleb's narrative as a means to destabilise history, which otherwise would have rested in the hands of Falkand's servant Collins who is more accepting of the *status quo*. Godwin brings into play 'the operation of human passions' and 'the empire of motives' that were neglected under the universal/general narrative of Scottish historiography. Godwin's psychological reading of history opens up a new textual site in which various contesting narratives strive for ascendancy, the judgment of which is finally left in the hands of the reader. Godwin, however, only embraces it in a half-hearted manner, for his relativist stance is finally overcome by his will to write what he considers to be real history; that is, to become 'the regenerator of a historical narrative interrupted by the fate of the 1642 revolution.'[27] With this end in mind, Godwin emphasises the significance of fiction as the only means to utilising history for the future:

> Laying aside the generalities of historical abstraction, we must mark the operation of human passions; must observe the empire of motives whether groveling or elevated; and must note the influence that one human being exercise over another, and the ascendancy of the daring and the wise over the vulgar multitude. It is thus, and thus only, that

> we shall be abled to add to the knowledge of the past, a sagacity that can penetrate into the depths of futurity. (362)

Mary Shelley follows this creed by carefully depicting the development of Castruccio's character in relation to his social environment and personal contacts so that his process of becoming a tyrant becomes clear to the reader. She begins by listing Castruccio's excelling qualities in a similar manner to Machiavelli's in 'The Life of Castruccio Castracani of Lucca'.[28] Her intention is not to provide them as a set of conditions that enabled him to distinguish himself as a military leader but as a basis to work on for the moulding of his character. First of all, Mary demonstrates that familial influence has a lasting effect on the protagonist, so that his father's ambition to form a political career for Castruccio outweighs the pacifist doctrine of Guinigi, his foster parent:

> 'Yes', cried Castruccio, 'You [Guinigi] have passed through life, and know what it is; but I would rather, while alive, enter my tomb, than live unknown and unheard of. Is it not fame that makes men gods? Do not urge me to pass my days in indolence; I must act, to be happy,—to any thing. My father did not wish me to become a farmer and a vine-dresser; but to tread in his steps, and go beyond them, and that is my purpose, which I would die to attain'. (27)

Mary Shelley also emphasises the Guelph-Ghibelline strife, which shapes the lives of those who are implicated in it, as an ulterior force that is fed by, but often beyond the control of, an individual. She then introduces power-crazed figures, such as Alberto Scoto and Galeazzo Vizconti, who encourage and eventually persuade Castruccio to follow his ambition at all costs:

> Scoto had been more successful than any other in the exercise of this policy [of an 'evil school'], and he now initiated Castruccio in the secrets of the craft. Hitherto his mind had been innocence, and his thoughts were honour. Frankness played on his lips; ingenuousness nestled in his heart; shame was ever ready to check him on the brink of folly; and the tenderness of his nature seemed to render it impossible for him to

> perpetrate a deed of harshness or inhumanity. [...] But nineteen is a dangerous age; and ill betides the youth who confides himself to a crafty instructor. If Castruccio listened at first with an inattentive ear to the counsels of Scoto, yet their frequent repetition, and the wax-like docility of his mind, quickly gave them power over him. (43)

Galeazzo Visconti's objective to tarnish the peace compact, which Castruccio made with Florence, and motivate him to further self-aggrandizement proves successful when he reminds him of his initial ambition to defeat the Guelph rule altogether:

> These were the lessons with which Galeazzo awakened the latent flame in the soul of Castruccio; a flame, covered, but not extinguished, and which now burned more fiercely than ever. He swore the destruction of the Guelphs, and interminable war to Florence; and his blood flowed more freely, his eyes shone brighter, his soul was elevated to joy, when he thought that one day he might be the master of that proud city [Florence]. (126)

What deserves attention in Shelley's delineation of the character development of Castruccio is that he willingly discards every piece of advice and guidance that would have prevented him from becoming a power-crazed tyrant. The interplay of necessity and contingency, complicated further by the effect of will fascinated Shelley as it did Godwin.[29] In the case of Castruccio, his inability to comprehend and embrace the doctrine of the more enlightened pacifists such as Guinigi and Euthanasia becomes the direct cause of tragedy.

As Caleb is meant to represent the new man who represents the new age in Godwin's novel, Euthanasia is theoretically that alternative history in *Valperga*. Mary likewise adopts multiple narratives, in order to first fracture a given history, and then reconstruct it. Euthanasia and Beatrice tell their own stories, which effectively override the life and psychological development of Castruccio Castracani. If the narrator, who probes into the inner secrets and developments of the hero, recapitulates Caleb's curiosity about Falkland and his will to restore what becomes unwritten in history, the heroines' narratives denote an alternative mode of history, which can be described as being uniquely feminine. In other words, if 'The Life and Adventures of Castruccio, Prince of Lucca' suggests a linear development in time that becomes recorded in public history, then 'Valperga' represents a space that cannot be assimilated into time. Mary Shelley herself tells us of her deliberate distinction at the end of the novel:

> The private chronicles, from which the foregoing relation has been collected, end with the death of Euthanasia. It is therefore in public histories alone that we find an account of the last years of the life of Castruccio. (323)

Godwin, however, was the one who gave the final shape to the original title of 'Castruccio, Prince of Lucca', by tagging 'The Life and Adventures' on to the name of the historical figure, and contesting it with an alternative history, 'Valperga'.[30] That the life of the heroine Euthanasia is not the alternative to Castruccio's life and adventures deserves attention: for Euthanasia is not a female participant in the act of making history, nor does she strive to become one.[31]

The name Valperga 'is generally thought to be related to that of the abbess Walburga', who was 'an Englishwoman from Wessex who became head of the German monastery in Heidenheim in 761'; her body 'was said to be the source of a healing oil which flowed from her rock-tomb in Germany'; and her interment was celebrated on 1 May 'with popular rites surviving from an older natural-religion'.[32] In the novel, Valperga is the name of the castle, which Euthanasia inherits from her mother (as the original heir before her marriage to Adimari); it is worth noting that it may possibly signify a female descent. That 'Valperga' is associated with space, rather than the linear temporality, which the other half of the title—'The Life and Adventures of Castruccio'—suggests, is reminiscent of the gendered demarcation Kristeva makes between the feminine '*space* generating and forming the human species' and masculine '*time*, becoming of history' (Kristeva 190–1). Furthermore, based on the female role of motherhood and re-production, Kristeva names 'repetition' and 'eternity' as the two defining conceptions of time in female subjectivity. In creating an imaginary space to embody an alternative conception of time, Mary Shelley likewise gives Valperga both a sense of cyclic continuity and a-temporality or eternal moment: the former arises from the generational inhabitation of the site, whereas the latter, from the figurative body of St. Walberga with which the name is associated, and more importantly, from Euthanasia's apocalyptic vision based on 'love' and 'imagination'. Historically speaking, it was the second generation of feminists who came after 1968 who emphasised their difference from, rather than their assimilation to, 'the linear time of history and politics' (187). Mary Shelley shares the attitude of these second-generation feminists in that she deliberately makes a distinction between the two conceptions of time based on gender.

The belief that the body of St. Walburga was the source of healing oil permeates the novel through Euthanasia: her space denotes a realm of spiritual purging in which the physically and emotionally battered prophetess Beatrice temporarily receives healing and regains her sanity. Castruccio, even in his acts of cruelty, considers Euthanasia as the means to his salvation:

> She knew, she must have known, that in spite of absence and repulse, she was the saint of my life; and that this one human weakness, or human virtue, remained to me, when power and a strong will had in other respects metamorphosed me. (312)

It is only when she is found guilty of taking part in a conspiracy against Castruccio that her fate leads her to death;[33] even then, it is not the same death to which Castruccio is subjected: as the inscription on his tomb symbolises, his life is understood in terms of time, which enables his name to be remembered at the cost of it being subsumed under the linearity of history:

> 'Lo, by the fame of my deeds, I live and shall live, the glory of Italian soldiery, the paragon of the Lucchese, the pride of Tuscany, Castruccio son of Gerio, of the family of the Antelminelli. I lived, I sinned, I suffered; I yielded to Nature. Men of good will, help a devout soul in need, mindful that in short while ye are to die.' (326)

Euthanasia, by contrast, falls into oblivion; but just as her name was never recorded in history, she emblematises the eternal space that cannot be violated by time, and from which she emerged and to which she is eventually submerged, literally:

> She was never heard of more; even her name perished. She slept in the oozy cavern of the ocean; the sea-weed was tangled with her shining hair; and the spirits of the deep wondered that the earth had trusted so lovely a creature to the barren bosom of the sea, which, as an evil step-mother, deceives and betrays all committed to her care. (322)

Because Euthanasia becomes an idea of a republican ideal that cannot be confined to time and space, the novel does not preclude its future recursion; in other words, we interpret the value of her life on the basis of that hope.

The negotiation of history and romance enabled Valperga to map out imaginary sites in which Shelley could experiment with historical material without becoming enslaved by it. Shelley follows Scott in so far as he utilises the technique of documentary history in order to re-create a believable past but relies on romance as a particularly useful tool in the process of his myth-making. In other words, his stereotyped characters and predictable happy ending carry a certain faith in the homogeneous and ordered world of the Middle Ages. Shelley, in the end, deviates from Scott's medievalist views, but she shares his technique in adopting romance as an integral part of her novel: for it likewise allows her to create her own myth. The romance that Shelley placed at the heart of the history of Castruccio Castracani enables us to understand how Shelley engaged in history; that is, as a female participant in an essentially masculine tradition. The alienation and abjection that the two heroines experience reflect not only Shelley's experience in writing history that was commonly attributed to men but her own response to her immediate literary circle. Although it is far-fetched to conclude that her early novels are all feminist critiques of masculine Romanticism, there is no doubt that her surrounding male Romantics helped to shape the corpus of her works. In other words, the act of writing history for Shelley was to come to an understanding of her relationship with them, and more importantly with their works that expressed their commitment to the Enlightenment ethos and Promethean aspiration, both of which were to be realised in the political and social sphere. Shelley was as much an accomplice of their enterprise as she was a fierce critic of them, as demonstrated in the ambivalent portrayal of the two heroines.

Shelley's preoccupation with past, present and future in all her early novels bears particular significance here: as a historical novel, *Valperga* seeks to communicate across these three time spans with the realisation that only a dialectical dialogue between them can lead us to the truth of history, which is never objective but always subjective. The myth she encodes in her novel is, on the one hand, the fate of a female writer whose professional position had become threatened to the point of being silenced; on the other, the eclipse of liberalism, firstly due to the failure of the French Revolution and the counter-Revolutionary climate that followed it.[34] A more immediate cause for dismay would have been the series of failed attempts to liberate European countries from the rule of imperialist regimes.

Shelley also appropriates Godwin's revisionary attempt at writing history: hers is not so much to democratise it but to reflect on the recent republican failure as an inevitable step toward further progress. Shelley's historiography can also be understood as a gendered argument that the conception of history is fundamentally different for women as opposed to men, and that women's history requires its own representation in order to render it satisfactorily. Mary thus follows Godwin's re-working of genre—that is, of the historical novel—for different reasons but for a similar end, which is to destabilise history and to re-construct it.

Medievalism and Republicanism

If nostalgia and trauma are 'two characteristic patterns of historicity for Romanticism' as Gary Handwerk asserts, then *Valperga* provides a perfect example of it.[35] The novel relies on nostalgia to recuperate an

Arcadian past that is emotionally charged: the narrative account of Euthanasia's love for Castruccio works to that effect:

> [...] the words and looks of Castruccio replied to her [Euthanasia], and she felt happier than she had ever been. There was no doubt, no sorrow; all was security and calm; and her heart softened, until tears sprang forth under the weight of unmitigated pleasure. She was frank, generous and fearless; therefore she instantly believed and trusted; while the master-passions which ever ruled her life were not forgotten, but, mingling with and heightened by love, glowed with greater energy. They passed several months in the enjoyment of this intercourse; they hoped, they felt, that their destinies were intertwined never to be separated; and their union was only deferred until Castruccio should free his country. (79)

When Euthanasia narrates her own upbringing to Castruccio, her account is similarly imbued with a sense of nostalgia for an ideal past:

> You left me at Florence the favourite daughter of a father I adored: I was ever near him reading and conversing with him; and if I have put order in my day dreams, and culled the fruit of virtue and some slight wisdom from my meditations, it is to his lessons that I owe this good. (80-81)

> But he, whether he taught me to consider the world and the community of man, or to study the little universe of my own mind, was wisdom's self, pouring out accents that commanded attention and obedience [...] I learned from him to look upon events as being of consequence only through the feelings which they excited, and to believe that content of mind, love, and benevolent feeling ought to be the elements of our existence; while those accidents of fortune or fame, which to the majority make up the sum of their existence, were as the dust of the balance. (82)

What separates the present from the nostalgic past, however, is not time or space, but trauma, which creates an interiority that disrupts the mental process of assimilating experience into a linear sequence of events. In the novel, Castruccio's acts result in the alienation of both heroines from their own past, the consequence of which is their inability to re-engage in historical discourse. Consequently, Shelley has no choice but to end the novel with their deaths. Trauma dictates the way history is to be understood in the novel: that is, as a projection of pathological subjectivity that resists being assimilated into linear narrative.

Medieval Italy does not have an immediate effect of evoking a nostalgic past for the English reading public, and it is this deliberate displacement of tradition that Shelley exploits in order to write her own history. It is not so much the national past that bears significance but the locality of Italy as the 'Paradise of Exiles', as she herself characterised it, which suited her project of writing about 'the Elect' of which she was a part, and their further involvement with the socio-political milieu of the early nineteenth century.[36] *Valperga* is invested with Promethean ideals and emotions of masculine Romanticism that Shelley experienced through her father William Godwin, her husband P.B. Shelley, and her friend Lord Byron; it is with this understanding that the novel should be read. In other words, Shelley records her engagement with the Romantic circle and its committed agendas—their exploration of the imagination, their fascination with the relationship of art and society, history and polity. That this involvement was, in the end, tragic is the symbolic significance of the novel. As Euthanasia stresses the significance of memory as being a characteristically human trait that connects the minds of the people of the past, present, and future, Shelley, likewise, makes her novel a site of memory that will enable the reader to participate in her nostalgic past.[37]

In so doing, Shelley also harnesses nostalgia, which had a particular relevance to medievalism in the nineteenth century: there was a distinct voice that expressed longing for an old world that manifested itself in England in the feudal society of the middle ages. Its rhetoric can be traced back to Edmund Burke's *Reflections on the Revolution in France*; and its full articulation found in the nineteenth century, in the historical novels of Scott, Tennyson's poetry on the Arthurian legend, Pugin's Gothic architecture, and Newman's theological tracts that initiated the Oxford Movement, to name a few instances. Although *Valperga* does not concern itself with English medievalism and works under the aegis of Italian republicanism, it effectively utilises the nostalgia that came in vogue with medievalism. Shelley, for example, recreates a colourful and vivid past that is congenial with the medieval world of some of these texts.

Mary is known to have taken pains to re-create a faithful past: she worked on the novel over several years, and although it is somewhat inaccurately acclaimed by Percy Shelley that she researched into 'fifty books' for its historical setting, she consulted both medieval and renaissance texts in their original for her historical material.[38] Opinion, however, was divided over her efforts: *The Literary Gazette* praised the section on Euthanasia's court 'for its vivid picture of the manners of the age', and *La Belle Assemblé* likewise singled out its 'intimate acquaintance with the history and manners of the times', *The Literary Register of the Fine Arts, Sciences, and Belles Lettres* went as far as to say that 'The principal merit of this novel consists [...] in its faithful delineation of the character and manners of the people of the age of which it treats'. *Blackwood's Edinburgh Magazine*, however, gave unfavourable views on the novel 'stepping aside for ten pages, *merely* for the purpose of letting us see, that the writer knows the way in which the *Mysteries* of the middle ages were represented'.[39] On matters of characterisation, both *Blackwood's* and *Monthly Review* reached a similar conclusion that Mary did injustice to Castruccio's character but successfully rendered the two female characters.[40] It can be inferred from this that her contemporary reviews found *Valperga* persuasive in its description of the historical setting and of the fictional female characters as plausible types of the age but unconvincing in its characterisation of Castruccio as the historical figure. This is highly ironic in that they are, in reality, saying that what makes the novel historical in the first instance (i.e. the treatment of the life of Castruccio Castracani), is the most unhistorical thing about the novel. They share a dissatisfaction with Mary's liberty to move away from the historical figure yet call it history. What they fail to notice is that *Valperga* is not so much about Castruccio Castracani, but a site of historical deconstruction, and a platform on which to work toward the future.

This is not to say that *Valperga* is a democratic history in the sense that *Caleb Williams* is: Falkland who represents the ruling class is equipped with stereotypical virtues only to be unmasked by Caleb; Euthanasia, on the other hand, is depicted as an ideal ruler who demonstrates *noblesse oblige* by looking after her dependents.[41] There is nothing in the novel to suggest political subversion, and it comfortably accommodates the hierarchical social system. We are led to believe in the ideal ruler-ruled relationship that once existed, enabling nostalgia to play a central part as it does in other medievalist texts. The object of nostalgia, however, is not the social system of the middle ages nor its religious faith, but the Arcadian world in which Euthanasia first finds her love for Castruccio. Her philosophical education by her father and appreciation of nature bring her, both intellectually and emotionally, to full bloom; furthermore, her union with Castruccio promises her complete womanhood. That this sense of glory becomes betrayed and demolished is the other half of history, which the novel seeks to communicate.

There is nothing remarkable about Mary's choice of medieval Italy as the novel's setting, considering the reverence with which the Romantics regarded the republican state of medieval Italy, and its by-product, Dante.[42] It is, however, worth noting that the novel concerns republicanism in its decline rather than in its full-blown glory. Historically speaking, it is not even that: the two political parties, which were engaged in an endless conflict over the dominion of the Italian city-states, were not as clear-cut in their ideological positions as their political banners suggest, and they were often interchangeable depending on the circumstances.[43] Even when she sides with the Guelphs through Euthanasia, Mary is careful not to impose her ideological preference in depicting the political reality of medieval Italy. For example, Ferrara suffers under the Guelph rule that exposes the tyranny of the Dominican inquisitors, which only becomes relieved by the acquisition of power by a Ghibelline leader. Mary's subtle handling of the two factions makes it clear that it is not always partisan favouritism that she is exercising in the novel but personal judgment that enables one to remain committed to the ends toward which political parties strive without succumbing to self-interest.[44]

In this sense, the novel does not concern itself with recuperating a historical moment; rather, it evolves around a transcendent idea that escapes historical reality.[45] As embodied by the heroine Euthanasia, its creed remains a highly personal one that cannot be systematically implemented in society. That Dante was the main source of inspiration for the Romantics' dwelling on medieval Italy is unquestionable; however, to what extent the Italian poet influenced their re-construction of his society requires further examination. For the Florentine's patriotic sentiment is projected onto the imaginary plane of the *Divine Comedy*—a work that was a result of political exile. In other words, medieval Italy may have offered the perfect distance (both in terms of time and geography) that enabled the Romantics to exercise their imagination freely.

Their immediate republican model was, of course, associated with the French Revolution. Although Mary never admitted to a direct reference to contemporary politics,[46] it was fairly obvious to the reader who the modern Castruccio was: Percy Shelley, for one, saw in the political career of Castruccio, a resemblance to that of Napoleon.[47] Even if Mary had no intention of writing about Napoleon, his impact on the Romantic imagination was undeniable. Napoleon readily became a Romantic prototype. Byron, for example, identified himself with the figure for his political potential and his theatricality.[48] Mary was no exception, and a failed hero, of whom no doubt Napoleon was seen to be the greatest example, dominates her early novels.

The kind of republicanism that Mary attempts to delineate in the novel stresses its elusiveness rather than its concrete status in history: that is why the novel is haunted by it without being able to be situated in time. It is also a recursive concept, which implies the English Commonwealth and French republicanism under the guise of medieval Italian republicanism.[49] As much as Godwin's history is determined by the fate of the Commonwealth in that he seeks to re-write it, the history of the second-generation Romantics is shaped by the failure of the French Revolution and Napoleon's usurpation of power.[50] Thus, it is only too plain that Mary should choose 'the misguided hero who turns villain';[51] however, that this betrayal of expectation is voiced in the form of a trauma deserves attention. For Mary expresses it most directly through the two heroines who suffer from Castruccio's misconduct. By creating two women who become involved with the hero, Mary both personalises and internalises the political crisis initiated by Castruccio's military aggression.

Trauma is caused by a charged moment that continually returns to the victim because it cannot be processed intellectually: its mode of expression is characteristically cyclic, and it resists assimilation into linear history.[52] Godwin effectively takes this up as the main theme in *Mandeville*, a historical novel that he wrote at the time of Mary's conception of *Valperga*. Mandeville suffers from the effect of political persecution that his parents faced in Ireland, by imagining that he is the victim of conspiracy until he is driven to madness. The novel, which is written in the first person narrative, gives away his pathological state, only to make the act of narration impossible to complete. Its implication is that there is no rational way of depicting the traumatised self but to do so internally, that is, through the voice of the victim.

Mary likewise follows Godwin's example in creating a pathological narrator for her novella *Mathilda*:[53] the heroine becomes traumatised, firstly owing to her discovery of her father's incestuous love for her and secondly by his death as the result of his guilt at his passion and its disclosure. That Mary temporarily left *Valperga* to write *Mathilda* in the summer of 1819 is suggestive: for the emotional interiority of the two heroines in *Valperga* that dominate the novel can be traced back to *Mathilda*. In the novella, not only do the emotions dominate but they also govern the plot: there is no story independent of Mathilda's emotional outburst directed at her father and friend who, in the first instance, appears to hold the potential of becoming a counsellor-lover for Mathilda. In *Valperga*, Mary re-engages with the thematic preoccupation with trauma that led to the collapse of narrative in *Mathilda*; the outcome is a disruption of historical continuity that can only be patched up by the alternation of private and public histories.

It is particularly useful to apply trauma to the representation of history in *Valperga*: for both Euthanasia and Beatrice become unable to re-engage in a healthy historical discourse after traumatic experiences that leave them emotionally scarred. For both Euthanasia and Beatrice, their narrative hinges on the moment of Castruccio's betrayal, which proves to be equally traumatic as his acts lie beyond their comprehension: Beatrice is convinced that her union with Castruccio is the result of divine intervention; Euthanasia cannot imagine her lover abandoning her own ideological choice. Even if Euthanasia is able to rationalise the events when Beatrice cannot, she is equally susceptible to trauma, as her counsellor-patient relationship with Beatrice reveals. In her active role to comfort and re-educate Beatrice, we are told that her numb senses are revitalised, which suggests previous emotional malfunction: 'Euthanasia found her heart, which was sinking to apathy, awake again, as she listened to Beatrice' (248). What is more, the personal trauma effectively becomes a social trauma: Euthanasia's defeat and exile signal that of the republican ideal, while Beatrice's victimisation and death through insanity symbolise that of proleptic Protestantism.[54]

Despite her liberty with historical facts, Mary's historical sense is apt: to locate the republican ideal in the Guelph politics is not, in the end, convincing, for the Guelphs were as party-spirited as the Ghibellines with their interest in self-aggrandizement, which is precisely what the politics of the novel works against. Her critique of imperial aggression aligns more with Godwin's and Percy's attempt to unlock the 'mind-forged manacles', the result of which will supposedly be a Utopian society, as most clearly manifested in *Prometheus Unbound*. Godwin talks of a 'euthanasia of government' in *Political Justice*, meaning an ideal political state when 'weakness and ignorance' of society have been cured, and thus, the government itself has become unnecessary.[55] It is this Enlightenment epistemology that underlies the liberal ethos of *Valperga*; yet it also remains deeply affected by the politics of the early nineteenth century, which overshadowed its healthy progress. The name Euthanasia, for instance, is given an ironic ring in *Valperga*, as the complete opposite happens: Castruccio's ignorance and weakness destroy what ought to be cherished as the means to achieving an ideal polity. Euthanasia becomes an emblem in the novel of what might have been, rather than what actually happens; it is this negative knowledge that the novel embraces and seeks to communicate.

ROMANTICISM AND FEMINISM

Distinguishing Mary's portrayal of Castruccio from those of her predecessors, *Blackwood's Edinburgh Magazine* notes that 'far too much reliance has been laid on thoughts and feelings, not only modern, but modern and feminine at once' (284). The review is quick to sense the intellectual and aesthetic climate that the novel reflects; but it is particularly instructive that it brings in the issue of gender. For Mary effectively uses gender to contrast the public history of Castruccio and the private lives of Euthanasia and Beatrice. It is interesting that she channels fiction into 'private chronicles' while retaining the 'public histories' as facts (although this distinction is only maintained on a superficial level).[56] That flux of thoughts and feelings deserves recording as much as actions echo Godwin's psychological approach to history. It is also a challenge to the masculinist history, which had so far dictated how history should be written; that is, as a series of events and actions surrounding men of social distinction. Both Godwin and Mary give voice to marginalised individuals who had hitherto been silenced and pave the way to a subversive writing of history. Despite their shared agenda—that is, to re-write history—*Valperga* goes one step further to include the destiny of such an attempt, so that the novel reads as a self-defeating project. In other words, the 'thoughts and feelings' of Euthanasia cannot change Castruccio in the way that Caleb Williams succeeds with Falkand.[57] The tragic ending of *Valperga* seems to combine the fate of Romanticism and that of female autonomy, as Mary understood these.

What Mary describes under the rubric of 'private chronicles' is not merely the lives of the two female characters who otherwise would have had no voice in the 'public histories', but also the fate of those male writers who surrounded her. The division of knowledge, which developed in accordance with the division of labour necessitated by the Industrial Revolution, was increasingly becoming a threat to poets and writers alike who were being ushered into the private domain of emotions. In effect, they were losing the former ground on which they exercised their moral/political influence over society; instead, they were forced to participate in the consumer market as providers of entertainment.[58] Political economy was at the pivot of this re-distribution of knowledge as well as of wealth, aimed at 'The greatest happiness for the greatest number'.[59] Malthus, for example, dismissed Godwin's *Political Justice* as Utopian gibberish—a result of the philosopher's transgression into the realms of political economy, ignoring the statistical results of facts.[60] P.B. Shelley clearly saw this debate in terms of the new politico-economic system called capitalism around which society was evolving. Shelley sought to influence the political direction and check the morality of a nation, arguably for the last time in history with full faith as a poet; such an endeavour was, however, in the end, hopeful but visionary. For the imagination, which enables poets to achieve such ends as argued in *A Defence of Poetry*, turns destructive in his dark vision of 'The Triumph of Life'.

It is possible to connect the fate of Euthanasia in *Valperga* to the central anxiety that preoccupied the minds of the second-generation Romantic poets (namely Shelley and Keats). They attempted to write their own history, not of the past, however, but of their future through similar devices: the persona of Shelley's 'The Triumph of Life' and Keats's 'The Fall of Hyperion' both seek to resolve their state of limbo through a dialectic discourse with another (Rousseau in the case of 'The Triumph', and Moneta in 'The Fall'); yet, it remains unresolved because their texts demand an audience which their contemporary age did not allow them; or, to put it more accurately, the literary reviewers (who exercised a significant influence over the sales of books) made it difficult for them to gain one.[61] Because the kind of poetry that Shelley, in particular, was engaged in as a means to social change required the existence and active participation of real readers, his failure and disappointment with his audience had a destructive effect on his poetic career.

It is clear from her letters that if she did not base her heroine on him Mary Shelley identified Euthanasia with Percy Shelley.[62] Her career as a countess depicts a pure, high-minded struggle to maintain herself politically in a world governed by self-interest; and just as Euthanasia became prey to Castruccio's aggression, Shelley was eclipsed by the indifference of the general reading public.[63] Euthanasia's father, whose creed echoes that of Godwin, likewise falls to obscurity despite his philosophical excellence. As a daughter and wife of visionary Romantics who sought to change society through their writings, the gap between reality and their ideal must have been particularly acute for Mary. Using the gender argument, Mary subtly writes the fate of those Romantics who surrounded her.

Beatrice offers a more complex case, as a socially oppressed and sexually abused victim. Mary uses throughout her early novels a character who is displaced from society and in effect becomes prey to social abuses, whose connection to society is with the hero alone but who is not saved by him: in *Frankenstein*, the monster is created by Victor Frankenstein only to wander on his own, and to be driven to revenge; Beatrice in *Valperga* is the daughter of a heretic, who becomes ruined owing to Castruccio's betrayal; in *The Last Man*, the Greek princess Evadne falls from her high station in society to poverty and eventually death owing to her attachment to Raymond. That Mary repeatedly created characters suffering from social oppression is of interest; it equally deserves attention that they are all intimately connected with the hero. This is where a feminist reading has the strongest hold on Mary's novels, concluding that her treatment of an oppressed heroine problematises the repression of female imagination in a masculine society.[64]

Mary's attitude, however, seems divided on this issue: on the one hand, her characters demonstrate her fascination with dominating men, but on the other, they also prove her awareness of these men's egotism, which she seeks to reform.[65] Thus, the relationship between the heroine and the hero is double-edged, which Mary portrays through the device of creating two heroines: if Beatrice represents blind submission to masculine power, Euthanasia symbolises female heroism at the cost of sacrificing her own happiness.

Castruccio figures not only as a spectre of Napoleon, but also of Byron, who acted out the Romantic hero. Castruccio's will to power, which he ruthlessly executes, similarly characterises Raymond in *The Last Man*, who was clearly based on Byron.[66] Mary's fascination with Byron as the Dionysian hero also bears significance: Castruccio's political ambition is counter-balanced by his romantic attachments to the two heroines.[67] Whether Mary had more in common with Byron, to whom she seems to have been attracted physically, than with her husband is not of interest here; rather, that she repeatedly delineated a type of masculine dominance for which Byron stood as a ready model is a fact deserving attention.[68] That Mary was in two minds about such a figure is clearly demonstrated by her depiction of her two heroines in *Valperga*; furthermore, this contradiction is never resolved in the novel, and the two heroines are both in the end obliterated from Castruccio's history.

The only positive outcome of their fatal attraction to Castruccio is the bond that they establish with each other; but even then, it is Castruccio that connects them together, so Beatrice is never cured of her mental illness through the care of Euthanasia.

The novel presents two problems that disable it from functioning as a successful feminist history: firstly, Mary does not allow Euthanasia, who embodies the ideal balance of masculine rationality and feminine sensibility, to achieve her task of reforming Castruccio; secondly, Mary mimics masculine oppression in delineating Beatrice's character without giving her any hope for enlightenment. The failure of the two heroines to achieve their autonomy, however, extends to the novel's project to collapse the division between the 'private chronicles' and 'public histories' so that their integration enables a more holistic approach to history. This in itself is what Mellor identifies as Mary's target of critique, which she directs toward the masculine Romantics—that is, their efforts to work towards a unification of opposites by transcending the finite—but the very fact that *Valperga* is implicated in this vision allows us to realise that her anti-Romanticism is not as straightforward as it is sometimes believed to be.[69] That is to say, what appears as her critique of masculine Romanticism often takes the form of an inverted self-defeatism; it is not the transcendent Romantic vision that is being attacked here but that which prevents it from being realised in the public sphere. Mary deals with Romanticism in its feminine guise so that the fate of female autonomy, as depicted by the two female characters, effectively becomes that of its own. In this sense, the novel does not adhere to a strictly gendered politics; rather, she uses gender as the most effective device of presenting that destiny as she saw it, of Romanticism and republicanism.

NARRATIVE AND POWER

The novel's self-defeating attempt to re-write history must, in the end, be understood as a process that invites the readers to participate in its experience, and through the act of sympathy, to alter the way in which we interpret history. The text enables us to sympathise with all three characters, however different the degree may be. What the three characters have in common is that their lives, in one way or another, are a near miss: Castruccio loses Euthanasia in exchange for the fulfilment of his political ambition; Euthanasia sacrifices her female happiness in order to abide by her principles; and Beatrice exhausts her religious enthusiasm by misdirecting it to Castruccio. There is a sense of fruition *manqué*, to which the novel repeatedly returns as a point of reference.

In the beginning of the story, Beatrice is known as the prophetess who is revered by the people of Ferrara for her visionary powers. We are told that

> Beatrice herself is wrapt up in the belief of her own exalted nature, and really thinks herself the *Ancilla Dei*, the chosen vessel into which God has poured a portion of his spirit; she preaches, she prophesises, she sings extempore hymns, and entirely fulfilling the part of *Donna Estatica*, she passes many hours of each day in solitary meditation, or rather in dreams, to which her active imagination gives a reality and life which confirm her in her mistakes. (136–7)

Although Mary follows Muratori's sceptical treatment of inspired women in the Middle Ages as those who were mostly marked by 'ardent imagination, filled with ideas of religion and piety',[70] she nonetheless creates an emotional eruption in the text that cannot be subdued under the Papal control nor by Euthanasia's rationalism. That she resists being accommodated by either of the two implies her role as a proleptic Protestant; but as her insanity drives her to an early grave, the potentiality of her religious heresy becomes self-defeating without having any further effect on the Catholic orthodoxy.

If Beatrice is made to unconsciously act out her genealogy as the daughter of Wilhelmina, an impostor claiming to be 'the Holy Ghost incarnate upon earth for the salvation of the female sex', it is not without an ironic twist; for she becomes prey to sexual abuse due to her misguided notion of her spirituality that triggers her downfall. Beatrice's conversion to Paterinism after her betrayal by Castruccio and her self-induced victimisation to sadism suggest a scope for an alternative social critique of the Middle Ages to that given by Euthanasia; however, as Beatrice never recovers from her mental illness, Paterinism is understood as falling short of being the final solution to the existent social problems.[71]

Mary gives a sense of fatalism to Beatrice's destruction as an irreparable work that repeats her genealogical past: despite the efforts of the Bishop of Ferrara and Euthanasia to re-educate her, Beatrice can only follow her mother's footsteps. A similar kind of fatalism prevails over the lives of Euthanasia and Castruccio: the making of a tyrannical despot on the one hand, and of a defeatist idealist on the other, equally derives from their genealogical past. For example, Castruccio resists Guinigi's pacifism to embrace his father's strong partisan ambition. Euthanasia lives her life by her father's philosophical idealism, which he dictates to her during his retirement from the world of action. It may even be argued that the three characters are not *really* different but only act out their destiny. Mary, however, does not bow completely to such a deterministic view and distinguishes the three characters according to the degree of their self-knowledge. In *Valperga*, self-knowledge is used for subversive ends: those who possess it, namely Euthanasia and partly Beatrice, exercise power over the novel while Castruccio, who is deprived of it, has no control over the text and simply remains to be written by others.

Although the two heroines appear powerless in the male-dominated world, they are distinct from Castruccio in that they give their own narrative: Euthanasia tells Castruccio about her upbringing and the philosophical doctrine by which she was educated; Beatrice narrates to Euthanasia her love for, and betrayal by, Castruccio and the physical and mental abuses she was subjected to when captured by a sadist lord. Their stories are cohesive in that they are supported by a rationale that demands to be read on its own terms. Despite the different degrees to which their narratives prove to be convincing, they nevertheless actively shape the way in which we read the lives of the three characters.

The life of Castruccio, on the other hand, remains entirely dependent upon narratives other than his own. Moreover, the authorial voice, which incorporates the heroines' narratives into Castruccio's history, does not account for his thoughts or feelings: his character and actions are brought to our attention as mere objects of scrutiny. Such an attitude suggests a deliberate attempt to dehumanise Castruccio and to reduce him to a type; and its motives lie in the location of the cause of his character failure. In fact, most of the description concerning him is to do with its development; in other words, the making of a tyrant. Mary's Castruccio, who blindly lusts for power, makes a stark contrast to the prince written by other historians, who is honoured with praises for his military accomplishments. This is also a deliberate challenge to the Machiavellian hero whose forte is self-knowledge.[72]

Mary dictates, on the one hand, how we should read the life of Castruccio Castracani through the authorial narrative; yet she allows her two female heroines to tell their own stories, as contesting versions within the politics of the novel. In effect, Castruccio is silenced, while the two female characters share power over the novel. Such a reversal of power characterises Mary's subversive stance in writing history. Even if such gesture does not change history itself, in the sense that Castruccio outlives both Euthanasia and Beatrice after having destroyed them, it affects the way we read history by providing new grounds for historical judgment.

CONCLUSION

Mary follows Godwin's revisionary attempt at re-assessing the criteria of historical judgment. Military glory, which distinguished such historical figures as Alexander the Great, is in the hands of Godwin, reduced to a mere sign of barbarism. In *Caleb Williams*, Godwin makes the country squire and patron of the protagonist, Falkland, confront the democratic hero, Caleb, who questions the validity of his title, 'the Great', by citing some examples that counter it:

> Accursed blasphemy! Did these authors [Humphrey Prideaux and Henry Fielding] think that by the coarseness of their ribaldry they could destroy his well-earned fame? [...] Examine for yourself, and you will find in Alexander a model of honour, generosity and disinterestedness, a man who for the cultivated liberality of his mind and the unparalleled grandeur of his projects must stand alone the spectacle and admiration of all ages of the world.[73]

While Falkland stresses the impressive magnitude of his self-aggrandizement, Caleb brings to critical attention his acts of exploitation that enabled it:

> Ah, sir! It is very fine thing for us to sit here and compose his panegyric. But [would you have me] forget what a vast expense was bestowed in erecting the monument of his fame? Was not he the common disturber of mankind? Did not he overrun nations that would never have heard of him, but for his devastations? How many hundred thousands of lives did he sacrifice in his career? [...] Man is surely a strange sort of creature, who never praises any one more heartily than him who has spread destruction and ruin over the face of nations! (99)

Mary, likewise, rewrites history by playing down the military accomplishments of Castruccio, and voices a similar critique against military aggression through the words of Guinigi, the peasant protector of Castruccio:

> To my eyes, which do not now glance with the same fire as yours, the sight of the bounties of nature, and of the harmless peasants who cultivate the earth, is far more delightful than an army of knights hasting in brilliant array to deluge the fields with blood, and to destroy the beneficial hopes of the husbandman. (25)

That Mary changed Guinigi's occupation from a soldier to a peasant deserves attention: in Machiavelli's version, as an excelling soldier, Guinigi sees a great potential in Castruccio and adopts him to train him as one; Mary's Guinigi is an ex-soldier retired into the life of peasantry, who preaches peace and love in vain to Castruccio.

Mary plays down Castruccio's accomplishments as an excelling soldier and leader because she gives a different meaning to his political career as a near miss from that given by Machiavelli. His lost opportunity is not his sovereignty over Tuscany due to his premature death, but the chance to redeem himself and thereby work toward a better cause. That his ideological choice is further integrated with his love affair with Euthanasia assumes the structure of a romance. It is in this respect that Mary deviates the most from the previous historians: that is, the point of focus in the novel is how the familiar pattern of romance becomes disrupted through the misguided actions of the male protagonist. What appears as a feminist critique of masculine egotism bears political connotations that cannot be identified straightforwardly, for Mary's structural re-working of *Ivanhoe* locates Castruccio's self-aggrandizement (or his 'will to power') as the obstruction to the novel's happy ending; in this sense, it is not only the political binary of imperialism/republicanism that is being problematised here, but also the Machiavellian political sensibility set against the humanitarian values of *Ivanhoe*.

Bearing in mind the distinct political framework that *Ivanhoe* and *Valperga* took, it is only natural that they should, in the end, diverge in the historical ideology they promote: however, as the products of romance writers rather than historians, their foci converge on the act of myth-making rather than that of documenting history. Just as Scott's medieval past is invested with his own belief in the feudalistic order as a valid and healthy body politic, Mary creates an imaginary space, which is invested with Romantic idealism that resists masculine history of linear progress. That such a conception of time cannot in the end sustain itself and becomes subsumed in the 'public history' of marching events is yet another part of that myth. To conclude it as a defeatist enterprise is, however, to miss the point: for Euthanasia's judgment overrules any other narrative as the most satisfactory version of that story. We may understand Euthanasia's judgment as a social act that seeks to balance the 'demands of the head and the heart' by making use of the 'traditional iconic representations of a female Justice/Justizia—by a woman'.[74] It further reflects an attitude of the women critics of the Romantic period who 'set themselves up as *judges*, judges not just of aesthetic taste and literary excellence but also of cultural morality', and in so doing 'claimed the right to control the social sphere, that arena that mediates between the public and the private realms' (46, 47). Presumably, Mary gave her heroine the name Euthanasia meaning, 'good death' (eu-, thanatos) in Greek, with the faith that sound judgment outlives exterior actions and is privileged to a lasting life.

NOTES

1. Mary refers to her conception of the novel and its date in a letter of 30 June 1821 to Maria Gisborne: '[I]t has been a child of mighty slow growth, since I first thought of it in our library at Marlow' (*MWSL* 1:203).
2. Mary read Sismondi 'in January and February, 1819'; 'in the early spring of 1820, she read both Machiavelli's and Niccolò Tegrimi's biographies of Castruccio'; [I]n the autumn of that same year she read Sismondi again, along with Villani's history of Florence, continuing with the latter through the winter and into the spring of 1821' (Walling 53). Walling furthermore brings to our attention Godwin's suggestion to Mary of writing 'a series of biographies that would be called "The Lives of the Commonwealth's Men", a collection that would deal inevitably with the political conflicts of seventeenth-century England' in the summer of 1818 that might have provided an incentive for Mary to write on Castruccio instead of the 'Commonwealth men' (62).

   Godwin took an active part in Mary's composition of *Valperga*, the publication of which was intended to assist him financially (*PBSL* 2:352–53). Godwin's involvement, however, seems to have been limited to 'mostly just cuts' rather than 'major rewritings or insertions' (Crook 1996, p. xiii).
3. Lisa Vargo, for example, claims that '*The Triumph of life* marks the place where this conversation [i.e. a complex dialogue formed by the writings of the Shelleys] breaks off'; see 'Close Your Eyes and Think of Shelley: Versioning Mary Shelley's *Triumph of Life*' (Clark and Hogle 215).
4. Percy Shelley took great interest in *Valperga* and expressed his high views in his letters: 'I promise myself success from it [*Valperga*]; and certainly, if what is wholly original will succeed, I shall not be disappointed' (to Thomas Love Peacock, 8 November 1820; *PBSL* 2: 245); 'I flatter myself you have composed something unequalled in its kind, & that not content with the honours of your birth & your hereditary aristocracy, you will add still higher renown to your name' (to Mary Shelley, 8 August 1821; *PBSL* 2: 320). See also Rossington 2000, p. xiv.
5. See P.B. Shelley's 'Devil, and devils' quoted in part in Chapter 1.
6. In *Prometheus Unbound*, a cosmological drama based on Æschylus's *Prometheus Bound*, Shelley uses 'cars' as agents of time and fate that will dethrone Jupiter from his throne and restore Prometheus's reign; a chariot in the 'Triumph of Life', likewise, controls the fate of 'The Wise,/The great, the unforgotten' as well as the multitude by making them its captives. Although 'cars' or 'chariots' do not appear in *Valperga* in a literal sense as they do in the previous two works, Shelley utilises the image to denote

fate. Euthanasia, on her decision to join the conspiracy against Castruccio, realises the inevitability of what is to follow: 'the path was narrow, and her chariot could not turn' (302); Castruccio, similarly, characterises his chosen life as having selected 'these hell-hounds to drag my car of life' (312). See the note for 'car of life' in Rajan 1998, p. 466.

7. As the original working title of William Godwin's *Caleb Williams*, 'Things as They are', and its ending become projected onto a probable terrain, the Shelleys likewise wrote with an acute sense of the necessity and possibility that negotiate history.
8. See note to 3.3.64–68 in Everest et al. 2000.
9. The Romantic concept of the mind as an active agent, with its locus in the imagination, as opposed to the passive role assigned to it by the empiricists (e.g. Locke) is relevant here; for Rousseau singles himself out as being marked by 'the spark which Heaven lit my spirit' to denote a semi-god status in his capability to create through the imagination. For a materialist reading of Rousseau, see Hamilton 1997. Hamilton argues that it is Rousseau's subjectivity that compels him to resist being assimilated into 'the body politic' in which he ought to play a democratic part.
10. For the influence of Dante's *Divine Comedy* on 'The Triumph' see Chapter 1; references to it in *Valperga*, firstly given by the narrator at the beginning of the novel, then repeatedly mentioned by Euthanasia in relation to her idealism based on her love for liberty and beauty, not to mention the name 'Beatrice', which Shelley chose for her other heroine, are the obvious ones.
11. Mary Poovey reads *Frankenstein* as Mary Shelley's critique of her contemporaries' egotism for failing to take responsibility for their own creation. Poovey's argument is further developed by Anne K. Mellor who relates it to politics as well as science in *Mary Shelley*. Betty T. Bennett succinctly summarises the political issue of the novel: 'Frankenstein's failure, then, is a parable for the failure of the nineteenth-century socio-political structure to take responsibility—material and spiritual—for the greater populace'. See 'General Introduction' in *The Novels and Selected Works of Mary Shelley* (1: xxxi).
12. I mean hypothetical in two ways: firstly, in its treatment of human creation; secondly, in the novel's association of death with Romantic quest as a trope, which was literally realised with the lives of the second—generation Romantics. For the much-debated 'life-principle' on which Mary based her story, see the introduction to Butler 1993, pp. xv–xxi.
13. 'Appendix A: Author's Introduction to the Standard Novels Edition (1831)' in Butler 1993, p. 197.
14. Blumberg 76.

15. Mary worked on *The Last Man* from February 1824 into November 1825; it eventually came out in 1826, four years after Percy Shelley's death and two years after Byron's. Mary writes in her journal of 14 May 1824: 'The Last Man! Yes I may well describe the solitary being's feelings, feeling myself as the last relic of a beloved race, my companions extinct before me' (*MSJ* 2:476–77).
16. The story of human extinction by the plague, and consequently the destruction of the intimate circle, of which the narrator is a member, is imbued with a sense of fatalism: '"Am I for ever", he [Raymond] cried, "to be the sport of fortune! Must man, the heaven-climber, be for ever the victim of the crawling reptiles of his species! [...] But I am about to die!—nay, interpret me not—soon I shall die. From the many-peopled earth, from the sympathies of man, from the loved resorts of my youth, from the kindness of my friends, from the affection of my only beloved Perdita, I am about to be removed. Such is the will of fate! Such the decree of the High Ruler from whom there is no appeal: to whom I submit"'; 'I [Lionel] again felt, that we were enchained to the car of fate, over whose courses we had no control. We could no longer say, This we will do, and this we will leave undone. A mightier power than the human was at hand to destroy our plans or to achieve the work we avoided'. See *The Last Man* 154, 243.
17. As I have already argued, the novel leaves open the possibility of Walton re-working his future so as not to repeat Victor Frankenstein's mistakes; in fact, Walton, at the end of the novel, abandons his expedition to the North Pole for humanitarian reasons. In *The Last Man*, Lionel narrates what has passed already in the light of the present; also, the very fact that what Lionel records belongs to the future gives the novel a predetermined character.
18. Beatrice becomes disillusioned and mad when she is betrayed by Castruccio; Castruccio's cruelty and lust for power intensify and become uncontrollable when he exiles Euthanasia; Euthanasia literally becomes 'lost' in the sea on her way to Sicily.
19. Blumberg, for instance, criticises Elizabeth Nitchie's 'simplistic approach', which argues 'that the character of Castruccio is based almost entirely on Byron' (Blumberg 84). Amongst various influences that may be noted in the novel, one that will not be discussed further but deserves attention is Castruccio's egocentric actions that prevent him from winning his domestic happiness with Euthanasia, which echo that of Godwin's fictional character St. Leon, who likewise sacrifices his family for his whim and then curiosity. Pamela Clemit argues that the central theme of domesticity in *St. Leon* derives from the works of Mary Wollstonecraft, which Godwin

was re-reading and editing at the time of its composition. Introduction to *St. Leon*, p. xv.

20. For Mary's revision of Scott's *Ivanhoe*, see introduction to *Valperga* (Curran 1997). While Curran stresses Mary's re-working of the characters and plot in *Ivanhoe*, her novel also reflects Scott's techniques in portraying the past. According to Georg Lukács, 'Scott's greatness lies in his capacity to give living human embodiment to historical-social types' and his historical authenticity, which is 'the quality of the inner life, the morality, heroism, capacity for sacrifice, steadfastness etc. peculiar to a given age' that 'reawaken the spirit of the age' (Lukács 1976, pp. 34, 53). For Godwin's influence on the novel, see Clemit 1993: 'while the historical scope of Valperga owes much to Scott's more naturalistic, documentary art, its central imaginative threads reflect the selective and theoretical concerns of earlier Godwinian novels' (177).
21. Mary Shelley read *Ivanhoe* on 10 and 11 June 1820; the dates fall in between 'the formal start' of writing *Valperga* and her intense 'reading and note-taking and writing' that followed her visit to Lucca on 11–12 August 1820. See *MSJ* 312–3,321; Crook 1996, p. xi.
22. Browning refers to both the 'Cathari, or Albigensians, a heretical sect well established in Provence' and the 'Paulician or Paterine heresy', which resembled each other: in the poem (ii 616–17), Sordello complies with the popularity of Montfort's crusade against the former sect by singing his eulogy as a means to gaining his own (unlike the real Sordello who shared his fellow troubadour's disgust at Montfort's barbaric act); Browning makes a brief remark on the favouritism which Eccelin II showed toward the latter sect (ii 860–1). See Woolford and Karlin 1991, 1:503, 517.
23. Friedrich Schlegel makes a similar point:

    > These two great historical parties—the Guelphs and Ghibellines, are the same which we meet with in other periods of history, and even in our own times, though under other names [...] There is ever the one party aspiring after greater freedom, and the other immovably attached to the ancient faith, and to the principles it inculcates. (369)

    Schlegel, however, reverses the conventional understanding of the party banners by associating, 'freedom' with the Ghibellines, and 'ancient faith' with the Guelphs (Schlegel 1848, pp. 369–70).
24. The relationship between republicanism and feminism is a complicated one that had been seen as being incompatible in the past; however, this mutual exclusivity is now being questioned as the formulation of republicanism

underwent a change. For the classical model of masculine republicanism, see Pocock 98–100; in relation to feminism, see Phillips 2000.

25. 'Of History and Romance' 367, 362. This previously unpublished essay was composed, according to Godwin's manuscript note, 'while the Enquirer (1797) was in the press, under the impression that the favour of the public might have demanded another volume' (359).
26. One of the reasons for focusing my argument on *Caleb Williams* is that Godwin exploits history in order to render 'Things as they are'; and his use of history seems particularly pertinent to Mary Shelley's *Valperga*. Gary Kelly similarly reads it as a historical representation of the present:

    > Godwin's novel [*Caleb Williams*] was, from the evidence of the natures and names of its characters, an allegory of Protestant not to say Dissenting history [...] with *Things As They Are* Godwin had already written a historical novel, set, paradoxically, in the present, but dealing nevertheless with the moral history of man.

    See Kelly 1976, p. 208. The more overt historical novels written by Godwin, such as *St. Leon* and *Mandeville*, engage in the problematic history of Protestantism characterised by social alienation and persecution.
27. Jon Klancher, 'Godwin and the Genre Reformers: on Necessity, and Contingency in Romantic Narrative Theory' in Rajan 1998, p. 32. Tilottama Rajan similarly writes:

    > Godwin frees the reader from an auxiliary role and makes history the site of difference rather than of an atemporal vindication of authorial identity [...] At the same time, he is reluctant to give away to a complete relativism. Hence, his historicizing of intention takes the form of a divinatory hermeneutics, which imposes ateleological direction on the history of reception, consistent with his own notions of perfectibility. (Rajan 1990, p. 169)

28. Niccolò Machiavelli, 'The Life of Castruccio Castracani' (2: 533–59).
29. See Tilottama Rajan, 'Between Romance and History: Possibility and Contingency in Godwin, Leibniz, and Mary Shelley's *Valperga*' in Bennett 2000, pp. 88–102.
30. Crook cites an account given by Thomas Medwin and Mary Shelley's letter of April 1823 for the basis of its assumption (xiii); see Medwin 374; *MWSL* 1: 331.
31. Betty T. Bennett reads the title as representing two alternative ideologies: 'The two cannot exist; confrontation must erupt' (Reiman 1978, p. 358). This is true given the framework of the novel (i.e. Guelph/Ghibelline strife); however, it is also possible to read Euthanasia's political stance,

which is dependent on 'love' and 'imagination', as a deliberate retreat from that power struggle without being an abdication of her struggle against it.

32. See note to *Valperga* (Crook 1996, p. 10; Rajan 1998, p. 446).
33. Daniel E. White elaborates on this in '"The god undeified": Mary Shelley's *Valperga*, Italy and the Aesthetic Desire'. *Romanticism on the Net* 6 (May 1997).
34. The harsh reality that female writers faced can be ascribed to the 'remasculinization of writing' that took place in the beginning of the nineteenth century; see Siskin 1998, pp. 206, 208. James Chandler takes *The Quarterly*'s reception of Anna Laetitia Barbauld's 'Eighteen Hundred and Eleven' as an example that demonstrates the extent to which a female writer such as Barbauld was excluded from engaging in such activity as the '[r]epresentations of the state of the nation' (McCalman 357–58).
35. See 'History, Trauma, and the Limits of the Liberal Imagination: William Godwin's Historical Fiction' in Rajan 1998, pp. 64–85.
36. Mary Shelley mentions 'Paradise of Exiles' in a letter dated 9 September 1823, addressed to Leigh Hunt; she also refers to her 'having made a part of the Elect' in a letter of 3 October 1824 addressed to Thomas Jefferson Hogg (*MWSL* 1:377, 450).
37. Euthanasia cites the Romans and the Greeks as being privileged to a mental historical past that enables them to tap into the liberal ethos that gave birth to their writings in the first place; the close connection between writing and political freedom further suggests that the latter could be achieved through the former in the future, as Percy Shelley envisaged (81).
38. Percy Shelley writes in his letter to Thomas Love Peacock: 'Mary is writing a novel, illustrative of the manners of the Middle Ages in Italy, which she has raked out of fifty old books' (*PBSL* 2:245). Mary Shelley herself refers to it in her letter to Maria Gisborne: '[I]t has indeed been a work of some labour since I have read & consulted a great many books' (*MWSL* 1: 203). Her list of references included in the preface to the novel includes: Niccolò Machiavelli's *La Vita di Castruccio Castracani da Lucca*, J.C.L. Sismondi's *Histoire des républiques italiennes au moyen âge*, Niccolò Tegrimi's *Vita Castrucci Castracani* (5).
39. *Literary Gazette, and Journal of the Belles Lettres* 319 (1 March 1823): 132–33; *La Belle Assemblée, or Court and Fashion Magazine*, n.s. (August 1823): 83–84; *The Literary Register of the Fine Arts, Sciences, and Belles Lettres* 36 (6 March 1823): 151–52; *Blackwood's Edinburgh Magazine* 13 (March 1823): 283–93.
40. John Gibson Lockhart, reviewing for *Blackwood's* writes: 'Our chief objection, indeed, may be summed up in one word—Mrs Shelley has not done justice to the character of Castruccio'. *Monthly Review* 101 (May 1823)

expresses similar views that 'the real Castruccio was little fitted to be converted into the hero of the novel, and the present writer has not been able to give any additional interest to his character' (105). In reviewing the female characters, *The Literary Gazette* notes that 'the female pictures are exquisite, both from their contrast and in themselves' (132); *Monthly Review* praised that 'Euthanasia, the heroine, is on the whole finely drawn' and '[t]he story of Beatrice, also, an enthusiastic girl, who believes herself to be divinely inspired, possesses considerable interest' (105). *The London Chronicle* 133 (8–10 March 1823) praises the character of Beatrice as 'a fine piece of painting of the Rembrandt School' (240).

41. Blumberg brings to our attention Euthanasia's role as a benevolent ruler (87).
42. For the influence of Dante on the Romantics, see Brand. Sismondi's *Histoire des Républiques Italiennes de l'Age Moyen* also contributed to the marriage of nineteenth-century republican sympathies and medieval Italy. See, for example, John Herman Merivale's review of Sismondi's *Histoire.*
43. 'Ghibellines and Guelfs allegiances were dictated wholly by local convenience and ambition. The *fideles* of the rival powers readily changed or mixed sides (and not only with revolutions of regime), defied their nominal leaders, and fell out among themselves' (Jones 348).
44. Mary expresses her disapproval of 'republican principle & liberty, if Peace is not the offspring' (*MWSL* 2:183).
45. See Michael Rossington, 'Future Uncertain: the Republican Tradition and Its Destiny' (Bennett 2000, pp. 103–18).
46. Mary Shelley's own views are referred to in a letter of (c. Nov.–Dec.) 1825 from David Lyndsay (a pseudonym of Mary Diana Dods) to William Blackwell: 'She [Mary Shelley] was much gratified by your review of Valperga, but declar'd that in her delineation of Castruccio Bonaparte (whom she hates) never enter'd her mind' (*MWSL* 1:534).
47. Percy Shelley refers to Castruccio, in a letter to his publisher Ollier, as 'a little Napoleon, and, with a dukedom instead of an empire for his theatre' (*PBSL* 2:353). Lockhart complains about the novel's 'perpetual drumming at poor Bonaparte' in his review in *Blackwood's.*
48. See *Ode to Napoleon Buonaparte, Childe Harold's Pilgrimage* (3.17–45, 4.89–92) for Byron's depiction of, and personal investment in, Napoleon. Simon Bainbridge discusses the impact of Napoleon on the Romantic imagination (including Byron's identification with the historic figure) in Bainbridge 134–52.
49. In the introduction to Shelley's research notes for *Valperga* included in *The 'Charles the First' Draft Notebook,* Nora Crook writes: '[t]he English Civil War and the Commonwealth had been urged as a theme for Mary Shelley by Godwin as early as 8 June 1818'; William Walling 'whose account of the

making of [...] *Valperga* [...] is still the most complete to date [...] suggests that Mary Shelley undertook *Valperga* as an alternative to Godwin's proposal'; see BSM 12: xxx; Walling 62.

50. In the preface to his *History of the Commonwealth of England*, William Godwin begins by addressing the neglect and mistreatment from which English history between 1640 to 1660 has suffered and makes it the 'object of the present work to remedy this defect, to restore the just tone of historical relation on the subject, to attend to the neglected, to remember the forgotten, and to distribute an impartial award on all that was planned and achieved during this eventful period'; see Godwin 1824, 1: v–vi.
51. *BSM* 12: xxx.
52. I am drawing on Cathy Caruth's argument in *Unclaimed Experience: Trauma, Narrative, and History*, which brings texts, of psychoanalysis, of literature, and of literary theory together to investigate how they 'both speak about and speak through the profound story of traumatic experience' (4):

    > At the core of these stories, I would suggest, is thus a kind of double telling, the oscillation between a *crisis of death* and the correlative *crisis of life*: between the story of the unbearable nature of an event and the story of the unbearable nature of its survival. (7)

    What seems particularly relevant to Mary Shelley's case is her own traumatic experience of losing her children in a short period. Both *Mathilda* and *Valperga* were written around the time of her tragic loss. That Mary Shelley blamed P.B. Shelley for their children's death and accused her father of indifference may explain the feminist critique of masculine egotism in *Valperga*.
53. For the continuity of Mary's interest in the pathology as the subject matter, see Rajan 1994, pp. 43–68.
54. Handwerk writes: 'Presbyterianism represents for him [Godwin] exclusion and isolation, a radicalized Protestant interiority that places him beyond the reach of rational discourse' (77).
55. Godwin 1976, p. 248.
56. Mary, for example, takes liberties in making changes to Castruccio's biographical details: he is born eight years later than the account given by both Sismondi and Tegrimi, Castruccio's first biographer; he remains single when, in fact, he was married and had three children of his own. See Green 1986.
57. The original ending of the novel extant in the form of a manuscript concludes with Caleb's mad soliloquy during his imprisonment following the court case in which he accuses Falkland of murder; it naturally gives a different sense to the meaning of the novel compared to that of the final version. See 'Appendix I' (McCraken 327–34). For Gary Kelley's argument that

Godwin's alteration was based on the political milieu of the time, and especially on the court case of Joseph Gerrald, see *English Jacobin Novel* 198.

58. John Barrell writes on 'the idea of the division of labour', which

> 'functioned as a fully articulated discourse, offering a comprehensive account of human history that could be appealed to by aestheticians, linguists, literary critics and speculative historians. It was predominantly associated, however, with the institution of political economy: with the celebration of economic expansion and industrial improvement, and with the attempt to vindicate the structure of modern commercial societies as, precisely, a structure, as something which, despite its arguably chaotic appearance, was available to be known, to be comprehended.' (Barrell 89)

Although Barrell concentrates his argument on the picturesque and its discourse, which he sees in contest with that of the division of labour, a similar case may be put forward for poetics and the poets' attempt to establish an independent cognitive role from that of political economists. A good example of this would be Percy Shelley's *Defence of Poetry* written in response to Thomas Love Peacock's essay that denounced poetry's utility in a modern, commercial society.

59. This phrase, which Jeremy Bentham found in Joseph Priestley's pamphlet *Essays on Government*, became the central principle of utilitarianism, as Bentham tells us: '[I]t was by that pamphlet and this phrase in it that my principles on the subject of morality, public and private, were determined'; see 'Introduction' to *Utilitarianism* (Warnock 7).

60. Donald Winch glosses one of Malthus's criticisms targeted at Godwin and Condorcet:

> They had endangered the very notion of science as a progressive enterprise by infringing Newtonian precepts. In arriving at conclusions based solely on extrapolation, they had reasoned from causes to possible effects rather than from observed effects to possible causes.

See the 'Introduction' to T. R. Malthus, *An Essay on the Principle of Population; or, A View of Its Past and Present Effects on Human Happiness; With an Inquiry into our Prospects Respecting the Future Removal of Mitigation of the Evils Which it Occasions* (xii).

61. The most notorious review, which was falsely believed to have caused Keats's death, was John Wilson Croker's review of Keats's *Endymion* (1818); equally malicious was John Taylor Coleridge's review of Percy Shelley's *The Revolt of Islam* (1818); see Reiman 1972, 2: 751, 767–76.

62. In a letter of 12 January 1823 addressed to Jane Williams, Mary notes the uncanny twist of fate by which her husband, like her heroine Euthanasia,

drowned at sea: 'Is not the end of mine wondrous—the fate—the shore—how miserably foretold—it is very strang[e]'; she likewise wrote to Maria Gisborne in May 1823: 'Is not the catastrophe strangely prophetic' (*MWSL* 1:307, 336).

63. Shelley's letters express his disappointment regarding his public reception. See my Introduction.
64. Barbara Jane O'Sullivan reads Beatrice as a Cassandra figure whose story can be interpreted as 'the troubled history of female spiritual and imaginative power which is buried alive beneath the surface of Western culture' (141). See 'Beatrice in *Valperga*: A New Cassandra' (Fisch et al. 140–58).
65. Paul A. Cantor brings to our attention the possibility of a dialogue taking place between the works of Mary and Byron, suggesting that Mary seeks to 'transform' the 'hidden ugliness of the male', which 'is' his aggressiveness and will to power'; see 'Mary Shelley and the Taming of the Byronic Hero': "Transformation" and "*The Deformed Transformed*" (Fisch et al. 103).
66. In *The Last Man*, Mary Shelley brings out the resemblance of Raymond, Castruccio, and Byron, on the one hand, and Adrian, Euthanasia, and Shelley, on the other: 'With all the incongruities of his character, Raymond was emphatically a man of the world. [...] He looked on the structure of society as but a part of the machinery which supported the web on which his life was traced. The earth was spread out as an highway for him; the heavens built up as a canopy for him'; 'Adrian felt that he made a part of a great whole. [...] His soul was sympathy, and dedicated to the worship of beauty and excellence' (Blumberg 38). Mary Shelley writes in her letter of 20 August 1827 addressed to Teresa Guiccioli: 'have you read my Last Man—You will find in Lord Raymond and Count Adrian faint portraits but I hope not displeasing to you of B. and S—but this is a secret'; see *MWSL* 1:566 (its original in Italian 564).
67. In *The Last Man*, Raymond also becomes emotionally attached to two women: Perdita, whom he marries, and Evadne, who becomes both financially and emotionally dependent on him.
68. For Mary's fascination and sympathy with Byron, see Blumberg 57–75 and Moore 426.
69. See Mellor 1993; Beer 29–48.
70. Mary Shelley's quote from Muratori (136).
71. See 'The Paterin Beatrice' in Rieger 111–28.
72. Self-knowledge is used in a different meaning by Machiavelli who stresses the significance of a successful political and military manoeuvre: 'It is in this world of great importance to know oneself, and to be able to measure the forces of one's spirit and of one's position' (554).
73. *Caleb Williams* (Clemit 1992, pp. 98–9).
74. Mellor in Beer 1995, p. 30.

Chapter 3

Browning's *Sordello*

Introduction

Robert Browning's narrative romance *Sordello*, which is based on the life of a troubadour of the Middle Ages, similarly draws on the factional contest between the Guelphs and the Ghibellines of the Italian city-states. As Mary Shelley utilised the historical material to tell her own story, much of Browning's knowledge of medieval Italy, which derived from chronicles of that period of Italian history, was used to create a setting that would prove convincing in its 'local color', but in the end, no more than a mere platform on which to engage in his own poetic concerns. Robert Browning, writing in 1863, over twenty years after the first publication of *Sordello*, explained his intentions in his poem in his dedication to his friend Joseph Milsand:

> The historical decoration was purposely of no more importance than a background requires; and my stress lay on the incidents in the development of a soul: little else is worth study.[1]

Browning had already faced this dilemma back in 1837 during his compositional stage as testified by Harriet Martineau in her diary:

> [Browning] Denies himself preface and notes. He must choose between being historian or poet. Cannot split the interest. I advised him to let the poem tell its own story.[2]

It is hardly surprising that Browning chose the latter, not simply because he was writing in verse, but also because he was more concerned with writing about the future rather than merely about the past as Aristotle had outlined.[3] *Sordello* demonstrates his continuing interest in the intellectual, emotional, and spiritual aspects of human existence, which can be seen in his earlier poems such as *Pauline* and *Paracelsus*. Browning's preoccupation with 'the incidents in the development of a soul' took various expressions—from a confessional fragment to a Romantic drama, and to a romance narrative—during the course of which his poetic style gradually emerged. That it had something to do with his shifting weight from 'subjective' to 'objective' poetry is one way of explaining it; another attempt at understanding this trajectory is to see it as rites of passage that enabled Browning to regain his Christian faith as the informing ethos of his poetry.

In his celebrated essay on Shelley, Browning not only identifies his poetry with the 'subjective' type of poetry, but he also highlights its religious nature as being the predominant characteristics as opposed to the worldly matter that concerns 'objective' poetry. Browning's high praise of Shelley, however, does not conceal the extent to which he had moved away since his adolescent years, when Shelley was his idol to worship and to emulate. That Shelley's atheism was now a problem rather than a novelty is clear: rather than distancing himself from it, however, Browning is more concerned about exonerating him from the misunderstandings that such labelling is likely to invite. He does this by arguing that Shelley mistook every wrong for the great principles, thereby 'mistaking Churchdom for Christianity, and for marriage, "the sale of love" and the law of sexual oppression' (1009).[4] Browning, however, insists that Shelley would not have remained in error for long and that '[g]radually he was raised above the contemplation of spots and the attempt at effacing them, to the great Abstract Light, and through the discrepancy of the creation, to the sufficiency of the First Cause' (1009). According to Browning, Shelley had already embodied 'the capital dogmas of Christianity'; he simply had not come around to admitting it.

Insightful as this is, if one examines Shelley's later poems against his preoccupation with Plato and Calderón, one need not look far to see where he was heading. Although Browning can with some comfort assert his position in 1852 as having moved away from Shelley by objectifying his life and poetry, Browning was still struggling to shake off Shelley's influence when writing *Sordello*. To word it differently, Browning's account of Shelley is equally about his own completion or closure of the Shelleyan legacy that burdened him as much as it is about Shelley. The 'Essay on Shelley' is thus informative of Browning's own poetic process.

Browning's repeated attempt at creating a guilt-ridden artist who, for one defect or another, cannot accomplish what he is out to achieve, derives from his immediate precursors, Shelley and Byron. The Faustian theme, which appealed to both these poets, was also the source for Browning's first major attempt at public success, *Paracelsus.*[5] Goethe, who was at the heart of German Romanticism, no doubt, captured the imagination of the second-generation Romantics and Browning who was under their immediate influence; however, equally deserving of attention is Pedro Calderón de la Barca, whose dramatic plays Shelley was rigorously reading and even attempting to translate toward the end of his life. Calderón's plays offer a useful way into some of the aesthetic and spiritual concerns that dominate Shelley's later works, and furthermore, become translated into those of Browning. Considering the similarities that are detectable in Calderón and Shelley's poetry, it is not hard to imagine how the Spanish dramatist fascinated Shelley; at the same time, it does not take much effort to speculate how congenial their works must have seemed in the eyes of Browning.[6]

Denis Florence McCarthy, who was one of the pioneer translators of the dramatic plays of Calderón, succinctly summarises this point. Shelley's translation is referred to as the exemplary attempt so far at bringing Calderón's plays to life; this, McCarthy argues, is owing to Shelley's own lyrical skills as a poet:

> In his [Calderón's] pages we feel the dazzling glory of the sun that we can scarce behold, the deep blue of the sky, the azure freshness of the sea, the snow-white foam of the waves, the myriad colours of the flowers, all blended, contrasted, confused in a brilliant maze of splendour, which, in its combination, Nature itself does not equal, and in its separate beauties cannot surpass. It is because the poetry of Shelley partakes more largely of this characteristic of Calderon than that of any other writer with whom I am acquainted (totally opposed as the two poets are in every other respect), added to his wonderful command of language and exquisite lyrical harmony, that I believe he was pre-eminently fitted for complete success in a task which, while it contained much of the charm of his own original compositions, would be totally free from those peculiarities of opinion and expression which must always be an obstacle to their universal popularity.[7]

Browning's own assessment of the 'subjective' poetry for which Shelley is seen to be a representative is not far off from McCarthy's statement:

> [T]he subjective poet, whose study has been himself, appealing through himself to the absolute Divine mind, prefers to dwell upon those external scenic appearances which strike out most abundantly and uninterruptedly his inner light and power, selects that silence of the earth and sea in which he can best hear the beating of his individual heart, and leaves the noisy, complex, yet imperfect exhibitions of nature in the manifold experience of man around him, which serve only to distract and suppress the working of his brain. (1003)

As Browning here explains, it is essentially the religious mind in search of the 'Divine' that instructs the 'subjective' poet and for whom Nature is its direct manifestation. Therefore, the ability to capture the external nature best qualifies the poet to achieve his purpose. In direct opposition to this is the 'objective' poet who 'in his appeal to the aggregate human mind, chooses to deal with the doings of men' (1003).

This polarisation of poetry into the 'subjective' and the 'objective' was a current notion in the 1830s that was being voiced in England by authors who came in contact with German Romanticism.[8] In his 'Lectures on Dramatic Art', Schlegel singles out Calderón next to Shakespeare as the two greatest dramatists whose works deserve full attention.[9] Although he sees the two poets on an equal footing, he also views them as embodying two very different worlds. While Calderón's dramas are 'founded on the religious passion', Shakespeare's derive from 'his knowledge of the human heart'.[10] Schlegel's further assessment is suggestive: 'Calderón is to be considered as the last summit of the romantic poetry' (xxi). The antithetical nature of the dramatic works of Calderón and Shakespeare, no doubt, enabled the Romantics and Victorians alike to identify at once the aesthetic orientation of Romanticism and its counter-movement that was gradually emerging. Even if one took the accounts given by Browning himself or of his biographers at face value—that 'he knew neither the German philosophers nor their reflection in Coleridge'—it is more than likely that similar comparison between Calderón and Shakespeare (whom Lockhart equally claimed to be 'the greatest dramatists the modern world has produced') would have been made by Browning himself.[11]

Shelley is much in accordance with the debate that was being initiated by Schlegel when he singled out Calderón for his ability to incorporate religion into drama—a tradition that had been long lost since the Athenian drama—in *A Defence of Poetry*:

> Calderon in his religious Autos has attempted to fulfil some of the high conditions of dramatic representation neglected by Shakespeare; such as the establishing a relation between the drama and religion, and the accommodating them to music and dancing [. . . .] (519)

Despite Calderón's religious dogmatism, which he goes on to criticise in the very succeeding lines of the quote, Shelley was essentially attracted to the religious nature of his works.[12]

Calderón's dramas often concern the spiritual conversion from disbelief or spiritual inertness to active Christian faith.[13] What Browning described as 'the incidents in the development of a soul' regarding his poem *Sordello*, would be much at home in the plays of Calderón, which, according to McCarthy, focus their interest on the 'inward workings of the soul' (xvi). There is much in *Sordello* to suggest that the kind of influence that Calderón's dramas exercised upon Shelley's poetry are also present in Browning's poem. Take for example the world which Sordello inhabits in the beginning: Sordello feeds on his narcissistic desire in a womblike haven that denotes a dream rather than a realistic locale. That the outer surrounding becomes a space for the projection of the 'inward workings of the soul' is a characteristic that I have already mentioned in relation to both Shelley's and Calderón's works.[14] Although *Sordello* is a narrative with a concrete plot, this dreamlike vision, which Sordello entertains throughout, makes the poem both obscure and disruptive. In other words, there are two conflicting forces at work: the poet's will to tell a story (in a conventional sense) and his almost compulsive desire to diverge from it in order to narrate 'the development of a soul'. The mixture of these two aesthetics—one visionary and the other pertaining to realism—creates discordance within the poem that cannot simply be explained away by Browning's eccentricities. For instance, Sordello's view of the world is not dissimilar to that adopted by Shelley's narrator of 'The Triumph of Life': their deliberate distancing and isolation from the real world enables an aestheticised view of the world that is seen as a pageant.[15] Yet, Browning demonstrates that he can turn to realism if he wishes to do so: the pillage scene of Ferrara presents one such example that counter-balances the dreamlike vision of Sordello's Goito days.

The inner process whereby one gains active faith through humility is necessarily a private and personal experience that belongs to the realm of 'subjective' poetry. It is the way in which Calderón successfully rendered that experience in drama that attracted Shelley despite 'the rigidly-defined and ever-repeated idealisms of a distorted superstition' (490). For all his Catholicism, Calderón's poetry is not merely a means to communicate dogma but also merit artistic value: his ability to depict nature as a live organism in its full splendour; the power of sensuality that appealed so much to Shelley, and Calderón's utilisation of rich metaphors that sparked off Shelley's creativity are a few of such examples. In relation to Browning, one may even add the baroque style as a possible influence on his poetry.[16] What is of particular interest is Calderón's playful use of metaphors (i.e. Calderónization as Shelley coined it), which will be discussed in the next section. That Calderón demonstrated that poetry could serve as an effective means of engaging in religious experience without becoming subjected to theology no doubt served as an inspiration to Shelley's later poems such as 'Ode to the West Wind', *Adonais*, and 'The Triumph of Life'. In *Sordelleo*, Browning thematises such a gesture—to depict religious experience in poetry—so that it becomes more poignant. On a latent level, *Sordello* tells a story of a vain artist who mistakes himself to be the godhead but becomes humbled to accepting his role in the service of mankind. It is the kind of rite of passage that Calderón illustrates in his dramas. However, Browning tells us in his poem that such a subjective narrative is what he seeks to leave behind in order to embrace Shakespearean drama in which the subjective self is expunged. It is almost as if he *had* to write about 'the inner development of the soul' and objectify the act within the poem as a way forward to writing the 'objective' poetry of Shakespeare's kind. This practice—the expunging of the self—which took the most obvious shape in *Pauline*, was, therefore, ever to remain an excruciating memory for Browning.[17] Calderón's dramas arguably served as an antithetical model to Shakespeare's, which appealed to Browning for the very same reason that attracted him to Shelley as 'the last of Romantic poetry'.

The Problem of Audience

Shelley's influence on Browning as a young man has become a cornerstone in judging the literary works of the latter's early years; yet, the story that is being repeated has somewhat stereotyped this to a simple equation of Browning's emulation of lyrical self-expression and his eventual abandonment of it. This may well be the obvious conclusion to be drawn after examining Browning's earlier works, such as *Pauline*, *Paracelsus*, and *Sordello*, in comparison to his dramatic monologues;

a more complex picture emerges, however, if one takes a closer look at these early works and assesses them in their own right. *Sordello*, which is regarded as the crux of Browning's swerve away from Shelleyan Romanticism, largely concerns his poetics: the narrator provides an outline of poetical history, of which the last form looks to what he would later term as the dramatic monologue, in the process of which lyricism is abandoned.[18] It is generally agreed that Browning identified in the Romantic bard a self-gratifying stance in the lyrical self-expression and a Promethean ambition to act as a self-elected god; that he consequently searched for a poetical form that would embody his newfound ethos. My aim is to attempt to re-consider some of the assumptions that have been made about what is often acknowledged to be Browning's finding or innovation while engaging in Browning's revisionary programme. In some cases, the germ already exists in Shelley's works.[19] As an example of this, I would like to focus my examination on Shelley's *Letter to Maria Gisborne* in relation to *Sordello*. In doing so, it is particularly useful to look at the *Letter* as a result of Shelley's intensive reading of the works of the Spanish dramatist Calderón, which provide a leeway to the shifting attitude reflected in the *Letter*.

Letter to Maria Gisborne was written in 'late June 1820', approximately a year after Shelley first mentions Calderón in a letter to Hogg, praising him as the 'great dramatic genius', whom he was to compare to Shakespeare soon after.[20] References to Calderón occur sporadically in his letters throughout the following months, and his enthusiasm for Calderón was never to waver until the very end of his life, when he produced a translation of an excerpt from *El Mágico Prodigioso*. Of all his later works that are marked by Calderón's influence, such as *The Cenci*, 'Ode to the West Wind', 'To a Skylark', *The Sensitive Plant*, *Hellas*, *Adonais*, and 'The Triumph of Life', the Letter deserves attention, not simply because it serves as a document of his immersion in Spanish studies, but more importantly because it dramatises the writer-reader dynamics in a manner similar to Browning's *Sordello*.[21]

What distinguishes the Letter from Shelley's other works is that it is a verse epistle addressed to a specific individual: the poem was, in fact, initially written as a private letter to Maria Gisborne without any intention on Shelley's part to publish it. It was supposedly written when the Shelleys were staying at Leghorn in a house owned by the Gisbornes, who were then visiting London. The intimacy and the easy flow of the poem can be accounted for by the real audience that Shelley had in mind when writing it. Shelley begins the poem by presenting a 'spider' or 'silk worm' metaphor, which I will come back to later. He then moves on to the workshop that belongs to the Gisbornes' son, Henry Reveley, a nautical engineer who was at the time designing a steam-boat. Various pieces of mechanical equipment and mathematical calculations are mentioned with a certain playfulness that infuses figures taken from diverse sources, such as the Bible, classical mythology, and history. He then subtly slips into his own mind through the analogy of machinery for the human brain; at which point, we learn that his jocular spirit with which he began the poem, in fact, barely disguises his inner trouble. His scorn for the scathing reviews that he endured, namely for his epic poem *The Revolt of Islam* (although not specified as such in the poem itself), emerges as the poet's main preoccupation here. At this very moment, he reverts to addressing Maria Gisborne: 'You are not here!' (63). His disappointment with the public reception of his work compels him to retreat to those treasured moments that were spent in blissful harmony with the addressee, among the long list of which was their reading of Calderón:

> Or how I, wisest lady! then indued
> The language of a land which now is free,
> And winged with thoughts of truth and majesty,
> Flits round the tyrant's sceptre like a cloud,
> And bursts the peopled prisons, and cries aloud,
> 'My name is Legion!'—that majestic tongue
> Which Calderon over the desart flung
> Of ages and of nations; and which found
> An echo in our hearts, and with the sound
> Startled oblivion;—thou wert then to me
> As is a nurse—when inarticulately
> A child would talk as its grown parents do.
>
> (*Posthumous Poems* 64–5)

Shelley then draws his attention to 'London' where the Gisbornes are presently situated. It is not the critics whom he associates 'London' with, but rather his close-knit friends. The scope of his ideal audience widens at this stage from the Gisbornes to encompass those other friends whom he considers to be 'treasures' in 'that great sea, whose ebb and flow/At once is deaf and loud, and on the shore/Vomits its wrecks, and still howls on for more' (65). His humorous accounts of them not only demonstrate Shelley's warm regard for them, but they also strengthen the solidarity that exists among them based on mutual understanding and respect.

Shelley's thoughts of his friends in London make him realise that he is alone in Italy. The poem, at this point, becomes that of an invitation for the Gisbornes to return to Italy. He appeals to them by making a contrast between what they would encounter in Italy—the idyllic lovers with their 'serenade'—to the cursing prostitute that roams in the streets of London. In the last verse paragraph, Shelley insists on their company: 'Next winter you must pass with me' (68). It is not, however, the Gisbornes alone, but 'Hunt, Hogg, Peacock and Smith,' the entire band, that he wants near him. Such occasion of merriment alone will raise him from his despondency and see him through to the spring.

Despite the light-hearted tone with which Shelley moves from one topic to another by whimsical association, his latent anxiety cannot be entirely disguised. In fact, Shelley encodes his deepening problem regarding the public reception of his works in the first verse paragraph, using the 'spider' and 'silkworm' metaphor:

> The spider spreads her webs, whether she be
> In poet's tower, cellar, or barn, or tree;
> The silkworm in the dark green mulberry leaves
> His winding sheet and cradle ever weaves;
> So I, a thing whom moralists call worm,
> Sit spinning still round this decaying form,
> From the fine threads of rare and subtle thought—
> No net of words in garish colours wrought
> To catch the idle buzzers of the day—

> But a soft cell, where when that fades away,
> Memory may clothe in wings my living name
> And feed it with the asphodels of fame,
> Which in those hearts that must remember me
> Grow, making love an immortality. (59)

Shelley works on the Romantic model of a caterpillar's transformation into a butterfly, which signifies the inner working of the artist that will manifest itself outwardly. He also combines this with the denigrating status of a 'worm' that was imposed upon him by the 'moralist' who criticised his private morality in the *Quarterly Review*. The effect of this is that instead of being sheltered and nourished for the great transformation to take place, the 'worm' will perform the secretive task on his own despite the hostile environment in which he is placed. Furthermore, when the transformation does take effect, it will be owing to the 'wings' of 'Memory' and not as the direct result of his inner workings.

What deserves attention here is that Shelley's growing weariness about appealing to the public as an enlightening bard and successive attacks on the obscurity and morality of his works have done enough to discourage him from taking on that role. Instead, in the Letter, he assumes the voice of a friend who writes to Maria Gisborne for her sympathy and understanding;[22] he then extends the circle to include his other close friends such as 'Hunt, Hogg, Peacock and Smith.' Only in their memories can Shelley's name hope to live on and to 'Grow'; the decisive factor for this being that he can depend on their 'love,' which will enable him, in return—as the embodiment of love—to become immortal.

The *Letter*, in spite of its playful tone, reveals a significant change in the poet's stance that cannot be explained only by the genre in which it is written. He dismisses himself as the chosen bard who will enact social change through his poetry; instead, he shows vulnerability and humanity that prove him to be no different from any other person. It is no coincidence that he presents himself as such—a human being with worries and joys—in a poem that is closely linked with Calderón. Furthermore, it is significant that he is dependent on his friends for the effect of his creativity to take place: his faith that the influence he intends his poetry to exercise over his readers will be automatically realised is replaced by a mutual co-operation whereby the writer must rely on the reader for sympathetic and active participation. What differentiates his small but friendly audience from his critics, for example, is love: the dynamics of the writer-reader relationship cannot blossom, as Shelley claims, without mutual respect and understanding. The critics who attempt to tarnish his reputation are not driven by love, but hatred—what Shelley understood as a misguided emotion that is also a distortion of love. Equally harmful to the creator as the unsympathetic critics are the indifferent masses that simply dismiss his works. As the complete absence of a public reader testifies, the way literature has come to be consumed in the nineteenth century presents a grave problem for poets such as Shelley.

This very problem—that writers were losing their hold on readers at a symbolic level that helped shape the latter's moral, political, and aesthetic taste—is the central theme of Robert Browning's narrative poem *Sordello*. Browning began the poem in the more 'popular' vein of a narrative combined with a romance in the hope that he might gain a wider audience. The outcome, however, could not be any more different: the poem was condemned to obscurity, and even his fellow-poet Tennyson is alleged to have grumbled over its unintelligibility.[23] What Tennyson is known to have said regarding the poem—that 'there were only two lines in it that he understood, the first and the last, and that both were lies'—is not far from the truth; for Browning, on one level, and by far the most important, utilises romance as a decoy for attracting the audience so that he may engage their attention on issues he considers more important while their interest, temporarily as it may be, is sustained. Browning's attitude in doing so is never didactic: he does not attempt to instruct as the more enlightened philosopher or poet, but rather seeks the reader's help—that is, to enable the writer-reader dynamics to work. What I mean by this is that by imagining a sympathetic audience, which he in fact does, Browning is able to establish a dialectical discourse within himself that enables him to experiment and develop his ideas; on the part of the reader, one is expected to engage in that process by attempting to make sense of not only what he means but also what one makes of it. The poem begins open-ended with a series of interruptions and digressions, and is nearly abandoned at one stage; because the very nature of the poem is to work out the poetics that the poem is engaged in; the story ends not when the plot is complete but when Browning has reached the end of that process. Browning, to a certain extent, exploits his protagonist in order to complete his own initiation as a poet, and thereby sacrifices the plot for his own means to accomplish this. The readers may arguably be drawn into this process unnecessarily; however, given the central role they play in Browning's creativity, they are automatically implicated in it and his theoretical digression becomes an apologia for doing so.

Browning's radical stance in *Sordello* is the way in which he defines his ideal audience, which the general reader is expected to emulate. Browning does not look to the future for its maturation, as is often the case with Shelley; instead, he maps out an a-temporal condition that will make his ideal audience. It is not necessarily the enlightened and knowing reader that will accomplish the task of a co-operative partner, but his 'willing' 'friends' who can help him develop his inner life by actively participating in it. If we are to take 'fate' as a measuring stick for the quality of his audience along the lines of the Enlightenment ethos to see how much it meets the demand of the writer, Browning's following comment makes it fairly clear that he has other criteria in mind:

> 'tis not for Fate to choose
> Silence or song because she can refuse
> Real eyes to glisten more, real hearts to ache
> Less oft, real brows turn smoother for our sake:
> I have experienced something of her spite;
> *But there's a realm wherein she has no right*
> *And I have many lovers*: say but few
> Friends Fate accords me? (i 37–44)
> [emphasis added]

In other words, Browning does not simply settle for the audience that his age can(not) provide but seeks to actively create his own, firstly by recruiting his own friends or those he would consider metaphorically to be his friends:

> Here they are; now view
> The host I muster! Many a lighted face
> Foul with no vestige of the grave's disgrace;
> What else should tempt them back to taste our air
> Except to see how their successors fare?
> My audience: and they sit, each ghostly man
> Striving to look as living as he can,
> Brother by breathing brother; thou art set,
> Clear-witted critic, by ... but I'll not fret
> A wondrous soul of them, nor move Death's spleen
> Who loves not to unlock them. Friends! I mean
> The living in good earnest—ye elect
> Chiefly for love—suppose not I reject
> Judicious praise, who contrary shall peep
> Some fit occasion forth, for fear ye sleep,
> To glean your bland approvals. (i 44–59)

Browning's good humour, which adds colour and life to the band of elect, is however not entirely devoid of anxiety. Even those whom he considers as his 'friends' are susceptible to 'sleep' ('but friends,/Wake up'; vi 869–70) and their response is not enthusiastically promising ('To *glean* your *bland* approvals'). This cannot be dismissed merely as Browning's humility concerning his creativity if we examine how the writer-reader relationship is reflected in the case of his own poet-protagonist: Sordello lives in social seclusion and is burdened with a paramount task to reveal himself—a state approximating godhead—through words, which he is never able to accomplish. His tragedy is that he cannot successfully communicate his thoughts to anyone; even when his poem wins him a laurel crown, he is still misunderstood and praised for the wrong reasons.[24] Sordello's life becomes one endless succession of misreading by everyone who comes into contact with him, including Palma, his 'out-soul.' Browning is not moderate in the degree of Sordello's failure, and his insistence on the total collapse of communication between writer and reader weighs heavily on the poetics that he is out to scrutinise. Therefore, his summoned audience should not be understood as an act of mere decoration but as a device on Browning's part to seriously engage in the relationship with his reader.

Given the friendly audience Browning introduces at the beginning of the poem, which maintains its ghostly presence as his immediate listener until the very end of the poem, *Sordello* possibly echoes Shelley's Letter in more ways than one. The most apparent influence of Letter on *Sordello* can be detected in the imageries and choice of words. The first such example is the analogy of machinery for life (or more specifically that of an artist), for which Browning harnesses the mechanical vocabularies used in the Letter.[25] Although both poets employ 'engine/machine' to denote the process and product of their (artistic) work, their attitudes differ significantly. Whereas Shelley emulates the god-like status in that the speaker may 'breathe a soul into the iron heart/Of some machine portentous, or strange gin' (ll. 8–9), Browning's account suggests a process of gradual construction:

> simply experiment
> Each on the other's power and its intent
> When elsewhere tasked, if this of mine were trucked
> For thine to either's profit,—watch construct,
> In short, an engine (iii 811–15)

It is of particular interest that the section of Letter that shows the greatest example of Calderónization invites different religious views from both poets.[26] To Shelley, the Spanish dramatist and his works cannot evade Catholic dogmatism and its related acts of tyranny in the form of the Spanish Inquisition, with which 'thumbscrews, wheels, with tooth and spike and jag' (60) are associated. Browning, unlike Shelley, focuses on the temporary status of the workmanship, which can benefit, but remain subordinate to, the real work that is to be done in one's afterlife ('When elsewhere tasked'):

> We die: which means to say the whole's removed,
> Dismounted wheel by wheel that complex gin,
> To be set up anew elsewhere, *begin*

A task indeed but with a clearer clime
Than the murk lodgment of our building-time (iii 824–28)
[emphases added]

Browning's humble view sees his earthly work as not without value but inevitably limited in its scope compared to what is achievable in one's afterlife; his *weltanschauung* is grounded in Christianity, which gives weight to the value of life after death, determinable according to how one's life is spent on earth.

Browning's analogy of (artistic) life with machinery is, however, prompted as a response to his critic's accusation of 'Presumptuous' behaviour in comparing himself with Moses, to which he retaliates reversely—it is his critics who 'marvel at and magnify/Mine [his] office' (iii 808–9). If Browning means to humble his critic on the philosophical grounds that human creativity is inevitably limited and therefore should not be compared to divinity, then Shelley's rebuke of his critic takes on board a different set of values:

And here like some weïrd Archimage sit I,
Plotting dark spells, and devilish energy,
The self-impelling steam-wheels of the mind
Which pump up oaths from clergymen, and grind
The *gentle spirit* of our *meek reviews*
Into a powdery foam of salt abuse,
Ruffling the ocean of their self-content (62)
[emphases added]

Shelley's critique is targeted at the hypocritical stance of reviewers who claim to be 'gentle' and 'meek' but in reality are malicious ('a powdery foam of salt abuse') if 'their self-content' is ever shaken up. He does not see himself on par with his critics; but rather, he takes the moral high ground to point out the misguided passion with which they pass their judgments. As a rationalist who thoroughly embraces love as the end to all things, Shelley reminds his critics that their verbal abuse is not called for in a case of public failure:

> Whatever talents a person may possess to amuse and instruct others, be they ever so inconsiderable, he is yet bound to exert them: if his attempt be ineffectual, let the punishment of an unaccomplished purpose have been sufficient; let none trouble themselves to heap the dust of oblivion upon his efforts; the pile they raise will betray his grave, which might otherwise have been unknown.[27]

The second example of verbal echo that can be detected in *Sordello* occurs in a passage that describes Sordello's immature creativity when secluded in Goito as a page in the 'secret lodge of Adelaide's'. Browning, following Shelley's use of the 'silkworm' analogy, utilises the transformation of a caterpillar into a butterfly to denote the inner development and manifestations of an artist:

> Like the great palmer-worm that strips the trees,
> Eats the life out of every luscious plant,
> And when September finds them sere or scant
> Puts forth two wondrous winglets, alters quite
> And hies him after unforeseen delight (i. 632–36)

The significance of this is that Sordello does not succeed in his potential development: 'So fed Sordello, not a shard disheathed' (i 637). Sordello is merely feeding his imagination with fanciful associations of things that amount to nothing:

> He o'er-festooning every interval
> As the adventurous spider, making light
> Of distance, shoots her threads from depth to height,
> From barbican to battlement; so flung
> Fantasies forth and in their center swung
> Our architect (i 664–69)

The 'silkworm' and 'spider' imageries that Shelley himself employs in *Letter* are used by Browning in almost exactly the same sense in *Sordello*: not only do they symbolise the artist and his engagement in the creative process, but in both texts, they also imply their failures.

It is not difficult to account for the presence of *Letter* in *Sordello* given their shared interest and anxiety. The influence of the former does not simply stop at a verbal echo but extends to the very problem and resolution that the *Letter* adopts. For example, the analogy of machinery for artistic work (of linguistic construction) invites us, in both cases, to speculate on the poet's anxious relationship with his critic; the caterpillar denotes unrealised potential that does not see the day of public success (except that gained by a whim in the case of Sordello). What is more, this deep sense of anxiety is couched in playful humour, as in the depiction of their respective immediate audiences; but this is not to say that they are ornamental devices. Their imaginary audience is a crucial part of their dialectical process to make their art work (which is figuratively represented in the opening verse paragraph of *Letter*). If *Sordello* can be considered as the first step toward Browning's dramatic monologues based on his re-working of lyrical self-expression, then the *Letter* offered a compelling model of the writer-reader relationship that was based on love and co-operation.

POETS, POETICS, AND POETIC INFLUENCES

Much of *Sordello* concerns the writing process of poetry, the various types of which Browning discriminates mainly through Sordello, but also Eglamor, and the relation of poetry to society at large.[28] Browning's poetic experiment, which encompasses his stylistic as well as moral probing, takes on an eccentric choice of narrative. That it was his intention to gain a wider audience by adopting this poetic form demonstrates the urgency with which Browning sought public success; however, its outcome suggests that the pressure, rather than accommodating him to popular taste, exposed him to his poetic crisis. That is to say, *Sordello* takes us on an initiation tour that enables him to discover his poetic identity, which Browning attains by negotiating with his predecessors—namely, the Romantic poets. As most of his early works are discussed in relation to Romanticism, *Sordello* is also about Browning's emulation of, and revisionary attempt at, its poetic ethos.

Sordello's initial alienation from society and receptivity toward nature is given as a ready model of a Wordsworthian Poet who is gifted with 'deep feelings' and 'active power to fasten images/Upon his brain' when brought into contact with nature.[29] If the Poet readily responds to nature, he does so as a means to identify his inner self, which is manifested in it. Browning acknowledges Sordello as being of this type that seeks self-revelation through others, whereas Eglamor is the 'temple-worshiper' who devotes himself to others.[30] Eglamor, no doubt, figures as a formalist of poetic limitation; however, that Browning is more interested in the serious flaws that accompany the first type of poet attests to the extent of his engagement with the Romantic poet. Browning was not the first to experiment with such introverted temperaments, and his Romantic precursors themselves provide the central issues that Browning raises in his poem.

The most immediate example is Shelley's *Alastor; or, The Spirit of Solitude*. Critics have been divided over not only the meaning of the poem in relation to its preface but also as to whom Shelley is talking about if he did model the poet on someone; but, as Peter Butter reminds us in his annotation to the poem, it enhances our understanding of it if we accept that it is made up of a hybrid of ideas and personal experiences (as all works are) rather than reflecting a coherent material.[31] Couched in such loose terms, what is recognisable in *Alastor* is the presence of Wordsworth, and in the *Alastor* volume as a whole, that of the first-generation Romantic poets, namely Wordsworth and Coleridge. Shelley read Wordsworth's *Excursion* in 1814, which confirmed his views on the older poet. As Mary Shelley testifies in her journal (dated 14 September) of Shelley's disappointment with his former idol, much of Wordsworth's influence over Shelley at this time had been negative: '[Shelley] calls on Hookham and brings home Wordsworths Excursion of which we read a part—much disappointed—He is a slave.'[32] It explains the background 'To Wordsworth' in which Shelley denounces Wordsworth even when he still acknowledges his poetic genius. This has led some critics to conclude that *Alastor* is about the 'decay of genius' of which Wordsworth is the prototype.[33] Shelley, however, understood it differently: Wordsworth's failing poetic energy was not to do with his autumnal decline but rather to do with his political apostasy. This is after all what constitutes his disappointment in 'To Wordsworth.'

In *Sordello*, Browning portrays a solipsistic poet not unlike the *Alastor* poet: the difference being that with the latter, the *Alastor* poet does not alter his course of pursuit (i.e. to seek ideal vision) that leads him to his untimely death, whereas Sordello temporarily enters the political sphere only to fail of its own accord. The intriguing turning-point occurs for both Browning and his protagonist-poet when politics becomes at stake: that is, just at the point when Sordello looks as if he might succumb to Palma's political ambition by making it his own, Browning breaks off his narrative to reinstate his political position. He likens Sordello's narrow escape to that of Rome from the siege of Brennus at the rescue of Manlius Marcus (iii 574–6), which provides a subtext to the poem.[34] In Venice, where Browning is reviewing his vocational significance as a poet, he encounters a 'disheveled ghost' that is an emblem, for him, of 'suffering humanity'; consequently, its presence reminds him of his commitment to serve the people;[35] his recovered republicanism thereafter enables him to continue his narrative, in which the author's political choice is reflected in Sordello's.

It is of interest that Sordello's 'Will' to self-projection, which he sought through nature and people, becomes translated into his political ambition to rule: that is, Browning's portrayal of a nature poet who is characterised by 'his roves/Among the hills and valleys, plains and groves' (ii 270–1) not only suggests an anti-social behaviour but that his self-serving egotism contains a potential danger of his succumbing to the seduction of political power if given the chance. The association of the two strongly implies Wordsworth as Shelley understood him. Two factors can be brought to critical attention in order to endorse this view. Firstly, refined nature poetry is not celebrated as a quality worth one's praise but is seen as a consequence of evading commitment to more important (especially political) issues. Secondly, self-absorbed poetry that puts oneself as the primary object of interest is attacked as a sign of egotism that disables one from identifying with others. Shelley succinctly puts this in 'Peter Bell the Third'—a parody of Wordsworth's own 'Peter Bell':

He [Wordsworth] had a mind which was somehow
 At once circumference and centre
Of all he might or feel or know;

Nothing went ever out, although
  Something did ever enter.

He had as much imagination
  As a pint-pot;—he never could
Fancy another situation,
From which to dart his contemplation,
  Than that wherein he stood.[36]
(Shelley 1840; 3: 241)

As an example of the former, Browning makes a scathing remark on the kind of nature poetry that is suggestive of Wordsworth when distinguishing true poets from false ones; he does this by illustrating an example taken from the Bible 'where the Israelites travel through the wilderness of Zin (or 'Sin') and cry out for water' (iii 778–806n.).[37] While 'water', as a metaphor of 'enlightenment', is only accessible to a limited few, the ignorant poets claim equal access to it but are denied the production of meaningful poetry, in which context occurs his comment: 'Meantime, just meditate my madrigal/O' the mugwort that conceals a dewdrop safe!' (iii 788–9). The irony is that the speaker cannot extend his concerns beyond the aesthetics that may be 'exquisite' in themselves but are irrelevant to the moral issue at stake.

Wordsworth wrote a series of nature poems based on flowers, which could well have offered Browning the material for this comment.[38] Of the total three poems that Wordsworth composed on the small Celandine, two—'To the Small Celandine' and 'The Small Celandine'—in particular offer some further insight into their possible influence. If Browning did have these poems in mind when inserting these lines, he, no doubt, intended a satirical attack on the original poems. For example, Wordsworth's exaggerated insistence on the significance of the finding of the flower becomes highly ironic when referred to in the context of seeking true enlightenment ('The water of life') in *Sordello*:

Eyes of some men travel far
For the finding of a star;
Up and down the heavens they go,

Men that keep a mighty rout!
I'm as great as they, I trow,
Since the day I found thee out,
Little flower—I'll make a stir,
Like a great astronomer. (ll. 9–16)[39]

Shelley quotes the last two lines of the stanza in a letter dated 6 July 1819 addressed to Thomas Love Peacock; for which Peacock provides a gloss by quoting it in full and adding the explanation that

> It [Little Celandine] blossoms from the end of February to the end of April. It is so far connected with the arrival of the swallow, that it ceases to blossom when the swallowwort [Celandine] begins. This probably was the reason for its being called celandine, though the plants have nothing in common. But I think, in honour of Wordsworth, its old name should not have been entirely banished from botanical nomenclature. It might have been left, in Homeric phraseology, as the flower which men call Pilewort and Gods call Celandine.[40]

If Browning had access to these letters (which he no doubt did to some), this explanatory comment may have provided him with the choice of a 'mugwort' as a result of a slight alteration from 'pile-' to 'mug-', perhaps out of embarrassment.[41] Furthermore, 'mugwort that conceals a dew-drop safe' strongly suggests the physical make-up of a small Celandine as Wordsworth describes in 'The Small Celandine':[42]

When hailstones have been falling, swarm on swarm,
Or blasts the green field and the trees distressed,
Oft have I seen it muffled up from harm,
In close self-shelter, like a Thing at rest. (ll. 5–8)

Another plausible source of influence is Shelley's 'Verses written on receiving a Celandine in a letter from England', which was '[i]n language and imagery unmistakably reminiscent of Wordsworth's poems to the celandine'.[43] Mary Shelley dates the poem to 'July—1816' but is counter-claimed by the Longman editors as early spring owing to the unavailability of the flower at that time.[44] If Shelley sent a copy of this poem, which was 'written on receiving a Celandine' from Peacock, back to the addresser, there is again a chance that Browning may have seen it.[45] The significance of this slightly increases compared to the original poems by Wordsworth, as Shelley again engages in a critique of Wordsworth's political apostasy. Shelley likens the flower to Wordsworth and laments their transformation with the difference being that the former 'grows grey from age' whereas 'Wordsworth's own decay is seen as inward, corrupting the achievement of his prime':[46]

Yes, gentle flower, in thy recess
None might a sweeter aspect wear:
The young bud drooped so gracefully,
Thou wert so fair—
Among the fairest ere the stress
Of exile, death, and injury
Thus withering and deforming thee
Had made a mournful type of thee;

A type of that whence I and thou
Are thus familiar, Celandine—
A deathless Poet whose young prime
Was as serene as thine,
But he is changed and withered now,
Fallen on a cold and evil time;
His heart is gone—his flame is dim,
And infamy sits mocking him.

Celandine! thou art pale and dead,
Changed from thy fresh and woodland state.
Oh! that thy bard were cold, but he
Has lived too long and late.
Would he were in an honoured grave;
But that, men say, now must not be
Since he for impious gold could sell
The love of those who loved him well. (17–40)

Shelley, once again, emphasises Wordsworth's growing conservatism as the direct cause of his poetic decline and his disappointment in which manifests itself toward the end of the poem:

> That he, with all hope else of good,
> Should be thus transitory
> I marvel not—but that his lays
> Have spared not their own glory,
> That blood, even the foul god of blood,
> With most inexpiable praise
> Freedom and truth left desolate
> He has been brought to celebrate!
>
> They were his hopes which he doth scorn,
> They were his foes the fight that won;
> That sanction and that condemnation
> Are now forever gone.
> They need them not! Truth may not mourn
> That with a liar's inspiration
> Her majesty he did disown
> Ere he could overlive his own.
>
> They need them not, for Liberty,
> Justice and philosophic truth
> From his divine and simple song
> Shall draw immortal youth
> When he and thou shall cease to be,
> Or be some other thing, so long
> As men may breathe or flowers may blossom
> O'er the wide Earth's maternal bosom.
>
> The stem whence thou wert disunited
> Since thy poor self was banished hither,
> Now by that priest of Nature's care
> Who sent thee forth to wither
> His window with its blooms has lighted,
> And I shall see thy brethren there,

And each like thee will aye betoken
Love sold, hope dead, and honour broken.

Although Shelley's critical attack on his political views is, to a certain extent, counter-balanced by his reverence for the poetical genius of Wordsworth, it is also more acute because of his deference for him. Wordsworth's acceptance of a governmental post in 1813 officially symbolised the departure from his service to the people, which was further confirmed by his accession of his laureateship in 1843. Browning reiterates his condemnation of Wordsworth's public roles in 'The Lost Leader' five years after the publication of *Sordello*;[47] his views demonstrate that he was much in line with Shelley and there is no reason to doubt that it is also manifested in *Sordello*.

When Browning breaks off from his narrative to engage in his own crisis as a poet, his digression alternates between his concern for the style and the content of the kind of poetry he seeks to write. His recovered sense of political responsibility through his encounter with the 'sad disheveled ghost' necessitates him, in return, to consider an appropriate form that will best accommodate it: the self-revelatory poetry that Sordello aimed at will not do. Browning provides us with three types of poetry that ascend in the degree of their importance: 'The worst of us, to say they so have seen;/The better, what it was they saw' and 'the best,/ Impart the gift of seeing to the rest' (iii 840–3). The last type are further given a religious connotation as 'the Makers-see', 'Who ply the pullies' (iii 907), so that they can mediate between heaven and earth. What deserves attention here is that Browning subtly denounces the self-deified poet that is characteristic of the Romantic poet, such as Shelley, by emphasising the subordinate status of poets: they may impart knowledge that can help people to become more enlightened, but they can never be the godhead.

Sordello's initial attitude toward the world is one of arrogance, which the narrator interrupts to criticise:

Dear monarch, I beseech,
Notice how lamentably wide a breach
Is here! Discovering this, discover too

What our poor world has possibly to do
With it! As pigmy natures as you please—
So much the better for you; take your ease;
Look on, and laugh; style yourself God alone (ii 415–21)

Sordello's appropriation of Apollo accentuates his desire to become the godhead and to be worshipped by nature and the people as such, the model of which can be found in Romantic poetry. Shelley's 'Song of Apollo' is particularly pertinent with regard to the static and sovereign power that Apollo is associated with in *Sordello*:

I am the eye with which the Universe
  Beholds itself, and knows itself divine.
All harmony of instrument or verse,
  All prophesy, all medicine are mine,
All light of art or nature;—to my song,
Victory and praise in their own right belong.[48]

Not only did Browning read the poem in the pirated edition of *Miscellaneous Poems,* but he also wrote 'Splendid' at the top of the poem in his own copy.[49] Given his initial favourable impression of the poem, it is not beyond feasibility to speculate that Browning chose 'Apollo' as a way of critiquing the Romantic poet with whom he had initially identified but from whom he was increasingly distancing himself.

Instead of assuming an exalted stance for the poet, Browning insists on a shared humanity that humbles the poet to the level of ordinary people to whom he owes responsibility and service. Browning's poetics here emulate that which Wordsworth put forward in the preface to the *Lyrical Ballads*: 'Among the qualities which I have enumerated as principally conducing to form a Poet, is implied nothing differing in kind from other men, but only in degree' (p. 607).[50] The problem for Browning that seems to keep Wordsworth at bay despite his affinity with the latter's aesthetics is again Wordsworth's political apostasy, which cannot be excused given his initial commitment to the people.

Shelley suggests an interesting connection between Wordsworth's political stance and character that is detectable in his poetry and is not entirely irrelevant to *Sordello*. Three years after the publication of the *Alastor* volume, Shelley again attempted to reassess Wordsworth's contribution by parodying the latter's published poem *Peter Bell*. The outcome, however, is not entirely of a satirical nature but contains some of his matured views on Wordsworth:

He had a mind which was somehow
  At once circumference and centre
Of all he might or feel or know;
Nothing went ever out, although
  Something did ever enter.

He had as much imagination
  As a pint-pot;—he never could
Fancy another situation,
From which to dart his contemplation,
  Than that wherein he stood.

Yet his was individual mind,
  And new created all he saw
In a new manner, and refined
Those new creations, and combined
  Them, by a master-spirit's law,

Thus—though unimaginative,
  An apprehension clear, intense,
Of his mind's work, had made alive
The things it wrought on; I believe
Wakening a sort of thought in sense.[51]
(Shelley 1840; 3: 241)

As Wordsworth's primary shortcoming, Shelley singles out his inability to go out of himself and identify with others: 'Nothing went ever out, although/Something did ever enter'; 'he never could/Fancy another situation,/From which to dart his contemplation'. Despite an 'individual mind' with 'apprehension clear, intense', Shelley deprives him of 'imagination'—the sovereign faculty, as he states in *A Defence of Poetry*.[52]

Again, Hazlitt's assessment of Wordsworth's poetry is instructive in the demarcation that Shelley is creating here: '[h]e exemplifies in an eminent degree the power of *association*; for his poetry has no other source of character'.[53] Hazlitt's choice of word—*association*—denotes the working of Coleridgian poetics that distinguishes 'imagination' from 'fancy'. Whereas the former 'dissolves, diffuses, dissipates, in order to re-create', the latter works under 'the law of association' with 'fixities and definites'.[54]

Further, this has moral implications, so that Wordsworth, unlike the 'objective poet', cannot enter into the life of others through imagination but can only appropriate them to his inner self; he represents a kind of genius that concerns oneself as the primary subject;[55] therefore, while his mind may be a mine of 'deep feelings' and 'deep thoughts', he cannot become all things like Shakespeare.[56] For Shelley, however, self-identification with the other implies political as well as moral improvement by the very act of self-involvement with others:

> The great secret of morals is Love; or a going out of our own nature, and an identification of ourselves with the beautiful which exists in thought, action, or person, not our own. A man, to be greatly good, must imagine intensely and comprehensively; he must put himself in the place of another and of many others; the pains and pleasures of his species must become his own. The great instrument of moral good is the imagination; and poetry administers to the effect by acting upon the cause.[57]

If we understand 'imagination' to be the mediator of identifying with others as Shelley explicitly does, then it is not difficult to see how his critique of Wordsworth's political position and his lack of 'imagination' are closely linked. Wordsworth's obsession with introverted characters and his conservative views in *The Excursion* are not unrelated factors for Shelley.

The poetical and political failings of Sordello, on the other hand, are more complex: although his introspective nature is being critiqued at in the beginning, Sordello is not entirely a 'subjective poet' whose concerns are of himself alone, for his soul encompasses every type of life. What deters him from realising different identities are his physical limitations that will not allow him to be all at once:

> Happiness must be
> To feed the first by gleanings from the last,
> Attain its qualities, and slow or fast
> Become what one beholds; such peace-in-strife
> By transmutation is the Use of life,
> The Alien turning Native to the soul
> Or the body—which instructs me; I am whole
> There and demand a Palma (iii 162–9)

He fails to put 'such peace-in-strife' into practice out of contempt for his 'Means' and thereby decides to choose his own (poetical) death. This does not necessarily mean that such an attempt will altogether die with him; in fact, others will follow in his footsteps. Dante is being evoked here as the one who will successfully override him in history.

Dante's *Divine Comedy* bears significance not simply as the epic-scale poetry that succeeded Sordello's failed attempt (i.e. to write in the vernacular),[58] but also because Dante was successful in imagining his own spiritual journey, which led him to paradise with the help of a female figure. Palma ought to have been for Sordello what Beatrice was to Dante, only she turns out to be destructive for his inner development. Sordello's political failure, after he decides to try out his ambition in the world of action, is not unconnected to Palma's political ambition to make him a king: his political will to serve the people could not find the body, that is Palma, through which to work it out, and thereby destroyed itself.[59] Again, the *Alastor* volume lurks in the background for a gloominess that owes its mood to failed relationships and unsatisfied political idealism.

Alastor, no doubt, sets the dominant tone of the volume with its solipsistic poet who is driven by an ideal beauty that evades his grasp and is in the end avenged for turning his back on real human relationships. The poet fails in his quest; firstly, because he attempts to seek a realm beyond his mortal reach; secondly, because he undermines the significance of human sympathy. 'O! there are spirits of the air', a poem included in the same volume with similar themes (e.g. the futility of pursuing shadows), allows a more overtly biographical interpretation than *Alastor*. For example, it is possible to identify parts that relate to Shelley's loss of Harriet Grove and his estrangement from his first wife, Harriet Westbrook.[60] Mary Shelley, however, singles out Coleridge as the inspiration behind it:

> The poem beginning, 'Oh, there are spirits in the air', was addressed in idea to Coleridge, whom he never knew; and at whose character he could only guess imperfectly, through his writings, and accounts he heard of him from some who knew him well. He regarded his change of opinions as rather an act of will than conviction, and believed that in his inner heart he would be haunted by what Shelley considered the better and holier aspirations of his youth.[61]

Although Mary Shelley's gloss here stresses Coleridge's change of political views, the poem, like *Alastor*, dramatises personal unhappiness that derives from his failure to find a soul partner:

> *And thou hast sought in starry eyes*
>   *Beams that were never meant for thine,*
> *Another's wealth*; –tame sacrifice
>   To a fond faith!
>
> Yes, all the faithless smiles are fled
>   Whose falsehood left thee broken-hearted;
> The glory of the moon is dead;
>   Night's ghosts and dreams have now departed;
> Thine own soul still is true to thee,
> But changed to a foul fiend through misery.

This fiend, whose ghastly presence ever
  Beside thee like thy shadow hangs,
Dream not to chase; —the mad endeavour
Would scourge thee to severer pangs.
Be as thou art. Thy settled fate,
Dark as it is, all change would aggravate.
(Shelley 1839; 3: 7)
[emphasis added]

The account given above is reminiscent of *Alastor*, where we are told of the Poet whose 'self-centred seclusion was avenged by the furies of an irresistible passion pursuing him to speedy ruin.'[62] Notably, his 'soul', which has maintained its integrity, is 'changed to a foul fiend through misery' and not through 'self-centred seclusion'. Unlike the Poet in *Alastor*, the addressee of the poem did look for worldly happiness but failed to attain it.

The influence of Coleridge on *Alastor* has been previously noted by critics such as Joseph Raben who makes a rather extreme case by suggesting that Shelley identified himself with Coleridge.[63] Raben's argument that the shared temperament and background of the two poets provide ample basis for the poetic influence of one over the other is not convincing; however, as 'O! there are spirits of the air' demonstrates, his presence in the volume is undeniable and offers useful areas where Shelley did identify with him. If Wordsworth's poetry, for Shelley, was tainted by self-absorption in conjunction with political apostasy, then Coleridge's poetry joined in the latter with self-afflicted despondency. Coleridge mentions 'Halfness' and 'Other half' to denote 'something that is without, that has the property of Outness' which he feels he is in need of but cannot find in reality. That Coleridge's personal misery owes something to the lack of such existence, which further prompts him to turn his back on his earlier self (that is, with respect to his political beliefs) bears resonance to the inner development of Sordello. Sordello's inability to fulfil his potential as a liberal leader, which reflects his inner change, can partly be explained by his failure to find his 'out-soul' who will assist him in achieving the ideal vision.

FEMINISM

Browning's revisionary attempt in *Sordello*, by means of reconsidering some of the implications of Romantic poetry, does not restrict itself to the poetic subject and its formal make-up; but its workings can be located in the least suspected area. As one such example, I would like to focus on Browning's treatment of the muse.

The muse is a problematic concept, not only in *Sordello*, but also in other nineteenth-century poetry, which, arguably, reflects the destabilisation of poetic tradition and social marginalisation of poetry as a literary genre. For instance, Wordsworth grapples with the idea in the preface to *The Excursion* by insisting at first that

> Urania, I shall need
> Thy guidance, or a greater Muse, if such
> Descend to earth or dwell in highest heaven! (ll. 25–7)[64]

His gesture, however, to invoke a traditional muse soon turns hollow when he cannot actually name his source of inspiration other than as 'prophetic Spirit'. Byron in *Don Juan* mocks it in the same spirit in which he downplays epic as a viable genre: 'For me who, wandering with pedestrian Muses,/Contend not with you on the wingèd steed.'[65] In Shelley's *Revolt of Islam*, which is clearly modelled on Spenser's epic romance in terms of poetic form (Spenserian stanza) and subject (national upheaval), Mary Shelley figures as his muse:

> So now my summer-task is ended, Mary,
> And I return to thee, mine own heart's home;
> As to his Queen some victor Knight of Faëry,
> Earning bright spoils for her enchanted dome;[66]

Keats is perhaps an exceptional case whose romance narrative successfully incorporated a muse who acts as the source of inspiration for *Endymion*. The 'sovereign power' of love is the central theme of the poem; Diana, who acts both as the ideal lover of Endymion and a muse for the poet, enacts a traditional role whereby she responds to the poet's need to create a believable world; that is, of Love. The identification of the muse with a lover, which is also seen in Shelley's 'The Triumph of Life' in a more problematic guise, raises some issues surrounding the concept of a muse, as I will demonstrate later with Browning's *Sordello*.

The generic packaging of *Sordello* as a narrative romance was an intentional choice by Browning to gain a wider audience;[67] however, its disruption soon becomes clear with his numerous digressions, which in turn provide an apologia for it. The most notable divergence occurs toward the end of Book Three when Browning himself interrupts the narrative to reinstate his political stance. The significance of his suspension of narrative is explored, firstly by his comparison to 'An archimage' who conjures up a fantastic display then aborts it in order to effect greater pleasure for his audience. That Spenser's *Faerie Queene* is being glanced at seems fairly obvious in his staging of the 'archimage' providing entertainment for the 'novice-queen'.[68] Browning's immediate abandonment of such a venture ought to be understood not only on an artistic but also on a socio-political level on which the significance of his digression is eventually determined.

After an interlude of Browning's own poetics that is intermixed with Sordello's—as an antithesis of Eglamor's that 'judge the song and singer One' (iii 604)—Browning attempts to resume the poem by invoking a muse that will inspire him to continue his narrative: 'Who's adorable/ Enough reclaim a—no Sordello's Will/Alack!—be queen to me?' (iii 659–61) This is not lip service to the poetic genre in which he writes, as clearly shown by his choice firstly of the Italian peasant-girls followed by the 'sad disheveled ghost'.[69] The fact that Browning does not introduce the muse until halfway through the poem, however, complicates his intentions. There are a number of male poets and writers who are either invoked, or referred to in the poem (e.g. Dante, Cervantes, Shelley, Walter Savage Landor and Sydney), but those who fit Browning's description just quoted above would be Queen Victoria and 'My English Eyebright' (Fanny Haworth) in addition to the Italian peasant girls and the 'sad disheveled ghost'. That the central focus is on the 'ghost' is unquestionable given its significance in the re-orientation of the poem.

Browning's gesture to emulate a narrative romance is undercut by his own voice, which will not allow *Sordello* to be consumed as one: that is, the evolving aesthetics that come to fruition during the course of the composition expose his scepticism regarding the genre. In other words, Browning has little interest in delineating the life of his protagonist, which, according to some historical sources, was marked by chivalric accomplishments and romantic intrigue, the two most important factors that make up a medieval romance.[70] Instead, Browning's Sordello suffers from inaction: he starts out as an indulgent hedonist in a secluded environment, becomes Palma's minstrel by a whim only to lapse back to his original state; he attempts to enter the world of action but that also fails. It is ironic that Browning should choose a troubadour-poet of the Middle Ages for this rift; for his thematic concern is far from courtly love or knightly gallantry.[71] What alone may single out Sordello as an appropriate persona for the author is his reputed philosophical nature, which Browning exploits to the full.[72]

One of the notable differences between Browning's muse and a conventional one is that the former figure is devoid of any attractive attributes:

> You, no doubt,
> Have the true knack of tiring suitors out
> With those thin lips on tremble, lashless eyes
> Inveterately tear-shot (iii 715–18)

It is possible to read this in two ways: firstly, that poets who gave their initial commitment to the cause of the people (that is, the 'disheveled ghost' as the emblem of 'suffering humanity') eventually abandon it; or literally, that men cannot maintain their interest in a female who does not give them aesthetic pleasure. The latter reading becomes more pertinent when the narrator goes on to say that

> there, be wise
> Mistress of mine, there, there, as if I meant
> You insult! Shall *your friend (not slave)* be shent

For speaking home? Beside care-bit erased
Broken-up beauties ever took my taste
Supremely, and I love you more, far more
Than she I looked should foot Life's temple-floor—(iii 718–24)
[emphases added]

There is a strong implication here that what is being under attack is the way male poets have exploited the female in the form of a worship underpinned by self-gratifying desire.[73] The narrator's insistence on being her 'friend' separates him from a 'slave' that implies a hierarchical bind that is sexually defined. As criticisms on the male treatment of the female, either in the form of a muse or an ideal woman as the object of chivalric devotion, have demonstrated, such constructs have barely concealed the sexual economy that sustains it.[74] In other words, such acclaimed selfless devotion is dependent on the sexual desire without which it has no effect. Browning clearly takes on a feminist perspective by exposing such hidden agenda and reinstating his relationship with his muse. What he sees in the 'disheveled ghost' is not the absence of female beauty, which of course becomes tied in with male sexual desire, but the external circumstances that compelled her to undergo such change; and she thereby becomes the emblem of 'suffering humanity'. If the Romantic poets saw their muse as their aid to seek ideal beauty, then Browning is directly challenging this stance by offering himself to the service of others rather than appropriating the muse to himself.

Browning is alleged to have swerved away from his former idol Shelley by dismissing him at the beginning of the poem: 'thou, spirit, come not near/Now—nor this time desert thy cloudy place/To scare me, thus employed, with that pure face!' (i 60–2)[75] Although Browning openly disclaims him, there is much in the text to suggest that his influence is still very prominent. For example, in the quoted section above, the narrator tells the 'disheveled ghost' that he prefers her to the muse who 'should foot Life's temple-floor'. This, of course, can be taken in a general sense to mean 'dance in the temple of life',[76] but when bearing in mind the last fragment poem that Shelley wrote, it is possible to read Browning's ongoing engagement with his poetry.

Shelley's 'The Triumph of Life' as it stands is a dark vision that encapsulates the history of Western Civilisation from the Hellenic and Hebraic societies to contemporary Europe in the aftermath of the French Revolution. The subtext of the poem, however, concerns his private life and his anxiety, which he represses throughout.[77] The speaker is guided by Rousseau who narrates to him the fate of 'The Wise,//The great, the unforgotten' (81); and more importantly, tells him of his own life in the form of an allegorical dream. Rousseau, who is reduced to an 'old root' as a consequence of his disheartenment by becoming involved in the pageant of Life, serves as a warning for the speaker who is yet to awake from his dream to experience it in reality. In the culminating episode of his story, he encounters a 'Shape all light'

which with one hand did fling
Dew on the earth, as if she were the dawn,
And the invisible rain did ever sing

'A silver music on the mossy lawn;
And still before me on the dusky grass,
Iris her many-coloured scarf had drawn:

'In her right hand she bore a chrystal glass,
Mantling with bright Nepenthe; the fierce splendour
Fell from her as she moved under the mass

'Out of the deep cavern, and with palms so tender,
Their tread broke not the mirror of its billow;
She glided along the river, and did bend her

'Head under the dark boughs, till like a willow,
Her fair hair swept the bosom of the stream
That whispered with delight to be their pillow.

'As one enamoured is upborne in dream
O'er lily-paven lakes mid silver mist,
To wondrous music, so this shape might seem

'Partly to tread the waves with feet which kissed
The dancing foam; partly to glide along
The airs that roughend the moist amethyst,

'Or the slant morning beams that fell among
The trees, or the soft shadows of the trees;
And her feet, ever to the ceaseless song

'Of leaves, and winds, and waves, and birds, and bees,
And falling drops, moved to a measure new
Yet sweet, as on the summer evening breeze,

'Up from the lake a shape of golden dew
Between two rocks, athwart the rising moon,
Dances i' the wind where never eagle flew;
(*Posthumous Poems* 88–89)

What is immediately recognisable is the sensuality of the 'shape all light' who suspends Rousseau's thoughts 'between desire and shame' (89). Critics have been divided over the interpretation of the 'shape'—from an evil seductress to an emblem of the human imagination—and Shelley's use of the female figure is deliberately ambiguous. The 'shape' in the beginning seems to represent Rousseau's imagination, as demonstrated by the co-operative work of his eyes, the sun and the well, which are the counterparts of human imagination in Shelley's symbolism. Her significance, however, soon becomes questionable:

'And still her feet, no less than the sweet tune
To which they moved, seemed as they moved, to blot
The thoughts of him who gazed on them; and soon

'All that was, seemed as if it had been not;
And all the gazer's mind was strewn beneath
Her feet like embers; and she, thought by thought,

'Trampled its fires into the dust of death; (89)[78]

Rousseau responds to her shifting influence on him—from sensuality to destructiveness—by asking her a series of ontological questions—'Shew whence I came, and where I am, and why' (l. 398); she then urges him to drink from her cup, the effect of which he sees a 'Vision never seen before'. That this new vision is the pageant of Life that compels him to despair proves that irreparable damage has been done and that the 'shape' may possibly be its cause. Rousseau, however, insists on her benevolent influence:

> 'So knew I in that light's severe excess
> The presence of that shape which on the stream
> Moved, as I moved along the wilderness,
>
> 'More dimly than a day-appearing dream,
> The ghost of a forgotten form of sleep;
> A light of heaven, whose half-extinguished beam
>
> 'Through the sick day in which we wake to weep,
> Glimmers, forever sought, forever lost; (91)

Rousseau's inconsistent narrative makes it impossible to interpret the 'shape' as denoting either the good or the evil: as her initial existence owes to Rousseau's own visual participation, her moral valorisation is dependent on Rousseau's interpretation. After claiming that 'like day she came,/Making the night a dream', he says that 'the fair shape waned in the coming light/As veil by veil the silent splendour drops/From Lucifer, amid the chrysolite//Of sunrise' (90). The deliberate reversal of her attributes in the space of a few lines demonstrates how self-contradictory his testimony is.

Paul de Man has introduced a groundbreaking reading of the poem by suggesting that there is no causal sequence involved in this scene and that the 'shape' 'as the figure for the figurality of all signification' dramatises the inevitable erasure of its own imposition, which he calls disfiguration.[79] It is also worthwhile deliberating why this trope takes a female form. De Man's argument, which focuses on the duplicity of thought—that is, 'thought's empire over thought' that 'destroys thought in its attempt to forget its duplicity'—is pertinent to the narcissistic use of the female in Shelley's poetry.[80] Its genealogy can be traced back to the 'veiled maiden' of *Alastor* whose 'voice was like the voice of his own soul/Heard in the calm of thought' (*Posthumous Poems* 274) and Cythna in *The Revolt of Islam* who adopts her lover's name and becomes the female Laone.[81] Shelley furthermore provides us with his own definition of Love, which is clearly defined by narcissistic desire:

> We dimly see within our intellectual nature a miniature as it were of our entire self, yet deprived of all that we condemn or despise, the ideal prototype of every thing excellent or lovely that we are capable of conceiving as belonging to the nature of man. Not only the portrait of our external being, but an assemblage of the minutest particulars of which our nature is composed: a mirror whose surface reflects only the forms of purity and brightness: a soul within our soul that describes a circle around its proper Paradise which pain and sorrow or evil dare not overleap. To this we eagerly refer all sensations, thirsting that they should resemble or correspond with it.[82]

In other words, 'Love tends' to its antitype that can be found in another, who is equipped 'with an understanding [...] an imagination [...] a frame' like our own that corresponds 'in such proportion as the type within demands' (504).

As recent feminist criticism has highlighted, the Freudian model of narcissistic desire is based on a phallogocentric construct of the subject that precludes women as the Other. Whereas man has no choice but to forsake 'the narcissistic perfection of his childhood' when he grows up and becomes 'disturbed by the admonitions of others and by the awaking of his own critical judgment', women remain in their narcissistic bliss. According to Freud, it is this narcissistic 'essence of woman' that attracts and invites the male to project his 'ego ideal' onto her.[83] The problematic way in which the female becomes unwritten in this equation is where feminist criticism has most to say.[84] Luce Irigaray, for example, comments on the absence of the female sex that is not only relevant to the writings of Freud but also to the way language has heretofore operated:

> We are luminous. Neither one nor two. I've never known how to count. Up to you. In their calculations, we make two. Really, two? Doesn't that make you laugh? An odd sort of two. And yet not one. Especially not one. Let's leave *one* to them: their oneness, with its prerogatives, its domination, its solipsism: like the sun's. And the strange way they divide up their couples, with the other as the image of the one. Only an image. So any move toward the other means turning back to the attraction of one's own mirage. A (scarcely) living mirror, she/it is frozen, mute. More lifelike. The ebb and flow of our lives spent in the exhausting labor of copying, miming. Dedicated to re-producing—that sameness in which we have remained for centuries, as the other. (207)

Shelley's self-gratifying depiction of the female therefore inevitably destroys itself as a figment of the poet's imagination at best, and more problematically as 'the unattainable reflection and completion of the male ego'.[85]

Browning, as he repudiates the solipsistic poet of *Alastor* in *Sordello*, equally condemns the Shelleyan muse as a projection of masculine egotism. It is apt that his muse should figure as a 'ghost', for the ideal woman as the muse in the works of his Romantic predecessors exists only to the extent that she aids the poet in his pursuit of self-completion and thereby is given no entity of her own. Browning recovers the female voice, which is often erased at the end of such a narrative, enabling the male-ego to re-assert itself. By so doing, he subtly condemns the irresponsibility of such a self-gratifying act and his deliberate choice not to partake in the repeated act of complicity to exploit the female becomes the radical stance of his romance. The 'ghost' does not merely remain as an emblem but is also given a human voice; for, in fact, she retorts to the poet's depiction of her as 'ravishingest lady' as his response makes clear: 'And hear/Me out before you say it is to sneer/I call you ravishing' (iii 745–7). Under the same token, 'suffering humanity', which reveals itself in the masses, historically had no place in romance let alone could hope to be the source of its inspiration. It seems fairly clear that Browning is keen to re-write the tradition of romance and its political as well as gender implications: if traditional romance dealt with the lives of the nobility alone within the secure confines of the feudal system, then *Sordello* introduces a democratic impulse that is mediated through Italian republicanism.[86]

Following the lead of the Romantics for their feminisation of the male protagonist, Browning also characterises Sordello as a sensitive youth who is primarily a poet (although he temporarily enters into the world of action in vain) rather than a valiant knight. Browning reverses the stereotypical gender assumptions so that, in *Sordello*, the female (such as Adelaide and Palma) represents the sterility of power-crazed ambition whereas the male characters demonstrate sensibility and even vulnerability. Not only does Browning experiment by upsetting some of the conventional expectations of a romance, but he also mobilises gender roles so that they can be adopted by either of the sexes.

Browning attempts to redefine his audience and his relation to them by summoning a fraternal community at the beginning of the poem. He uses 'friend' and 'brother' in order to address his elected audience throughout the poem as a strategic means to establish a writer-reader relationship based on love and co-operation. That this is an alternative stance to the Romantic bard as 'a nightingale, who sits in darkness, and sings to cheer its own solitude with sweet sounds' or 'the unacknowledged legislator[s] of the World' who heralds 'the awakening of a great people' clearly signifies his divergence from Shelley.[87] Yet, Browning's revisionary attempt at Shelley's poetics does not stop here: by inserting 'the disheveled ghost', Browning humanises his poetic exercise and thereby makes accessible the inaccessibility of his poetics. If it remains inaccessible, it is only because the reader is neglecting his/her duty just as Browning must appropriate himself to the 'ghost' in order to serve his muse:

> Ah, had I, judge,
> Or no, your secret? Rough apparel—*grudge*
> All ornaments save tag or tassel worn

To hint we are not thoroughly forlorn—
Slouch bonnet, *unloop* mantle, *careless go*
Alone (that's saddest but it must be so)
Through Venice, *sing now* and *now glance aside*,
Aught desultory or undignified,
And, ravishingest lady, will you pass
Or not each formidable group, the mass
Before the Basilike (that feast gone by,
God's day, the great June Corpus Domini)
And wistfully foregoing proper men
Come timid up to me for alms? (iii 729–42)
[emphases added]

As imperatives such as 'grudge', 'Slouch', 'unloop', 'go', and 'sing' demonstrate, Browning specifically states what he should do to attract the 'ghost': it is only because he has discovered the secret, which he puts into practice, that he is able to gain his muse. Browning gives a different sense here to the act of tapping the source of poetic inspiration. If Shelley's 'shape all light' was the last celebratory act of the imagination that deified man, it was also a reminder of his inescapable mortality. The futility of aiming to achieve godhead as demonstrated by Sordello himself in the poem instead leads Browning to the palpable, the real, lives of people whom he must study in order to discover the secret mechanism by which they work. Unlike his predecessors, whom the muse favours for their beauty or intellectual pursuits, his encounter with the 'ghost' has a religious significance: Browning's recognition of the 'suffering humanity' as the overriding importance in his poetic subject becomes tied in with Moses who effectively 'smites/The rock' (iii 800–1) and proves his accessibility to true enlightenment. For fear of arrogance of having compared himself to Moses, Browning initiates another argument that levels men (including himself) as being preoccupied in the same task of constructing 'an engine' that is life. Browning's democratising impulse is grounded on his religious faith, which humbles him to embrace his shared humanity with others: the 'ghost' acts as a catalyst to the poet who self-willingly but unknowingly (as regards its significance) adopts that gesture.

Politics

Sordello emulates the polemics put forward by the radicals of the early nineteenth century in their attempt to re-orient themselves in the aftermath of the French Revolution. The extent to which the liberal cause had suffered as a consequence of the bloody terror that succeeded the Revolution cannot be overemphasised: it was enough to convince the first-generation Romantics to renege on their radicalism; the poetry of Byron and Shelley was defined, to a large extent, by the legacy of their predecessors' abandonment of the liberal cause, and by their struggle against the reactionary climate of the nineteenth century. Although Victorianism is perceived as a cultural force that no longer directly concerns the radicalism of the 1790s, it owes much of its political and philosophical debate to the re-orientation of ideas and attitudes that took place in the first three decades of the nineteenth century. Radicalism in the 1830s, of which Browning was one of the leading spokesmen, was a continuation, therefore, of the Romantic endeavour to salvage liberalism in a climate that was decidedly hostile and discouraging to those who promoted it.[88] My objective is to localise that influence by examining the works of the Shelleys in comparison to *Sordello*.

As I have argued in the previous sections, Shelley's continuing influence and presence in *Sordello* makes it only natural that some of his political ideas should emerge in the poem. Although little (if any) commentary has been made on the literary influence of Mary Shelley's writings on Browning, *Valperga* shares much of the thematic preoccupation, not to mention the historic setting, of *Sordello*. Also, in considering the politics of the Shelleys, Godwin's radicalism based on gradualism deserves full attention.

The need to commit oneself politically in order to sustain gradual social progress runs as a leitmotif in the last three books of *Sordello*: after Sordello's awakening to republican Rome as the archetype of an ideal polity that must be recreated, he learns that it can only be realised by an accumulation of gradual efforts through the course of successive historical stages. To a certain extent, he suffers from being placed prematurely in time and cannot carve out a heroic role for himself, as Dante was able to. Browning introduces the idea that historical leaders in the past have merely been the effect of a collective power that only matures with time in order to emphasise 'that collective man/Outstrips the individual!' (v 95–6).[89] Browning neither devises nor undermines the achievements of great men; but he also refuses to overlook the contribution of unknown people in the process of shaping history. In outlining the two dominant political forces that were led and inspired by Charlemagne and Hildebrand, Browning reminds the readers that

> —but, link on link,
> Why is it neither chain betrays a chink?
> How coalesce the small and great? Alack,
> For one thrust forward, fifty such fall back! (v 179–82)

In other words, without the continuous efforts of the numerous unknown people who carried out the will of great men such as Charlemagne and Hildebrand, there would not have been any progress; it would merely have been a collection of isolated individuals however great they might have been. Although the argument concerning the interactive relationship between individual and collective power would have been topical enough for Browning in the thirties (for instance, through Mill), he would have already encountered the idea in the writings of Shelley, who took pains to illustrate the importance of collective enlightenment in the face of political progress.

Shelley's central enterprise was to engage with the public with the intention of providing a rationale that would explain the cause of the failure of the French Revolution so that the public may have a more active role in the future making of societal changes. *Revolt of Islam* was the first of such attempts. In the 'Preface' to the originally titled *Laon and Cythna*, Shelley makes it clear from the very beginning that it is 'an experiment on the temper of the public mind', the intention of which is not to court a popular audience. The 'Preface', however, carefully manipulates the way in which the poem ought to be read by providing a guideline that will discriminate readers who hold 'a virtuous enthusiasm for those doctrines of liberty and justice' from those who do not (32). It is on those whose 'faith and hope in something good' are alive that its polemic would have any effect. Shelley importantly assigns the cause of the failure of the French Revolution to the discrepancy between existing knowledge and action:

> The French Revolution may be considered as one of those manifestations of a general state of feeling among civilized mankind, produced by a defect of correspondence between the knowledge existing in society and the improvement, or gradual abolition of political institutions. (ix)

If such a polemic should be applied to the reading of *Sordello*, then it can be said that what Sordello psychologically undergoes—from his conception of 'Rome' to its collapse followed by his realisation of the need to commit himself to a cause that will only materialise itself gradually—*is* the liberalist struggle of the early nineteenth century, as Shelley understood it:

> Can he who the day before was a trampled slave, suddenly become liberal-minded, forbearing, and independent? This is the consequence of the habits of a state of society to be produced by resolute perseverance and indefatigable hope, and long-suffering and long believing courage, and the systematic efforts of generation of men of intellect and virtue. Such is the lesson which experience teaches now. But on the first reverses of hope in the progress of French liberty, the sanguine eagerness for good overleapt the solution of these questions, and for a time extinguished itself in the unexpectedness of their result. Thus many of the most ardent and tender-hearted of the worshippers of public good, have been morally ruined by what a partial glimpse of the events they deplored, appeared to shew as the melancholy desolation of all their cherished hopes. Hence gloom and misanthropy have become the characteristics of the age in which we live, the solace of a disappointment that unconsciously finds relief only in the wilful exaggeration of its own despair. [. . .] But mankind appear to me to be emerging from their trance. I am aware, methinks, of a slow, gradual, silent change. (x–xii)

Sordello reiterates the pessimistic view one is prone to adopt in the seemingly hopeless contest of the 'enthusiastic sort' against 'The careless tribe':

> Remark
> Why schemes wherein cold-blooded men embark
> Prosper, when your enthusiastic sort
> Fails: for these last are ever stopping short—
> (Much to be done—so little they can do!)
> The careless tribe see nothing to pursue
> Should they desist; meantime their scheme succeeds.
> (iv 823–9)

In *Sordello*, the re-orientation of political and philosophical radicalism in favour of gradualism becomes internalised so that the transition takes place within the mind of Sordello. The extent to which the visionary failure of the Revolution scarred and immobilised the liberal imagination can account for the paralytic state in which the protagonist remains for most part of the poem; however, Sordello is not entirely static and the small (of external visibility) yet profound progress within that he does make is what may count as the 'slow, gradual, silent change'.

Both P.B. Shelley's 'The Triumph of Life' and Mary Shelley's *Valperga* can be read in the light of early nineteenth-century politics—mainly as a response to the Revolutionary failure and as a reflection of the impasse into which liberal imagination had fallen. In so doing, they create a dichotomy between 'Men of Action' (v 414) and philosophers/poets: history reads as a tragedy—a pageant that consists of those who possess power or knowledge (but rarely the two combined), and those who have neither (as in the masses). Browning likewise dramatises this dichotomy in the confrontation scene that takes place between Salinguerra and Sordello: Salinguerra, in response to Sordello's plea to work for the Guelph cause, scorns his politics as being 'a trite censure of the minstrel tribe' (v 392). Salinguerra's dismissal of Sordello as one of the 'burr-heads for the joust' as opposed to the 'spear-heads for battle' (v 394) is the legacy of the failure of Romantic poets to successfully integrate their poetry into politics. The threat for poets to be classified as mere 'dreamers' is voiced most prominently in Keats's 'The Fall of Hyperion', for example. The speaker of that poem undergoes a visionary transformation after which he is brought into contact with Moneta, the mother of the muses, who, in response to the speaker's probing questions, addresses him as 'a dreaming thing/A fever of thyself' (i 168–9). Keats's anxiety to prove otherwise is voiced through the speaker:

> tell me: sure not all
> Those melodies sung into the world's ear
> Are useless; sure a poet is a sage,
> A humanist, physician to all Men.[90] (i 187–90)

The need to retain the poet's role in the social arena is echoed in *Sordello*, however, with a difference that moves beyond the mapping of two camps—men of action and poets/philosophers.

As part of his gradualist schema, Browning discourses on the significance of time and what is materially accomplishable in it, as opposed to the infinite moment that is self-contained. Sordello's inability, or unwillingness, to commit himself to the former, instead of fantasising over the latter, is the fatal mistake he makes:

> Sordello, wake!
> Where is the vanity? Why count you, one
> The first step with the last step? What is gone
> Except that aery magnificence—
> That last step you took first? (v 84–88)[91]

Sordello must learn to take 'The first step' if he seeks to achieve 'men's whole work'. Underlying the emphasis laid on the temporal is Browning's faith in societal progress, glossed through the privileged vantage point of the nineteenth century over the preceding ages. If primitive societies were based on the principle of 'Strength by stress/Of strength' (v 126–7), then a more advanced society supersedes it in its gradual transition from 'strength' to 'knowledge': 'still by stress/Of Strength, work

Knowledge! (v 168–9). Although Browning is able to place partial historical judgments on past events, such as the 'People's Crusade' ('trick of breeding strength by other aid/Than strength [v 188–89]) and the formation of the 'Lombard League' ('trick of turning strength/Against pernicious strength' [v 191–2])—both examples of political progressiveness—he is unable to negotiate 'that second road' by which 'Knowledge by stress of Knowledge' (v 201) becomes accomplished. It indicates a future condition yet to be realised while 'for the next age/Or two, of Knowledge, part by Strength and part/By Knowledge!' (v 216–7).

The pessimism that lies at the heart of 'The Triumph of Life' and *Valperga* derives from their historical outlook, which compels them to see history as being essentially cyclic: in 'The Triumph', Rousseau imposes upon the speaker his view of 'Life', which is to despair at the human folly that recurs throughout history; by allowing the power-crazed Castruccio to lay siege to peace-loving Valperga without any salvation for Euthanasia, Mary Shelley infers Napoleon's usurpation of power as the most recent example that overshadowed liberal aspiration. Although Browning shares a cyclic outlook on history to a certain degree when he discourses on 'strength' and 'grace' that dominate alternately (v 106–111) past literary scenes, he also emphasises the progress that has been made in his deliberate distancing from the Middle Ages.[92] The readers are not invited merely to experience historical repetition, but also to discriminate what exactly makes them contemporaries against the medieval world. On both literary and societal levels, we are led to believe that things *have* progressed despite human shortcomings. Browning does not allow the absolute state of idealism to become the measuring stick for the real world and insists on focusing on the relative value by comparing the past with the present.

History is portrayed as a tragedy in 'The Triumph' and *Valperga* because they seek an apocalyptic transition from a society based on 'strength' to one based on 'knowledge'. They suggest, furthermore, that this societal change lies in the hands of few individuals whose level of enlightenment defines the course of history. Browning counters the emphasis they place on individual power by critiquing Sordello's will to self-fulfilment: the poet-protagonist's mistaken identity as the godhead discourages him from accepting his limited historical role. In his oscillation between collectivism and individualism, Browning dramatises the dynamics of the interrelationship as that of co-operation rather than contestation.

Browning challenges the Shelleys' understanding of history by creating a poet who was, historically speaking, also a man of action, unlike Dante. The significance of his choice and his development of the protagonist is that Browning does not share the Shelleys' aversion to men of action. In fact, he values Sordello's potential contribution as combining poet and politician. In the greater framework of the poem, Salinguerra is Sordello's other half who represents the Dionysian energy that will complement his Apollonian reason.[93] It is only when the two converge that successful political action can be taken: Sordello lacks the passion and volition to act with which Salinguerra pursues Romano's interest, whereas Salinguerra does not have a rational motive for committing himself to the Ghibelline party other than revenge for having been deprived of his first bride. That Browning took equal pains to delineate the character of Salinguerra attests to the significance of his role in relation to Sordello.

Sordello's failure to make something of his given opportunity is given a different meaning from that of Euthanasia in *Valperga*. Mary Shelley in no way suggests that Euthanasia should have married Castruccio to weaken his tyrannical actions; rather, she criticises such a lack of integrity in Beatrice, who expresses her wish to do so if given the chance.[94] Mary Shelley's criticism is mainly targeted at Castruccio, who fails to exploit his prowess to work for a better cause. To convert potential Castruccio figures into enlightened individuals who are able to embrace liberty and peace (as in the case of Euthanasia) is the overriding motive of the novel; it is to this end that Mary Shelley devotes her analysis of Castruccio's character and the environment that contributed to its formation. The tragedy of the novel lies in Castruccio's unrestrained passion for power that dehumanises him in the end. Mary Shelley's critique becomes targeted at the inhumanity that politics can be reduced to when it loses sight of its primary objectives (i.e. to serve the people):

> It is strange, that man, born to suffering, and often writhing beneath it, should wantonly inflict pain on his fellows; but however cruel an

> individual may be, no one is so remorseless as a ruler; for he loses even within himself the idea of his own individuality, and fancies that, in pampering his inclinations, and revenging his injuries, he is supporting the state; the state, a fiction, which sacrifices that which constitutes it, to the support of its mere name. (176)

In his 'Sonnet: Political Greatness', Shelley reiterates Mary Shelley's scepticism toward a ruler whose will is to extend power over others:

> Man who man would be,
> Must rule the empire of himself; in it
> Must be supreme, establishing his throne
> On vanquished will, quelling the anarchy
> Of hopes and fears, being himself alone.[95]

If will to power signifies a temptation that should be averted as in the case of the Shelleys, then Browning unravels a complicated argument that is in direct response to this problem by questioning Sordello's rash attempt to 'dash/This badge to earth and all it brought' (vi 193–4). Browning does not readily excuse Sordello for opting out from taking political responsibility:

> Before
> He dashes it, however, think once more!
> For, was that little truly service? Ay—
> I' the end, no doubt; but meantime? (vi 197–200)

Sordello engages in the very question of how to forward the liberal cause precisely when placed in an adverse position as in the case of Sordello. Browning does not speculate on the possibility of turning Salinguerra into a crusader for the people as Mary Shelley implies with Castruccio; rather, Browning is more interested in probing a realistic outlet that can *lessen* rather than *solve* the dilemma.

As Sordello acts out Browning's political re-orientation in books iv to vi, the reader is faced with a dilemma that is not easy to solve: for Browning does not make it entirely clear what Sordello should have done when compelled to choose between his loyalty to the Guelph cause and his acceptance of the badge that would have ensured his becoming the Imperial Perfect, thereby enabling him to exercise power freely.[96] That the ideal polity, in the form of a republican state, had been overshadowed by the failure of the French Revolution does much to account for the criticism that is directed at the construction of 'Rome' in the poem, is clear; Browning reiterates, for example, what Shelley had already articulated in the preface to *The Revolt of Islam* by alerting himself and his protagonist to the pitfall of believing that Rome was built in a day. Even if Browning's gradualist stance begs no explanation, still the means by which one is to achieve such an end is ambiguous. Browning presents a scenario that fails either way: Sordello would have most likely been corrupted by power had he accepted the badge; yet, due to his abdication of power, he gave way to Eccelin III, who notoriously tyrannised his people and pillaged the land, and thereby deterred the social progress from taking place. Then what was Sordello to do?

Sordello reflects to a large degree the actual political scene of the 1830s during which the poem took its shape. The radicalism that gained momentum around the Reform Act of 1832 but considerably lost its life-source soon after the turn of the decade to be absorbed by a more class-based movement (such as the Chartism) has much to do with the complicated status in which radicalism features in the poem. The philosophic radicals who took active initiative in agitating public opinion on behalf of the 'people' were those who were most closely associated with the parliamentary activities and informed the public through the periodical press such as the *Westminster Review*. The philosophic radicals were faced with a dilemma that would prove frustrating either way: if they held to the integrity and independence of their ambition to see progress of liberal reform and be the agents through which this reform would be achieved, then this would mean allowing the Tories to gain office and losing their opportunity of further reform, however small and slow this might be; if on the other hand, they were to commit themselves to reform regardless of its scale or agent, then they would have to support the Whig government on their own terms. Consequently, they adopted hostile rhetoric and aggressive tactics to guarantee their independence from the

Whigs; however, they had no choice but to support the Whig government when faced with no alternative way to press on with reform. The ultimate failure of their attempt to realign existing parties by creating a new radical party have something in common with the fate Browning imposed on Sordello's political career: the philosophic radicals were acting prematurely in time and could not herald the next political stage whereby the masses would actively take part in supporting parliamentary reform. As much as this failure is owing to an illusionary belief in the existence of 'the people', Sordello's can be explained by the collapse of communication (i.e. his inability to convey his ideals to Salinguerra and Palma).

On a different level, the problem of power seems to have fascinated Browning as he repeatedly dealt with it in works such as *Strafford, King Victor and King Charles, The Return of the Druses, Colombe's Birthday, Parleying with George Bubb Dodington*. In these works, Browning raises questions either about the nature of leadership (i.e. its accession and retention), apostasy, or the interrelationship between one's public and private will. That Browning was deeply sceptical of a political leader in the way that the Shelleys were is obvious:[97]

> Even when their impulse to lead appears in itself noble and disinterested, they find themselves, once in or near power, compelled to degrade their own integrity and deceive their followers in order to maintain their position. (Woolford 1988, p. 17)

In *Sordello*, this dilemma (i.e. one's access to power is crucial in order to make political changes; but at the same time, it also puts one's integrity in danger) is not solved, nor does Browning provide a definite answer to this problem in his later works. What deserves attention is the urgency with which he stressed the significance of retaining one's social and political responsibility; anything that falls short of that becomes a target of his critique.

As the exercise of one's political power becomes translated into a question of one's moral integrity, similarly, the combat between 'strength' and 'knowledge' that determine one's societal progress depends upon the level of spirituality that each age manifests in the form of (a) political action(s). That Christianity is bound up with political radicalism in *Sordello* is hardly surprising given the role Christianity played in the socialist movement of the nineteenth century.[98] What deserves attention, however, is Browning's swerve away from Shelleyan radicalism that owes much to the tradition of eighteenth-century materialism, in order to embrace political progressiveness that is inspired by the Bible.[99] The evolution of Sordello's political views does not take place solely under the Enlightenment ethos that informs Rousseau in 'The Triumph' or Euthanasia in *Valperga*. Sordello follows the Guelph cause not only because of his republican sympathies but also because it recognises the significance of spiritual authority over a secular one. The Enlightenment ethos that promotes the idea of human perfection is undermined by Christian humility that obliges one to realise the fractured and imperfect state of life in which it remains; therefore one must not

> to display completely here
> The mastery another life should learn,
> Thrusting in time eternity's concern (i 564–6)[100]

Although such a visionary end sought by the Enlightenment thinkers should not be abandoned, one ought to seek its realisation in human terms. As Browning rightly expressed his work as concerning 'the development of the soul', *Sordello* does not merely relate the rite of passage to become a republican poet but also a Christian poet.[101] What motivates Sordello to reconfirm his humanism, which thereby collapses his sense of self-importance, is the scene of human devastation caused by the pillage of Ferrara (iv 332ff). Sordello's eventual commitment to the fate of the people over Salinguerra and Palma's dynastic pursuit signifies a democratic impulse that is based on the Bible.[102] Nor does Sordello strive after a Godwinian Utopia where enlightened citizens govern themselves without the imposition of secular institutions; rather, it is a just society that is inspired by one's Christian faith. The motivating factor of choosing republicanism over imperialism is that, as a social infrastructure, it best resembles the teaching of Christ.

Sordello's rite of passage to become a poet of the people is to first recognise the 'idea of the Incarnation of Christ as the basis of his own creativity':[103]

> A Power above him still
> Which, utterly incomprehensible,
> Is out of rivalry, which thus he can
> Love, tho' unloving all conceived by Man—
> What need! And of—none the minutest duct
> To that out-Nature, nought that would instruct
> And so let rivalry begin to live—
> But of a Power its representative
> Who, being for authority the same,
> Communication different, should claim
> A course the first chose and this last revealed—
> This Human clear, as that Divine concealed—
> The utter need! (vi 589–601)

Sordello's mistake was to assume an identity that was beyond his rivalry (i.e. the godhead); rather, he should have worked out his creativity in human terms in a similar manner to the Incarnation of Christ, which represents divinity in a human form.

It is significant that Browning saw the main power struggle in history in terms of secular and religious strife, which accounts for his characterisation of Sordello's potential as a socially committed Christian poet. Such re-orientation of Enlightenment radical philosophy, which was secular in nature, develops into the Christian socialism of the nineteenth century whereby political action and spirituality can sit comfortably together. The most immediate example of this for Browning would have been W.J. Fox and his *Monthly Repository*, which contributed to the dissemination of political radicalism and Christianity (dissenting) as a combined cultural force. In view of Shelley's influence on Browning, his most significant challenge to Shelley occurs here when Browning rejects his materialist adhesion to reason as the underlying principle of levelling politics, but instead substitutes for it the Bible. Browning's political radicalism cannot be understood without taking into account his Christian faith; in that sense, *Sordello* is as much about spiritual regeneration as it is about the revamping of political liberalism.

Rome and Venice

In *Sordello*, Browning makes full use of 'place' in its geographical as well as symbolic signification.[104] For example, Sordello initially emerges from, and returns to, Goito, a womblike haven where he is allowed to indulge in his own narcissistic world. Within a political framework, cities are divided into either Guelph or Ghibelline strongholds; the demarcation of the two camps, however, often becomes violated, which offers material for tragedy, as in the case of Sordello.[105] What is surprising given Browning's choice of Sordello as his poet-protagonist, which was most likely inspired by his account given by Dante in *The Divine Comedy*, is that Browning makes little use of Sordello as a Mantuan poet.[106] As Browning's numerous historical digressions attest to motives other than factual faithfulness, Sordello is made into a troubadour whose potential not only rivals the artistic achievements of Dante and Petrarch, but also Rienzi's political aspiration.[107] That 'Rome' signifies an idea inherent in Sordello is Browning's own making; it is calculated to elevate the troubadour from a purely regional celebrity to that of a more universal one even if it was confined to his potential.[108] What is more, Browning's use of 'Rome' and 'Venice' directly draws on the works of the Romantics—namely Byron and Shelley.

My reason for focusing on 'Rome' and 'Venice' is that although they do not literally figure in the story of the poem, they become its cruces. When Browning breaks off from his narrative in Book iii, the first thing he informs the reader is of the locale: 'I sung this on an empty palace-step/At Venice' (iii 656–57). This break, the significance of which becomes assimilated into the story itself in the following Books, is solely dependent on Browning's direct experience of Venice. In other words, what Browning was later to develop in Sordello when witnessing the devastation of Ferrara owes its inspiration to his own encounter with Venice. Furthermore, it is a mediated one that evokes the speaker of

Byron's *Childe Harold.* Just as 'Venice' can be associated with Byron, it is equally useful to examine Browning's conceptualisation of 'Rome' in the light of Shelley's works. For the latter, with its strong tradition of Roman republicanism and imperialism, it might seem a needless analogy at first glance; however, it is pertinent that, after all, Browning's initial high regard for Shelley's poetry as works of idealism par excellence (e.g. *Prometheus Unbound*) did provide an immediate example for the metaphor of 'Rome' as an ideal polity. It is my objective to re-examine Browning's engagement with Shelley and Byron.

Browning's immediate model for his idea of reconstructing 'Rome' (i.e. of republican Rome) would most likely have been Edward Bulwer-Lytton's *Rienzi*, which was published in 1835. Rienzi, as depicted by Bulwer-Lytton, must have struck a chord in Browning who was then attempting a narrative of a troubadour, renowned for his poetry and prowess. Rienzi was, above all, a scholar, who was not only able to use the past as a means to the future, but who effectively used poetry as the vehicle to influence the public:

> The wonderful rise of Rienzi had excited an extraordinary enthusiasm in his favour through all the free populations of Italy. And this had been yet more kindled and inflamed by the influential eloquence of Petrarch, who, at that time, possessed of a power greater than ever, before or since, (not even excepting the Sage of Ferney), wielded by a single literary man, and had put forth his boldest genius in behalf of the Roman Tribune. (211)

It deserves attention how Bulwer-Lytton refers to Petrarch as the advocator of liberty and a vital accompaniment to Rienzi's political leadership throughout the novel. That literary scholarship and sensibility seem vital in recreating the ideal polity of republican Rome owes its articulation to Shelley: by elevating the status of a poet to that of a seer or even to that of 'the unacknowledged legislator of the world,' Shelley argues in *A Defence of Poetry* that '[t]he most unfailing herald, companion, and follower of the awakening of a great people to work a beneficial change in opinion or institution, is Poetry' (*SPP* 535). In the context in which Shelley advocates the poets (i.e. not necessarily as versifiers but those who appertain to the laws shared by them), it is particularly useful to look at Mary Shelley's *Valperga*, which delivers a similar kind of apotheosis of poetry. Dante figures as the equivalent of Petrarch in *Rienzi*, whose poetry becomes the breathing spirit of the republican Florentines, including the heroine, Euthanasia:

> I must date my enthusiasm for the liberties of my country, and the political welfare of Italy, from the repetition of these Cantos of Dante's poem. The Romans, whose writings I adored, were free; a Greek who once visited us, had related to us what treasures of poetry and wisdom existed in his language, and these were the productions of freemen: the mental history of the rest of the world who are slaves, was a blank, and thus I was irresistibly forced to connect wisdom and liberty together; and, as I worshipped wisdom as the pure emanation of the Deity, the divine light of the world, so did I adore liberty as its parent, its sister, the half of its being. Florence was free, and Dante was a Florentine; none but a freeman could have poured forth the poetry and eloquence to which I listened: what though he were banished from his native city, and had espoused a party that seemed to support tyranny; *the essence of freedom is that clash and struggle which awaken the energies of our nature, and that operation of the elements of our mind, which as it were gives us the force and power that hinder us from degenerating, as they say all things earthly do when not regenerated by change.* (81–82) [emphases added]

Mary Shelley's argument over 'the essence of freedom' is not merely to justify Dante, who was a Ghibelline and therefore a supporter of the Emperor: rather than defining it by the political banner (which was often taken up arbitrarily depending on one's convenience), she judges it on the basis of one's breadth of mind. That poets are regarded as best at qualifying to maintain such a level of mental freedom, again, reiterates Shelley's argument in the *Defence*.

Given Browning's leaning towards Shelley, and the influence which the second-generation Romantics exerted over the early Victorians, it is not difficult to rationalise why Browning was tempted to politicise *Sordello*. If one compares it with a work of an exact same title concerning the life of Sordello, published in 1837, by Mrs. Busk, it is fairly clear that

Browning is working under a different set of objectives than to tell a love-romance of a troubadour. Browning sets Sordello apart from others, not only by his lethargic seclusion, but also by the breadth of his mind. Salinguerra, Palma, Ecelin, and the rest are depicted as characters whose minds are set in a framework that disables them from seeing things in any other light but in their own; it is only Sordello whose mind undergoes significant change, from an egocentric hedonist to a humanitarian philanthropist, because he *is* capable of change. What becomes problematic is when Sordello chooses to retain his mental freedom from the shackles of power that will lead to his spiritual degeneration.[109] Bulwer-Lytton explores the consequences of Rienzi's seizure of power, however, with a more sympathetic reading than is usually given to the downfall of the tribune. More emphasis is placed on the selfishness and cruelty of the barons, on the one hand, and the self-interested ignorance of the masses, on the other, which make them a ready prey to individuals who exploit their weaknesses to their own ends.[110] The historical outlook of both *Rienzi* and *Valperga* best resembles a pageant that repeats its tragedy throughout the course of history.[111]

Such reading of history is precisely what comes under attack in *Sordello*. Browning does not commend Sordello's narrow escape from spiritual corruption; rather, he condemns him for his irresponsibility in forsaking the people. Browning does not look to others (i.e. Salinguerra, Palma, and the Ferrarese) in order to defend Sordello's failure, and is much subtler than Bulwer-Lytton in placing judgment on the ignorant masses: he does not willingly partake in denigrating their human value, as Bulwer-Lytton is prone to do.[112] Again, Browning advocates gradualism with a faith that time and effort would bear fruit in social progress:

What difference betwixt
This Rome and ours? Resemblance what between
The scurvy dumb-show and the pageant sheen—
These Romans and our rabble? Rest thy wit
And listen: step by step,—a workman fit
With each, nor too fit,—to one's task, one's time,—
No leaping o'er the petty to the prime,

When just the substituting osier lithe
For bulrushes, and after, wood for withe
To further loam and roughcast work a stage,
Exacts an architect, exacts an age,—
Nor tables of the Mauritianian tree
For men whose maple-log's their luxury,—
And Rome's accomplished! (v 46–59)

In the succeeding lines, Browning introduces a voice of those who claim that it is 'Better (say you) merge/At once all workmen in the demiurge,/All epochs in a life-time, and all tasks/In one' (v 59- 62) to emphasise the shortcoming of Sordello's vision that seeks to transform the world overnight: ''twas happy to conceive/Rome on sudden' but 'for the rest, her spite/Is an old story' (v 67–8, 69–70). As Latané argues, Browning's critique is aimed at the Romantic construct of 'Rome' that is dependent on an 'apocalyptic or utopian, that attempts to evaporate history's contingencies' (Latané 1987, p. 89), the most notable example of which is Shelley's *Prometheus Unbound.*

In the 'Preface' to *Prometheus Unbound*, Shelley explains the objective of his drama, which is to 'produce a systematical history of what appear to me to be the genuine elements of human society' (xiv). It is, furthermore, a revolutionary history, whether one interprets it as being political or psychological, that is grounded on the author's 'passion for reforming the world'. In so doing, the drama draws its inspiration from the ancient ruins of Rome, as the author specifies in the 'Preface'. What is of particular interest is the way in which Shelley stages his composition:

> This Poem [*Prometheus Unbound*] was chiefly written upon the mountainous ruins of the Baths of Caracalla, among the flowery glades, and thickets of odoriferous blossoming trees, which are extended in ever winding labyrinths upon its immense platforms and dizzy arches suspended in the air. The bright blue sky of Rome, and the effect of the vigorous awakening of spring in that divinest climate, and the new life with which it drenches the spirits even to intoxication, were the inspiration of this drama. (ix)

This account, despite its striking image of Rome, does not add up to Shelley's compositional record: Kelvin Everest argues that his 'emphasis on the Roman spring of 1819 as the inspiration for the drama is however misleading' (Everest 2000, p. 457). If this were the case, it would mean that Shelley's staging for his cosmological drama was an intentional device; it would make sense to have his epic, which concerns the liberation of Prometheus from the tyranny of Jupiter grounded in a soil that stood as an emblem of two forces (i.e. liberty and tyranny). Mary Shelley reinforces this point by again stressing the importance of their Roman experience in connection with Shelley's epic drama:

> At last, when at Rome, during a bright and beautiful Spring, he gave up his whole time to the composition. The spot selected for his study was, as he mentions in his preface, the mountainous ruins of the Baths of Caracalla. [. . .] The charm of the Roman climate helped to clothe his thoughts in greater beauty than they had ever worn before. And, as he wandered among the ruins made one with nature in their decay, or gazed on the Praxitelean shapes that throng the Vatican, the Capitol, and the palaces of Rome, his soul imbibed forms of loveliness which became a portion of itself.[113]

For the Shelleys, among other Romantics, 'Rome' becomes 'a contemporary trope for history itself' and 'a representation of the atemporal Ideal, and as the ruinous physical reminder of the passage of time in which cityscape blends with nature to make an architectural palimpsest'.[114] By using this trope as the prelude to his cosmological drama, Shelley effectively maps out a mental space beyond time in which the battle between liberty and tyranny is being fought.

In *Sordello*, 'Rome' 'figures as the ideal polity',[115] either of the Republic, or the Empire;[116] however, there is no doubt that its ideological preference lies with the former. Browning's discourse on Charlemagne and Hildebrand goes to some length to prove his case; but as Bulwer-Lytton likewise entertains this struggle as being one of civic and moral superiority superseding the other, this schism had great currency within the time of his composition and the liberals were keen to identify themselves with the Guelphs as the more progressive party.[117] In *Rienzi*, Bulwer-Lytton, furthermore, develops the spiritual side of the Guelph party in their alliance with the Pope:

> The Republics of the Middle Ages grew up under the shadow of the Church; and there, as elsewhere, it was found, contrary to a Vulgar opinion, that Religion, however prostituted and perverted, served for the general protection of civil freedom,—raised the lowly, and resisted the oppressor. (203)

Religion becomes a central issue in *Rienzi* for reasons that partly concern Bulwer-Lytton's repeated reference to the English Civil War and the Puritans led by Cromwell as the immediate example of English republicanism.[118] In delineating the character of Rienzi, Bulwer-Lytton emphasises 'his religious enthusiasm' as 'the most singular feature of his character', which he goes on to compare with 'the intense fanaticism of our own Puritans of the Civil War, as if similar political circumstances conduced to similar religious sentiments' (234).

Browning likewise underpins the religious contribution to the regeneration of polity in *Sordello*: his discourse on Hildebrand is an obvious instance of this while Sordello's awakening to the idea of the reincarnation of Christ is a subtler account of it. If Adrian, in *Rienzi*, holds a key to the collapse of contest between 'Force and Intellect', 'Order and Strife' (281), then Browning approaches this dilemma on an entirely different footing: whereas Lytton emphasises the significance of Adrian's aristocratic background that enables him to intuit the weight of 'Order' yet at the same time appreciate Rienzi's 'Intellect' and 'Strife', Browning does not interest himself with a practical measure that will remedy social malfunction but rather focuses on the ontological question of 'good' and 'evil' that gives rise to moral judgment. His agonistic view that actively affirms the significance of 'evil' in the face of 'good' owes its critical force to Milton's *Paradise Lost*, but also to Shelley, who expounded a similar view in 'On the Devil, and Devils'.[119] The issue then is to elude the illusion that 'evil' can be severed to be eliminated; instead, one should entertain the idea that 'a partial death is every joy;/The sensible escape, enfranchisement/

Of a sphere's essence' (vi 262–4). For all his collectivism, what Browning commends is, in fact, individualism based on personal judgment:

Since
One object viewed diversely may evince
Beauty and ugliness—this way attract,
That way repel, why gloze upon the fact?
Why must a single of the sides be right?
Who bids choose this and leave its opposite?
No abstract Right for me—(vi 439–45)

That Shelley associated 'Rome' with his Zoroastrian drama that plays out the struggle between 'good' and 'evil' may arguably have provided material for Browning's philosophical digression in the face of re-constructing 'Rome'. Shelley's deliberate choice to use the Roman Jupiter instead of the Greek Zeus 'suggests a connection in his mind between patriarchal religion and "Roman" imperialism', and to transport the setting of the drama from the traditional Georgian Caucasus to the Hindu Kush, and to change 'its principal female protagonist, the Greek Io, for a female figure called Asia' attest to the Manichean influence under which he composed his Greek drama.[120] Such aesthetic re-orientation must have made an impression on Browning whose poem goes halfway in emulating the revolutionary regeneration of republican polity. If *Sordello* can be understood as being at once a critique of apocalyptic history, and an exponent of agnosticism, then Shelley's mythmaking in *Prometheus Unbound* played some part in encoding that faith.

'Rome' figures in the poem, primarily as an *idea* rather than as a historical reality; its cerebral function in the poem makes a striking contrast to the more palpable 'Venice'. Whereas 'Rome' is fed by literature based on its historical past, Browning takes particular care in representing 'Venice' as *real life*, which consists of real people in everyday life:

That Bassanese
Busied among her smoking fruit-boats? These
Perhaps from our delicious Asolo

Who twinkle, pigeons o'er the portico
Not prettier, bind late lilies into sheaves
To deck the bridge-side chapel, dropping leaves
Soiled by their own loose gold-meal? Ah, beneath
The cool arch stoops she, brownest-cheek!

that Paduan girl
Splashes with barer legs where a live whirl
In the dead black Giudecca proves sea-weed
Drifting has sucked down three, four, all indeed
Save one pale-red striped, pale-blue turbaned post
For gondolas. (iii 661–68,71–76)

That 'Venice' has little to do with the story of *Sordello* except that his visit there prompted an aesthetic re-orientation of the poem, explains its unusual presence in the poem. Browning's mode of narrative is almost documentary: 'I sung this on an empty palace-step/ At Venice' (iii 656–7). Not only does this recall Byron's own account in the beginning of Canto IV of *Childe Harold's Pilgrimage*—'I stood in Venice, on the Bridge of Sighs'—but it also mimics Byron's mode of delivery: as much as the poem narrates the story of Childe Harold, it also documents Byron's own experience as in a travelogue. In considering the compositional process of *Sordello*, the Italian trip, which Browning undertook in 1838, is of particular significance, partly because it provided him with the local colour of the places he was depicting, but more importantly because it brought him in direct contact with the *present* as it relates to his subject matter; what he was formerly imagining as the remote world of medieval Italy suddenly bore a temporal import:[121]

(At home we dizen scholars, chiefs and kings,
But in this magic weather hardly clings
The old garb gracefully: Venice, a type
Of Life, 'twixt blue and blue extends, a stripe,
As Life, the somewhat, hangs 'twixt nought and nought (iii 695–9)

Browning's association of 'Venice' with 'Life' is not confined to his aesthetics, but also extends itself to his political as well as moral commitment to the present society, as his encounter with the 'sad disheveled ghost' proves. The 'Life' that 'Venice' comes to represent offers both its joys—in the instance of the Italian peasant-girls and the pleasure that Browning gains by observing them—and its sad reality as personified by the 'ghost', which he encounters in the streets of Venice (whether a real person or an emblem). What is compelling is the way in which earthly sensuality and brutal reality converge in the name of 'Venice' to function as an antithesis to 'Rome', which is represented as being essentially cerebral and idealistic. As Sordello reiterates it in the pillage-scene of Ferrara, Browning's experience of human depravation in Venice provided the source of pessimism that runs throughout the poem. It is useful, at this point, to look at the Romantics' account of 'Venice', but in particular, Byron's and moreover Shelley's identification of Byron with 'Venice'.

Byron, of all the Romantics, arguably had the strongest association with Venice. He went there in late 1816 for the first time, spent three carnival seasons in the city, and led, what his friends considered, a dissolute life. The fact that he had exiled himself from England for good when he went to live on the continent in the spring of 1816, accounts for the gloominess, bitterness, and pessimism (despite his wit and humour) that run throughout his works. His life in Venice was infamously characterised by debauchery, but of an escapist kind, that resulted in a near self-destruction, both physical and moral. As is often the case with the Romantics, the personal drama is seen against the backdrop of the political scenery so that private disappointments readily translate to those of political failures:

> The two cantos [cantos III and IV of *Childe Harold's Pilgrimage*] were consciously written against the background of the defeat of Napoleon and the restoration of the monarchies in 1814–15. The whole comprises an autobiographical journey into and through a deep personal malaise which Byron represents as a symbol of the condition of Europe between 1809 and 1818.[122]

This is particularly true in the case of Venice, which was placed under the rule of Francis I of Austria in 1814. In 'Venice. An Ode', Byron employs four verse paragraphs to take the readers through his lament over the degradation of Venice, the historical struggle between freedom and tyranny, the glorious past of Venice contrasted to her present inverse position, and finally, his political hope in America. Although Byron ends on a hopeful note, the poem as a whole can hardly be characterised as being optimistic:

> There is no hope of nations!—Search the page
> Of many thousand years—the daily scene,
> The flow and ebb of each recurring age,
> The everlasting *to be* which *hath been*,
> Hath taught us nought or little. (56–60)

Byron was to reiterate this in canto IV of *Childe Harold*:

> There is the moral of all human tales;
> 'Tis but the same rehearsal of the past,
> First Freedom, and then Glory—when that fails,
> Wealth, vice, corruption,—barbarism at last.
> And History, with all her volumes vast,
> Hath but *one* page (964–9)

That Byron regarded Venice as yet another example that exhibits past glory in the face of present degradation, is clear from both of these poems; however, it is of particular interest that he invests his own personal life in his depiction of Venice. In *Childe Harold*, Byron's own identification with Venice becomes acute when he recognises himself 'A ruin amidst ruins' (4.219). Byron's gaze at Venice does not stop at being that of a passer-by; his immersion in its fall becomes that of his own self.

Shelley's poetry grounds in this identification that Byron had himself made with 'Venice'; furthermore, in the process of this, he discerns its aesthetic and philosophical implications by contrasting them to his own. In the most notable example, 'Julian and Maddalo', the propensities of two differing minds—that is, his own and Byron's—are examined through a conversation that takes place in Venice. That Byron's persona,

Maddalo, is described as 'a Venetian nobleman of ancient family and of great fortune', as opposed to Shelley's, 'Julian', who 'is an Englishman of good family', reveals Shelley's identification of Byron with Venice. Furthermore, Shelley's delineation of his character deserves attention:

> He [Maddalo] is a person of the most consummate genius; *and capable, if he would direct his energies to such an end, of becoming the redeemer of his degraded country*. But it is his weakness to be proud: he derives, from *a comparison of his own extraordinary mind with the dwarfish intellects that surround him*, an intense apprehension of the nothingness of human life. His passions and his powers are incomparably greater than those of other men, and instead of the latter having been employed in curbing the former, they have mutually lent each other strength. *His ambition preys upon itself, for want of objects which it can consider worthy of exertion.*[123]
>
> [emphases added]

This description of Maddalo is not dissimilar to Browning's account of Sordello: the troubadour likewise *could have been* a 'redeemer of his degraded country' but proved otherwise; his initial arrogance correspondingly compelled him to regard the world 'As pigmy natures' (ii 419); Sordello is also unable to find his 'out-soul'—'Power to uplift his power'—for which 'His sensitiveness idled . . . grew/And dwindled at caprice' (vi 42, 51). Although it is unlikely that Browning modelled Sordello on Shelley's account of Byron, what Shelley identified in Byron with 'Venice' is of relevance. Maddalo demonstrates not only unfulfilled potential but also resignation in the face of reality. Maddalo refutes Julian's 'aspiring theories' as 'Utopia' and introduces the Maniac in order to disprove Julian's philosophy. The poem can also be read on a more allegorical level:[124] 'life' for Julian's type is continual strife against the compelling evidences that disprove his idealistic beliefs; Maddalo, on the other hand, despite his potential to do otherwise, acquiesces in the demoralised world that surrounds him. It is instructive that Julian visits Maddalo on his native soil (i.e. Venice) where he is taught that 'History, with all her volumes vast,/Hath but *one* page' by being taken to see the Maniac who held similar 'aspiring theories' to Julian's, that eventually led him to insanity.[125] Like Rousseau in 'The Triumph of Life', the Maniac represents the negative potential of the speaker, which he must resist in order to maintain his idealistic aspirations. 'Venice' figures as a seductive pessimism that tempts one to resignation.

Browning exploits this identification of Byron and 'Venice' that Shelley repeatedly made, not by emulating Shelley but by converting it into a cause for his humanitarian philanthropy.[126] Browning's choice to court the 'sad disheveled ghost' instead of the Italian peasant-girls is not only a gesture to dissociate himself from the amorous affairs that become tied in with Venice but to distance himself from the self-serving egotism of Byron, whose behaviour in Venice was notorious.[127] Essentially, Browning is rewriting the Romantic texts (of Shelley and Byron) by replacing them with his own interpretation: 'Rome' and 'Venice' come to bear a different meaning in *Sordello* because he modifies the Romantics' reading of them.

NOTES

1. Browning 1863; 3: 251.
2. Martineau 3: 207.
3. It is also clear from what has been said that the function of the poet is not to say what *has* happened, but to say the kind of thing that *would* happen; that is, what is possible in accordance with probability or necessity. The historian and the poet are not distinguished by their use of verse or prose; it would be possible to turn the works of Herodotus into verse, and it would be a history in verse just as much as in prose. The distinction is this: the one says what has happened, the other the kind of thing that would happen. (5.5 *Universality*; Aristotle 16)
4. All citations of 'Essay on Shelley' are from Collins 1996.
5. *Paracelsus* has been called 'the English Faust', and Browning draws upon both Marlowe's and Goethe's versions of the Faust legend. Browning certainly knew Part One of Goethe's *Faust*, which was in his father's library; he also knew of Abraham Hayward's 1834 translation.

   See the editor's notes to *Paracelsus* (Woolford 1991, p. 103).
6. Browning also read Calderón from his early days; the Spanish dramatist's influence on him deserves attention in itself but will not be dealt with in this book. In a letter dated 5 December 1834 (MS, private collection) addressed to Monclar, Browning mentions his knowledge of Spanish and his ability to read some Calderón; Browning refers to 'that wild Drama of Calderón's which frightened Shelley just before his death' (*El Purgatorio de San Patricio*) in a letter to Elizabeth Barrett Browning dated 13 May 1845. Browning also owned a copy of Calderón'. See Maynard, p. 447; *Correspondence* 10: 214; *Collections* 49 (A557).
7. Calderón 1853, 1: xiii, xiv.
8. See Mason, pp. 258–60. Mason lists Henry Crabb Robinson, de Quincy, and Coleridge as disseminating the terms 'subjective' and 'objective' for current use.
9. Schlegel 1815, p. 98.
10. See Schlegel 1815, p. vi; 1840, p. xx.
11. Lockhart's comment is from McCarthy, p. xxv.

    The quote on Browning's knowledge of German is from A.S. Orr, *A Handbook to the Works of Robert Browning*, 7th ed., 1896, p. 108. Browning has also made remarks that are in accord with her comment: 'I am more & more possessed by a perfect antipathy for the North & its sights & sounds [. . .] I *will* not learn German for instance' (a letter addressed to Monclar dated

5–7 December 1834); 'I never read a line, original or translated, by Kant, Schelling, or Hegel in my whole life' (in a letter to F.J. Furnivall dated 25 April 1882). See *Correspondence*, 3: 111; *Trumpeter*, p. 51. However, Browning admits to consulting Schlegel & Tieck's translation of Shakespeare in order to help his reading of German; it is more than likely that he came across Schlegel's *A Course of Lectures on Dramatic Art and Literature.*

12. Webb 1976, p. 210.
13. Alexander A. Parker writes thus on Calderón's *autos*:

> He [Calderón] holds the view that the aim of all Christian poetry is to present the reconciliation of the 'eternal' with the 'earthly'. This can be done only by symbolism. Dante's symbolism is 'from above downwards': the Christian conception of life is comprised in a 'poetic dogma' which is applied to all the individual manifestations of the 'earthly'. Calderón's symbolism is 'organic' and employs the contrary method: all the things of this life, including legends and myths, are raised on to the spiritual plane and given a universal significance. His *autos* are, as a result, essentially a poetry of the invisible beauty which can be vaguely yearned for on earth but never found, and which is not accessible to the senses apart from symbols; and all true poetry is an allegorical symbol of transcendent truth and beauty. Calderón has seized on the perfect method of conveying the mysterious and incomprehensible through the senses. Eternal truths should not be presented in the cold formulæ of metaphysical abstractions: they should be fused with the poetic form in such a way that the allegory comes to life, and allegorical characters do not only mean something but become real living beings. And it is precisely this that Calderón is able to achieve. In his *autos*, therefore, the divine in human form, with the collaboration of a God-intoxicated nature becomes the symbol of the supersensible. (Parker 28)

Not only his *autos* but also his tragedies and comedies concern the spirituality of human existence; among the works that Shelley read and admired, *El Principe Constante, El Mágico Prodigioso,* and *El Purgatorio de San Patricio* are such examples.

14. See chapter 1.
15. Browning employs words such as 'pageant' (i 855) and 'pageantry' (ii 564) to denote the way in which Sordello sees the world around him; he also uses it within a context of a larger time span thereby designating a specific time in history: 'while there fleets/Outside the screen a pageant time repeats/Never again!' (iii 209–11).

16. See 'A Possible Echo of Calderón in Browning' by Lawrence Poston, pp. 26–9. In the article, Poston suggests three areas of research useful to Browning scholars one of which being 'a comparison of the baroque in Calderón and Browning' (29).
17. J.S. Mill's comment on *Pauline* famously pointed out the introspective tendency of Browning's early work: 'With considerable poetic powers, this writer seems to me possessed with a more intense and morbid self-consciousness than I ever knew in any sane human being'. The copy, which was annotated by J.S. Mill and further responded by Browning, is in the Forster-Dyce Collection in the Victoria and Albert Museum (Woolford 1991; 1: 17).
18. Sordello predicts the poetic development from epic, drama, and what amounts to the dramatic monologue (v 560–631). Lyricism is never explicitly acknowledged in the poem; however, the fact that Sordello's main concern is self-revelation strongly implies it.
19. In shedding light on the Victorian inheritance of Romanticism in its fractured state, John Woolford writes: 'What Victorians represent as their own conflicts *with* Romanticism normally pre-exist *within Romanticism itself*, and are indeed constitutive features of Romantic thought' (private communication).
20. Webb 1995, p. 413.
21. Browning most likely read the 'Letter' in the *Postumous Poems*. All citations of the 'Letter' are from this volume.
22. Of the stance that Shelley adopts in the *Letter*, Tim Webb writes: 'It is as if this practice [the ease of the whole poem, the obvious delight with which Shelley develops his images] provided a kind of therapy which gave wing to his creative faculties' (Webb 1976, p. 230).
23. For Tennyson's response to *Sordello*, see Sharp 1890, p. 110.
24. Browning expresses similar thoughts in his letter of 11 February 1845 to Elizabeth Barrett Browning: 'what I laughed at in my "gentle audience" is a sad trick the real admirers have of admiring at the wrong place—enough to make an apostle swear! *That* does make me savage [...]' (*Correspondence* 10: 71).
25. Examples of vocabularies appearing in both texts are 'engine(s)' (L, p. 60; *S*, iii 815) 'wheel(s)' (L, p. 60; *S*, iii 825), 'gin' (L, p. 59; *S*, iii 825), 'tooth('s)' (L, p. 60; *S*, iii. 820), and 'brass'(L, p. 60; *S*, iii 833). See Shelley 1839; Woolford 1: 582.
26. Shelley's coinage to mean the elaboration of metaphor in the manner of Calderón.
27. Shelley is more cautious here than in his bold 'Preface' to *The Revolt of Islam*, which incorporates his 'response to the *Quarterly Review*'s attack on

him for plagiarism'; see editor's commentary and 'Preface' to *Prometheus Unbound* (Everest 2000, pp. 460, 476).

28. Lionel Stevenson describes *Sordello* as a 'poem about a poet writing a poem about a poet writing poems' in 'The Key Poem of the Victorian Age', p. 278.
29. *Excursion*, 1.136; ll. 145–6; quoted from Wordsworth 1936.
30. 'The two categories strongly anticipate the 'subjective' and 'objective' poets of *Shelley* (1852)'; see Woolford 1991; 1: 425.
31. For the past opposing views on the relation between the 'Preface' and the text, see Evan K. Gibson, 'Alastor: A Reinterpretation', p. 1108.

    Butter writes with regard to the model of the poet:

    > It is interesting to compare the *Alastor* poet with various real characters (Shelley himself, Wordsworth, Coleridge) and fictional ones (Wordsworth's Wanderer and Solitary in *The Excursion*, Coleridge's Ancient Mariner); but the poem should be read as an independent imaginative creation. (Butter 238)

32. *MSJ* 1:.25.
33. Mueschke 229–45.
34. The poem's historical framework, the Guelph-Ghibelline strife, is represented by the ideological polarities of republicanism and imperialism.
35.

    > the sad
    > Disheveled form wherein I put mankind
    > To come at times and keep my pact in mind
    > Renewed me (iii 942–5)

36. Shelley's critique targeted at Wordsworth's egotism in 'Peter Bell the Third' will be discussed later in further detail.
37. Browning's attack on Wordsworth here seems to be conscious of what Hazlitt wrote of Wordsworth in *The Spirit of the Age* (1825)—not only in his use of the example from *Exodus* but also in his use of metaphor (i.e. 'dewdrop' on a flower):

    > He [Wordsworth] gathers manna in the wilderness, he strikes the barren rock for the gushing moisture. He elevates the mean by the strength of his own aspirations; he clothes the naked with beauty and grandeur from the stores of his own recollections. […] the dewdrop glitters on the bending flower […].

    Hazlitt 1932; 11: 88. The relevance of this passage to Browning's particular choice of metaphor and wording is mentioned in Woolford 1991; 1: 581–82.

Hazlitt's depiction here possibly echoes Colderidge's first impressions of hearing Wordsworth's unpublished manuscript poem being recited to him by the poet himself, the account of which he gives in *Biographia Literaria*:

> It was the union of deep feeling with profound thought; the fine balance of truth in observing with the imaginative faculty in modifying the objects observed; and above all the original gift of spreading the tone, the *atmosphere*, and with it the depth and height of the ideal world around forms, incidents, and situations, of which, for the common view, custom had bedimmed all the luster, had dried up the sparkle and the dewdrops. (Ch. 4; Coleridge 1983; 1: 80)

38. The Longman editors state that 'the author of To the Daisy and The Small Celandine is being glanced at' (580).
39. All quotations from the Celandine poems are from Wordsworth 1969, pp. 126–27.
40. See Peacock 1909, pp. 191–2.
41. It was called a Pilewort because it was used as a cure for piles (*OED*).
42. See Wordsworth 1969, p. 447.
43. Mueschke 232.
44. Matthews 1989; 1: 512.
45. Although Mueschke and Griggs claim that 'Shelley sent Peacock a copy of *The Celandine*', there is no hard evidence to prove it (232).
46. See the notes in Matthews 1989, p. 514. The quoted text is from this edition.
47.

> Just for a handful of silver he left us,
> Just for a ribband to stick in his coat—
> Got the one gift of which fortune bereft us,
> Lost all the others she lets us devote;
> They, with the gold to give, dole him out silver,
> So much was their's who so little allowed:
> How all our copper had gone for his service! (ll. 1–7)

See Woolford 1991; 2: 177–8.

48. *Miscellaneous Poems* 53.
49. See Pottle 1965, p. 52. Pottle lists the poem as one of Browning's favourites from the entire volume (27). The copy, which was owned by Browning, is currently in the Taylor Collection at Princeton University; see *Collections* 178 (A2109).
50. Early on in the 'Preface' Wordsworth writes:

> He [Poet] is a man speaking to men: a man, it is true, endued with more lively sensibility, more enthusiasm and tenderness, who has

> a greater knowledge of human nature, and a more comprehensive soul, than are supposed to be common among mankind; a man pleased with his own passions and volitions, and who rejoices more than other men in the spirit of life that is in him [. . .] (603).

'Preface to *Lyrical Ballads* (1802)' in Wordsworth 2000.

51. 'Peter Bell the Third' was not published until 1840 (although erroneously advertised as 1839) in the one-volume edition of *The Poetical Works of Percy Bysshe Shelley*; however, Browning may have seen it at a prior date through Leigh Hunt to whom Mary Shelley entrusted its manuscript for advice (her letter to Hunt is dated around 5 October 1839); see the 'Publication and History of the Text' in *BSM*, vol. 1; *LMWS* 2: 325–6. M.Y. Mason furthermore contends that '[t]here was evidently some kind of literary relationship between the two men [Hunt and Browning] in the years immediately preceding 1840, and this may have left its mark on *Sordello*' (268). Alternatively, Browning may have come across it through Moxon whom he was assisting for the 1839 and 1840 editions of Shelley's *Poetical Works*. See *Correspondence* 4: 113; Thomas, p. 87.
52. 'The great instrument of moral good is the imagination; and poetry administers to the effect by acting upon the cause' (*SPP* 517).
53. *The Spirit of the Age* 89.
54. For Coleridge's distinction of the two terms, see *Biographia Literaria* 1: 304–5.
55. Robert Langbaum argues that Wordsworth's choice of subject owes to a greater current of thought in which the subjective had to be exhausted before the objective could be attempted:

> Wordsworth wrote *The Prelude*, the model in English of the subjective or autobiographical poem, not because he believed in autobiographical poetry but in order to prepare himself for a long philosophical poem treating of the 'mind of man'. He wrote it because he felt as yet inadequate to the objective undertaking, out of 'real humility'. (28–9)

56. Coleridge writes: 'Shakespeare becomes all things, yet for ever remaining himself'. See *Biographia Literaria* 2: 28.
57. *SPP* 517.
58. Sordello's contribution to vernacular Italian is noted:

> How he sought
> The cause, conceived a cure, and slow re-wrought
> That Language, welding words into the crude
> Mass from the new speech round him, till a rude

Armour was hammered out, in time to be
Approved beyond the Roman panoply
Melted to make it, boots not. (ii 573–9)

However, 'Thrusting in time eternity's concern' (i 566) proves linguistically unfeasible:

Piece after piece that armour broke away
Because perceptions whole, like that he sought
To clothe, reject so pure a work of thought
As language (ii 588–91)

Sordello thereby neglects to make the effort and becomes subjected to oblivion.

59. Browning makes it clear that Palma is operating on different principles to Sordello as his comment after 'She [Palma] spoke' (iv 901) makes clear in *Syracuse* (a copy of *Sordello* which Browning used for his revision of the poem in 1855–6; currently at Syracuse University): 'Ghibellinism & selfishness' (Woolford 1991; 1: 645).
60. See the notes in Matthews 1989, p. 448.
61. See 'Note on the Early Poems' by Mary Shelley in Shelley 1839; 3: 15–6.
62. Quoted from the 'Preface' in Shelley 1839; 1: 109.
There is also a verbal echo in the text itself:

While day-light held
The sky, the Poet kept mute conference
With his still soul. At night the passion came,
Like the fierce fiend of a distempered dream,
And shook him from his rest, and led him forth
Into the darkness. (*Posthumous Poems* 276)

63. See Raben 278–92. For its reply, see Webb 1967, pp. 402–11.
64. *The Excursion* in Wordsworth 1969, p. 590.
65. 'Dedication' 8.1–2; see Byron 5: 5.
66. 'Dedication' in *The Revolt of Islam* (Shelley 1839; 1: 155).
67. The opening of the poem, beginning with 'Who will, may hear Sordello's story told', 'is characteristic of romance narrative'; see Woolford 1991; 1: 395. Browning also emulates the formulaic pattern of romance by adopting a six-book structure and a medieval romance motif whereby the protagonist appears anonymous at first but proves his noble birth at the end of the story.
68. While Archimago, 'the great master of false image' in *The Faerie Queene* provides a possible source for 'archimage' (Woolford 1991; 1: 563), the word also appears in Shelley's *Letter to Maria Gisborne* subsequently to his reference to Spenser: 'And here like some weird Archimage sit I,/Plotting dark spells, and devilish energy'. See *The Faerie Queene*, p. 1079; 'The Letter to Maria Gisborne' in Shelley 1839; 3: 280.

69. When compared to Edmund Spenser's *The Faerie Queene*, Browning's deviation from the traditional use of a muse becomes apparent: at the beginning of the poem, Spenser invokes Calliope, the muse of epic poetry for her assistance ('Helpe then, ô holy Virgin chiefe of nine' (1.2.1); although Gloriana is the heroine of the poem, she also figures as the poet's inspiration in her combined persona as 'the one of the most royall Queene or Empresse, the other of a most virtuous and beautifull Lady, this latter part in some places I doe expresse in Belphœbe, fashioning her name according to your owne excellent conceipt of Cynthia (Phœbe and Cynthia being both names of Diana)' (15).

Browning's muse is a further reworking of the Romantic model; for example, both Shelley and Keats often invoke an ethereal agent (in the form of a female) as the source of inspiration (e.g. Shelley's *Alastor; or, The Spirit of Solitude*, *Hymn to Intellectual Beauty*, *Prometheus Unbound*, *Epipsychidion*, Keats's *Endymion: A Poetic Romance*, and 'The Fall of Hyperion'). In making the 'Italian peasants' or a 'female beggar' his muse, Browning swerves away from the ideal in order to embrace the real: that in itself tells much of the aesthetic valorisation of the poem.

70. Benevenuto d'Imola ('14th-century commentator on Dante') Aliprandi, and Platina (a poet and a historian, respectively, of the fifteenth century) are some of the key contributors to the legend that Sordello was 'a hero of chivalry' as an 'accomplished soldier and courtier'. *Biographie Universelle* (Paris 1811–22) confirms Sordello's abduction of the wife of the Count of Saint Boniface, which provides the material for various versions of the episode including Browning's. See Woolford 1991; 1: 381.

71. In describing the spirit of Provençal poetry (under which Sordello's works are classified), Sismondi relates it to the rise of chivalry:

> It [chivalry] was, in a manner, the soul of the new literature, and the character which is thus given to the latter, so different from any thing in antiquity, and so rich in potential invention, is one of the most important matters of observation in the history of modern literature [. . . .] Its [of chivalry] essential character is devotion to woman and to honour.

See Sismondi 1823; 1: 87.

As Sordello participates in the Court of Love as a competitor and is expected to perform his extempore on 'Elys', one of the two main themes for troubadours was idealised love: 'This beautiful language [Provençal] was exclusively employed, for a long time, in those compositions to which it was so peculiarly appropriate—in amatory and martial songs' (Sismondi 1: 127).

72. According to an account given by Nostradamus, Sordello 'composed songs on subjects of philosophy, not love' (Woolford 1991, 1: 381).
73. The primary example of this is 'The Triumph of Life' as I will demonstrate in the following argument; but other works such as Shelley's *Alastor* and Keats's *Endymion* and 'La belle dame sans merci' may be included.
74. For example, Swann engages in the question of the Romantic woman by focusing on the lady in Keats's 'La belle dame sans merci' whose depiction suggests that 'her only function is to be a lure, not simply for the knight, but for the reader' (83); Dyer contends that Scott's romance *Ivanhoe* undercuts the ideology of chivalry by showing how the chivalric protection of women is not disinterested but rather is dependent on sexual desire' (349).
75. In the running-titles, which first appeared in the *Poetical Works*, 3 vols. (1863) and were later retained in *Poetical Works*, 6 vols. (1868, 1870, 1875,) Browning specifies the 'spirit' as Shelley: 'Shelley departing, Verona appears' (Woolford 1991; 1: 394).
76. Woolford 1991; 1: 577.
77. See Ch. 1.
78. There is a verbal echo of this section in *Sordello* (Woolford 1991; 1: 529): 'Every spark/Of Mantua life was trodden out; so dark/The embers' (iii 73–5).
79. De Man 116–9.
80. Barbara A. Schapiro contends that 'the Alastor quest, the hopeless search of the wounded narcissist for his ideal maiden/self, is the most central shaping situation of Shelley's poetry' (32). The first chapter, which she devotes on Shelley, focuses on *Alastor* and 'The Triumph of Life.'
81. The poem, which was initially called *Laon and Cythna* (taken after the names of the hero and heroine), was suppressed owing to their incestuous relationship and later republished as *The Revolt of Islam* with their kinship omitted (*SPW* 31).
82. 'On Love' quoted from *SPP* 504.
83. Freud 14: 73–102.
84. For further argument, see Lacan, Jacobus, Kofman.
85. Mellor 1988, p. 7.
86. On the influence of Browning's political re-orientation of history, John Woolford wirtes:

> In a famous series of essays in *Fraser's Magazine* during the 1830s, Carlyle had systematically attacked the assumption that history consists of stories of kings and nobles rather than the doings of the whole people; and the historiography of *Sordello*, particularly in passages highlighting the suffering of the common people under

feuding aristocratic dynasties (Book iv, for instance), clearly echoes this polemic. (Woolford 1988, p. 4)

87. *A Defence of Poetry* in *SPP* 516, 535.
88. Although the terms 'liberalism' and 'radicalism' are not used interchangeably here but are distinguished on the basis of loosely defined meanings (e.g. the general political attitude and political position respectively), these terms need to be discriminated carefully when applied in their strictest sense. In the eighteenth century, for example, 'liberalism' was associated with Whig politics that supported the dethronement of James II in favour of William the Orange (as opposed to the Tories); in the nineteenth century, the close association between 'liberalism' and Whiggism remained the same, but came to re-position itself (as the century progressed) so that it no longer was seen to be in direct conflict with the Tories, but instead, of a party of moderate reform that embraced progress out of self-interest or fear. During the period of the Reform Act, 'radicalism,' on the other hand, 'harboured the memory of the victims of the Peterloo massacre, the imprisonment of Horne Tooke for supporting the French Revolution, and beyond that the anarchism of Godwin's *Political Justice*' in their endeavour to achieve an ideal society based on ideology (160). Therefore, what the Shelleys and Browning understood by these two terms (especially 'liberalism') would have been slightly different. See the chapter on 'Politics' in Woolford and Karlin 1996, pp. 158–65.
89. Its polemics (v 95–6) suggest the influence of utilitarian ethics that was to dominate the nineteenth century. J.S. Mill notably argued for 'the importance of the masses' that 'becomes constantly greater' while 'that of individuals less'; see 'Civilization' in Mill 1977; 18: 121.

    Although Browning introduces this idea as a universal principle to be applied to all ages rather than as a recent development (i.e. the collective power is present in any age), his delineation of poetic progress (through the voice of Sordello) suggests that the masses will play a greater role in the transmission of ideas and in the appreciation of art in the coming age.
90. Cook 2001, p. 295.
91. Browning inserts the following lines between lines 84 and 85 in his revision of the poem (1863, 1868, 1888; the only alteration being 'stay,' in 1888), which clarifies 'The first step' and 'the last step':

    God has conceded two sights to a man—
    One, of men's whole work, time's completed plan,
    The other, of the minute's work, man's first
    Step to the plan's completeness: what's dispersed
    Save hope of that supreme step which, descried
    Earliest, was meant still to remain untried

> Only to give you heart to take your own
> Step, and there stay—leaving the rest alone?

See Woolford 1991; 1: 661.

92. The story is framed so that the distance from the Middle Ages is self-evident from the beginning ('the dim/Abysmal Past divide its hateful surge' [i 18–9]); additionally, Browning's digression on poetic progress underlined by historical development emphasises the differences that exist between the Middle Ages and his own age. Browning seems particularly sensitive to this as he wrote in the 'Preface' to *Strafford* of his 'eagerness to freshen a jaded mind by diverting it to the healthy natures of a grand epoch' as the reason for abandoning *Sordello* ('Preface' to the first edition of *Strafford* in Jack 1984, p. 500).
93. The association of Apollo with Sordello and Bacchus with Salinguerra infers this polarisation of character. Apollo is introduced as Sordello's object of emulation (i 926–7); 'Bacchus!' occurs in Salinguerra's speech (iv 720).
94. In response to Euthanasia's reproach on Castruccio's conduct, Beatrice argues that

    > 'Forms, forms,—mere forms, my mistaken Euthanasia. *He* remained, and was not that every thing? Methinks, it would please me, that my lover should cast off all humanity, and be a reprobate, and an outcast of his species. Oh! then how deeply and tenderly I should love him; soiled with crimes, his hands dripping blood, I would shade him as the flowering shrub invests the ruin; I would cover him with a spotless veil;—my intensity of love would annihilate his wickedness [. . .]' (250)

95. *Miscellaneous Poems* 21.
96. Browning, on one level, implies that Sordello should have accepted the 'badge' with a mind to work toward the Guelph cause:

    > How dispute
    > The Guelphs were fitliest maintained in rule?
    > That made the life's work: not so easy school
    > Your day's work—say, on natures circumstanced
    > So variously, which yet, as each advanced
    > Or might impede that Guelf rule, it behoved
    > You, for the Then's sake, hate what Now you loved,
    > Love what you hated (vi 206–213)

97. *Prince Hohenstiel-Schwangau, Saviour of Society* recounts the political career of Napoleon III, which would be the most contemporary topic of them all. Browning probes into the enigmatic character of Napoleon III (who infamously betrayed his involvement in the Italian cause) and suggests how casually his ideals were compromised in the end.

98. John Woolford argues that much of Browning's egalitarian politics derives from 'extreme Puritan theory' as embraced by 'John Lilburne, leader of the Levellers in the English Civil War' (Woolford 1988, ch. 1).
99. See William Whitla, *The Central Truth: the Incarnation in Robert Browning's Poetry* (Toronto: University of Toronto Press, 1963):

    [T]he assaults on faith which presented themselves as very real problems to Browning came partially out of the nineteenth-century inheritance from Eighteenth-century 'rationalism [. . .]'. (3)

100. See Browning's letter addressed to Dowden dated 5 March 1866 for the significance of these lines in *Sordello*. Talking of Sordello, Browning asserts that

    [I]t is the second [subjective poet] 'enervated' and modified by the impulse to 'thrust in time's eternity's concern'—*that*, or nothing. This is just indicated in the passage where these words occur, and the rest of the poem is an example of the same. (Hood 92)

101. In Browning's dedication of the poem in 1863 to Joseph Milsand, he writes: 'my stress lay on the incidents in the development of the soul: little else is worth study'; see note 1.

    See also Grube 413–29.
102. Erich Auerbach sees the fundamental difference between the Bible and Classical literature as being that of politics: the former is levelling (by emphasising the common humanity), whereas the latter is elitist (in discriminating taste based on class) (41–9).
103. See Woolford 1991; 1: 751.

    John Woolford writes in *Browning the Revisionary*:

    Browning here [*The Ring and the Book* i 709–19] rejects, once again, the Romantic preoccupation with a poetics of unmediated vision, and defines his aesthetics as being in and for the world. And as before, it is an aesthetic of love, a love like that manifested through Christ towards man, that replaces Romantic vision and motivates poetic utterance. (129)

    William Whitla's *The Central Truth* concerns Browning's treatment of the conception of the Incarnation as being a model of human creativity: 'Browning was beginning to see how the Incarnation closely linked God's action with the poet's function of discerning and clothing in language the "pure white light"' (17). For Browning's later reticence about making this direct analogy, see *Browning the Revisionary* (128–9).
104. Michael Mason emphasises the significance of '[p]lace, rather than time or character' as 'the organizing and discriminating factor in the poem' (33).

105. Sordello becomes orphaned when the entire Ghibellin faction gets expelled from Vicenza owing to the joint forces of Azzo and the Count of Saint Boniface who anticipated the military move of Taurello and Ecelin there.
106. See *A Browning Handbook*:

> [I]t is probable, I think, that Browning's attention was first attracted to the poet Sordello by Angelo Cerutti's edition of Danielo Bartoli's *De' Simboli Trasportati al Morale* [. . . who] had directed the reader to the part which Sordello played in Dante's *Purgatorio*. (70)

Browning later referred to the cantos in question in a letter dated 22 December 1845 to Elizabeth Barrett.

Although Sordello becomes a famous troubadour in Mantua after winning the prize at a 'Court of Love' held by Count Richard of Saint Boniface, he soon becomes disillusioned with his success and moves back to Goito.
107. Mrs. Sutherland Orr writes:

> I cannot therefore help thinking that recent investigations of the life and character of the actual poet [Sordello], however, in themselves praiseworthy and interesting, have been often in some degree a mistake; because, directly or indirectly, they referred Mr. Browning's Sordello to an historical reality, which his author had grasped, as far as was then possible, but to which he was never intended to conform. (1908, pp. 99–100)

Sordello's artistic ambition rivals that of Dante and Petrarch in their achievements to write in the vernacular; Sordello's political aspiration emulates that of Rienzi who was the last tribune to create a Roman republic.
108. 'And Rome, indeed,/Robed at Goito in fantastic weed,/The Mother-City of those Mantuan days' (iv 975–7).
109. Sordello predicts his own downfall from the role of a tribune of the people to a sovereign: 'who sits alone in Rome' (vi 351).
110. The Barons—the Colonna, Orsini, and Savelli—are described as being vengeful by waging petty wars upon one another in the beginning; but they unite in power after one of their members becomes condemned to death by Rienzi as a consequence of a fair trial, in order to protect their self-interest based on privilege. The plebeians likewise only show support where their interest lies; when faced with responsibility (e.g. providing men to protect themselves from outside invaders and paying tax in order to support the militia), they turn their backs on Rienzi to support a demagogue, Baronecelli, who appealed to their immediate interests.

111. Both *Rienzi* and *Valperga* evoke Napoleon in their depiction of their heroes (i.e. Rienzi and Castruccio). Whereas the connection between Castruccio and Napoleon is only referred to in a review of *Valperga* and by P. B. Shelley in his letter as self-evident, Bulwer-Lytton makes a direct comparison of the two:

> The marked outline of the face, and the short, firm upper lip, were not concealed by the beard and moustachios usually then worn; and, in the faded and antique portrait of the person now described, still extant at Rome, may be traced a certain resemblance to the popular pictures of Napoleon, not indeed in the features, which are more stern and prominent in the portrait of the Roman, but in that peculiar expression of concentrated and tranquil power which so nearly realizes the ideal of intellectual majesty. (83)

112. Sordello affirms his own neglect as the cause of failure to 'build another Rome':

> Impotent to build
> Another Rome, but hardly so unskilled
> In what such builder should have been as brook
> One shame beyond the charge that he forsook
> His function! (v 547–61)

Bulwer-Lytton characterises the plebeians as simply ignorant, self-interested, and short-sighted throughout the novel as epitomised by the smith, Cecco del Vecchio, whom he describes as 'honest, but uneducated—impracticable, and by nature a malcontent' (265).

113. 'Note on Prometheus Unbound, by Mrs. Shelley', Shelley 1839; 2: 132, 139.
114. Latané 1987, p. 88.
115. See the note in Woolford 1991; 1: 651.
116. 'Guelph Rome or Ghibellin Rome'; see the reprinted texts of 1863, 1868, 1888.
117. Sismondi's *Italian Republics* was instrumental in giving a contemporary currency to the Guelph-Ghibelline strife; Mrs. Busk, for example, responded to Sismondi in the form of an attack in *Blackwood's Magazine* (Oct. 1832).
118. For example, 'Cromwell's Dream'.
119.
> Shall we suppose that the Devil occupies the centre and God the circumference of existence, and that one urges inwards with the centripetal, whilst the other is perpetually struggling outwards from the narrow focus with the centrifugal force, and that from their perpetual conflict results that mixture of good and evil, harmony and discord, beauty and deformity, production and decay [....]

'On the Devil, and Devils', Julian edition 7: 100

120. Leask argues that '*Prometheus Unbound* functions by an antithetical movement [to Shelley's earlier work, *The Revolt of Islam*, that 'pulled its

(suppressed) Indian setting westwards into the Hellenistic world, and sought to homogenize the Orient in occidental terms'], namely in the orientalization of Greek myth'; he further contends that *Prometheus Unbound* was written under the influence of Rammohun Roy, 'founder in 1829 of the Hindu reform movement Brahmo Sabha'. See sections on *Prometheus Unbound* in Leask 1992, pp. 135–54 (141, 144).

121. Browning in a letter (dated 1838) to Fanny Haworth writes: 'I went to Trieste, then Venice—then through Treviso and Bassano to the mountains, delicious Asolo, all my places and castles, you will see'. Quoted in Mrs. Sutherland Orr 1908, p. 93.
122. McGann 2000, p. 1026. See the editor's notes to *Childe Harold's Pilgrimage*. All citations from this poem will be from this edition.
123. *Posthumous Poems* 3.
124. Julian and Maddalo converse while 'o'er the lagune/We glided' (8) effectively uses 'water' as a metaphor for 'life' in Shelley's symbolism. The notable example of this is *Alastor; or, The Spirit of Solitude*: 'O stream!/ Whose source is inaccessibly profound,/Whither do thy mysterious waters tend?/Thou imagest my life' (*Posthumous Poems*, p. 285; ll. 508–11). Evan K. Gibson reads the poet's boat journey across the Caspian Sea 'down a yawning cavern of winding depth, and finally through a tremendous maelstrom into a quite cove' as allegories of death and life; see Gibson 1022–42.
125. *Childe Harold's Pilgrimage* 4. 968–9.
126. After dwelling on the degraded state of Venice 'where human forms,/Like pollution-nourish'd worms/To the corpse of greatness cling,/Murdered, and now mouldering', Shelley refers to Byron as 'One remembrance, more sublime/Than the tattered pall of Time' who found 'refuge' in Venice; see 'Lines Written Among the Euganean Hills' in Shelley 1839; 3: 132–33.
127. Browning experimented with this aspect in 'In a Gondola' based on his first-hand experience of Venice, which 'was traditionally associated with erotic intrigue'; see commentary in Woolford 1991; 1: 118.

   Byron's self-importance in employing the imagery of crucifixion, for example, could not have impressed Browning, to say the least: 'The thorns which I have reaped are of the tree/I planted,—they have torn me,—and I bleed:/I should have known what fruit would spring from such a seed' (*CH* 4. 88–90).

   Shelley 'disapproved of Byron's life in Venice and the poetry he was writing there' (Everest 2000; 2: 658); it is documented in a letter he wrote to Peacock (dated 17 or 18 December 1818) on Byron's *Childe Harold*, Canto IV; see *LPB S* 2: 58.

AFTERWORD

P.B. Shelley's 'The Triumph of Life' succinctly brings some of the central Romantic concerns and engagements to a culmination: its interest in origins, the legacy of the Enlightenment, the workings of the imagination and the problem of subjectivity, man's relationship with nature, history, the political role of the poet in the making of future society, and love as the transforming principle of life. If Shelley's high-Romanticism suffers in the end from solipsism, Mary Shelley's *Valperga* offers a historicist reading of its failure that enables the reader to understand the social and political limitations of their age that worked against Shelley's aspirations. In so doing, Mary Shelley also introduces a gendered argument that is not only pertinent to the cultural exclusion that beset professional women writers of her age, but is also useful in delineating the eclipse of poets as a source of political influence. Robert Browning's *Sordello* directly takes up these issues: his concern with the audience, the solipsist poet, and the problem of power are some of the legacies of the failure of Romanticism to assimilate poetry into politics. The poem's Victorian sensibility also reflects the change in climate of the 1830s from the years in which the Shelleys spent writing their works in question. One way of putting it is to see Browning as embracing a utilitarian ethos over the Godwinian doctrine of individual freedom.

Despite their gradational shift in perspective, all three texts nonetheless place ultimate weight on the effort of the individual, that is, the protagonists. Rousseau in 'The Triumph' figures as the guide to the speaker-narrator, as an exponent of the Enlightenment, and the inspirer of the French Revolution, not to mention the leading voice of sentimentalism. Euthanasia in *Valperga* is a Shelleyan idealist who seeks to transform society through 'love' and 'imagination' even at the expense of her own happiness. Browning's Sordello likewise attempts to work toward the cause of the people against the opposition set by those who surround him. Sordello's transformation from a hedonist egotist to a liberator of the people tragically proves to be of little significance in its actual influence on society. That the Promethean effort becomes consumed by history rather than the other way around is the central problem in all three texts.

In communicating their histories as trauma—as obstructed narratives that suffer from repetitive rehearsal of their inability to assimilate and overcome a catastrophic event—they do so ultimately through their gesture of departure: whereas 'The Triumph of Life' uncannily acts out the dying voice through the author's own death, both *Valperga* and *Sordello* seek to salvage historical value in the act of the hero(ine)'s death. Cathy Caruth, commenting on Freud's letter written to his son, makes a point of the significance of departure:

> Freud's freedom to leave [Vienna to bring forth his book in England] is, paradoxically, the freedom not to live but to die: to bring forth his voice to others in dying. Freud's voice emerges, that is, as a departure. And it is this departure that, moreover, addresses us. (Caruth 23)

The deaths of Euthanasia and Sordello compel us to read the works as hinging on this kind of departure that seeks to recover meaning in the very act of dying. The double perspective—of the history that could have been and what became of it—create a tension that does not affect the past but the future toward which the present is continuously working in its process of 'becoming'. Therefore, the symbolic death of an alternative history heightens the present historical consciousness, as Marx famously put it, that 'Men make their own history, but they do not make it just as they please [...] but under circumstances directly encountered, given, and transmitted from the past' (Marx 300). The historicist understanding of all three writers in their act of textual creation is what makes their works compelling testimonies of their dialectical negotiation of the past and present in their attempt (for the future) to make that very alternative history that did not, because it could not, materialise in the past. 'The Triumph of Life', *Valperga*, and *Sordello* still speak to us for that very reason.

Bibliography

Primary Sources

Browning, Robert. *The Brownings' Correspondence.* Edited by Philip Kelly, Ronald Hudson, and Scott Lewis. 14 volumes. Winfield, K.S.: Wedgestone Press, 1984.

___. *Browning's Trumpeter: the Correspondence of Robert Browning and Frederick J. Furnivall 1872–1889.* Edited by William S. Peterson. Washington, D.C.: Decatur House Press, 1979.

___. *Letters of Robert Browning Collected by Thomas J. Wise.* Edited by Thurman L. Hood. London: John Murray, 1933.

___. *New Letters of Robert Browning.* Edited by William Clyde De Vane and Kenneth Leslie Knickerbocker. London: John Murray, 1951.

___. *The Poems.* Edited by John Pettigrew, supplemented and completed by Thomas J. Collins. Revised edition. 2 volumes. London: Penguin, 1996.

___. *The Poems of Browning.* Edited by Daniel Karlin, Joe Phelan (Vols. 3, 4), and John Woolford. 4 volumes. London: Longman, 1990, 1991, 2007, 2012.

___. *The Poetical Works of Robert Browning.* 3rd edition. 3 volumes. London: Chapman and Hall, 1863.

___. *The Ring and the Book: Books I–IV.* Edited by Stefan Hawlin and T.A.J. Burnett. Oxford: Clarendon Press, 1998.

___. Foreword. *Robert Browning's Prose Life of Strafford.* By F.J. Furnivall. London: Kegan Paul, 1892.

___. *Strafford.* Edited by Ian Jack and Margaret Smith. Oxford: Clarendon Press, 1984.

Shelley, Mary. *Frankenstein, or The Modern Prometheus, the 1818 Text.* Edited by Marilyn Butler. The World's Classics. Oxford: Oxford University Press, 1994.

___. General Introduction. *Frankenstein, or The Modern Prometheus.* By Betty T. Bennett. Edited by Nora Crook. Volume 1 of *The Novels and Selected Works of Mary Shelley.* Nora Crook and Pamela Clemit, general editors. 8 volumes. London: William Pickering, 1996.

___. *The Journals of Mary Shelley: 1814–1844*. Edited by Paula R. Feldman and Diana Scott-Kilvert. 2 volumes. Oxford: Clarendon Press, 1987.
___. *The Last Man*. Edited by Jane Blumberg and Nora Crook. Volume 4 of *The Novels and Selected Works of Mary Shelley*. Nora Crook and Pamela Clemit, general editors. 8 volumes. London: William Pickering, 1996.
___. *The Letters of Mary Wollstonecraft Shelley*. Edited by Betty T. Bennett. 3 volumes. Baltimore: Johns Hopkins University Press, 1980–1988.
___. *Valperga, or, The Life and Adventures of Castruccio, Prince of Lucca*. Edited by Nora Crook. Volume 3 of *The Novels and Selected Works of Mary Shelley*. Nora Crook and Pamela Clemit, general editors. 8 volumes. London: William Pickering, 1996.
___. *Valperga*. Edited by Stuart Curran. New York: Oxford University Press, 1997.
___. *Valperga*. Edited by Tilottama Rajan. Peterborough, Ontario: Broadview, 1998.
___. *Valperga*. Edited by Michael Rossington. Oxford World's Classics. Oxford: Oxford University Press, 2000.
Shelley, Percy Bysshe. *Alastor and Other Poems: Prometheus Unbound With Other Pomes; Adonais*. Edited by P.H. Butter. London: Collins, 1970.
___. *The Complete Works of Percy Bysshe Shelley*. Edited by Roger Ingpen and Walter E. Peck. Julian editions. 10 volumes. London: Ernest Benn, 1926.
___. *The 'Charles the First' Draft Notebook*. Edited by Nora Crook. Volume 12 of *The Bodleian Shelley Manuscripts*. New York: Garland, 1991.
___. *'Peter Bell the Third' and 'The Triumph of Life'*. Edited by Donald H. Reiman. Volume 1 of *The Bodleian Shelley Manuscripts*. London: Garland, 1986.
___. *'Prometheus Unbound Notebook'*. Edited by Neil Fraistat. Volume 9 of *The Bodleian Shelley Manuscripts*. London: Gardland, 1991.
___. *The Letters of Percy Bysshe Shelley*. Edited by Frederick L. Jones. 2 volumes. Oxford: Clarendon Press, 1964.
___. *Miscellaneous Poems by Percy Bysshe Shelley*. London: William Benbow, 1826.
___. *Poems and Prose: Percy Bysshe Shelley*. Edited by Timothy Webb, critical selection by George E. Donaldson. Everyman Library. London: J.M. Dent, 1995.
___. *The Poems of Shelley*. Edited by Geoffrey Matthews and Kelvin Everest. Jack Donovan, Ralph Pite, Michael Rossington, and Cian Duffy (Vol. 3 only), contributing editors for volumes 2, 3.3 volumes. London: Longman, 1989, 2000, 2011.
___. *The Poetical Works of Percy Bysshe Shelley*. Edited by Mrs. Shelley. 4 volumes. London: Edward Moxon, 1839.
___. *The Poetical Works*. Edited by Mrs. Shelley. 2 volumes. London: Edward Moxon, 1840.

___. *The Poetical Works: Shelley*. Edited by Thomas Hutchinson and corrected by G.M. Matthews. Oxford: Oxford University Press, 1970.
___. *Posthumous Poems of Percy Bysshe Shelley*. Edited by Mrs. Shelley. London: John and Henry L. Hunt, 1824.
___. *Prometheus Unbound: A Lyrical Drama With Other Poems*. London: C. and J. Ollier, 1820.
___. *The Revolt of Islam; A Poem*. London: C. and J. Ollier, 1817.
___. *Shelley's Poetry and Prose*. Edited by Donald H. Reiman and Neil Fraistat. 2nd edition. New York: Norton, 2002.

SECONDARY SOURCES

Allott, Miriam, ed. *Essays on Shelley*. Liverpool: Liverpool University Press, 1982.
Aristotle. *Poetics*. Translated by Malcolm Heath. London: Penguin Books, 1996.
Armstrong, Isobel. *Language as Living Form in Nineteenth-Century Poetry*. Brighton: Harvester, 1982.
___. *The Major Victorian Poets: Reconsiderations*. London: Routledge & Kegan Paul, 1969.
___. *Victorian Poetry: Poetry, Poetics and Politics*. New York: Routledge, 1993.
Auerbach, Erich. *Mimesis: the Representation of Reality In Western Literature*. Translated by Willard R. Trask. Princeton: Princeton University Press, 1968.
Bainbridge, Simon. *Napoleon and English Romanticism*. Cambridge: Cambridge University Press, 1995.
Baker, Lee C.R. 'The Diamond Necklace and the Golden Ring: Historical Imagination in Carlyle and Browning'. *Victorian Poetry* 24.1 (1986): 31–46.
Bakhtin, Mikhail. *Rabelais and His World*. Translated by Hélèn Iswolsky. Bloomington: Indiana University Press, 1984.
Bann, Stephen. *The Clothing of Clio*. Cambridge: Cambridge University Press, 1984.
Barrell, John. *The Birth of Pandora and the Division of Knowledge*. Basingstoke: Macmillan, 1992.
Beer, John. *Questioning Romanticism*. Baltimore: Johns Hopkins University Press, 1995.
Behrendt, Stephen C. *History and Myth: Essays on English Romantic Literature*. Detroit: Wayne State University Press, 1990.
Benjamin, Walter. *Illuminations*. Translated by Harry Zorn. Edited by Hannah Arendt. London: Cape, 1970.

Bennett, Betty T., and Stuart Curran, eds. *Mary Shelley in Her Times.* Baltimore: Johns Hopkins University Press, 2000.

Berkeley, George Fitz-Hardinge. *Italy in the Making 1815–1846.* 3 volumes. Cambridge: Cambridge University Press, 1968.

Bloom, Harold. *A Map of Misreading.* Oxford: Oxford University Press, 1975.

___. *Poetry and Repression, Revisionism from Blake to Stevens.* New Haven: Yale University Press, 1976.

___. *The Ringers in the Tower: Studies in the Romantic Tradition.* Chicago: University of Chicago Press, 1971.

___. and Adrienne Munich, eds. *Robert Browning: A Collection of Critical Essays.* Englewood Cliffs, N.J.: Prentice-Hall, 1979.

___. *Shelley's Mythmaking.* New Haven: Yale University Press, 1959.

Blumberg, Jane. *Mary Shelley's Early Novels: 'this child of imagination and misery'.* Basingstoke: Macmillan, 1993.

Blunden, Edmund. *Shelley: A Life Story.* London: Collins, 1946.

Brand, C.P. *Italy and the English Romantics: The Italianate Fashion in Early Nineteenth-Century England.* Cambridge: Cambridge University Press, 1957.

Brinkley, Robert, and Keith Hanley, eds. *Romantic Revisions.* Cambridge: Cambridge University Press, 1992.

Butler, Marilyn. 'Myth and Mythmaking in the Shelley Circle'. *ELH* 49.1 (1982): 50–72.

___. *Romantics, Rebels and Reactionaries: English Literature and Its Background 1760–1830.* Oxford: Oxford University Press, 1981.

Byron, George Gordon. *The Complete Poetical Works.* 6 volumes. Edited by Jerome J. McGann. Oxford: Clarendon Press, 1980–91.

___. *Lord Byron: the Major Works.* Edited by Jerome J. McGann. Oxford World's Classics. Oxford: Oxford University Press, 2000.

Calderón. *Dramas of Calderón, Tragic, Comic and Legendary.* 2 volumes. Translated by Denis Florence McCarthy. London: Charles Dolman, 1853.

Cambon, Glauco. *Ugo Foscolo: Poet of Exile.* Princeton, N.J.: Princeton University Press, 1980.

Caruth, Cathy. *Unclaimed Experience: Trauma, Narrative, and History.* Baltimore: Johns Hopkins University Press, 1996.

Castle, Terry. *Masquerade and Civilization: the Carnivalesque in Eighteenth-Century English Culture and Fiction.* Stanford: Stanford University Press, 1986.

Chaffee, Alan J. 'Dialogue and Dialectic in Browning's *Sordello*'. *TSLL* 23.1 (Spring 1981): 52–77.

Chandler, James. *England in 1819: the Politics of Literary Culture and the Case of Romantic Historicism.* Chicago: University of Chicago Press, 1998.

Chase, Cynthia, ed. *Romanticism.* London: Longman, 1993.

Clark, Timothy. *Embodying Revolution.* Oxford: Clarendon, 1989.

___. and Jerold E. Hogle, eds. *Evaluating Shelley*. Edinburgh: Edinburgh University Press, 1996.

Clemit, Pamela. *The Godwinian Novel: the Rational Fictions of Godwin, Brockden Brown, and Mary Shelley*. Oxford: Oxford University Press, 1993.

Coleridge, S.T. *Biographia Literaria or Biographical Sketches of My Literary Life and Opinions*. Edited by James Engell and W. Jackson Bate. 2 volumes. Number 7 of *The Collected Works of Samuel Taylor Coleridge*. 16 numbers. London: Routledge & Kegan Paul, 1983.

Collins, Tomas J. 'Shelley and God in Browning's *Pauline*: Unresolved Problems.' *Victorian Poetry* 3 (1965): 151–60.

Columbus, Robert R. and Claudette Kemper. '*Sordello* and the Speaker: A Problem of Identity.' *Victorian Poetry* 2 (1964): 251–67.

Condorcet, Marie Jean Antoine Nicolas, Marquis de. *Sketch for a Historical Picture of the Progress of the Human Mind*. Translated by June Baraclough. London: Weidenfeld & Nicolson, 1955.

Culler, A. Dwight. *The Victorian Mirror of History*. New Haven: Yale University Press, 1985.

Cundiff, Paul. *Robert Browning: A Shelley Promethean*. St. Petersburg, Florida: Valkyrie Press, 1977.

Curran, Stuart. 'The Political Prometheus.' *Studies in Romanticism* 25.3 (1986): 429–455.

___. *Shelley's Cenci: Scorpions Ringed with Fire*. Princeton: Princeton University Press, 1970.

Dawson, P.M.S. '"The Mask of Darkness": Metaphor, Myth, and History in Shelley's "The Triumph of Life".' Included in Behrendt ed., *History and Myth* 235–244.

___. *The Unacknowledged Legislator: Shelley and Politics*. Oxford: Clarendon Press, 1980.

Deane, Seamus. *The French Revolutions and Enlightenment in England 1789–1832*. Cambridge, Mass.: Harvard University Press, 1988.

De Man, Paul. *The Rhetoric of Romanticism*. New York: Columbia University Press, 1984.

De Vane, W. C. *A Browning Handbook*. 2nd edition. New York: Appleton-Century-Crofts, 1955.

___. 'Sordello's Story Retold.' *Studies in Philology* 27 (1930): 1–24.

Duff, David. *An Exposition of Browning's 'Sordello' with Historical and Other Notes*. Edinburgh: William Blackwood, 1906.

Duggan, Christopher. *A Concise History of Italy*. Cambridge: Cambridge University Press, 1994.

Dyer, Gary. 'Irresolute Ravishers and Sexual Economy of Chivalry in the Romantic Novel.' *Nineteenth-Century-Literature* 55.3 (2000): 340–368.

Eliot, T.S. 'Talk of Dante'. *Adelphi* 27 (1951): 110–112.

Ellis, Steve. *Dante and English Poetry: Shelley to T.S. Eliot*. Cambridge: Cambridge University Press, 1983.

Everest, Kelvin, ed. *Shelley Revalued: Essays from the Gregynog Conference*. Leicester: Leicester University Press, 1983.

Feldman, Burton, and Robert D. Richardson, eds. *The Rise of Modern Mythology: 1680–1860*. Bloomington: Indiana University Press, 1972.

Fisch, Audrey A., Anne K. Mellor and Esther H. Schor, eds. *The Other Mary Shelley: Beyond Frankenstein*. New York: Oxford University Press, 1993.

Foucault, Michel. *The Foucault Reader*. Edited by Paul Rainbow. New York: Pantheon, 1984.

Fraistat, Neil. *The Poem and the Book: Interpreting Collections of Romantic Poetry*. Chapel Hill: University of North Carolina Press, 1985.

Freud, Sigmund. *The Standard Edition of the Complete Psychological Works of Sigmund Freud*. Translated by James Strachey et al. 24 volumes. London: Hogarth Press, 1953–74.

Gibbon, Edward. *The Decline and Fall of the Roman Empire*. London: David Campbedd, 1993.

Gibson, Evan K. 'Alastor: A Reinterpretation'. *PMLA* 62 (1947): 1022–42.

Gilbert, Sandra M. and Susan Gubar. *The Madwoman in the Attic: the Woman Writer and the Nineteenth-Century Literary Imagination*. New Haven: Yale University Press, 1979.

Godwin, William. *Caleb Williams*. Edited by David McCracken. Oxford: Oxford University Press, 1982.

___. *Caleb Williams*. Edited by Pamela Clemit. Volume 3 of *The Collected Novels and Memoirs of William Godwin*. Mark Philip, general editor. 8 volumes. The Pickering Masters. London: Pickering, 1992.

___. *Enquiry Concerning Political Justice and Its Influence On Modern Morals and Happiness*. Edited by Issac Kramnick. Harmondsworth: Penguin, 1976.

___. *History of the Commonwealth of England: From Its Commencement to the Restoration of Charles the Second*. 4 volumes. London: Richard Taylor, 1824.

___. 'Of History and Romance'. *Things As They Are, or, The Adventures of Caleb Williams*. Edited by Maurice Hindle. Penguin Classics. Harmondsworth: Penguin, 1988.

___. *St. Leon*. Edited by Pamela Clemit. Oxford World's Classics. Oxford: Oxford University Press, 1994.

Goldsmith, Steven. *Unbuilding Jerusalem: Apocalypse and Romantic Representation*. Ithaca, N.Y.: Cornell University Press, 1993.

Grabo, Carl. *A Newton Among Poets: Shelley's Use of Science in Prometheus Unbound*. Chapel Hill: University of North Carolina Press, 1930.

Green, Louis. *Castruccio Castracani: a Study on the Origins and Character of a Fourteenth-century Italian Despotism*. Oxford: Clarendon Press, 1986.

Griffin, W. Hall, and H.C. Minchin. *The Life of Robert Browning*. 3rd edition. London: Methuen, 1938.

Grube, John. 'Sordello, Browning's Christian Epic'. *English Studies in Canada* 4 (1978): 413–29.

Hamilton, Paul. 'A French Connection: From Empiricism to Materialism in Writings by the Shelleys'. *Colloquium Helveticum* 25 (1997): 71–93.

___. *Historicism*. London: Routledge, 1996.

Handwerk, Gary. 'History, Trauma, and the Limits of the Liberal Imagination: William Godwin's Historical Fiction'. Included in Rajan ed., *Romanticism, History and the Possibilities of Genre* 64–85.

Hawthorne, Mark D. 'Browning, *Sordello*, and *Don Quixote*'. *MLA* 92 (1977): 1-33-37.

Hazlitt, William. *The Complete Works of William Hazlitt*. Edited by P.P. Howe. 21 volumes. London: J.M. Dent, 1930–34.

___. 'Sismondi and the Trescentisti'. *Italian Poets and English Critics, 1755–1859*. Edited by Beatrice Corrigan. Chicago: University of Chicago Press, 1969.

Hobhouse, John. *Historical Illustrations of the Fourth Canto of Childe Harold: Containing Dissertations on the Ruins of Rome; and an Essay on Italian Literature*. 2nd edition. London: 1818.

Holmes, Richard. *Shelley: the Pursuit*. London: Penguin, 1987.

Holt, Edgar. *Risorgimento: The Making of Italy 1815–1870*. London: Macmillan, 1970.

Hume, David. *An Enquiry Concerning Human Understanding*. Edited by Tom L. Beauchamp. Oxford: Clarendon Press, 2000.

Hunt, Leigh. *Descent of Liberty, A Mask*. New edition. London: S. Hamilton, 1816.

Hutchinson, J. *The Families of Flower Plants*. 2 volumes. 2nd edition. Oxford: Clarendon Press, 1959.

Irigaray, Luce. *This Sex Which Is Not One*. Translated by Catherine Porter and Carolyn Burke. Ithaca, N.Y.: Cornell University Press, 1985.

Jacobus, Mary. 'Is There A Woman in This Text?' *Reading Woman: Essays in Feminist Criticism*. London: Methuen, 1986.

Jameson, Frederic. *The Political Unconscious: Narrative as a Socially Symbolic Act*. London: Methuen, 1981.

Johnson, Alan P. 'Sordello: Apollo, Bacchus, and the Pattern of Italian History'. *Victorian Poetry* 7 (1969): 321–38.

Jones, Philip. *The Italian City-State: From Commune to Signoria*. Oxford: Clarendon Press, 1997.

Jordan, Frank, ed. *The English Romantic Poets: A Review of Research and Criticism*. New York: MLA, 1985.

Keats, John. *The Major Works: John Keats*. Edited by Elizabeth Cook. Oxford World's Classics. Oxford: Oxford University Press, 2001.

Keenan, Richard C. 'Browning and Shelley'. *Browning Institute Studies* 1 (1973): 119–45.

Kelley, Philip and Betty A. Coley. *The Browning Collections: A Reconstruction with Other Memorabilia*. Winfield, K.S.: Wedgestone Press, 1984.

Kelly, Gary. *English Fiction of the Romantic Period 1789–1830*. London: Longman, 1989.

___. *The English Jacobin Novel, 1780–1805*. Oxford: Clarendon Press, 1976.

Kofman, Sarah. 'Narcissistic Woman'. *The Enigma of Woman: Woman in Freud's Writings*. Translated by Catherine Porter. Ithaca, N.Y.: Cornell University Press, 1985.

Korg, Jacob. *Browning and Italy*. Athens, Ohio: Ohio University Press, 1983.

Kristeva, Julia. *The Kristeva Reader*. Edited by Toril Moi. Oxford: Basil Blackwell, 1986.

Lacan, Jacques. *Feminine Sexuality: Jacques Lacan and the école freudienne*. Translated by Jacqueline Rose. Edited by Juliet Mitchell and Jacqueline Rose. London: Macmillan, 1982.

Landor, Walter Savage. *The Poetical Works of Walter Savage Landor*. Edited by Stephen Wheeler. 3 volumes. Oxford: Clarendon Press, 1937.

Langbaum, Robert. *The Poetry of Experience: the Dramatic Monologue in Modern Literary Tradition*. Harmondsworth: Penguin Books, 1974.

Latané, David E. *Browning's Sordello and the Aesthetics of Difficulty*. ELS Monograph Series. Victoria, B.C.: University of Victoria, 1987.

___. '"See You?": Browning, Byron, and the Revolutionary Deluge in Sordello, Book I'. *Victorian Poetry* 22.1 (1984): 85–91.

___. 'Shelley's "Baleful Influence"'. *Studies in Browning and His Circle* 11.2 (1983): 31–36.

Leask, Nigel. *British Romantic Writers and the East: Anxieties of Empire*. Cambridge: Cambridge University Press, 1992.

Levinson, Marjorie, ed. *Rethinking Historicism: Critical Readings in Romantic History*. Oxford: Blackwell, 1989.

Lovejoy, A.O. *Essays in the History of Ideas*. Baltimore: Johns Hopkins University Press, 1948.

Liu, Alan. *Wordsworth: the Sense of History*. Stanford: Stanford University Press, 1989.

Lukács, Georg. *The Historical Novel*. Translated by Hannah and Stanley Mitchell. Harmondsworth: Penguin, 1976.

Lyles, W.H. *Mary Shelley: An Annotated Bibliography*. New York: Garland, 1975.

Lytton, Edward Bulwer. *The Poetical and Dramatic Works of Sir Edmund Bulwer Lytton*. London: Chapman and Hall, 1854.

___. *Rienzi, The Last of the Roman Tribunes*. 3 volumes. London: Saunders and Otley, 1835.

Machiavelli, Niccolò. *Machiavelli: the Chief Works and Others*. Edited and translated by Allan Gilbert. 3 volumes. Durham, N.C.: Duke University Press, 1965.

Macready, William Charles. *The Diaries of William Charles Macready 1833–51*. Edited by William Toynbee. 2 volumes. London: Chapman & Hall, 1912.

Maddox, Donald L. 'Shelley's *Alastor* and the Legacy of Rousseau'. *Studies in Romanticism* 9 (1970): 82–98.

Malthus, T.R. *An Essay on the Principle of Population*. Edited by Donald Winch. Cambridge: Cambridge University Press, 1992.

Marshall, Linda E. '"The Shape all Light" in Shelley's "The Triumph of Life"'. *English Studies in Canada* 5 (1979): 49–55.

Marin, Loy D. *Browning's Dramatic Monologues and the Post-Romantic Subject*. Baltimore: Johns Hopkins University Press, 1985.

Martineau, Harriet. *Harriet Martineau's Autobiography*. 3rd edition. 3 volumes. London: Smith, Elder, 1877.

Marx, Karl. *Selected Writings*. Edited by D. McLellan. Oxford: Oxford University Press, 1977.

Mason, M.Y. 'A Study of Browning's Poem *Sordello*'. B.Litt. thesis. Oxford, 1966.

Matthews, G.M. 'On Shelley's "The Triumph of Life"'. *Studia Neophilologica: A Journal of Germanic and Romance Philology* 34 (1962): 104–34.

___. 'Shelley and Jane Williams'. *RES* n.s. 12 (Feb. 1961): 40–48.

___. '"The Triumph of Life": A New Text'. *Studia Neophilologica* 32 (1960): 271–309.

Maynard, John. *Browning's Youth*. Cambridge, M.A.: Harvard University Press, 1977.

___. 'Robert Browning: A Reading of the Early Narratives'. *ELH* 26.4 (Dec. 1959): 531–48.

McCalman, Iain, ed. *An Oxford Companion to the Romantic Age: British Culture 1776–1832*. Oxford: Oxford University Press, 1999.

McGann, Jerome. *Romantic Ideology: A Critical Investigation*. Chicago: University of Chicago Press, 1983.

___. 'Rome and Its Romantic Significance'. *The Beauty of Inflections: Literary Investigations in Historical Method and Theory*. Oxford: Clarendon University Press, 1985.

Medwin, Thomas. *The Life of Percy Bysshe Shelley*. Edited by H. Buxton Forman. Revised edition. London: Oxford University Press, 1913.

Mellor, Anne K. 'A Criticism of Their Own: Romantic Women Literary Critics'. Beer, *Questioning Romanticism* 29–48.

___. *Mary Shelley: Her Life, Her Fiction, Her Monsters*. New York: Routledge, 1988.

___. ed. *Romanticism and Feminism*. Bloomington, IN: Indiana University Press, 1988.

___. *Romanticism and Gender*. New York: Routledge, 1993.

Merivale, John Herman. 'Review of Sismondi's *Histoire des République Italiennes du Moyen Âge*'. *The Quarterly Review* 7 (1812): 357–74.

Mill, J. Hillis. *The Disappearance of God: Five Nineteenth-Century Writers*. Cambridge, MA: Harvard University Press, 1975.

Mill, J.S. *Collected Works of John Stuart Mill*. J.M. Robson, general editor. 33 volumes. Toronto: University of Toronto Press, 1963–1991.

Miller, Betty. *Robert Browning: A Portrait*. London: John Murray, 1952.

Mineka, F.E. *The Dissidence of Dissent: The Monthly Repository 1806–1838*. Chapel Hill: University of North Carolina Press, 1944.

Moore, Doris Langley. *The Late Lord Byron: Posthumous Dramas*. London: John Murray, 1976.

Morton, Timothy. 'Shelley's Green Desert'. *Studies in Romanticism* 35 (1996): 406–30.

Mueschke, Paul, and Earl L. Griggs. 'Wordsworth as the Prototype of the Poet in Shelley's *Alastor*'. *PMLA* 49 (1934): 229–45.

Nesbit, George Lyman. *Benthamite Reviewing: The First Twelve Years of 'The Westminster Review' 1824–1836*. New York: Columbia University Press, 1934.

Nietzsche, Friedrich. *Untimely Meditations*. Translated by R.J. Hollingdale. Cambridge: Cambridge University Press, 1983.

Nitchie, Elizabeth. *Mary Shelley: 'Author of Frankenstein'*. New Brunswick: Rudgers University Press, 1953.

Norman, Sylvia. *Flight of the Skylark: the Development of Shelley's Reputation*. London: Marx Reinhardt, 1954.

O'Brien, Karen. *Narratives of Enlightenment: Cosmopolitan History From Voltaire to Gibbon*. Cambridge: Cambridge University Press, 1997.

O'Neill, Michael, ed. *Literature of the Romantic Period: A Bibliographical Guide*. Oxford: Clarendon Press, 1998.

___. *Romanticism and the Self-Conscious Poem*. Oxford: Oxford University Press, 1997.

___. *Shelley*. London: Longman, 1993.

Orr, Mrs. Sutherland. *A Handbook of the Works of Robert Browning*. 6th and revised edition. London: George Bell, 1892.

___. *Life and Letters of Robert Browning*. Revised and partly rewritten by Frederick G. Kenyon. New edition. London: Smith, Elder, 1908.

Parker, Alexander A. *The Allegorical Drama of Calderón*. Oxford: Dolphin Book, 1943.

Peacock, Thomas. *Peacock's Memoirs of Shelley With Shelley's Letters to Peacock.* Edited by H.F.B. Brett-Smith. London: Henry Frowde, 1909.

Peckham, Morse. *Romanticism and Behavior: Collected Essays II.* Columbia: University of South Carolina Press, 1976.

Peterson, Linda H. 'Biblical Typology and the Self Portrait of the Poet in Robert Browning'. *Approaches to Victorian Autobiography.* Edited by George P. Landow. Athens: Ohio University Press, 1979.

Petrarch, Francesco. *Triumphs.* Translated by Ernest Hatch Wilkins. Chicago: University of Chicago Press, 1962.

Philips, Anne. 'Feminism and Republicanism: Is This a Plausible Alliance?' *The Journal of Political Philosophy* 8.2 (2000): 279–293.

Pite, Ralph. *The Circle of Our Vision: Dante's Presence in English Romantic Poetry.* Oxford: Clarendon Press, 1964.

Pocock, J.G.A. *Virtue, Commerce, and History: Essays on Political Thought and History, Chiefly in the Eighteenth Century.* Cambridge: Cambridge University Press, 1985.

Poovey, Mary. *The Proper Lady and the Woman Writer: Ideology as Style in the Works of Mary Wollstonecraft, Mary Shelley, and Jane Austen.* Chicago: University of Chicago Press, 1984.

Poston, Lawrence, Jr. 'A Possible Echo of Calderón in Browning'. *Browning Society Notes* 4.3 (1974): 26–29.

___. 'Browning's Political Skepticism: Sordello and the Plays'. *PMLA* 88.2 (1973): 260–70.

Pottle, Frederick A. *Shelley and Browning: A Myth and Some Facts.* 1923. Hamden, C.T.: Anchor Books, 1965.

Pyle, Forest. *The Ideology of Imagination: Subject and Society in the Discourse of Romanticism.* Stanford: Stanford University Press, 1995.

Quinney, Laura. 'Skepticism and Grimness in Shelley'. *Colloquium Helveticum* 11–12 (1990): 169–82.

Quint, David. 'Representation and Ideology in 'The Triumph of Life'. *Studies in English Literature 1500–1900* 18 (1978): 639–57.

Raben, Joseph. 'Coleridge as the Prototype of the Poet in Shelley's *Alastor*'. *RES* 17 (1996): 278–92.

Rajan, Tilottama. *The Dark Interpreter: the Discourse of Romanticism.* Ithaca, N.Y.: Cornell University Press, 1980.

___. 'Mary Shelley's *Mathilda*: Melancholy and the Political Economy of Romanticism'. *Studies in the Novel* 26.2 (1994): 43–68.

___, and Julia M. Wright, eds. *Romanticism, History, and the Possibilities of Genre: Re-formation Literature 1789–1837.* Cambridge: Cambridge University Press, 1998.

___. *The Supplement of Reading: Figures of Understanding in Romantic Theory and Practice.* Ithaca, N.Y.: Cornell University Press, 1990.

Reiman, Donald H., Michael C. Jaye and Betty T. Bennett, eds. *The Evidence of Imagination: Studies of Interactions Between Life and Art in English Romantic Literature.* New York: New York University Press, 1978.

___, ed. *Shelley, Keats, and London Radical Writers.* 2 volumes. Part C of *The Romantics Reviewed: Contemporary Reviews of British Romantic Writers.* New York: Garland, 1972.

___. 'Shelley's "The Triumph of Life": The Biographical Problem'. *PMLA* 78 (1963): 536–50.

___. *Shelley's 'The Triumph of Life': A Critical Study Based on a Text Newly Edited from the Bodleian Manuscript.* Urbana: University of Illinois Press, 1965.

Ricouer, Paul. 'The Metaphorical Process as Cognition, Imagination, and Feeling'. *Critical Inquiry* 5 (1978): 143–159.

Rieger, James. *The Mutiny Within: The Heresies of Percy Bysshe Shelley.* New York: George Braziller, 1967.

Roberts, Hugh. *Shelley and the Chaos of History: a New Politics of Poetry.* University Park, P.A.: Pennsylvania State University Press, 1997.

Rousseau, Jean Jacques. *A Confessions of Jean-Jacques Rousseau.* Translated by J.M. Cohen. Harmondsworth: Penguin, 1954.

___. *A Discourse on the Origins of Inequality.* Translated by Maurice Cranston. Harmondsworth: Penguin, 1984.

___. *The First and Second Discourses Together With the Reply to the Critics, and the Essay on the Origin of Languages.* Edited and translated by Victor Gourevitch. New York: Harper & Row, 1986.

Ryals, Clyde De L. *Becoming Browning: The Poems and Plays of Robert Browning, 1833–1846.* Columbus: Ohio State University Press, 1983.

___. 'Browning's *Pauline*: the Question of Genre'. *Genre* 9 (1976): 231–45.

___. *The Life of Robert Browning.* Oxford: Blackwell, 1993.

Schapiro, Barbara A. *The Romantic Mother: Narcissistic Patterns in Romantic Poetry.* Baltimore: Johns Hopkins University Press, 1983.

Schlegel, August William. *A Course of Lectures on Dramatic Art and Literature.* Translated by John Black. 2 volumes. London: C. Baldwin, 1815.

___. *Course of Lectures.* 2nd edition. London: 1840.

Schlegel, Friedrich. *The Philosophy of History.* Translated by James Burton Robertson. 6th and revised edition. London: Henry G. Bohn, 1848.

Shakespeare, William. *The Tempest.* Edited by Anne Righter (Anne Barton). Harmondsworth: Penguin Books, 1968.

Sharp, William. *Life of Robert Browning.* [S.I.]: Walter Scott, 1890.

Shelley, Bryan. *Shelley and Scripture: The Interpreting Angel.* Oxford: Clarendon Press, 1994.

Simpson, David. *Irony and Authority in Romantic Poetry.* London: Macmillan, 1979.

Siskin, Clifford. *The Works of Writing: Literature and Social Change in Britain, 1700–1830*. Baltimore: Johns Hopkins University Press, 1998.
___. *Historicity of Romantic Discourse*. New York: Oxford University Press, 1988.
Sismondi, J.C.L. Simonde de. *Histoire des Républiques Italiennes du Moyen Âge*. 16 volumes. Paris: Chez H. Nicolle, 1809–1818.
___. *Italian Republics: or, The Origin, Progress and Fall of Italian Freedom*. The Cabinet Cyclopœdia. London: Longman, 1832.
___. *Historical View of the Literature of the South of Europe*. 4 volumes. Translated by Thomas Roscoe. London: Henry Colburn, 1823.
Smith, Denis Mack. *Mazzini*. New Haven: Yale University Press, 1994.
Spenser, Edmund. *The Faerie Queene*. Edited by Thomas R. Roche, Jr. and C. Patrick O'Donneell. London: Penguin Books, 1978.
Stevenson, Lionel. 'The Key Poem of the Victorian Age'. *Essays in American and English Literature Presented to Bruce McElderry, Jr.* Edited by Max F. Schulz, William D. Templeman and Charles R. Metzger. Athens: Ohio University Press, 1968.
Sustein, Emily W. *Mary Shelley: Romance and Reality*. Baltimore: Johns Hopkins University Press, 1991.
Swann, Karen. 'Harassing the Muse'. Included in Mellor ed., *Romanticism and Feminism*. Bloomington, IN: Indiana University Press, 1988. 81–92.
Teich, Milulàš, and Roy Poter, eds. *The National Question in Europe in Historical Context*. Cambridge: Cambridge University Press, 1993.
Thomas, Donald. *Robert Browning: A Life Within Life*. London: Weidenfeld and Nicolson, 1982.
Trumpener, Katie. 'National Character, Nationalist Plots: National Tale and Historical Novel in the Age of Waverly, 1806–1830'. *ELH* 60.3 (1993): 685–731.
Tucker, Herbert F. *Browning's Beginnings: The Art of Disclosure*. Minneapolis: University of Minnesota Press, 1980.
Waley, Daniel. *The Italian City-Republics*. 3rd edition. London: Longman, 1988.
Walling, William A. *Mary Shelley*. Boston: Twayne, 1972.
Warnock, Mary. *Utilitarianism*. Glasgow: William Collins, 1962.
Webb, Timothy. 'Coleridge and Shelley's *Alastor*: A Reply'. *RES* 18 (1967): 402–11.
___. *Shelley: a Voice Not Understood*. Atlantic Highlands, N.J.: Humanities Press, 1977.
___. *The Violet In the Crucible: Shelley and Translation*. Oxford: Clarendon Press, 1976.
Wellek, Réne. 'The Concept of Romanticism in Literary History'. *Approaching Literature: Romantic Writings*. Edited by Stephen Bygrave. London: Routledge, 1996.
White, Daniel E. '"The god undeified": Mary Shelley's *Valperga*, Italy and the Aesthetic of Desire'. *Romanticism on the Net* 6 (May 1997).

White, Hayden V. *Metahistory: The Historical Imagination in Nineteenth-century Europe*. Baltimore: Johns Hopkins University Press, 1975.
Whitla, William. *The Central Truth: The Incarnation in Robert Browning's Poetry*. Toronto: University of Toronto Press, 1967.
Wicks, Maragret Campbell Walker. *The Italian Exiles in London 1816–1848*. Manchester: Manchester University Press, 1937.
Wollstonecraft, Mary. *Mary, and, The Wrongs of Woman*. Edited by Gary Kelly. The World's Classics. Oxford: Oxford University Press, 1976.
Woodman, Ross Greig. *The Apocalyptic Vision in the Poetry of Shelley*. Toronto: University of Toronto Press, 1966.
Woolford, John. *Browning the Revisionary*. Basingstoke: Macmillan, 1988.
___. and Daniel Karlin. *Robert Browning*. London: Longman, 1996.
Wordsworth, William. *William Wordsworth: the Major Works*. Edited by Stephen Gill. Oxford World's Classics. Oxford: Oxford University Press, 2000.
___. *Wordsworth: Poetical Works*. Edited by Thomas Hutchinson and revised by Ernest De Selincourt. London: Oxford University Press, 1969.
Yetman, Michael G. 'Exorcising Shelley Out of Browning: Sordello and the Problem of Poetic Identity'. *Victorian Poetry* 13.2 (1975): 79–98.
Young, Louise Merwin. *Thomas Carlyle and the Art of History*. Philadelphia, P.A.: University of Pennsylvania Press, 1939.

INDEX

早稲田大学学術叢書 23

Negotiating History
From Romanticism to Victorianism

2012年 6 月25日　　初版第 1 刷発行

著　者……………………鈴木 理恵子
発行者……………………島 田　陽 一
発行所……………………株式会社 早稲田大学出版部
169-0051 東京都新宿区西早稲田 1-1-7
電話 03-3203-1551　　http://www.waseda-up.co.jp/
装　丁……………………笠 井 亞 子
印刷・製本……………精文堂印刷株式会社

© 2012, Rieko Suzuki. Printed in Japan　ISBN978-4-657-12703-7

無断転載を禁じます。落丁・乱丁本はお取替えいたします。

刊行のことば

早稲田大学は、2007年、創立125周年を迎えた。創立者である大隈重信が唱えた「人生125歳」の節目に当たるこの年をもって、早稲田大学は「早稲田第2世紀」、すなわち次の125年に向けて新たなスタートを切ったのである。それは、研究・教育いずれの面においても、日本の「早稲田」から世界の「WASEDA」への強い志向を持つものである。特に「研究の早稲田」を発信するために、出版活動の重要性に改めて注目することとなった。

出版とは人間の叡智と情操の結実を世界に広め、また後世に残す事業である。大学は、研究活動とその教授を通して社会に寄与することを使命としてきた。したがって、大学の行う出版事業とは大学の存在意義の表出であるといっても過言ではない。そこで早稲田大学では、「早稲田大学モノグラフ」、「早稲田大学学術叢書」の２種類の学術研究書シリーズを刊行し、研究の成果を広く世に問うこととした。

このうち、「早稲田大学学術叢書」は、研究成果の公開を目的としながらも、学術研究書としての質の高さを担保するために厳しい審査を行い、採択されたもののみを刊行するものである。

近年の学問の進歩はその速度を速め、専門領域が狭く囲い込まれる傾向にある。専門性の深化に意義があることは言うまでもないが、一方で、時代を画するような研究成果が出現するのは、複数の学問領域の研究成果や手法が横断的にかつ有機的に手を組んだときであろう。こうした意味においても質の高い学術研究書を世に送り出すことは、総合大学である早稲田大学に課せられた大きな使命である。

「早稲田大学学術叢書」が、わが国のみならず、世界においても学問の発展に大きく貢献するものとなることを願ってやまない。

２００８年１０月

早稲田大学

「研究の早稲田」 早稲田大学学術叢書シリーズ

中国古代の社会と黄河

濱川 栄 著 476頁 ¥5,775

東京専門学校の研究
——「学問の独立」の具体相と「早稲田憲法草案」
真辺 将之 著 380頁 ¥5,670

命題的推論の理論
——論理的推論の一般理論に向けて
中垣 啓 著 444頁 ¥7,140

一亡命者の記録
——池明観のこと
堀 真清 著 242頁 ¥4,830

ジョン・デューイの経験主義哲学における思考論
——知性的な思考の構造的解明
藤井 千春 著 410頁 ¥6,090

霞ヶ浦の環境と水辺の暮らし
——パートナーシップ的発展論の可能性
鳥越 皓之 編著 264頁 ¥6,825

朝河貫一論
——その学問形成と実践
山内 晴子 著 655頁 ¥9,345

源氏物語の言葉と異国

金 孝淑 著 304頁 ¥5,145

経営変革と組織ダイナミズム
——組織アライメントの研究
鈴木 勘一郎 著 276頁 ¥5,775

帝政期のウラジオストク
——市街地形成の歴史的研究
佐藤 洋一 著 456頁＋巻末地図 ¥9,765

民主化と市民社会の新地平
——フィリピン政治のダイナミズム
五十嵐 誠一 著 516頁 ¥9,030

石が語るアンコール遺跡
——岩石学からみた世界遺産
内田 悦生 著 下田 一太（コラム執筆） 口絵12頁＋266頁 ¥6,405

モンゴル近現代史研究：1921 ～ 1924 年
——外モンゴルとソヴィエト，コミンテルン
青木 雅浩 著 442頁 ¥8,610

金元時代の華北社会と科挙制度
――もう一つの「士人層」
飯山 知保 著　460頁　¥9,345

平曲譜本による近世京都アクセントの史的研究
上野 和昭 著　568頁　¥10,290

Pageant Fever
― Local History and Consumerism in Edwardian England
YOSHINO, Ayako 著　296頁　¥6,825

全契約社員の正社員化
――私鉄広電支部・混迷から再生へ（1993年～2009年）
河西 宏祐 著　302頁　¥6,405

対話のことばの科学
――プロソディが支えるコミュニケーション
市川 熹 著　250頁　¥5,880

人形浄瑠璃のドラマツルギー
――近松以降の浄瑠璃作者と平家物語
伊藤 りさ 著　404頁　¥7,770

清朝とチベット仏教
――菩薩王となった乾隆帝
石濱 裕美子 著　口絵4頁＋342頁　¥7,350

ヘーゲル・未完の弁証法
――「意識の経験の学」としての『精神現象学』の批判的研究
黒崎 剛 著　700頁　¥12,600

日独比較研究 市町村合併
――平成の大合併はなぜ進展したか？
片木 淳 著　240頁　¥6,825

Negotiating History
― From Romanticism to Victorianism
SUZUKI, Rieko 著　266頁　¥6,195

すべてA5判・価格は税込